The Mamm...
SERIOUSLY COMIC FANTASY

Also available

The Mammoth Book of Ancient Wisdom
The Mammoth Book of Armchair Detectives & Screen Crimes
The Mammoth Book of Arthurian Legends
The Mammoth Book of Battles
The Mammoth Book of Best New Horror 99
The Mammoth Book of Best New Science Fiction 12
The Mammoth Book of Chess
The Mammoth Book of Comic Fantasy
The Mammoth Book of Dogs
The Mammoth Book of Erotica
The Mammoth Book of Gay Erotica
The Mammoth Book of Gay Short Stories
The Mammoth Book of Heroic and Outrageous Women
The Mammoth Book of Historical Detectives
The Mammoth Book of Historical Erotica
The Mammoth Book of Historical Whodunnits
The Mammoth Book of How It Happened
The Mammoth Book of International Erotica
The Mammoth Book of Jack the Ripper
The Mammoth Book of Lesbian Short Stories
The Mammoth Book of Men O'War
The Mammoth Book of New Erotica
The Mammoth Book of New Sherlock Holmes Adventures
The Mammoth Book of Nostradamus and Other Prophets
The Mammoth Book of Puzzles
The Mammoth Book of Tasteless Lists
The Mammoth Book of the Third Reich at War
The Mammoth Book of True Crime (new edition)
The Mammoth Book of True War Stories
The Mammoth Book of 20th Century Ghost Stories
The Mammoth Book of Unsolved Crimes
The Mammoth Book of War Diaries and Letters
The Mammoth Book of the Western
The Mammoth Book of the World's Greatest Chess Games

The Mammoth Book of

SERIOUSLY COMIC FANTASY

Edited by
Mike Ashley

ROBINSON
London

Robinson Publishing Ltd
7 Kensington Church Court
London W8 3SP

First published in the UK by Robinson Publishing 1999

Reprinted 1999

A copy of the British Library Cataloguing in
Publication data is available from the British Library.

ISBN 1-84119-089-6

Printed and bound in the EC

CONTENTS

COPYRIGHT AND ACKNOWLEDGMENTS

INTRODUCTION:
The Second Most Serious Page in This Book

Mike Ashley

I'm delighted to be able to compile a second volume of comic fantasy. As before, in *The Mammoth Book of Comic Fantasy*, there is a blend of old and new. There are thirty-four stories, eight of which are being published here for the first time. Most of the others have long been out of print, or available only in small-circulation magazines, and I believe most of them will be new to you.

I've kept my definition of fantasy broad, so you will find some stories that drift towards science fiction and others that defy definition entirely. I need only point you in the direction of "How I Got Three Zip Codes" by Gene Wolfe, "Uncle Henry Passes" by Esther Friesner and "The Eye of Tandyla" by L. Sprague de Camp to give you an idea of the diversity of fiction you will find here. As before, I have tried to alternate fantasies set in other worlds with fantasies set in this world, and I've also grouped together pairings of stories where there is some common thread.

The purpose of all of these stories is to entertain you and make you laugh. As I said in my introduction to the earlier volume, not everyone's sense of humour is the same, and that's another reason for the diversity presented here. I have tried to find something for everyone. Just about all of these stories made me laugh out loud at some point, and even those that didn't made me think about them many times afterwards, usually bringing a smile to my face.

Have fun.

Mike Ashley

NEANDER-TALE

James P. Hogan

James Hogan (b. 1941) is better known for his hard science fiction, especially the Minervan sequence which started with Inherit the Stars *(1977). But the following story shows that, when he chooses, he can take the mickey out of scientists – or the rest of humankind for that matter.*

"Artificial fire!? Waddya mean 'artificial fire'? What the hell is artificial fire?" Ug scowled down from beneath heavy close-knit Neanderthal brows at the tangle-haired, bearskin-clad figure squatting in front of him. Og was leaning forward to peer intently into the pile of sticks and twigs that he had built between two stones in the clearing where the trail from the stream widened on its way up towards the rock terrace fronting the caves. He seemed unperturbed by Ug's pugnacious tone; Ug was standing with his club still slung across his shoulder, which meant that, for once, he was not in a trouble-making mood that day.

"It's the same as you get when lightning hits a tree," Og

replied cheerfully as he began rubbing two sticks vigorously
together in the handful of moss which he had placed underneath the twigs. "Only this way you don't need the lightning."

"You're crazy," Ug declared bluntly.

"You'll see. Just stand there a couple of seconds longer and
then tell me again that I'm crazy."

A wisp of smoke puffed out from the moss and turned into a
blossom of flame which quickly leaped up through the twigs
and engulfed the pile. Og straightened up with a satisfied
grunt while Ug emitted a startled shriek and jumped backwards, at the same time hurriedly unslinging his club.

"Now tell me again that I'm crazy," Og invited.

Ug's gasp was a mixture of terror, awe and incredulity.

"Holy sabre-cats, don't you know that stuff's dangerous? It
can take out a whole block of the forest in the dry season. Get
rid of it for chrissakes, willya!"

"It's okay between those rocks. Anyhow, I don't want to get
rid of it. I was wondering if we could figure out how to use it
for something."

"Like what?" Ug continued to stare nervously at the crackling pile and kept himself at a safe distance. "What could
anybody do with it, besides get hurt?"

"I don't know. All kinds of things . . ." Og frowned and
scratched his chin. "For instance, maybe we wouldn't have to
kick people out of the caves and make them trek a half-mile
down to where the hot springs are whenever they start to smell
bad."

"How else are they gonna clean up?"

"Well, I was thinking . . . maybe we could use this to make
our own hot water right there in the caves and save all the
hassle. Think what a difference that would make to the girls.
They wouldn't –"

"WHAT!" Ug cut him off with a shout that echoed back
from the rocks above. "You wanna take that stuff *inside* the
caves? You are crazy! Are you trying to get us all killed? Even
the mammoths take off like bats outa hell if they catch so much
as a whiff of that stuff. Anyhow, how could you make water
hot with it? It'd burn through the skins."

"So you don't put it in skins. You put it in something else . . . something that won't burn."

"Such as what?"

"Hell, I don't know yet," Og yelled, at last losing his patience. "It's a brand new technology. Maybe some kind of stone stuff . . ."

The sounds of running feet and jabbering voices from just around the bend in the trail above interrupted them. A few moments later Ag, the Vice-Chief, rushed into the clearing, closely followed by about twenty of the tribespeople.

"What's going on down here?" Ag demanded. "We heard shouting . . . ARGH! FIRE! There's fire in the valley. FLEE FOR YOUR LIVES! FIRE IN THE VALLEY!" The rest took up the cry and plunged back into the undergrowth in all directions. The trees all around reverberated with the sounds of colliding bodies and muffled curses, while Og continued to stare happily at his creation and Ug watched nervously from a few paces back. Then silence descended. After a while bearded faces began popping one by one out of the greenery on all sides. Ag re-emerged from behind a bush and approached warily.

"What's this?" he enquired, looking from Ug to Og and back again. "There hasn't been a storm for weeks. Where did that come from?"

"Og made it," Ug told him.

" '*Made* it'? What are you talking about – 'made it'? This some kinda joke or sump'n?"

"He made it," Ug insisted. "I watched him do it."

"Why?"

"He's crazy. He says he wants to take it inside the caves and –"

"INSIDE THE CAVES?" Ag clapped his hand to his brow and rolled a pair of wide-staring eyes towards Og. "Are you outa your mind? What are you trying to do? Haven't you seen what happens to the animals that get caught when the forest goes up? We'd all get roasted in our beds."

"Nobody's saying you have to sleep on top of it," Og said wearily. "You keep it out of the way someplace. Water pulls up trees when the river floods, but you can still take water inside without having to flood the whole goddamn cave. Well, maybe we can make our own fire and learn to live with it in the same sort of way."

"What's the point?" Ag challenged.

"It could be useful to have around," Og said. "The animals don't like it. It might stop the bears from trying to muscle into the caves every time the snow comes. Things like that . . . all kinds of things . . ."

Ag sniffed and remained unimpressed.

"All the people would have taken off for the hills too, so it wouldn't do much good," he pointed out.

"What about the smoke?" a voice called out from the circle of figures that had started to form around the edge of the clearing.

"What about it?" Og asked.

"You can't breathe it. How could people live in a cave full of smoke?"

"You fix it so the smoke goes outside and not inside," Og shouted in exasperation.

"How?"

"For Pete's sake, I don't know yet. It's a new technology. What do you want – all the angles figured out in one day? I'll think of something."

"You'd pollute the air," another voice objected. "If all the tribes in the valley got into it, there'd be smoke everywhere. It'd black out the sun-god. Then he'd be mad and we'd all get zapped."

"How do you know it isn't a she?" a female voice piped up from the back, only to be promptly silenced by a gentle tap on the head from the nearest club.

At that moment the circle of onlookers opened up to make way for Yug-the-Strong, Chief of the tribe, and Yeg-the-Soothsayer, who had come down from the caves to investigate the commotion. Yeg had been a great warrior in his youth and was reputed to have once felled an ox single-handed by talking at it non-stop until it collapsed in the mud from nervous exhaustion; hence Yeg's nickname of "Oxmire". For the benefit of the two elders Ag repeated what had been said and Ug confirmed it. Yeg's face darkened as he listened.

"It's not safe," he pronounced when Ag had finished. The tone was final.

"So we learn how to make it safe," Og insisted.

"That's ridiculous," Yeg declared flatly. "If it got loose it would wipe out the whole valley. The kids would fall into it. On top of that the fallout would foul up the river. Anyhow, you'd need half the tribe to be carrying wood up all the time, and we need the resources for other things. It's a dumb idea whatever way you look at it."

"You've got no business screwing around with it," Yug said, to add his official endorsement.

But Og was persistent and the arguing continued for the next hour. Eventually Yeg had had enough. He climbed onto a rock and raised an arm for silence.

"How this could be made safe and why we should bother anyway is still unclear," he told them. "Everything about it is unclear. Anyone who still wants to mess around with unclear energy has to be soft in the head." He turned a steely gaze towards Og. "The penalty for that is banishment from the tribe . . . forever. The law makes no exceptions." Yug and Ag nodded their mute agreement, while a rising murmur of voices from the tribe signalled assent to the decision.

"Throw the bum out!"

"I don't want no crazy people collecting free rides outa my taxes."

"Let the Saps down the end of the valley take care of him. They're all crazy anyway."

Og lodged a plea with the appeal-court in the form of Ag, who passed it on to Yug.

"Beat it," was Yug's verdict.

An hour later Og had drawn his termination pay in the form of two days' supply of raw steak and dried fish, and was all packed up and ready to go.

"You'll be sorry," he called over his shoulder at the sullen group who had gathered to see him on his way down the trail. "It won't do you any good to come chasing after me and telling me you've changed your minds when winter comes. The price to you will have gone out of sight."

"Asshole!" Ug shouted back. "I told you you'd blow it."

Over the months that followed, Og travelled the length and breadth of the valley trying to interest the other tribes in his discovery. The *Australopithecines* were too busy training kangaroos to retrieve boomerangs as a result of not having got their design calculations quite right yet. The tribe of *Homo Erectus* (famous for their virility) were preoccupied with other matters and didn't listen seriously, while *A. Robustus* declared that they had no intention of becoming *A. Combustus* by being ignited and becoming extinguished at the same time. And so Og found himself at last in the remote far reaches of the valley where dwelt the *H. Saps*, who were known for their strange ways and whom the other tribes tended to leave to their own devices.

The first Sap that Og found was sitting under a tree staring thoughtfully at a thin slice of wood sawn from the end of a log that was lying nearby.

"What's that?" Og asked without preamble. The Sap looked up, still wearing a distant expression on his face.

"Haven't thought of a name for it yet," he confessed.

"What is it supposed to do?"

"Not sure of that either. I just had a hunch that it could come in useful . . . maybe for throwing at hyenas." The Sap returned his gaze to the disc of wood and rolled it absently backwards and forwards in the dust a couple of times. Then he pushed it away and looked up at Og once more. "Anyhow, you're not from this end of the valley. What are you doing on our patch?" Og unslung an armful of sticks from his pack for the umpteenth time and squatted down next to the Sap.

"Man have I got a deal for you," he said. "You wait till you see this."

They spent the rest of the afternoon wheeling and dealing and ended up agreeing to joint-management of both patents. The Sap had got a good deal, so it followed that Og must have got a wheel, which was what they therefore decided to call it. The chief of the Saps agreed that Og's trick with the sticks constituted a reasonable share-transfer price, and Og was duly installed as a full member of the tribe. He was content to spend the remainder of his days among the Saps and never again ventured from their end of the valley.

*   *   *

The winter turned out to be a long one – over twenty-five thousand years in fact. When it at last ended and the ice-sheets disappeared, only the Saps were left. One day Grog and Throg were exploring far from home near a place where the Neanderthals had once lived, when they came across a large rock standing beside a stream and bearing a row of crudely carved signs.

"What are they?" Grog asked as Throg peered curiously at the signs.

"They're Neanderthal," Throg said.

"Must be old. What do they say?"

Throg frowned with concentration as he ran a finger haltingly along the row.

"They're like the signs you find all over this part of the valley," he announced at last. "They all say the same thing: OG, COME HOME. NAME YOUR PRICE."

Grog scratched his head and puzzled over the revelation for a while.

"So what the hell was that supposed to mean?" he mused finally.

"Search me. Must have had something to do with the guys who used to live in the caves behind that terrace up there. Only bears up there now though." Throg shrugged. "It might have had something to do with beans. They were always counting beans, but they were still lousy traders."

"Weirdos, huh? It could have meant anything then."

"Guess so. Anyhow, let's get moving."

They hoisted their spears back onto their shoulders and resumed picking their way through the rocks to follow the side of the stream onwards and downwards towards the river that glinted through the distant haze.

UNCLE HENRY PASSES

Esther Friesner

Esther Friesner (b. 1951) is undeniably the Queen of Comic Fantasy. She has written some of the best humorous short stories and novels of the last decade, including Here Be Demons *(1988),* Hooray for Hellywood *(1990),* Gnome Man's Land *(1991) and* Majyk by Accident *(1993). She has also edited the comic fantasy anthologies.* Alien Pregnant by Elvis *(1994),* Chicks in Chainmail *(1995) and* Did You Say Chicks? *(1996). The following is a new story, specially written for this anthology.*

It is with a heavy heart that I recall the death of my father's uncle Henry, my great-uncle of the same name, a man who served the town of Sutter, New Mexico, truly and well for many years. It's bad enough that he died like he did – by having an animal fall on him, though not from any great height – but now Daisy says it's my job to bring Dad up to speed on the tragic circumstances surrounding Uncle Henry's demise.

I don't want to do it.

Partly I don't want to do it because Dad and Mama are

enjoying their first real vacation in years and there is nothing like news of a favourite relative's expiration to make you realize that life is transitory, that death comes unexpectedly, and that drinking something blue out of a coconut shell with a flamingo-shaped swizzle stick and a lump of pineapple stuck in it won't stave off the Dark Angel worth shit.

Mostly, though, I don't want to do it because I don't know *how* to do it. There are certain circumstances surrounding Uncle Henry's passing which Dad'd find incredible if he were to hear them from someone other than me. And even with me telling him, I don't know how to make him believe it all. It would take a mighty long letter to explain the whole sorry affair, and a phone call is out of the question because it would cost too much. Maybe not at first, but once I tell Dad what happened he's going to say "No!" and I'll have to say "Yes, *honest!*" and then he's going to say "I don't believe it!" and I'll have to swear it's all true (which it is, though the truth doesn't convince some folks at all) and that's where the call's going to run into serious money.

That's why I'm writing down what happened, just to get it straight in my mind so I don't go breaking the bank when I finally do call Dad. I will, you know; I don't want to, but I will. I've got to. Daisy said that if I don't, she'll bite my ass.

It all happened this past Election Day, which dawned cold and clear and stuck with it until ten, ten-thirty, which was about when things began happening such as to make the casual observation of weather conditions immaterial. It was after the breakfast rush; I was taking care of business at the coffee shop, tending the counter and the cash register, with Daisy there to help me. Daisy's not much for conversation, except when she's telling me what to do or what I've already done wrong. Now me, I enjoy a nice friendly chat with just about anyone, so you can imagine how glad I was when the bell over the door tinkled and Mayor Wiley came in.

He was looking a mite nervous, seeing as how it was Election Day and all, plus for the first time in twelve years he actually had to head a campaign against an opponent who was geared up to give him a run for the money. (Daisy says I shouldn't try to be someone I'm not by showing off with fancy figures of speech, but considering as how everyone knows Mayor Wiley has been more than partial to awarding public works contracts to his near-and-dear-and-related-by-marriage, the money is in fact what he's always made a run for.) Anyway, I offered him a cup of coffee on the house. I figured it was the least I could do, seeing as how I'd voted for the other guy.

Mayor Wiley had promoted my offer into a free cup of coffee *plus* a free donut (and didn't Daisy growl at me for that!) when Merch Arnot came riding into town on the monster and all hell broke loose by degrees.

We got the first intimation that things were not as they ought to be when Mrs Pembleton's little six-year-old boy, Timmy, came running into the coffee shop, yelling about the beast and its rider.

"There, there, Timmy," Mayor Wiley said, getting his butt down off the stool and putting on that brandied fruitcake voice he uses when he's trying to impress the voters. "What do you mean, 'Old man Arnot's gone crazy'? That's kind of a given. You know you're going to have to be more specific than that." He tried to pat little Timmy on the head, but the kid jumped back and scowled at him.

"Touch me and I'll slap a child abuse suit on you so fast it'll make your head spin like a stripper's tit-tassels," the kid spat. "You want specific, you go out in the street and see for yourself what he's brought to town this time! Me, I'm hot-wiring the first car I find and getting my ass the hell to Albuquerque." And he ran back outside.

Well, it just tears your heart to hear a little child scared desperate enough to try something like that. Albuquerque, by God! Mayor Wiley and I traded a look, then headed after him. I called back over my shoulder for Daisy to cover for me – not that I expected many customers if the situation out in the street was as bad as little Timmy claimed.

Wouldn't you know, it was worse. It's no secret that our Main Street's not the widest stretch of pavement in the greater New Mexico area, but the downtown part's four lanes across, plus ample free parking. Well, parked amply across all four lanes plus with its rump resting on top of Gavin Ordway's prized and cherished humvee was the biggest damn Jackalo-pasaurus Rex I ever did see.

Also the only one, needless to say.

It was about as tall as a two-storey building, but that was measuring all the way up to the tips of its pronghorns. If you only took its height to the shoulder, it wasn't so much. Merch'd done better in the past. I don't think I'll ever forget that Christmas back in '69 when he dressed up like Santa and had that team of eight antlered armadillos the size of double-decker buses pulling his sleigh in the town parade. It took Dad and Mama a whole week to comfort me and Sis after the poor critters died from that accidental ginseng–garlic–vitamin C overdose he gave them to maintain their size. I still miss Rudolph.

Anyhow, what old Merch'd brought to town this time was no Rudolph. He was riding it like an elephant, straddling its neck and trying to steer it with a skinny little leather strap he'd got wound around the base of its horns. That contrivance didn't look likely to steer a dachshund, and when Daisy came out of the coffee shop to join the rest of us gawkers she said so.

There was quite a crowd. The first seriously contested election this town's seen in twelve years *will* fill the streets. By rights it should've been a banner day for us small business-men. How long does it take a person to vote? If a man's travelled any appreciable distance to pull that little lever, he's going to want to do something more to justify the trip, even if it's just having a ham sandwich at my place. That wasn't about to happen now, which displeased more than a few of my Better Business Bureau colleagues.

"Leave it to Merch to **** things up for everyone," said Miss Diderot from the yard goods store. (I'm sorry, I just can't bring myself to write some stuff down the way it was spoken. Unlike Daisy, I wasn't raised in a barn.)

Rory Vega from the Gulf station wiped an oil smear off his face with the back of his hand and whistled. "What in the hell *is* that?"

"Looks like it's a damn fine reason for you to start ordering humvee parts," Margaret Lee said, and she laughed. I guess she never did get over it when Gavin Ordway dumped her for that schoolteacher from Santa Fe. So at least one person in the crowd was on the monster's side.

"What does it *look* like it is?" Daisy snarled. "Another of Arnot's freaks!"

"Daisy!" I exclaimed, and gave her a little kick so she'd shut up. Everyone around us got real quiet and looked embarrassed, as if they'd been the ones to say that ugly thing instead of my Daisy. Merch Arnot's got his little quirks, but he's a good man, born and raised in Sutter, and there isn't a single decent human being in this town who'd ever use the f-word where he could maybe hear it.

Fortunately, he was too high up to catch wind of what Daisy'd said, or else he was too involved with more pressing problems to pay any mind to Daisy's yapping. I want to tell you, he really had done it this time.

Daisy'd asked what that thing looked like. It was not a real question on her part, but when I tell Dad about Uncle Henry, I bet he'll ask the same thing, so I better pull an answer together right now: To be honest, it looked like all *sorts* of things, mainly jackrabbit, until you got to the head. The head was where it started getting interesting. That was where the scales began, and the antlers, and the jaws. The jaws were what really held a person's attention, all filled up with sharp, white teeth, and bright, red tongue, and loud, ferocious roar, and Timmy.

Poor Timmy. No hot-wired getaway car for him, and no Albuquerque either. I guess you have to take the bad with the good. He wasn't dead yet, but judging from how the monster was tossing him around it was only a matter of time. Merch Arnot was tugging at that sorry little antler-leash, whacking the beast with the slack end and kicking its shoulders with his heels, and in general trying to make it drop the boy.

"Bad girl, Gretchen! *Bad* girl!" he hollered. "You let go now, you hear?"

That did about as much good as you might imagine. By then, someone had run to fetch Mrs Pembleton from her register at the Bag 'n' Bye-Bye. Could be they thought that a mother's screams of anguish would touch the monster's heart and make it let go of Timmy, maybe even have it set him down gently and lower that gigantic horned head so the boy could pat its nose and lay his soft little cheek against its big old scaly one and say something like, "It's okay, Gretchen, I love you," before he gave it a kiss and it sort of snorted tenderly at him and everyone watching went "Awwwww" because each of us is a monster until we find love.

I blame Spielberg for making people expect this kind of **** to happen. Naturally it never does, at least not in Sutter, except for the part about the anguished mother's screams. Mrs Pembleton held up her end of that real good. Too good. The noise spooked the monster. It took a jump backwards, with little Timmy still in its jaws, and rammed its fuzzy cottontail bunny butt into the front of the bank, smashing the plate-glass windows. A piece of broken glass must've jabbed the beast's rump because it let loose with a roar of pain, and that *did* make it drop little Timmy.

Lucky thing for him that my Daisy has her wits about her and a friend over at the firehouse. While the rest of us were standing around goggle-eyed, she'd run downstreet and fetched some firemen and one of the smaller nets. Sparky, the hose company Dalmatian, came along to help out, herding the men into position and barking like crazy. Little Timmy landed in the net, so he bounced but he didn't break.

I wish I could say that Merch Arnot was that lucky. When the Jackalopasaurus did the glass-up-its-ass leap, those powerful hind legs sent it sailing clear across Main Street and right into the front of the florist's. As Miss Ilse Doggett used to tell us in health class, this was an accident that could have been avoided. Legs like that, so perfectly built for leaping, could've lifted the beast right *over* the flower shop and into the next street, and they would've, if the poor ******* had been able to *see* the flower shop in the first place.

Yes sir, Merch's new monster had some of the worst eyesight I have ever witnessed in anything other than roadkill. I don't know how Merch decides which Part A off Animal One he is going to connect to which Part B off Animal Two, but he sure screwed it up this time. (While I'm on the subject of things I don't know, I am also bone ignorant as to where Merch obtains said parts, especially in the case of his source for the -saurus Rex portion of this specific monster, but I think I'm happier remaining uninformed.) Anyway, what we now had on our communal hands on Election Day in downtown Sutter was two or three tons of spooked, ferocious, merciless, reptilian, horned, fanged and near-sighted bunny rabbit.

****
.

Did I mention "uncontrollable"? I should have. Merch Arnot might have been riding the monster, but he was not in charge of it, or of anything except wetting his pants. The beast wasn't responding to his commands or his leash *before* it got stampeded, and it sure as hell wasn't paying him any mind after. When it collided with the flower shop it took another leap *back* to the bank side of Main Street, where it wiped out *La Croissanterie*, then *back* the other way to total the hardware store, then *back* again to smash – In short, it was the ping-pong ball of the Apocalypse.

And through it all, Merch Arnot kept his seat. He didn't have much choice. He'd got himself tangled in the reins so that he was tied to the beast's back to stay. It was like the last scene in *Moby Dick* where Gregory Peck drowns. He should've been wearing a bike helmet like Merch was. Merch Arnot is living proof that you can be a mad scientist *and* sensible. God bless America.

"Get help!" he hollered from way atop the bounding and rebounding monster.

"We already got the Fire Department here!" Rory yelled back up at him. "They got a net! Jump!"

"Holy ****ing **** on toast, Rory, I would if I could!" Merch called out as the beast ploughed into the drug store and boomeranged over to squash the Redi-Wash. Gretchen, as Merch called her, was moving in a zigzag pattern heading north, which was not good. If she didn't calm down or slow up soon, her trajectory was eventually going to bring her far enough up the street to hit the school. The kids weren't there, on account of the Board of Ed. having voted to give them Election Day off instead of Hogmanay, but the school is our town's polling place. What with an exciting election for once, the building would be packed, and forget about issuing an evacuation order: the Dems would claim it was just another Republican dirty trick and the old-line Republicans would start saying how you couldn't talk dirty tricks without mentioning the New Deal, and then Vince Scipio, who is *still* running on the Libertarian ticket every election for every office, meds or no meds, would go into his speech about the corruption of the two-party system, and by that time the damage would be done. Someone had to do something.

Fortunately, Merch himself came up with the answer. "Rory!" he gasped as the video rental place went up in flinders around him. "Rory, run to the Baptist church and fetch my wife! She raised Gretchen from a pup; she's the only one can do anything with her!"

"Your wife! Right! Yes, *sir!*" Rory whipped off a sharp salute and spun on his heel, ready to sprint for glory. Then he stopped himself, cupped his hands to his mouth, and shouted, "Which one is it this year?"

"Like it matters!" Daisy snapped. "Just bring 'em now and we'll sort it out later!"

Very few men in this town have what it takes to stand and argue with my Daisy. Rory Vega is not one of them. He took off and was back in less than three minutes with Merch Arnot's wife Beth and her sister Eliza.

I should be truthful and say Merch's wife Eliza and her sister Beth, because that's what I thought the situation was when they came barrelling up. I confess I'd forgotten which one he was married to this year, same as Rory. It's an honest error. Unless I'm looking right at them, I tend to forget which one is which. Even then I have the tendency to think of them as Lefty and Righty, and the unfortunate knack of sometimes calling them by those names to their faces. Daisy says I'm a blockhead and just because they're Siamese twins is no excuse for being rude. (Of course, when I point out that the correct term is "*conjoined* twins" and that it's *ruder* to call 'em "Siamese twins" like she does, she rips me a new asshole. Some of us just can't take friendly criticism.)

Like I already wrote, it was a cold day, so the girls were wearing that custom-made trout-fur coat Merch grew special for them on the occasion of his 1991 divorce from Beth and remarriage to Eliza. (Unless 1991 was the year he shed Eliza to remarry Beth. I know the man likes to keep it fair, but it's not only confusing, it's hard on the Town Hall database. At least we didn't have to wait until the year 2000 to have our system blown to Kingdom Come.) They both looked equally annoyed with Merch, so there was no need to distinguish between them on that score.

"Merch Arnot, what are you doing with Gretchen?"

"Merch Arnot, who told you you could bring Gretchen to town? She's only a baby!"

"I'm sorry –" (Gretchen jumped across Main Street again and turned the pizzeria into a pancake house) "– dear! I thought she was ready for her first outing," Merch called to his alternating spouses. "Could you please –" (Gretchen hopped back the other way and destroyed the nail salon *and* the law offices of Ordway and Ordway; Margaret Lee cheered) "– try to reason with her? She always listens to you!"

"I should hope so!" said one of either Eliza or Beth, putting their hands on their trout-fur-covered hips. They looked around at the crowd, which by this time had grown out of all knowledge. "Okay," I think it was Eliza said. "Somebody give me a newspaper."

Well, were our faces red. All that crowd, all those people, and nobody had a newspaper to bless themselves with. As usual it was my Daisy who saved the day. "You want a newspaper? I'll fetch a newspaper. I always fetch the ****ing newspaper." And she was off at top speed, dodging her way between the piles of rubble clogging Main Street and the wreckage from mashed-down cars, and the bounding and rebounding monster.

Rory Vega thumped me on the back and gazed after her with true admiration in his eyes. "Son, that's one hell of a dog you got there."

I told him yeah, at least *sometimes* Merch came up with an experiment that wasn't a walking (or leaping) disaster area. Mind, you can count those more-or-less successes on the fingers of one hand and still have a thumb left over: the fur-bearing trout, my dog Daisy, and those giant horned armadillos. Okay, stretch a point and say *maybe* the glow-in-the-dark hamster booklights, the ones that move along the page while you read. (Although Merch always swore that they were what you might call Found Science, just a little souvenir he picked up on his last visit to Los Alamos.)

So Daisy came back with the paper and passed it to Beth and/or Eliza, both of whom shucked the trout-fur coat and raced up the street to head off Gretchen at the pass, as it were. That was what you might call the turning point.

There's nothing like a determined woman, unless it's two determined women who happen to be sharing the majority of the same body, internal organs included. Eliza and Beth were no track star, but they understood the value of shortcuts and it didn't take them long before they'd ducked around the corner over to Cedar Street, run up a whole lot of blocks parallel to Main, and come out a good ten yards ahead of their lord and master on his fractious mount. They couldn't have hoped to do this but for the fact that the Jackalopasaurus Rex's upstreet progress was not only zigzag and catty-cornered, but also redundant. That is to say, the beast would sometimes take a south-ish leap that sent it back to re-crush a vehicle, building, or other object which it – I mean *she* – had already pulverized.

Mrs Arnot and her sister shinnied up a lamp-post and when Gretchen came barrelling past, they brought the rolled-up newspaper down hard on her nose. I didn't see how a little-bitty piece of paper was going to make any kind of impression on something *that* big, even rolled up tighter than a duck's dinghy, but it did. Just that one smack on the nose and the creature stopped dead in her tracks, looking around somewhat bewildered, like an old lady who can't recall where she put her house keys.

Everybody cheered.

Merch Arnot sat there astraddle for a time, just catching his breath. Then he finally untangled himself, dropped a rope ladder from Gretchen's shoulder, and climbed down to street level, holding the reins tight. I do believe that if there'd been a hitching post handy he would've tied off that monster just as natural as if he was Gary Cooper come riding into Dodge for a drink. Well, we never did have a hitching post on Main Street, but Merch found something to make do.

Mayor Wiley was there to greet him. "Merch, I hope that you weren't thinking of keeping this noble animal among us any longer than is really good for her health," he said in a way that indicated there was no two ways about it.

"Actually I was planning on having a cup of coffee before I took her and the missuses home. My throat's a little dry. What I could really use is a *serious* drink, but it being Election Day and all . . ." He shrugged.

"Election Day, my ****ing ***!" someone shouted. I blush to record that the person who expressed himself so freely in front of the ladies was our own Uncle Henry. He'd popped up like a prairie dog with hiccups, right in the middle of the crowd presently surrounding Merch Arnot and Mayor Wiley (to say nothing of Gretchen). He had a piece of paper in his hand and he was waving it around angrily. He looked ready to bust several major blood vessels, not all of them his.

Everyone knows how Mayor Wiley and Uncle Henry go way back, so it wasn't just on account of Uncle Henry's highly influential job as Chief Registrar of Voters that Mayor Wiley came right up to him and asked in his most tell-me-where-it-hurts tone, "What's the matter, old son?"

"I'll *tell* you what's the matter!" Uncle Henry barked, his wattles spanking in the breeze. "Merch Arnot and this monster have taken Election Day and turned it into a *mess*! A *travesty*! A *disgrace*! I was upstreet at the school, doing my civic duty, and I want to tell you that as soon as word reached us about the doings down at *this* end of town, we lost three-quarters of the voters! They just *had* to rush out and rubberneck. And then some other damn busybody ran in hollering that the monster was headed our way, my God, didn't we go and lose the *rest* of the voters plus every last one of my volunteers! Everyone except for old man Hackett, and the only reason he didn't take off was Mighty Alan stole his walker!"

Mayor Wiley shook his head. "Henry, Henry, Henry," he said patiently. "What've I told you about hiring superheroes? Just because they can do everything, they think they can get away with anything."

Uncle Henry was not to be distracted from his righteous wrath. "*You* try scaring up volunteers to man the polls in this town! No civic pride, none at all, and I can't do it all by myself. Mighty Alan is a citizen of Sutter, same as you and me, with all rights and privileges appertaining thereto. It's not his fault he can fly and fold rocks with his bare hands and repel most harmful projectiles. If he volunteers, I'll take him. I didn't hear anyone complaining when he did jury duty!"

"When he did jury duty, he got to *sit still*," Mayor Wiley explained. "When he mans the polls he's got to *do* things with the voting booths and you know what that means: he breaks them. Takes them apart like they were made out of small curd cottage cheese, and I don't need to tell you that they're expensive to replace. He can't help it. His strength is as the strength of ten because his heart is pure."

"Then find him a woman before next Election Day!" Uncle Henry shot back. "Get his ashes hauled once and for all, purity adjusted, problem solved. Why the hell do *I* have to think of everything?"

Everyone within earshot coloured up bright red and didn't say a word. I do believe that our late Uncle Henry was the only soul in Sutter who didn't know that Mighty Alan was gayer than a Liberace Vegas Special. Mayor Wiley recovered his natural aplomb enough to ask, "Henry, why *did* Mighty Alan steal old man Hackett's walker?"

Uncle Henry scowled. "He said he was going to use it to wedge open the jaws of the monster."

"Uh-*huh*." Mayor Wiley nodded, then he looked up- and downstreet, casual. "You know, an aluminium walker couldn't keep a 'gator's jaws wedged open any appreciable amount of time, let alone something that's got choppers like *that*." He nodded towards Gretchen. She did have an impressive set of mouthbones on her, no argument there.

"I know it," Uncle Henry replied. "You know it. But *you* try arguing with a superhero. Like talking to the less intelligent parts of a brick wall."

"True, true." Mayor Wiley stroked his chin and glanced up and down Main Street again. "So tell me, Henry: if Mighty

Alan stole old man Hackett's aluminium walker to use as a weapon against the monster, and he did it up at the school, and the school's an easy walk from here, and Mighty Alan can fly, then why wasn't he *here* with that damned walker at least thirty minutes *before* this whole mess got started?"

Margaret Lee patted him on the shoulder. "Maybe he got lost," she said.

"How in hell could a man who can fly like a ****ing bird get lost in *this* town?" Mayor Wiley roared.

Margaret Lee shrugged. "Men never ask directions."

As the saying goes, speak of the gay superhero and he shall appear. Rory Vega glanced up, pointed at the friendly skies over Main Street, and hollered, "Look! It's a bird! It's a plane! It's —"

"It's gonna be a copyright lawyer on your sorry ass if you don't shut up," little Timmy snapped, none the worse for his recent ordeal except for being covered in reptile spit. "You do this same dumb routine every time Mighty Alan shows up. Jesus in a jitney, Vega, get some new material!"

Rory's caustic reply to the child was lost in the roar of our own superhero's aerial passage, old man Hackett's walker giving off little semaphor flashes of sunlight in his hands. "Fear naught!" Mighty Alan thundered from on high. "I shall dispose of the monster post-haste!" And he zoomed in for the kill.

We all tried to stop him. The crowd hollered and yelled and waved things until we were hoarse and tired, but it didn't do any good. Mighty Alan is strong and brave and he can fly and he has the ability to communicate with desert marmots, but *you* try telling a superhero that he is a skosh too late to make his daring rescue. They got super-hearing out the wazoo but that doesn't mean they *listen* worth a damn. He came flying on in like a Sidewinder missile, despite our best efforts to dissuade him, and he hit poor Gretchen right in the snout.

Lucky thing for him that his aim was off, or he might've done some actual harm to the critter, and then there'd've been hell to pay, with Eliza and Beth Arnot as Beelzebub's top repo men. He hit Gretchen in the snout all right, like I said, but he didn't do it with the walker, just his shoulder. It was more a body-check than an actual damage-doer. The Jackalopasaurus Rex tossed her head back, scared, let out a squeal like three freight cars full of hogs, and jumped. It looked like the start of the Main Street Destruction Derby all over again, except for the fact that this time Merch Arnot had tied her to the biggest nearby object left standing, namely my pickup truck. Big as she was, it was impossible for her to take off with a whole Chevy pickup anchoring her to earth. She went about six feet straight for heaven, hit the end of her tether, jerked up short, and hit the dirt at speed.

Unfortunately it was the portion of dirt which Uncle Henry was occupying at the time. He was a good man and a tough man, but no man I know of is tough enough to withstand the impact of a bungee-jumping Jackalopasaurus Rex. Maybe in Texas.

Now so far we'd had one genuine tragedy (Uncle Henry), and one almost-tragedy (Merch Arnot thought Gretchen'd broken her leg and he'd have to shoot her but she hadn't so he didn't), and a lot of property damage, and not too much of anything out of the ordinary at all, but *this* is the part where it gets *weird*.

Uncle Henry's last official act as Chief Registrar of Voters was to close the polls early, on account of Gretchen. Since he died before he was able to re-open them, the votes as they then stood gave Mayor Wiley a clear-cut win. They announced the results that evening in the Parker Funeral Home, where most everyone in town had gathered anyway to mark Uncle Henry's passing. A couple of Mayor Wiley's supporters applauded as loudly as they could, considering the place and the circumstances.

Then Mayor Wiley got up and stood in front of Uncle Henry's coffin, which was closed for obvious reasons. He cleared his throat, he thanked everyone for their support, and then he dropped something on us that was bigger than Gretchen and nowhere near as likely: he said he wasn't going to accept the results of the election because that wouldn't be moral. He said that this is a democracy and it wouldn't be fair of him to take personal, political advantage of a municipal tragedy. He said that first thing in the morning he was going to do the only ethical thing and start an intensive effort to mandate a new election, pronto. He said it was the only honest thing to do.

Honest. Mayor Wiley, lifetime politician, honest. Ethical. Moral. ****. Even with it all written down like this, there's no way on God's good green earth I'm going to be able to make *that* sound believable to Dad. No way *anyone* could. Not at long distance rates, anyhow.

Maybe I'll just tell him Uncle Henry's sick.

A DEALING WITH DEMONS

Craig Shaw Gardner

The previous volume, The Mammoth Book of Comic Fantasy, *reprinted "A Malady of Magicks" by Craig Shaw Gardner (b. 1949) which introduced the wizard Ebenezum, who is allergic to magic. It was the first story in what subsequently developed into a popular series of books, which include* A Malady of Magicks *(1986),* A Multitude of Monsters *(1986),* A Night in the Netherhells *(1987),* A Difficulty with Dwarves *(1987),* An Excess of Enchantments *(1988) and* A Disagreement with Death *(1989). Gardner has written plenty of other fun novels since then, including the Cineverse series in which the worst of Hollywood's B-movies turn out to be reality – Slaves of the Volcano God *(1989),* Bride of the Slime Monster *(1990) and* Revenge of the Fluffy Bunnies *(1990). The following story takes us back to the early days of Ebenezum and his well-meaning apprentice, Wuntvor.*

I

"Every sorcerer should explore as much of the world as he can, for travel is enlightening. There are certain circumstances, such as a major spell gone awry or an influential customer enraged at the size of your fee, in which travel becomes more enlightening still."
                    – from *The Teachings of Ebenezum*, Volume 5

We were forced, at last, to leave our cottage and go seek outside assistance. My master realized he could not cure his own affliction – the first time, I think, that the wizard had to face up to such a circumstance. So we travelled to find another mage of sufficient skill and cunning to cure my master's sorcerous malady, though we might have to travel to far Vushta, the city of a thousand forbidden delights, before we found another as great as Ebenezum.

Still, ever since the wizard had contracted the malady that caused him to sneeze uncontrollably in the presence of magic, life had been something of a problem. The affliction had occurred shortly after my master encountered a certain powerful demon from the seventh Netherhell. Ebenezum banished the creature in the end, surely the most fearsome he had ever faced, but his victory was not without its cost. From his moment of triumph onward, should he be confronted by sorcery in any form whatsoever, Ebenezum sneezed.

I believe Ebenezum had coped better than many would have in similar circumstances, still managing to ply his trade in small ways, mostly through the use of his wits rather than spells. But, then, Ebenezum had always told me that nine-tenths of magic was in the imagination.

Now, however, I was worried.

Ebenezum walked before me along the closest thing we could find to a path in these overgrown woods. Every few paces he would pause, so that I, burdened with a pack stuffed with arcane and heavy paraphernalia, could catch up with his wizardly strides. He, as usual, carried nothing, preferring, as he often said, to keep his hands free for quick conjuring and his mind free for the thoughts of a mage.

But all was not right with my master. I saw it in his walk – the same long strides he always took, but something was missing – the calm placing of one foot in front of another, knowing that whatever lay in one's path, a wizard could handle it. He walked too swiftly now, anxious to be done with what I imagined he thought the most unsavoury of tasks: asking another wizard for aid. It threatened to affect his whole bearing. For the first time in my long apprenticeship I feared for my master.

The wizard stopped mid-path to gaze at the thick growth about us. "I will admit I'm worried, Wunt." He scratched at the thick, white hair beneath his sorcerer's cap. "My maps and guidebooks indicated this was a lively area, with much commerce and no dearth of farms and friendly inns. That is the prime reason I took this route, for though we have cash from our recent exploits, a little more wouldn't hurt in the least."

The wizard stared out into the dark wood, his bushy eyebrows knit in concern. "Frankly, I wonder now about the effectiveness of certain other preparations I made for our journey. You never know what you'll encounter when travelling."

There was a great crashing of underbrush to one side of the trail. Branches were rent asunder; leaves rustled and tore away; small forest creatures cried in fright.

"Doom!" cried someone from within the thicket. Something large fell between my master and myself. Ebenezum sneezed. There was sorcery in the air!

"Doom!" the voice cried again, and the dark brown object that had fallen between us rose again into the air. It was a tremendous club, I realized, for attached to the end nearest the thicket was a large hand, in turn attached to an arm that disappeared into the heavy greenery. Ebenezum fell back a few paces along the path and blew his nose on a wizardly sleeve, ready to conjure despite his affliction.

The club rose and fell repeatedly to crush the underbrush. A man appeared in the cleared space. He was enormous – well over six feet in height, with a great bronze helmet topped by ornamental wings that made him look even taller. And he was almost as wide as he was tall, his stomach covered by armour of the same dull bronze.

He stepped out to block our path. "Doom!" his deep voice intoned once more. Ebenezum sneezed.

There was no helping it. I dropped my pack and grabbed my stout oak staff in both hands. The armoured man took a step toward the helplessly sneezing wizard.

"Back, villain!" I cried in a voice rather higher than I would have liked. Waving the staff above my head, I rushed the fiend.

"Doom!" the warrior intoned again. His barbed club met my staff in mid air, shearing the sturdy oak in two.

"Doom!" The fiend swung once more. I ducked to avoid the blow and slipped on a pile of crushed leaves and vines littered beneath my feet. My left foot shot from under me, then my right. I fell into a bronze-plated belly.

"Doo-oof!" the warrior cried as he fell. His helmet struck the base of a tree, and he cried no more.

"Quick, Wunt!" Ebenezum gasped. "The club!"

He tossed a sack at my shoulder. I pushed myself off the armoured belly and managed to fit the cloth around the heavy weapon. The wizard let out a long sigh and blew his nose.

"Enchanted."

So it was the club, and not the warrior, that had caused my master's sneezing attack. I regarded our now-prone opponent with some curiosity. The warrior groaned.

"Quick, Wunt!" Ebenezum called. "Quit dawdling and tie the fellow up. I have a feeling we have more to learn from our rotund assailant than first meets the eye."

The big man opened his eyes as I tightened the final knot on his wrists. "What? I'm still alive? Why haven't you killed and eaten me, like demons usually do?"

"What?" Ebenezum stared down at him, his eyes filled with wizardly rage. "Do we look like demons?"

The huge man paused. "Now that you mention it, not all that much. But you must be demons! It is my doom to always confront demons, my fate to fight them everywhere I turn, lest I be drawn into the Netherhells myself!" A strange light seemed to come into the large man's eyes, or perhaps it was only the quivering of his massive cheeks. "You could be demons in disguise! Perhaps you wish to torture me – slowly, exquisitely – with a cruelty known only to the Netherhells! Well, let's get it over with!"

Ebenezum stared at the quivering warrior for a long moment, pushing his fingers through his great white beard. "I think the best torture would be to leave you talking to yourself. Wunt, if you'll shoulder your pack again?"

"Wait!" the stout man cried. "Perhaps I was hasty. You don't act like demons, either. And the way you felled me – lucky blow to the stomach! You must be human! No demon could be that clumsy!

"Come, good fellows, I shall make amends!" He tugged at his hands, bound behind him. "But someone's tied me up!"

I assured him it had only been a precaution. We thought he might be dangerous.

"Dangerous?" That look came into his eyes again, or perhaps it was the way his helmet fell to his eyebrows. "Of course I'm dangerous! I am the dread Hendrek of Melifox!"

He paused expectantly.

"You haven't heard of me?" he asked after neither of us responded. "Hendrek, who wrested the enchanted war club Headbasher from the demon Brax, with the promise that it would be mine forever? The cursed Headbasher, which drinks the memories of men? Yet I cannot rid myself of it, for the power it gives me! I need the club, despite its dread secret."

His sunken eyes turned to the sack that held his weapon. "The demon did not inform me of the terms!" The warrior began to shake. "No man can truly own Headbasher! He can only rent it! Twice a week, sometimes more, I am confronted by demons making demands. I must slay them or do their fearsome bidding! For Brax did not tell me when I won the club, I won it on the instalment plan!" He quivered uncontrollably, his armour clanking against his corpulent form.

"Instalment plan?" mused Ebenezum, his interest suddenly aroused. "I had not thought the accountants of the Netherhells so clever."

"Aye, clever and more than that! Poor warrior that I am, I

despaired of ever finding anyone to save me from this curse till I heard a song from a passing minstrel about the deeds of a great magician, Ebenezer!"

"Ebenezum," my master corrected.

"You've heard of him?" A cloud seemed to pass from before Hendrek's eyes. "Where can I find him? I am penniless, on the edge of madness! He's my last hope!"

I glanced at the wizard. Didn't the warrior realize?

"But he's –"

Ebenezum silenced me with a finger across his lips. "Penniless, did you say? You realize a wizard of his stature must charge dearly for his services. Of course, there is always barter –"

"But of course!" Hendrek cried. "You're a magician, too! Perhaps you can help me find him. I ask not only for myself, but for a noble cause – a curse that threatens the entire kingdom, emanating from the very treasury of Melifox!"

"Treasury?" Ebenezum stood silent for a long moment, then smiled broadly for the first time since we began our journey. "Look no farther, good Hendrek. I am Ebenezum, the wizard of whom you speak. Come, we will free your treasury of whatever curse has befallen it."

"And my doom?"

My master waved a hand in sorcerous dismissal. "Of course, of course. Wunt, untie the gentleman."

I did as I was told. Hendrek pushed himself erect and lumbered over to his club.

"Leave that in the sack, would you?" Ebenezum called. "Just a sorcerous precaution."

Hendrek nodded and tied the sack to his belt.

I reshouldered my pack and walked over to my master. He seemed to have the situation well in hand. Perhaps my concern had been misplaced.

"What need have you to worry?" I asked in a low voice. "Minstrels still sing your praises."

"Aye," Ebenezum whispered back. "Minstrels will sing anyone's praises for the right fee."

II

"A professional sorcerer must espouse a strict code of ethics; a position that is not as limiting as it first appears. Most things are still possible within these ethical restrictions, so long as the sorcerer takes every precaution that, whatever he may do, he does not get caught doing it."
                                                  – from *The Teachings of Ebenezum*, Volume 9

The warrior Hendrek led us through the thick underbrush, which, if anything, became more impassable with every step. The late-afternoon sun threw long shadows across our paths, making it difficult to see exactly where you placed your feet, which made the going slower still.

As we stumbled through the darkening wood, Hendrek related the story of the curse of Krenk, capital city of the kingdom of Melifox, and how demons roamed the city, making it unsafe for human habitation, and how the land all around the capital grew wild and frightening, like the woods we passed through now. How Krenk had two resident wizards, neither of whom had been able to lift the curse, so that as a last resort Hendrek had struck a bargain for an enchanted weapon, but had failed to read the infernally small print. But then their ruler, the wise and kind Urfoo the Brave, heard a song from a passing minstrel about a great wizard from the forest country. Hendrek had been sent to find that wizard, at any cost!

"Any cost?" Ebenezum echoed. His step had regained the calm dignity I was more familiar with, not even faltering in the bramble patch we were now traversing.

"Well," Hendrek replied, "Urfoo has been known to exaggerate slightly on occasion. I'm sure, though, that as you're the last hope of the kingdom, he'll –"

Hendrek stopped talking and stared before him. We had reached a solid wall of vegetation, stretching as far as the eye could see and a dozen feet above our heads. "This wasn't here before," Hendrek muttered. He reached out a hand to touch the dense green wall. A vine snaked out and encircled his wrist.

Ebenezum sneezed.

"Doom!" Hendrek screamed and pulled his great club Headbasher from the sack at his belt.

Ebenezum sneezed uncontrollably.

Hendrek's club slashed at the vine, but the greenery bent with the blow. The whole wall was alive now, a dozen vines and creepers waving through the air. They reached for Hendrek's massive form; his swinging club pushed them back. Ebenezum hid his head within his voluminous robes. Muffled sneezing emerged from the folds.

Something grabbed my ankle: a brown vine, even thicker than those that threatened Hendrek, winding up my leg toward my thigh. I panicked, tried to leap away but only succeeded in losing my footing. The vine dragged me toward the unnatural wall.

Hendrek was there before me, slashing in the midst of the gathered green. His strokes were weaker than before, and he no longer cried out. Vines encircled his form, and it was only the matter of a moment before he was lost to the leafage.

I yanked again at the creeper that held me captive. It still held fast, but I caught a glimpse of my master behind me as I was dragged the last few feet to the wall.

The vines crept all about the wizard but were only now pushing at his sorcerous robes, as if the animate vegetation somehow sensed that Ebenezum was a greater threat than either Hendrek or myself. A gnarled tendril crept toward the wizard's sleeve, groped toward his exposed hand.

Ebenezum flung the robes away from his face and made three complex passes in the air, uttering a dozen syllables before he sneezed again. The tendril at his sleeve grew brown and withered, dissolving into dust.

My leg was free! I kicked the dead vine away and stood. Ebenezum blew his nose heartily on his sleeve. Hendrek had collapsed in what had been the vegetable wall. Leaves crackled beneath him as he gasped in air.

"Doom," Hendrek groaned as I helped him to his feet. "'Tis the work of demons, set on extracting vengeance on me for nonpayment!"

Ebenezum shook his head. "Nonsense. 'Twas nothing more than sorcery. A simple vegetable-aggression spell, emanating from Krenk, I imagine." He started down the newly cleared path. "Time to be off, lads. Someone, it appears, is expecting us."

I gathered up my gear as quickly as possible and trotted after Ebenezum. Hendrek took up the rear, muttering even more darkly than before. I saw what looked like a city before us on a distant hill, its high walls etched against the sunset sky.

We reached the walls some time after nightfall. Hendrek pounded on the great oak gate. There was no response.

"They fear demons," Hendrek said in a low voice. Rather more loudly, he called: "Ho! Let us in! Visitors of Importance to the Township of Krenk!"

"Says who?" A head clad in an ornate silver helmet appeared at the top of the wall.

"Hendrek!" the warrior intoned.

"Who?" the head replied.

"The dread Hendrek, famed in song and story!"

"The dread who?"

The warrior's hand clutched convulsively at the sack that held the club. "Hendrek, famed in song and story, who wrested the doomed club Headbasher –"

"Oh, Hendrek!" the head exclaimed. "That large fellow that King Urfoo the Brave sent off on a mission the other day!"

"Aye! So open the gates! Don't you recognize me?"

"You do bear a passing resemblance. But one can't be too careful these days. You look like Hendrek, but you might be two or three demons, huddled close together."

"Doom!" Hendrek cried. "I must get through the gate, to bring the wizard Ebenezum and his assistant before the king!"

"Ebenedum?" The head's voice rose in excitement. "The one the minstrels sing about?"

"Ebene*zum*," my master corrected.

"Yes!" Hendrek roared back. "So let us in. There are demons about!"

"My problem exactly," the head replied. "The two others could be demons, too. With the three huddled together to masquerade as Hendrek, that would make five demons I'd be letting through the gate. One can't be too careful these days, you know."

Hendrek threw his great winged helmet to the ground. "Do you expect us to stand around here all night?"

"Not necessarily. You could come back first thing in the morni–" The head's suggestion was cut short when it was swallowed whole by some large green thing that glowed in the darkness.

"Demons!" Hendrek cried. "Doom!" He pulled his war club from the sack. Ebenezum sneezed violently. Meanwhile, up on the parapet, a second thing had joined the first. This one glowed bright pink.

What appeared to be an eye floating above the circular green glow turned to regard the pink thing, while the eye above the pink turned to look at the green. Something dropped from the middle of the green mass and writhed its way toward us down the wall. A similar tentacle came from the pink creature to grab the green appendage and pull it back up the wall. Both orbs grew brighter, with a whistling sound that rose and rose; then both vanished with a flash and a sound like thunder.

The door to the city opened silently before us.

The wizard turned away from Hendrek and blew his nose.

"Interesting city you have here," Ebenezum said as he led the way.

There was something waiting for us inside. Something about four and a half feet high, its skin a sickly yellow. It wore a strange suit of alternate blue and green squares, as if someone had painted a chessboard across the material. A piece of red cloth was tied in a bow around its neck. There were horns on its head and a smile on its lips.

"Hendrek!" the thing cried. "Good to see you again!"

"Doom," the warrior replied as he freed his club from the sack. Ebenezum stepped away and held his robes to his nose.

"Just checking on my investment, Henny. How do you like your new war club?"

"Spawn of the Netherhells! Headbasher will never be yours again!"

"Who said we wanted it? Headbasher is yours – for a dozen easy payments! And nothing that costly. A few souls of second-rate princes, the downfall of a minor kingdom, a barely enchanted jewel or two. Then the wondrous weapon is truly yours!"

The creature deftly dodged the swinging war club. Cobblestones flew where the club hit the street.

"And what a weapon it is!" the demon continued. "The finest war club to ever grace our showroom! Did I say used? Let's call it previously owned. This cream puff of a weapon sat in the arsenal of an aged king, who only used it on Sunday to bash in the heads of convicted felons. Thus its colourful name and its beautiful condition. Take it from me, Smilin' Brax –" the demon fell to the pavement as Headbasher whizzed overhead "– there isn't a finer used club on the market today. As I was saying just the other day to my lovely – *urk* –"

The demon stopped talking when I hit it on the head. I had managed to sneak up behind the creature as it babbled and knocked it with a rather large cobblestone. The creature's blue and green checked knees buckled under the blow.

"Easy terms!" it gasped.

Hendrek quickly followed with a blow from Headbasher. The demon ducked, but it was still groggy from the first blow. The club caught its shoulder.

"Easy payments!" the thing groaned.

Hendrek's club came down square on the sickly yellow head. The demon's smile faltered. "This may be – the last time – we make this special offer!" The creature groaned again and vanished.

Hendrek wiped the yellow ichor off Headbasher with a shabby sleeve. "This is my doom," he whispered hoarsely. "To be forever pursued by Smiling Brax, with his demands for Headbasher, which no man can own but can only rent!" That strange light seemed to come into his eyes again, though perhaps it was only the reflection of the moon on the cobblestones.

Ebenezum stepped from the shadows. "It doesn't seem as bad as all that – uh, put that club back in the sack, would you? That's a good mercenary; mustn't take any chances." He blew his nose. "The two of you defeated the demon tidily."

My master pulled his beard reflectively. "As I see it, the

effectiveness of any curse depends on how the cursed looks at it. Watching the proceedings very carefully, with a wizard's trained eye, mind you, I can state categorically that once we disenchant the treasury, you'll have nothing to worry about."

A weight seemed to lift from Hendrek's brow. "Really?"

"You may depend on it." Ebenezum brushed at his robes. "Incidentally, does good King Urfoo really consider us his last hope for rescuing his gold?"

III

"A wizard who wants to build his reputation rapidly should locate in a rural rather than an urban setting. Magic seems more majestic when set against the broad vistas of the countryside. Townspeople, on the other hand, are so used to the action of certain tradespeople and government officials in their midst that the average conjurer's trick pales in comparison."

– from *The Teachings of Ebenezum*, Volume 10

Hendrek led us through the silent, winding streets of Krenk to the castle of King Urfoo. Having grown up in the duchy of Gurnish, in and around Wizard's Woods, Krenk was the largest town I had ever seen, with walls and a gate, as many as five hundred buildings, even paved streets! But I saw nothing else as we walked. Where were the taverns at which we could stop and exchange pleasantries with the natives? Where were the town's attractive young women? How could I be prepared when we finally arrived in Vushta, the city of a million forbidden delights, if every town we came to was as dead as this?

There was a scream in the distance. Hendrek froze, but the scream was followed by a woman's laughter. At least someone was enjoying herself, I supposed. Was the whole town so afraid of demons?

We came to an open space, in the middle of which was a building twice as grand and five times as large as anything around it. There was a guard standing in front of the palace's huge door, the first human (not counting the head) we'd seen since entering Krenk.

"Halt!" the guard cried as we walked into the courtyard before him. "And be recognized!"

Hendrek kept on moving. "Important business with King Urfoo!" he replied.

The guard unsheathed his sword. "Identify yourself, under penalty of death!"

"Doom!" the immense warrior moaned. "Don't you recognize Hendrek, back from an important mission for the king?"

The guard squinted in the darkness. "Don't I recognize who? I didn't quite catch the name."

"The dread Hendrek, here with the wizard Ebenezum!"

"Ebenezus? The one they all sing about?" The guard bowed in my master's direction. "I'm honoured, sir, to meet a wizard of your stature."

The guard turned back to Hendrek, who was quite close to the door by now. "Now, what did you say your name was again? I can't let just anybody through this door. You can't be too careful these days, you know."

"Doom!" Hendrek cried, and with a speed amazing in one so large, pulled his club from its restraining sack and bashed the guard atop the head.

"Urk," the guard replied. "Who are you? Who am I? Who cares?" The guard fell on his face.

"Headbasher, the club that drinks the memories of men. He will recover anon but will remember none of this, or anything else, for that matter." Hendrek re-sheathed his club. "Come, we have business with Urfoo." He kicked the door aside and stormed into the castle.

I glanced at my master. He stroked his moustache for a moment, then nodded and said: "The treasury." We followed Hendrek inside.

We walked down a long hall. Sputtering torchlight made our shadows dance against huge tapestries that covered the walls. A breeze from somewhere blew against my coat to make me feel far colder than I had outside. This, I realized, was the castle with the curse.

Two guards waited before a door hung with curtains at the far end of the hall. Hendrek bashed them both before either could say a word.

Hendrek kicked this door open as well.

"Who?" a voice screamed from the shadow of a very large chair on a raised platform in the room's centre.

"Hendrek," the warrior replied.

"Who's that?" A head sporting a crown peered over the arm of the great chair. "Oh, yes, that portly fellow we sent off last week. What news, what?"

"I've brought Ebenezum."

There was a great rustling as people rose from their hiding places around the room. "Nebeneezum?" someone said from behind a chair. "Ebenezix?" came a voice from behind a pillar.

"Ebenezum," my master replied.

"Ebenezum!" a chorus of voices responded as a good two dozen people stepped from behind marble columns, tapestries and suits of armour to stare at my master.

"*The* Ebenezum? The one they sing about?" King Urfoo sat up straight in his throne and smiled. "Hendrek, you shall be justly rewarded!" The smile fell. "Once we take the curse off the treasury, of course."

"Doom," Hendrek replied.

King Urfoo directed us to sit on cushioned chairs before him, then paused to look cautiously at the room's shadow-hung corners. Nothing stirred. The ruler coughed and spoke. "Best get down to business, what? One can't be too careful these days."

"My thoughts exactly, good king." Ebenezum rose from his seat and approached the throne. "I understand there's a cursed treasury involved? There's no time to waste."

"Exactly!" Urfoo glanced nervously at the rafters overhead. "My money involved, too. Lovely money. No time to waste. I'd best introduce you now to my sorcerous advisers."

Ebenezum stopped his forward momentum. "Advisers?"

"Yes, yes the two court wizards. They can fill you in on the details of the curse." Urfoo tugged a cord by his side.

"I generally work alone." My master pulled at his beard. "But when there's a cursed treasury involved, I suppose one can adjust."

A door opened behind the king and two robed figures emerged, one male, one female. "No time to waste!" the king exclaimed. "May I introduce you to your colleagues, Granach and Vizolea?"

The newcomers stood at either side of Urfoo's throne, and the three wizards regarded each other in silence for an instant. Then Vizolea smiled and bowed to my master. She was a tall, handsome woman of middle years, almost my height, red hair spiced with grey, strong green eyes, white teeth showing in an attractive smile.

Ebenezum returned the gesture with a flourish.

Granach, an older man dressed in grey, nodded to my master in turn, something on his face half-smile, half-grimace.

"The problem," King Urfoo said, "is demons, of course." He cringed on the word "demons", as if he expected one of them to strike him down for mentioning their existence. "We're beset with them. They're everywhere! But mostly," he pointed a quivering hand toward the ceiling, "they're in the tower that holds the treasury!"

He lowered his hand and took a deep breath.

"Doom," Hendrek interjected.

"But perhaps," the king continued, "my court wizards can give you a better idea of the sorcerous fine points." He glanced quickly to either side.

"Certainly, my lord," Granach said quickly behind his half-grimace. "Although none of this would have been necessary if we had used the Spell of the Golden Star."

Urfoo sat bolt upright. "No! That spell would cost me half my funds! There has to be a better way. Doesn't there?"

Ebenezum stroked his moustache. "Most assuredly. If the other wizards are willing to discuss the situation with me, I'm sure we can come to some solution."

"Nothing's better than the Golden Star!" Granach snapped.

"Half my gold!" the king cried. He added in a whisper: "Perhaps you should all – uh – inspect the tower?"

Granach and Vizolea exchanged glances.

"Very good, my lord," Vizolea replied. "Do you wish to accompany us now?"

"Accompany you?" Urfoo's complexion grew paler still. "Is that completely necessary?"

Vizolea nodded, a sad smile on her face. "For the hundredth time, yes. It states directly in the sorcerer's charter that a member of the royal family must accompany all magicians on visits to the treasury."

"Signed right there," Granach added. "At the bottom of the page. In blood."

Urfoo pushed his crown back to mop his brow. "Oh dear. How could that have happened?"

"If you'll excuse me for mentioning it, my lord," Vizolea said with downturned eyes, " 'twas you who stipulated the terms of the pact."

The king swallowed. "There is no time to waste. I must accompany you."

Granach and Vizolea nodded. "There's no helping it, without the Golden Star," Granach added.

"And so you shall!" My master's voice broke through the tension around the throne. "We shall inspect the treasury first thing in the morning!"

Urfoo, who had been sinking slowly in his throne, sat up again and smiled. "Morning?"

Ebenezum nodded. "My 'prentice and I have just completed a long journey. How much better to confront a curse during the light of day with a clear head!"

"Morning!" Urfoo the Brave shouted. He smiled at the court-appointed wizards. "You are dismissed until breakfast. Ebenezum, I can tell you are a wizard of rare perception. I shall have my serving girls make your beds and serve you dinner. And in the morning you will end the curse!"

I sat up straight myself. Serving girls? Perhaps there was something of interest in the township of Krenk after all.

"We must plan, Wunt," my master said when we were at last alone. "We only have till morning."

I turned from arranging the pile of cushions and skins that I was to sleep on. My master sat on the large bed they had provided him, head in hands, one on either side of his beard.

"I did not expect wizards." He threw his cap on the bed then and stood. "But the accomplished mage must be prepared for every eventuality. It is of utmost importance, especially concerning the size of our fee, that no one learn of my unfortunate malady."

The sorcerer paced across the room. "I shall instruct you on certain items that have been stored in your pack. We must keep up appearances. And the business with that warrior's enchanted club has given me an idea. We'll best my affliction yet."

There was a knock on the door.

"I was expecting that," Ebenezum said. "See which one it is."

I opened the door to find Granach. He shuffled into the room, still wearing his grimace smile.

"Excuse me for interrupting at so late an hour," the grey-clad wizard began, "but I did not feel earlier that I had the opportunity to welcome you properly."

"Indeed," Ebenezum replied, raising one bushy eyebrow.

"And I thought there were certain things you should be informed of. Before we actually visit the tower, that is."

"Indeed?" Both eyebrows rose this time.

"Yes. First a quick word of advice about our patron, King Urfoo the Brave. It is fortunate for him that Krenkians prefer epithets added early during a ruler's reign, for since he gave up chasm jumping at the age of sixteen, Urfoo has spent all his time in his treasury tower, counting his gold. Note that I didn't mention spending. Just counting. If you were anticipating a large return for your services, you might as well leave now. Our ruler should rather be called Urfoo the Stingy. The payment won't be worth the risk!"

"Indeed." Ebenezum stroked his beard.

Granach coughed. "Now that you know, I expect you'll be on your way."

My master tugged the creases of his sleeves into place and looked up at the other magician. "Indeed, no. A travelling magician, unfortunately, cannot pick and choose his tasks in the same way a town mage might. He has to accept what clients come his way and hope that what small payment he might receive will be enough to take him farther on his journey."

The toothy grimace disappeared completely from Granach's face. "You have been warned," he snarled from between tight lips. "The payment you will receive will in no way compensate for the danger you will face!"

Ebenezum smiled and walked to the door. "Indeed," he said as he opened it. "See you at breakfast?"

The other magician slithered out. Ebenezum closed the door behind him. "Now I'm sure there's money to be made here," he remarked. "But to business. I shall instruct you as to the proper volume and page number for three simple exorcism spells. I wonder, frankly, if we'll even need them."

He pulled one of the notebooks he was constantly writing in from his pocket and began to tear out pages. "In the meantime I will prepare my temporary remedy.

"The idea came from Hendrek's enchanted club." He tore the pages into strips. "When Hendrek's club is in the open air, I sneeze. However, when the club is in the sack, my nose is unaffected. It can no longer sense the club's sorcerous aroma. Therefore, if I stop my nasal sensitivity to things sorcerous, I should stop my sneezing!" He rolled the first of the strips into a tight cylinder. "But how to accomplish this, short of standing in the rain till I catch cold?"

He held the cylinder aloft so I could get a good look at it, then stuffed it up his nose.

There was another knock on the door.

"High time," Ebenezum said, pulling the cylinder back out. "See who it is this time, Wunt."

It was Vizolea. She had changed from her stiff wizard's robes into a flowing gown with a low neckline. Her deep green eyes looked into mine, and she smiled.

"Wuntvor, isn't it?"

"Yes," I whispered.

"I would like to talk to your master, Ebenezum." I stepped back to let her enter the room. "I've always wanted to meet a wizard of your skill."

"Indeed?" my master replied.

She turned back to me, touched my shoulder with one long-fingered hand. "Wuntvor? Do you think you could leave your master and me alone for a while?"

I glanced at the mage. He nodded rapidly.

"Let me tell you about the Golden Star," Vizolea said as I closed the door behind me.

I stood in the hallway outside our room for a moment, stunned. I had a feeling from Vizolea's manner that she wanted to do more than talk. With my master? I had been known in recent months to keep company with a number of young ladies in my home district, but somehow Ebenezum had always seemed to be above that sort of thing.

But I was still only an apprentice, unaware of the nuances of a true sorcerer's life. I sat heavily, wondering how I would get to sleep on the hallway's cold stone floor, and wishing, for just a moment, that a serving maid of my very own might wander by and make my situation more comfortable.

She wanted to leave.

"Wait!" I cried. "I'm a sorcerer's apprentice. When will you get another chance to dally with anyone half as interesting?"

She wouldn't listen. She drifted farther and farther away. I ran after her, trying to shorten the distance. It was no use. She was oblivious to me. I grabbed at her low-cut serving gown, pushed the tray from her hands, begged her to give me a single word.

"Doom," she said in a voice far too low.

I awoke to see Hendrek's face, lit by torchlight.

"Beware, Wuntvor! 'Tis not safe to sleep in these halls! Demons roam them in the wee hours!" He leaned closer to me, his overstuffed cheeks aquiver, and whispered: "You moaned so in your sleep, at first I thought you were a demon, too!"

I saw then he held Headbasher in his free hand. "Some nights I cannot sleep, I fear the demons so. 'Tis strange, though. Tonight I've seen nary a one. Grab onto my club!" He helped me to my feet. "What brings you to moans in the hallway?"

I explained my dreams of serving maids.

"Aye!" Hendrek replied. "This place is full of haunted dreams. This cursed palace was built by Urfoo's doomed grandfather – some called him Vorterk the Cunning, others called him Mingo the Mad. Still others called him Eldrag the Offensive, not to mention those few who referred to him as

Greeshbar the Dancer. But those are other stories. I speak now of the haunted corridors Vorterk built. Sound will sometimes carry along them for vast distances, seemingly from a direction opposite to where it actually originates. Hush, now!"

I didn't mention that it was he who did all the talking, for there was indeed a voice in the distance, screaming something over and over. I strained to hear.

It sounded like "Kill Ebenezum! Kill Ebenezum! Kill Ebenezum!"

"Doom!" Hendrek rumbled. I took a step in the direction of the screams. Hendrek grabbed my coat in his enormous fist and dragged me the other way through the maze of corridors. He paused at each intersection for a fraction of a moment, waiting for the screams to tell him which way to turn. Sometimes it seemed we turned toward the sounds, other times away. I became lost in no time at all.

But the voices became clearer. There were two of them, and the one no longer shouted. Both were agitated, though.

"I don't think so."

"But we have to!"

"You want to move too fast!"

"You don't want to move at all! We'll have to wait for years before we get that treasury!"

"If I let you handle it, it will slip through our fingers! We should enlist Ebenezum!"

"No! How could we trust him? Ebenezum must die!"

"Perhaps I should join Ebenezum and do away with you!"

Hendrek stopped suddenly and I walked into him. His armour banged against my knee.

"There's someone out there!"

A door flung open just before us. I froze, waiting for the owners of the voices to emerge.

Something else came out instead.

"Doom," Hendrek muttered when he saw it crawl our way. It looked like a spider, except that it was as large as me and had a dozen legs rather than eight. It was also bright red.

Hendrek swung the club above his head. Headbasher looked far smaller than it had before.

The creature hissed and jumped across the hall. Something

else followed it out of the room. Large and green, the new-comer looked somewhat like a huge, bloated toad with fangs. It jumped next to the spider-thing and growled in our direction.

"Doom, doom," Hendrek wheezed. I considered running, but Hendrek's bulk blocked my only escape route.

The bloated toad leapt in front of the almost-spider. Its fangs seemed to smile. Then the red many-legged thing scuttled over it in our direction. The toad growled and pushed past the dozen legs, but four legs wrapped around the toad and flipped it over. The almost-spider moved in front.

Then the toad-thing jumped straight on top of the many-legged red thing. The almost-spider hissed, the toad-thing growled. Legs interlocked; they rolled. Soon we could see nothing but flashing feet and dripping fangs.

Both disappeared in a cloud of brown, foul-smelling smoke.

"Doom," Hendrek muttered.

Another door opened behind us.

"Don't you think it was time you were in bed?"

It was Ebenezum.

I started to explain what had happened, but he motioned me to silence. "You need your sleep. We've a big day tomorrow." He nodded at Hendrek. "We'll see you in the morning."

The warrior looked once more at the spot where the crea-tures had disappeared. "Doom," he replied, and walked down the hall.

"Not if I can help it," Ebenezum said as he closed the door.

IV

"Never trust another sorcerer is a saying unfortunately all too common among magical practitioners. Actually there are many instances in which one can easily trust a fellow magician, such as cases in which no money is involved or when the other mage is operating at such a distance that his spells can't possibly affect you."

– from *The Teachings of Ebenezum*, Volume 14

No one ate when we met for breakfast. I sat quietly, running the three short spells I had memorized over and over in my head. My master was quieter than usual, too, being careful not to dislodge the thin rolls of paper that packed his nose. Vizolea and Granach glared at each other from opposite sides of the table, while Hendrek muttered and the king quivered.

Ebenezum cleared his throat and spoke with the lower half of his face. "We must inspect the tower." His voice sounded strangely hollow.

"The tower?" Urfoo whispered. "Well, yes, there's no time to lose." He swallowed. "The tower."

Ebenezum stood. The rest followed. "Hendrek," my master instructed, "lead the way."

The mage strode over to the king. "As we go on our inspection, Your Majesty, I should like to discuss the matter of our fee."

"Fee?" Urfoo quivered. "But there's no time to lose! The treasury is cursed!"

Vizolea was by my master's side. "Are you sure you really wish to inspect the tower? There may be things there you really don't want to see." Her hand brushed his shoulder. "You do remember our conversation last night?"

"Indeed." Ebenezum tugged his moustache meaningfully. "I have a feeling there are things about this treasury that will surprise all of us."

"Doom!" came from the front of the line as the procession moved from the throne room.

"Do I really have to come along?" came from the end.

"The charter," Granach replied.

"Perhaps we *are* being a bit hasty." The king wiped his brow with an ornate lace sleeve. "What say we postpone this, to better consider our options?"

"Postpone?" Granach exclaimed. He and Vizolea looked at each other. "Well, if we must."

They turned and started back for the great hall.

"If you postpone this," Ebenezum said as he caught the eye of the king, "King Urfoo may never see his money again."

"Never?" The king positively shook. "Money? Never? Money? Nevermoney?" He took a deep breath. "No time to lose! To the tower!"

We climbed a narrow flight of stairs to a large landing and another thick oak door.

"The treasury," Hendrek intoned.

"Your Majesty. The incantation, if you would," Granach remarked.

Urfoo huddled in the rear corner of the landing, eyes shut tight, and screamed:

> Give me an O! O!
> Give me a P! P!
> Give me an E! E!
> Give me an N! N!
> What's that spell?
> Open! Open! Open!

The door made a popping noise and did as it was bidden. No sound came from within.

"Go ahead," Urfoo called. "I'll just wait out here."

Ebenezum strode into the treasury.

The room was not large, but it was not particularly small, either. And it was full – of orange boxes and stacks of gold, fantastic jewellery and unmarked sacks, piled waist high at least, shoulder height near the walls.

We waded into the midst of it.

"Doom," Hendrek murmured. "So where are the demons?"

An unearthly scream came from the landing. Urfoo entered, pursued by the spider.

"The Spider of Spudora!" my master cried. He held his nose.

"Granach!" Vizolea exclaimed. "We didn't talk about this!"

"Your Majesty!" Granach shouted. "There is only one hope! The Golden Star, performed by me!"

"No you don't!" Vizolea recited a few quick words beneath her breath. "If anyone recites the Golden Star, it will be me!"

The toad-thing hopped into the room.

"The Toad of Togoth!" my master said.

"Quick, Urfoo!" Granach cried. "Give me leave to perform the spell before it's too late!"

A red claw snapped out of a pile of jewels.

"The Crab of Crunz!" my master informed me.

"Not the crab!" Vizolea shrieked. "This time, Granach, you've gone too far! Bring on the Lice of Liftiana!"

Granach stepped aside to avoid the panting Urfoo, now pursued by the almost-spider, the bloated toad, and a grinning crustacean.

"Oh, no, you don't!" he cried. "Bring forth the Bats of Billilappa!"

The air was getting heavy with insects and wings.

"That won't stop me! I summon the Rats of Ruggoth!"

"So? See how you handle the Mice of Myrgoll!"

"You asked for it! I bring forth the dread Cows of Cuddotha!"

My master flung his hands in the air. "Stop this now! You'll cause a sorcerous overload!"

The air shimmered as the room was filled with a chorus of moos. A sickly yellow form solidified before us.

"Ah, good Hendrek!" Smiling Brax exclaimed. "How good to see you again. We of the demon persuasion like to check out areas of extreme sorcerous activity; see if we can do a little business, as it were. And boy, is there business here! Perhaps some of you folks would like to purchase an enchanted blade or two, before some of my folks arrive?"

"Doom," Hendrek muttered.

Urfoo ran past. "All right! All right! I'll think about the Golden Star!" A blue cow with bloodshot eyes galloped after him.

"The Lion of Lygthorpedia!"

"The Grouse of Grimola!"

"Stop it! Stop it! It's too much!" Ebenezum pulled back his sleeves, ready to conjure.

"How about you, lad?" Brax said to me. "I've got this nifty enchanted dagger, always goes straight for the heart. Makes a dandy letter opener, too. I'm practically giving it away. Just sign on this line down here."

"The Tiger of Tabatta!"

"The Trout of Tamboul!"

"Too much!" Ebenezum shouted and sneezed the most

profound sneeze I had ever seen. Paper showered over the newly materialized devil trout, while the force of the blow knocked Ebenezum back against a pile of jewels.

He didn't move. He was out cold.

"Doom," Hendrek intoned.

"Then again," Brax said, looking around the room, "maybe I'd better sell you an axe."

"The Antelope of Arasapora!"

Someone had to stop this! It was up to me. I had to use the exorcism spells!

"Sneebly Gravich Etoa Shrudu –" I began.

"The Elephant of Erasia!"

Wait a second. Was it "Sneebly Gravich Etoa" or "Etoa Gravich Sneebly"? I decided to try it the other way, too.

"All right! You force my hand! The Whale of Wakkanor!"

There was an explosion in the centre of the room. Instead of a materialized whale, there was a lightless hole.

Ebenezum stirred on his bed of jewels.

Brax looked over his shoulder as the black void grew. "Drat. This would have to happen now, right on the edge of a sale. Oh, well, see you in the Netherhells!" The demon disappeared.

It was suddenly quiet in the room. The two other magicians had stopped conjuring, and all the demon creatures, crabs and cows, tigers and trout, had turned to watch the expanding hole.

Ebenezum opened his eyes. "A vortex!" he cried. "Quick, we can still close it if we work together!"

A wind rose, sucked into the hole. The creatures of the Netherhells, bats and rats, mice and lice, were drawn into the dark.

Granach and Vizolea both gestured wildly into the void.

"Together!" Ebenezum cried. "We must work together!" Then he began to sneeze. He pulled his robes to his nose, stepped back from the vortex. It was no use. He doubled over, lost to his malady.

The darkness was taking the jewels now, and the sacks of gold. And I could feel the wind pulling me. Granach screamed at it, and was drawn in. Vizolea cried against it, then she was gone. The blackness reached out for Hendrek and the king, my master and me.

Ebenezum flung his robes away, shouted a few words into the increasing gale. A bar of gold skidded by me and was swallowed. Ebenezum made a pass, and the vortex shrank. He gestured again, and the vortex grew smaller still, about the size of a man.

Then Ebenezum sneezed again.

"Doom!" Hendrek cried. King Urfoo, wide-eyed, was skidding across the floor to the void.

The warrior and I pushed against the wind to his aid. Jewels scattered beneath our feet and were lost. I pushed a chest toward the gaping maw, hoping to plug a part of it, but it was sucked straight through.

"My gold!" Urfoo cried as he rolled for the hole. I snagged a foot, Hendrek grasped the other. I struggled for footing on the loose jewels, which were moving beneath my feet. I slipped and fell into the warrior.

"Doo–oof!" he cried and lost his balance, back into the hole. The wind stopped. Hendrek stood, half here and half somewhere else. His girth had plugged the vortex.

Ebenezum blew his nose. "That's better." He recited a few incantations, sneezed once more and the hole sealed up as we pulled Hendrek free.

My master then gave a brief explanation to the king, who sat glassy-eyed on the now-bare floor of the treasury. How his wizards had tried to cheat him of half the treasury by inventing a curse when they couldn't get the money any other way, thanks to the sorcerous charter that called for a member of the royal family to open the door. How he had discovered this plot, and how he should be amply rewarded for saving the king's money.

"Money?" King Urfoo the Brave whispered as he looked around the room, perhaps a dozen jewels and gold pieces left where once there was a room of plenty. "Money! You've taken my money! Guards! Kill them! They've taken my money! Urk!"

Hendrek hit him on top of the head.

"They've – what? Where am I? Oh, hello." The king lost consciousness.

"Doom," Hendrek murmured. "Headbasher does its hell-ish job again."

My master suggested it might be a good time to travel.

V

"A wizard's robes are his badge of office, and one should always wear them proudly, unless one is not proud at that moment of being a wizard. In that case an artisan's frock, a monk's cowl or a dancer's veil are probably preferable, at least until the wizard reaches a friendlier clime."
– from *The Teachings of Ebenezum*, Volume 17

We had to wait for some hours in the pouring rain before we could get a ride away from Krenk. Ebenezum had thought it best, in case of pursuit, to cover his wizardly robes with a more neutral cloth of brown, and passing wagons were reticent to pick up three characters as motley-looking as we were, especially with one the size of Hendrek.

"Perhaps," Ebenezum suggested with a pull on his beard, "we would have better luck if we separated."

"Doom!" Hendrek shivered and clutched at the bag that held Headbasher. "But what of my curse?"

"Hendrek." The wizard put a comradely hand on the large warrior's shoulder. "I can guarantee you'll see nothing of Brax for quite some time. The severity of that vortex was such that it shook through at least three levels of the Netherhells. Take it from an expert; their transportation lines won't even be cleared for months!"

"Then," rumbled Hendrek, "I'm freed of Brax and his kind?"

"For the time being. Only a temporary remedy, I'm afraid. I have a certain affliction" – he paused, looking Hendrek straight in the eye – "also temporary, I assure you, that keeps me from effecting a more permanent cure. However, I shall give you the names of certain sorcerous specialists in Vushta, who should be able to help you immediately." My master wrote three names on a page of his notebook and gave them to the warrior.

Hendrek thrust the piece of parchment in Headbasher's bag, then bowed low to my master. "Thank you, great wizard. To Vushta, then." His head seemed to quake with emotion, but perhaps it was only the rain pouring upon his helmet.

"We're bound to Vushta ourselves, eventually," I added. "Perhaps we'll meet again."

"Who knows what the fates will?" said Hendrek as he turned away. "Doom."

He was soon lost in the heavy downpour.

Once the warrior was gone, I looked again to my master. He stood tall in the soaking rain, every inch a wizard despite his disguise. If any doubts had assailed Ebenezum on our arrival in Krenk, his actions in the subsequent events seemed to have erased them from his mind. He was Ebenezum, the finest wizard in all the forest country. And in Krenk as well!

Finally I could bear it no longer; I asked my master what he knew about the plot against King Urfoo.

" 'Tis simple enough," Ebenezum replied. "Urfoo had the wealth that the wizards wanted but couldn't get to, because of the charm on the door, so they devised the Spell of the Golden Star, through which, by their definition, Urfoo would have to release half the gold from the charmed tower in order for the spell to work. I don't blame them, in a way. According to Vizolea, the king hadn't gotten around to paying them in all the years they were in his service. Unfortunately, they got greedy and didn't work in unison, and you saw what happened. They even considered working the Golden Star spell three ways; at least Vizolea suggested as much, although" – my master coughed – "I usually don't engage in such activities."

He looked up and down the deserted road, then reached in his damp coat to pull out a bar of gold. "Good. I was afraid I'd lost it in our flight. I have so many layers of clothing on, I could no longer feel it."

I gaped as he hid the gold again. "How did you get that? The floor of the treasury was stripped."

"The floor was." The wizard nodded. "The inside of my robes was not. A wizard has to plan ahead, Wunt. Sorcerers are expected to maintain a certain standard of living."

I shook my head. I should never have doubted my master for a moment.

A covered cart pulled over to the side of the road.

"Need a ride?" the driver called. We clambered into the back.

" 'Tis a dismal night," the driver continued. "I'll sing you a song to lift your spirits. That's what I am – a travelling minstrel!"

Ebenezum looked out from his hood in alarm, then averted his face so that it would be lost in shadow.

"Let's see, what would be appropriate?" The minstrel tugged the reins of his mule. "Ah! Just the thing for a night straight from the Netherhells. I'll sing you a song about the bravest wizard around; fellow from the forest country up Gurnish way – um – Neebednuzum, I think he's called. Now, this ditty's a little long, but I think you'll be struck by the fellow's bravery."

Ebenezum had fallen asleep by the third verse.

THE CASE OF JACK THE CLIPPER

or

A Fimbulwinter's Tale

David Langford

The range of David Langford's wit and wisdom is awesome. He is, by profession, a nuclear physicist, and his "wisdom" surfaces in a number of serious tomes such as War in 2080 *(1979) and* The Third Millennium *(1985). But he's best known for his "wit", often to be found in the science fiction fan magazines. He has received umpteen Hugo Awards for his fan writings, some of which have been collected as* The Dragonhiker's Guide to Battlefield at Dune's Edge: Odyssey Two *(1988),* Let's Hear it for the Deaf Man *(1992) and* The Silence of the Langford *(1996). Langford (b. 1953) enjoys spoofs. His first book,* An Account of a Meeting with Denizens of Another World, 1871 *(1979), was taken seriously by UFO devotees. He has also parodied nuclear research in* The Leaky Establishment *(1984), and the disaster novel in* Earthdoom! *(1987), written with John Grant (whom you'll find elsewhere in this anthology). In the following story Langford turns his spoofing skills to the fiction of H. P. Lovecraft.*

Life is filled with bodings and portents. When I encountered my old acquaintance Smythe in the High Street I sensed that my own life was about to take some strange new turning . . . specifically, into the King's Head lounge bar, where with old-fashioned courtesy the renowned specialist in the uncanny reminded me that it was my shout.

"Cheers," I said a minute later, as we sat and sipped our bitter.

"*Ph'nglui mglw'nafh Cthulhu R'lyeh wgah'nagl fhtagn*," he responded eruditely; these occultists know many unfamiliar toasts. "I have just been picking up my new business cards – here, allow me to present you with one."

I studied the ornately engraved slip of pasteboard. *Dagon Smythe, Psychic Investigator*. "I can only admire the Seal of Solomon hologram . . . but, *Dagon* Smythe?"

"It is often advantageous, in this hazardous line of work, to have been prudent in one's choice of godparents. But stay! As a trained observer, I see that you have torn the sleeve of your jacket, probably on a protruding nail. I am reminded . . ."

"Is *that* the time?" I cried with the spontaneity that comes of long practice. "Well, I really must –"

"I am reminded," said Smythe inexorably, placing a gentle but firm hand on my forearm, "of a certain rather curious investigation in which nails played an interesting role. Nails, and old gods, and the end of the world."

"Why, yes! I remember that case well. One of your finest. The crooked occult-supplies house that used scanning tunnelling microscope technology to dismantle a nail from the True Cross into its individual atoms, enabling them to flood the market with countless billions of genuine if very tiny talismans and . . ."

"A different case, my friend, and a different kind of nail. This was some years ago in the small old town of F————, which lies close to D———— in the county of B————. It was there that I investigated a weird reign of nightly terror.

You must imagine the town's twisty streets swirling with late autumn fogs, so that every passer-by appeared as an eerie, phantasmal silhouette. And any one of those shadows in the night might be the creature that had earned the nickname . . . Jack the Clipper."

"Ripper?" I enquired.

"Clipper. For, time and again, the men (never the women) of that accursed town would report dim memories of a particularly strange shape that loomed through icy fog. A shape with a hint of flickering flame about it, no sooner perceived than lost in a mysterious tumble into unconsciousness. Then, seconds or minutes afterwards, the victim would find himself sprawled on the chilly stone of the pavement, his shoes and socks mysteriously removed in that interlude of missing time, and – sinister and eldritch beyond all imagining – *his toenails neatly clipped*."

At this point, being caught in mid-gulp, I suffered a regrettable accident with my pint of bitter.

"You laugh, do you? You laugh?"

"Some of the beer went the wrong way," I lied, shaking my head determinedly.

"Shallow and innocent person that you are, ignorant of all occult implication, you laughed. It is not so funny when you recollect that nail-clippings – the *exuviae* coveted by witches – play an important part in rituals of binding, of magical domination. And this elusive Jack the Clipper had struck again and again, night after night, amassing these means of sorcerously controlling what might ultimately prove to be the entire male population of the town of F————." He shuddered dramatically. "The hidden hand that wielded such control had the potential for unleashing very great evil indeed, up to and including a by-election victory for the Conservative Party. No . . . this was indeed no laughing matter."

I nodded dutifully. "And, er, this kind of voodoo control with sympathetic magic and waxen dolls and toenails, this was indeed the secret behind what was happening?"

"Oddly enough, it was not." Smythe drained his glass and placed it meaningfully on the table. I did the same, a trifle more meaningfully. There was a short pause.

*   *   *

Abruptly he continued: "You will remember my fervent belief in the value of applying the full range of modern technology to problems of occult investigation. I pioneered the Laser Pentacle, which outdid dear old Carnacki's electric version by vaporizing the more susceptible ab-human manifestations even as they attempted to pass through the wards. It was I who designed what has become the standard electronic probe for registering demonic presences, the Baphometer. Now the town of F——— offered an opportunity to field-test my experimental, computerized zombie spotter."

"Pardon?" Sometimes my friend's uncanny intuitive leaps eluded me.

"This mechanism was inspired by what students of artificial intelligence call the Eliza Effect . . . a shorthand for a kind of mental blindness which most human minds share. ELIZA is a rudimentary computer program which tries to imitate a psychotherapist – you type in something like 'WOULD YOU LIKE A DRINK?' –"

"Yes please," I said, quick as a flash; and, quick as a flash, Smythe ignored me.

"– and the ELIZA program might come back with 'WHY DO YOU THINK I WOULD LIKE A DRINK?', or throw in some random question like 'WHAT MAKES YOU SAY THAT?' or 'INPUT ERROR $FF0021 REDO FROM START?' All very *mechanical* and uncreative. But such is the power of wishful thinking – the Eliza Effect – that it's incredibly easy to fall into the belief that the program's responses come from some real intelligence."

"From some real intelligence," I repeated intelligently.

"This, of course, is how zombies routinely pass in modern society: they have no more true conversation than ELIZA, but our natural, human weakness is to give them the benefit of the doubt. My zombie spotter, though, is a pocket computer with a speech-recognition facility. It lacks any power of wishful thinking. It analyzes conversations with cold logic, and reports when the responses are sufficiently simple, repetitious and content-free – as is the case with zombies, and with minds whose free will has been overlaid by some form of malign

poppetry, voodoo, or other sorcerous control. With this device —"

Here Smythe seemed to remember something, and
mumbled briefly in what I took to be Gaelic. I felt suddenly
impelled to carry the empty beer-glasses to the bar, order two
fresh pints of Ticklepenny's Old Ichorous, and bring them to
our table.

"With this device in my pocket," Smythe went on after
several grateful sips, "I sampled the population of F————,
entering into numerous conversations in the local public
houses, identifying victims of Jack the Clipper, and surrepti-
tiously assessing the speakers' Zombie Quotient."

"You bought drinks for 'numerous' people!?" I said, aghast.
Smythe's parsimony was famous in our little circle of friends.

"Er . . ." The eminent occultist looked momentarily embarrassed. "Actually I used an old Irish charm I'd learned in
my travels — a tiny *geas* that compels the hearer to acts of
senseless generosity. It's quite harmless, although it does
slightly lower the intelligence of the subject."

I didn't quite follow this odd explanation, and after puzzling
over it for a few moments I indicated that Smythe should
continue his fascinating narrative.

"On the whole, my zombie scan simply drew a blank. Of
course there were a few significant ZQ readings from individuals whose higher brain functions had been depressed by
excess alcohol, extreme fatigue or compulsive perusal of *The
Sun*. But there was just no sign of the widespread occult
control which I'd feared."

"Oh, bad luck. One of your rare failures, then."

"Failure? Am I not a scientific investigator? Was I to be
discouraged by the slaying of my initial hypothesis by ugly
fact? Never! However, I confess that I found myself momentarily at a loss; and so I determined to seek a new line of attack
by the traditional means of haruspication."

I pondered that word. "What, cutting out someone's entrails? Did you call for volunteers, or something? 'Intrepid
investigator needs men with guts.' "

"Tut, tut. Haruspication is the *examination* of entrails for
hints of things to come. The definition says nothing about

cutting them out. That was merely an unfortunate necessity imposed on the ancients by lack of appropriate technology. As you say, I called for an amply paunched volunteer, a recent victim of Jack the Clipper. The rest was merely a matter of a little influence and a little bribery at a convenient hospital which possessed . . ." he paused dramatically ". . . an ultrasound scanner."

"Excellent!" I cried.

"Elementary," said he. "Interpreting the convolutions of intestines which are quivering and peristalsing in real time is something of a specialist craft, I must remark, but well worth anyone's study. Long and hard I gazed into the ultrasound scan display, as one delusive word after another took shape in those loops and coils. And this –" he turned over the business card still lying on the table, and scribbled on its back "– *this* is the word that I finally read there."

I took up the card. "*Naglfar*? . . . You're quite sure it isn't a misprint?"

"That one word, my friend, should have told you the whole story, had you been the ideal reasoner which, in fact, I am."

"It's an anagram of 'flagrant'? Well, nearly."

"It was sufficient, when I had thought things through, to persuade me to make a few unusual purchases: scuba gear, cylinders of oxygen and halon 1301, the makings of a protective pentacle, and a small pair of toenail clippers.

"Picture me now, that night in my room at the town's one hotel, the Marquis of G————. I stood at the centre of an improvised defence pentacle which, for a particular reason, was picked out in ice cubes. I nervously checked the oxygen flow in the scuba rig, I struck a small flame from my cigarette lighter, and I cast my clipped toenails out across the psychic defences with the trembling words, 'An offering to you, oh Loki!'

"And, as I had hardly dared to hope, the god Loki appeared, emerging somehow from the fiery interior of the central heating pipes. Being a trickster deity, he had adopted the aspect of a used car salesman, but with hot flame flickering in his eyes. His questioning gaze seemed to burn through my skin.

" 'I read the clues,' I said. 'Jack the Clipper preys on men and never on women, and as the world's foremost occult investigator I know my Norse myths. The *Naglfar* is the ship made of men's nails which you are fated to steer through the sea that rises to engulf the land when all Earth is destroyed in the final days of Ragnarok. Of course you chose toenails rather than fingernails, owing to their superior quality as a maritime construction material. But I've no idea why you should collect the wherewithal to build that dread vessel in a dull town like this.'

" 'Trickster gods are allowed to be as silly and capricious as they like,' Loki explained, stepping forward: 'And *of course* I picked an obscure place where Odin wouldn't think to look.' The words emerged in individual gouts of flame, reminiscent of a circus fire-eater with hiccups. 'Ouch. By Niflheim!' Being also a fire god, my visitor did not relish the ice pentacle . . . but nevertheless slowly forced his way through my wards in a cloud of hissing steam. His nostrils literally flared. 'I should add that fire gods have this regrettable habit of slowly incinerating mortals who ask impertinent questions.'

"But I had already clapped the scuba mask to my face and released the valve on that halon 1301 cylinder. The occult words of banishment which I pronounced – the unknown last line of the Maastricht agreement – were drowned in the hiss of escaping gas and might or might not have been effective. But I think I have successfully ascertained that fire gods particularly detest an atmosphere that's rich in fire-inhibiting halon. Before he could reach me, Loki fizzled and shrank and went out like, if you'll excuse the cliché, a light.

"And so the mystery was solved. The town of F——— heard no more of Jack the Clipper. Perhaps the fiery prankster's sinister work continues elsewhere in the world . . ."

"A truly remarkable farrago," I mumbled, my head still spinning slightly.

"All of which explains my new-found interest in cryonics," said Smythe with an air of considerable smugness.

"Of course," I replied weakly, determined not to ask the obvious question. My friend was visibly too pleased with himself to prolong the suspense any further.

"I have a notion, you see, that Loki the trickster was also maliciously sowing trouble for the gods themselves. The whole Norse pantheon is notoriously bound up in chains of unescapable fate. That which is written will be . . . and one of the things clearly written about the *Naglfar* is that it will be made of *dead* men's nails. So, you see, the end of the world, Ragnarok, can't come to pass until all those victims of 'Jack the Clipper' – men whose toenails are built into the fateful ship – are safely dead."

"Oh, wonderful. The world's safe for another – what? – fifty years?"

"Forever, perhaps, if some of those toenail donors are kept cryonically preserved at liquid-nitrogen temperatures. You must know that some people actually *pay* to be frozen in hope of eternity. So I am currently working to make certain lucrative arrangements with sympathetic Scandinavian governments, in the hope of financing cryonics projects which could hold off Ragnarok indefinitely. You may be sitting with – and, indeed, about to buy another drink for – the saviour of this world." Smythe gave a little bow.

A single, tiny fragment of Norse myth had meanwhile floated to the surface of my own mind. "Ah . . . Smythe. According to those same legends, one of the fated circumstances that leads up to Ragnarok and the last battle is the Fimbulwinter. A deep, unnatural winter. A long period of intense and artificial cold. Um, are you sure your cryonics scheme isn't already part of what's written?"

For the first time since I'd known him, Smythe looked nonplussed.

THE SHOEMAKER
AND THE ELVIS

Lawrence Schimel

Lawrence Schimel (b. 1971) is a US writer currently resident in Spain, who has been astonishingly prolific since his first story sale in 1989. Just a few of his stories will be found in the collection The Drag Queen of Elfland *(1997). He has a skill for weaving a sharp spike of a story out of a splinter of an idea. The following is one of his longer pieces.*

We'd heard, of course, about that other shoemaker, the one who'd found, upon waking, a set of shoes already made upon his workbench. But who'd have thought it might be true? Or that it could happen to us? I wasn't even a shoemaker, really! I'm a podiatrist. Sometimes I'll fashion orthopaedic shoes, the whole shebang, but mostly I just make inserts for people to slip into their sneakers. So what I can't figure out is: Why me? But isn't that always the case when someone has an encounter with the supernatural? Why me?

It was Jane who found them. She comes in earliest of everyone, to turn on the coffee machine and get the office ready for the day's clients, to call and confirm people's appointments. She's got a seven-year-old son, Eric, and so she has to leave by three to pick him up from school.

"That's so cute, Dr Katzman," Jane said to me by way of greeting, while I was hanging up my coat. "Who's got the Elvis fetish?"

"What Elvis fetish?" I asked her.

"You know, the blue suede shoes," she said.

"What blue suede shoes?" I asked her. I stuffed my scarf into the sleeve of my jacket.

"The ones in Room 2."

I walked down the hall. I hadn't made any blue suede shoes. I hadn't had a call for a pair of shoes in weeks – not until Mrs Parker came in yesterday. And she certainly didn't request blue suede shoes, not that I'd have made them for her even if she had. Her arches have fallen so deeply that inserts wouldn't suffice: she practically needed a special set of shoes with full-scale scaffolding.

"What happened to Mrs Parker's shoes?" I cried.

There, on the counter, right where I'd left the soles of Mrs Parker's special full-scale support shoes to set and dry over-night before fashioning them into footwear wide enough for her splayed toes to fit into, was a pair of blue suede shoes.

"Didn't you make those for her?" Jane asked me, coming into the room behind me. She lifted a shoe and felt inside. "Feels just like Mrs Parker's prescription to me."

I picked up the other shoe and felt inside.

"You're right, it does feel like the right prescription. But I didn't make them."

"Well, it couldn't have been Nancy," Jane said.

Nancy was my other secretary. She wasn't the swiftest of girls, but she did try. She was my wife's niece, so I couldn't fire her. We just tried to keep her away from anything easily damaged, like the computer. Or the filing. Or the vacuum. Or – well, anything remotely mechanical.

"Who else could it have been?" I said. "You know how she's totally gone for Elvis." Another of Nancy's endearing charms. "Although I can't fathom why she'd have done something like this," I continued.

"Well, that's exactly why it must have been her: You can't fathom why. That's Nancy for you." Jane has been nagging me to hire someone else, someone competent that is, to help her with all the work. Preferably getting rid of the dead weight while I was at it.

"I don't understand how it could've been Nancy, though," I said, ignoring the problem of Jane's dissatisfaction for the moment. "We don't even carry blue suede. What could she have made them from? And how would she have made them? Nancy doesn't know how to listen to the answering machine, let alone sew a complicated pair of orthopaedic shoes like this."

"What are you proposing it was, then," Jane asked, "elves in the middle of the night?"

"I'd believe elves made this a lot sooner than I would Nancy did. Elves, or maybe Elvis." I almost waffled the joke trying to get the accents over the right syllables.

Jane groaned. "I'll call the *Weekly World News*. 'Elvis Sighted in Podiatrist's Office!' 'Blue Suede Shoes Found to Cause Pigeon Toe!' And I get to keep half the money." She smiled and disappeared back to the front desk to begin calling. Clients, that is, not the *Weekly World News*.

I went to the phones as well. I explained to Mrs Parker that there might be a slight delay in her shoes, unless she didn't mind blue suede. The wholesaler, I lied, had sent us a shipment of blue suede instead of ordinary brown leather, and it would be weeks before they could send us a replacement shipment.

Mrs Parker said she didn't care what colour they were so long as her feet stopped hurting.

Nonetheless, I felt the tip of my nose when I hung up, just to make sure it hadn't grown any from my white lie. I mean, if elves – or Elvises – were making shoes in the middle of the night, why not the rest of all those old stories? I couldn't believe it was Nancy, and I didn't have any other ideas.

Nancy, when she showed up at one, was totally ignorant. Of the shoes, as well, I mean.

"Dr Katzman!" Nancy squealed when I showed her the blue suedes in Room 2. "You've made a pair of Elvis shoes!"

"I told you so," Jane and I both sighed together.

I was totally baffled by the shoes. Who had made them? And from what material? They obviously used the soles that I had left to set and dry, they'd been moulded off Mrs Parker's feet. I'd done them myself, I knew the warped shape of those fallen arches. But everything else had been changed. And all the materials I'd used, or left ready to be used, were gone.

At least Mrs Parker didn't mind about the colour – and they were well-crafted shoes, it seemed. If a bit . . . unfashionable.

Before Jane left, I laid out a new pair of soles in Room 3. I locked the door, took the key off my keyring and handed it to her. "Don't open it tomorrow until I get here," I told her. "I have no way of getting in there without you, now, and I want to be there tomorrow when we prove that it wasn't elves."

I was late getting to the office, despite my best efforts. I was eager to find out what happened with the soles I'd left out, but the Long Island Expressway was doing its imitation of a parking lot that morning, and I was almost an hour late by the time I got there. The traffic didn't seem to have caught any of the morning's clients, who were thick as fleas in the waiting room, and between them and the phone ringing off the hook, Jane and I didn't get a chance to unlock Room 3 until Nancy had shown up and could cover the phones and the front desk while Jane and I had the unveiling. We both stood hesitantly before the door for a few moments, just staring at it, neither of us saying a word. But our doubt and disbelief were quite apparent in our expressions.

"Everything is going to be exactly as we left it," I said, as Jane handed me the key and I opened the door. Still, I couldn't make myself turn the knob, nervous about what I might find, the possibility that I was wrong.

"Until you open the door," Jane said, "both possibilities will continue to exist. On the other side there are either a pair of soles, like we'd left them, or a pair of finished shoes, fashioned by supernatural or other means. We must open the door and find out which scenario is real." She paused for breath. "You open the door and I'll turn on the lights, okay?"

I nodded, unable to find my voice, and flung open the door. Jane reached around the doorjamb and flicked the light switch. Together, we stared in through the open door.

There, on the counter, was a new pair of blue suede shoes, obviously different from the first pair of yesterday. (These were easily four sizes smaller.)

"Now what?" I asked.

"I don't know which is more preposterous," Jane said, "the fact that elves are real, or that we've had an Elvis sighting right here in our office."

"Not a confirmed Elvis sighting," I reminded her. We went out into the hallway, closing the door behind us. But out of sight, this mystery was hardly out of mind.

"What," I wondered aloud, "are we supposed to do, according to the fairy tale?"

I didn't remember the story too well. But Jane's got a seven-year-old son, so she'd read it more recently than any of the rest of us.

"I think this means the King wants a pair of shoes for himself," Jane said. "That's what happens in the story, the elves are all barefoot and naked.'"

"Naked! I missed a chance of seeing Elvis naked!" I caught Nancy as she swooned. Jane rushed and got her a paper cup of water. I was pleased to see her coming to Nancy's rescue, despite her dislike for the girl.

"I'm all right, I think," Nancy declared. "But I'm not leaving this office until I get a sight of him tonight!"

Jane looked at me. "I'm kind of curious, myself," she said. "To see this story through to the end. In the fairy tale, the shoemaker and his wife make clothes and tiny shoes for the elves for Christmas. And the elves never come back."

"I guess we can't really call an exterminator, so it may just come to that. If it really is elves. Or Elvis. I admit I am curious myself, to find out for sure."

"It's agreed then," Jane said.

"What fun!" Nancy cried. "An Elvis stakeout!"

Jane and I both sighed, and went back to work.

Jane called around and arranged for Eric to stay at his friend Peter's house that night. I had a bit more trouble convincing my wife.

"You're staying late at work," my wife said with this certain tone in her voice. "With your *secretary*."

"I'm hurt that you even suggest such a thing," I told her. "Besides, Nancy will be here, too."

"You're staying late at work," my wife repeated in that same tone, though her voice had gone up an octave, "with *both* of your secretaries!"

"Someone's been breaking into the office," I explained exasperatedly. "Nancy thinks it's Elvis, so she wants to stay and see him. Speaking of which, we really need to talk about Nancy one of these days."

"Don't change the subject," my wife said. "Are you having an affair with my niece or your secretary or both of them at once?"

I sighed. "Why don't you come spend a boring night staking out the office with us, and you'll see that I am not having an affair with my secretary, who has a seven-year-old son fercrissake, or," and here I dropped my voice for the next three words, "your brainless niece!"

Adele showed up promptly at 6.30 when the office closed. I treated us all to Chinese food. We rushed back because we didn't know when he'd show up. I'd left a pair of soles on the counter in Room 1 this time, just to keep our midnight visitor(s) on his or their toes. And also because Room 1 had a supply closet big enough to fit four people.

We hid inside, peeking through the slats every now and again to see if he'd arrived yet. Well, Jane and I only occasionally peered through; Nancy was riveted, peeping through the entire time.

Adele complained that she was bored.

"I *told* you to stay home," I told her.

"I thought you were having an affair. I mean, you were giving me all the right cues. What was I supposed to do?"

"An affair?" Jane said, with this certain tone to her voice. Even with no lights on, I just knew she was sneering. Adele knew it, too, and I could feel her relax even further. Seeing

Nancy over dinner had been reassurance enough to dismiss that worry.

"Hush," Nancy reminded us, "who knows when he'll show up."

Adele, Jane and I all sighed. Nancy really thought she was going to see the King.

I didn't know what I thought we would see. Although I guess I thought we'd see *something*. Or rather, some*one*. Otherwise I wouldn't have been spending a night squatting in a supply closet with my secretary, my wife, and her brainless, Elvis-sick niece.

Adele sat next to me on the floor and leaned against my shoulder. Pretty soon she was snoring. I wanted to take a nap myself, but only my leg fell asleep. I was afraid I'd miss all the action, if there was to be any, and I didn't want to have to go through all this bother and discomfort a second time.

After what seemed like hours, Nancy began to sort of squeal – her attempt to keep from shouting in excitement. I was proud of her for even making an attempt.

There was a humming and some fumbling outside the closet. Something clattered to the floor. Someone cursed. And then the lights went on in the room.

The four of us peeked through the slats.

It was the King all right. He hadn't changed a bit. He looked exactly as young as in the last known photos of him, as if decades had not passed.

Well, one thing was different, or at least I'd never noticed it before.

"Look at that," I whispered. "He's worn clear through the insides of his soles."

"Oh, the poor thing," Nancy said aloud, and she rushed forward from our hiding spot into the room.

If Elvis was surprised to find her there, he didn't show it.

"Ya gotta help me, Mama," he drawled. "I'm caught in a trap, I can't get out. La belle dame sans merci hath me in thrall," he explained.

Nancy, of course, would do anything he asked of her.

"La Belle Dumb is in thrall, too," Jane sighed, and followed Nancy out of our hiding spot to rescue her. Once again, I was proud to see her coming to the aid of my wife's brainless niece, despite her dislike of the girl.

And Jane had hit on something profound, I thought, remembering my Keats from the token English class they made us take in med school. I marvelled at the similarity of Elvis to the Queen of Elfland, trapping unsuspecting mortals in his glamour, keeping them oblivious to everything but himself, and leaving them senseless because of him.

But I didn't want to miss out on all the action, so I set aside these musings for later and revealed myself as well. "What seems to be the problem?" I asked.

"My feet," the King moaned.

"Yes, I see," I murmured, soothingly. "Why don't you sit up there while I take a look," I said. Elvis climbed onto the padded table and drummed his heels against the drawers.

"I just can't stop dancing," he continued. "It's all the Queen's fault. She makes me dance. But I don't got the same stamina these elves do."

Suddenly, at the same moment, it sank home to Jane and me what he'd said earlier. La belle dame, the Queen of Elfland, had *the King* in thrall, not the other way around as I'd earlier thought Jane had meant. At last, the mystery of Elvis' disappearance was solved! It was no wonder he looked as young and unchanged as ever; I remembered this story, still, and according to the poem time moved differently between the worlds. Seven years would pass in the real world, and only a day would have gone by in the fairy kingdom.

"*The Enquirer* will *never* believe this," Jane muttered. "But maybe Spielberg."

"For seven years, I am her slave," the King was saying, as I knelt down before him and unlaced his worn-through blue suede shoes.

"You poor thing!" Nancy cried. Adele took her niece's arm, as much to quiet her and prevent her from doing anything rash as to catch the girl should she faint again.

I pulled Elvis' socks off. His feet gave off that particular fungal odour.

"You need to change your shoes more often," I told him. I

was afraid Nancy might do me damage if I said his feet stank. "Rotate them."

"I can only do what she wants me to. And she always wants me to sing and shake my hips for her. I'm so tired. And my feet! Just look at my shoes! You've got to help me, Doctor."

"Yes, I can see that," I said.

"You've got to help him!" Nancy cried.

"How is it you could come here?" Jane asked. My ever-practical Jane. I don't know what I'd do without her. The whole office would fall apart without her. I didn't think I had to worry until Eric was old enough to go off to college, but I couldn't help thinking how I really needed to make sure I'd hired someone else, someone she'd have trained, before she left me. She was just too smart to stay my secretary for long – she deserved more from life.

"It's because of the stories," Elvis said. "The Queen's cast a spell on me, and it makes me more or less an elf while I'm in her thrall. Making shoes is one of the things elves do, and in return the mortals will make a pair of shoes for us. Please, Doctor, I'm begging you, make me a pair of shoes that will make my feet stop hurting."

I knelt down before the King's feet again, and began examining his soles. I couldn't help feeling like Mary Magdalene washing the feet of Christ. I'd have to tell Jane the analogy, I thought – but not right then. The mood was wrong, and I wasn't sure either Nancy or my wife would catch the irony of it all. Well, I *knew* Nancy wouldn't. I held my tongue, and instead poked and prodded and measured his feet.

"Yes," I murmured. "Pronating. Hmmm."

"Can you help me?" the King begged, in his love-me-tender voice.

"I think I have a solution," I said, and began assembling supplies to take a casting. A silence settled over the room as I worked. Jane immediately fell into helping me, handing me the things I needed as I needed them. Nancy all but vibrated with anxiety and erotic tension; she looked as though she might, at any moment, leap onto the table and tear Elvis' sequinned clothes from him. Adele just watched, holding onto her niece with a quiet but firm grip. Elvis began to hum.

Jane and I worked. I poured the soles. "We're not going to have time for these to set," I warned. "They need a full twenty-four hours before I can make them into shoes. You'll have to come back tomorrow."

Nancy made that not-quite-squealing sound again.

"Let me see them," Elvis said. He hopped down off the table, and stood next to me. He looked at them, holding them in his hands as he hummed along. Then he handed them back to me. "They'll be fine like that," he said.

They had dried already.

I didn't question it. So many strange things were happening already, this seemed like nothing special.

The normality of sewing a pair of shoes was the only thing that made sense. The fact that they were for Elvis seemed inconsequential. These were just another pair of tired feet that needed to be supported. They just happened to belong to one of the most famous men in history, a man who was surrounded by a mystery that we'd just unravelled.

Not that anyone would believe us, if we told them. I didn't believe it myself.

But I made the shoes anyway, even not believing what was going on. There had to be some sort of rational explanation, I thought, and one day it would all become clear.

Elvis put his socks back on, and tried the shoes on. "They're perfect," he said, shuffling a step or two.

The King was so happy not to have his feet hurting him, he turned and kissed Nancy, who was standing nearest to him.

Nancy fainted.

No one was there to catch her, and she banged her head against the edge of the counter. I bent over her, and checked to see if she was all right. A streak of red stained the linoleum. Jane ran to fetch bandages. Adele went to call an ambulance.

"Where's Elvis?" Nancy cried, when she opened her eyes as we were holding a gauze bandage to the back of her skull.

"Elvis?" I asked. I looked around me. In the commotion, he'd disappeared. Back to Elfland, or wherever he'd come from. However he'd gotten here. I had to wonder if he'd ever been there, and didn't know which questioned my sanity more. And as I caught Jane's eye, I knew she was wondering how much we should tell Nancy, if we'd ever live down the true story.

"You've hit your head, honey," Jane said. "Elvis has been missing for years. He's probably dead by now."

"He can't be dead!" Nancy cried. "I saw him, I swear I saw him. You were all here. He kissed me!" Her eyelids fluttered again, and she sort of hugged herself.

"It was just a dream," Jane explained, patiently. "From when you hit your head."

Adele came back in. "The ambulance is on its way," she said.

"Just a dream," Nancy whispered. You could see her deflate. "It all seemed so real."

It all seemed so real. That's how I felt, too. It seemed so real, but how could it be true? I'd seen him with my own two eyes, I'd touched his naked soles with my own two hands, I'd made blue suede shoes especially for him, shoes that would stand up to the supernatural pounding of elfin dances.

No one spoke while we waited for the ambulance to show up. Adele went with her niece to the hospital, and I promised to follow her there once Jane and I had had a chance to clean up and close down the office.

"What will we tell people?" I asked.

"I don't know that we *can* tell people. Who'd believe us? I don't believe it, myself, and I was there. But at least we got to the end of the story, brought this all to some sort of conclusion."

"I guess," I said, not quite sure I felt a sense of closure. I would never look at an Elvis on velvet painting the same way again, I knew, and every time I heard one of his songs, I'd always remember the feel of his feet beneath my hands. "I just feel there are so many mysteries left unsolved. Like, are all those other fairy tales true, as well? And especially: Why me? But I guess we'll never find out."

Jane took the casting. "All I know," she said, "is that *this* is going to put Eric through college."

I could hardly argue with that.

DANCES WITH ELVES

Cynthia Ward

Cynthia Ward (b. 1960) has been selling short stories regularly to magazines and anthologies since her first story, "The Opal Skull", in 1989. Born in Oklahoma, she has lived in Maine, Spain, Germany and San Francisco, before settling in Seattle.

"Elves!" called Rooso the Anvil. "O Fair Folk, hear my plea! I have given up my family and my trade! I have given up the human world! I want to join you!"

The Fair Folk were the greatest, purest, wisest people in the world. They lived in peace with one another, in accord with the spirits, and in harmony with nature. Where they lived, the forest bloomed all year with sweet-scented blossoms and sweet-tasting fruit. When they hunted, the animals came willingly to them. Sometimes, Rooso knew, they stole human babies. He did not understand why this caused the parents such sorrow; the Elves had given the children a gift beyond compare.

Rooso the Anvil waited, but no answer to his call came from

the surrounding forest. Finally he crouched, slowly, as though pressed down by the weight of the darkness around his small fire. Three nights and three days had he waited, alone in the wilderness, surviving on nuts and berries. He had brought no food into the forest and, though he was a blacksmith, he had brought no iron.

"Why couldn't I have been raised by the Fair Folk?" Rooso asked the night. He bowed his head. "O Gods," he prayed, "grant me my wish, to join the first and greatest of Your creations."

When he raised his head, he found his campfire ringed about by seven motionless Elves. He had been accounted "fair as an Elf" by the women of his town, but in the presence of the Elves he suddenly felt as ugly and gnarled as a hunchback.

The tallest of the tall Elves spoke, in the Old Tongue, in a voice as clear and flowing as a stream. "We have heard your cries, these last three nights. Why do you disturb us?"

"I called you because I wish to join you." Rooso heard his voice creak like an old chair, but made himself continue. "I have left the world behind, in pursuit of my desire. You are so wise and fair, I would give anything to be one of you."

The Elves smiled at one another, a brief flash of teeth whiter than a human smile could ever be.

The tallest Elf turned back to Rooso. "If you are willing, human, you may become one with the Elves."

"You *know* I am willing."

"I am known as Eagle Striking," said the tallest Elf. "Put out your fire, human, and follow us."

Rooso emptied his waterskin, extinguishing the small fire. He blinked in the blackness of night.

At dawn, the Elves led the human out of the forest, into a clearing overgrown with wild roses, strawberries, poppies, daisies, and a score of flowers Rooso did not recognize. In the middle of this field stood a grove of fruit and oak trees. The apple, pear and cherry trees were bowed under the weight of fruit. The Elves dwelt high in the branches of the oaks, in shelters woven of branches and grass. Among the several score Elves who greeted him, Rooso saw a few children, all as quiet, dignified and beautiful as the adults. He saw no human children – if there were changelings here, they had changed completely.

The Fair Folk prepared a feast of welcome. Some piled wood high in the centre of the grove, while others filled baskets with fruit and berries. Eagle Striking led Rooso out of the grove and deeper into the ancient forest. He bade Rooso stand quiet in the shadow of a shaggy pine. Then he drew his knife. Rooso's heart slammed against his chest. Eagle Striking turned away.

The Elf took up a position several yards from Rooso. He stood motionless, his white skin and butter-coloured buckskin tunic shading into the browns and yellows of tree boles and fallen leaves.

Within moments a red deer appeared, a great stag crowned with tined antlers. Head upraised, legs steady, the stag approached the Elf and stretched out its slender neck. Eagle Striking laid the stone knife across the jugular and sawed at the tough hide. When blood spurted like water from a fountain, Rooso felt faint, though he had poached the king's deer many times. He reminded himself that the animal had come to Eagle Striking in accord with the harmony of nature.

At the feast, Rooso the Anvil ate better than he ever had in his life. The venison was savoury, not gamy, and tender as veal. As the feast progressed, a group of Elves chanted wild strange songs Rooso couldn't understand over the bone-shaking throb of log drums. When other Elves rose up and made a ring around the fire, Rooso realized he was about to witness the legendary dance of the Elves. He could not believe his good fortune. He never expected to be invited to join them.

He shook his head at their beckoning gestures until Eagle Striking left the dance and grabbed his wrist and dragged him to the fire. "Human, do you see the pattern?"

Rooso shook his head. The pattern was far too complex and the drumming too fast. But the beat slowed, and the dancers shouted encouragement, and moved slowly so that he could learn. Eagle Striking pulled him into motion, and the drums beat fast again, and Rooso found himself dancing the ancient Elvish dance.

★   ★   ★

In the morning, Rooso ate as well as he had last night, breakfasting on fruit, wild-pig ham and wheat bread dipped in honey. He lay against a tree, his hands on his overfull stomach, somnolent, insensible of the passing hours.

Eagle Striking came up to him and pressed a scrap of dried fruit into his hand.

"I am not hungry," Rooso said apologetically.

"Eat this toadstool if you would see as we see," Eagle Striking said. "Eat, and know the harmony of the world."

Rooso examined the toadstool, a long, dirty-looking white stem topped with a small, tight-fitting brown cap. How could this shrivelled scrap give him the wisdom of Elves?

He felt his stomach tremble. He quickly thrust the mushroom into his mouth and bit down. The stem snapped like an old stick. As he chewed, his saliva softened the mushroom, but the foul taste blotted up the moisture in his mouth. He swallowed with difficulty. He could not imagine how he could gain knowledge in this manner, and the attempt to imagine it made his stomach queasy. He calmed his mind and lay still.

After a while he realized the trees of the grove made a pattern. The pattern included all the trees he could see, and all the trees he could not see. He understood the pattern of the forest: the harmony of the trees with the animals, with the birds that flew above, with the worms that burrowed below. He understood the necessity of the deer eating the leaves and the wolf eating the deer. He turned to look at the huge oak he leaned against, and traced the furrows in the bark, following the pattern. *Everything* was part of the pattern. Rooso the Anvil laid his cheek against the rough bark, spread his arms as wide as they could stretch, and embraced the tree.

When evening thickened in the grove, the Elves built their bonfire. The human stared into the fire, watching the flames leap and twist in a dance as beautiful and meaningful as the dance of the Elves, or the pattern of the world.

Rooso realized Eagle Striking stood beside him, and the other Elves stood close around him. Eagle Striking laid his hand gently on Rooso's shoulder. "Human, do you see the pattern?"

Rooso spoke slowly. "Yes."

Eagle Striking asked, "Are you ready to be one with the Elves?"

Rooso smiled dreamily. "I am," he replied.

And so the Elves cooked and ate him.

A HEDGE
AGAINST ALCHEMY

John Morressy

In the previous volume I reprinted the story "Alaska" featuring
the wizard Kedrigern and his odd retinue of acquaintances. For
this volume I've dug back to the very first Kedrigern story, "A
Hedge against Alchemy", published in 1981. Since then there
have been five Kedrigern books: A Voice for Princess *(1986),*
The Questing of Kedrigern *(1987),* Kedrigern in Wanderland
(1988), Kedrigern and the Charming Couple *(1990) and* A
Remembrance for Kedrigern *(1990). John Morressy (b. 1930)*
is a retired US professor of English, and is working on further
Kedrigern stories.

Kedrigern took his wizardly studies seriously, but he was a
sensible man withal. On a beautiful morning in early spring he
saw greater wisdom in sitting comfortably in his dooryard,
soaking up the sunshine, than in conning ancient lore in his
dim, cobwebby study.

He sprawled back in pillowed comfort, feet up on a cushion, and rang with languid gesture a little silver bell. From within-indoors came the sound of sudden motion, and soon the slapping of huge feet on the flagstones. A small, hideous creature appeared at Kedrigern's side.

It was almost all head, and a very ugly head, too, with its bulging eyes and tangled brows and scarcity of forehead; with its great hook of nose, like a drinking horn covered with warts; with its ledge of chin and hairy ears like wide-flung shutters. Two great dirty flat feet splayed at the ends of the creature's tiny legs, and great hands like sails jutted out from its sides. The top of its mottled, warty, scurfy head reached just to the level of Kedrigern's footstool, and there the creature shuddered to a halt, trembling with the eager will to serve.

"Ah, there you are," Kedrigern said mildly.

The creature wildly nodded its monstrous head, spraying saliva about in generous quantities, and said, "Yah! Yah!"

"Good fellow, Spot. Listen carefully, now."

"Yah! Yah!" said Spot, bouncing up and down excitedly.

"I will have, I think, a small mug of very cold ale. Bring the pitcher, in case my thirst is greater than I anticipate. And bring with it a morsel of cheese just of a size to cover the lid of the pitcher, and a loaf of bread. And ask Princess if she'd care to join me."

"Yah! Yah!" said Spot, and windmilled off about his duties.

Kedrigern looked after him affectionately. Trolls were a bad lot, it was true, but if one got them young and trained them properly, they could be devoted servants. Excellent mousers, as well. They were hopeless when it came to good table manners, but one could not have everything.

He settled back among the cushions, closed his eyes, and emitted a sigh of quiet pleasure. This was the life for a sensible man, he thought snugly. Not like your damned alchemy.

Kedrigern could not understand the fascination of alchemy. It was all the rage these days, everyone was talking it up, but to him it was nothing more than a lot of smoke and stink and a horrible mess and pompous jargon about things no one understood but everyone felt obliged to speak of with solemn authority. Yet it seemed to be catching on. The bright young people were not interested in traditional wizardry any more. It was alchemy or nothing for them.

Just one more sign of the times, he believed, and bad times they were, with barbarians sweeping in from the east and burning the churchmen, churchmen issuing anathemas and burning the alchemists, and alchemists burning everything they could lay their hands on in their wild desire to turn lead into gold. Smoke and howling and destruction, that's all anyone cared about these days.

Except for Kedrigern, who was learning more and more about temporal magic and becoming rather good at it. He had reached into the future several times and established solid linkage with a specific time-point, though he was not quite certain just what point it was. He had even managed to pluck curious artifacts from that unformed age and retain them for study. There was much yet to learn, of course . . . but there would be time for that . . . much to learn . . .

Kedrigern fell into a light doze, awakening with a frown when a shadow fell upon him. He opened his eyes and saw a great hulking figure standing before him, blocking out the sun.

It took his eyes a moment to accustom themselves to the light, and his wits another moment to reconvene in the here-and-now, and then Kedrigern saw that the creature before him was a man of a kind he had hoped never to encounter.

He was twice the wizard's height and four times his bulk. Bare arms like the trunks of aged hornbeams hung from his beetling shoulders. Torso and thick legs were encased in coarse furs. A tiny head was centred between the bulging shoulders with no sign of a neck intervening. About him hung an effluvium of rancid animal fat and venerable perspiration. He was a barbarian, no doubt, and barbarians were no friends of wizards. Or of anyone else, for that matter.

"This road to Silent Thunder Peak?" the barbarian asked. His voice was like a fall of stone deep within a cave.

"Yes, it is," Kedrigern said politely. He pointed to his left. "Just follow the uphill track. If you hurry, you can reach the peak by sunset. Marvellous view on a day like this. I'd offer you a drop of some cool refreshment but I'm —"

"You wizard?" the barbarian rumbled.

That was the sort of question one did not rush to answer. Far too many people were wandering about these days with the notion that slaying a wizard was somehow a deed of great merit. It was the churchmen put them up to that, Kedrigern knew. Churchmen never had a good word for anyone. Barbarians, alchemists and wizards were condemned alike, in outbursts of chilling zeal and remarkably poor judgment. All the same, this specimen did not look like someone who took his orders from a holy man.

"Wizard?" Kedrigern asked, squinting up. "Do I understand that you're inquiring after the whereabouts of a wizard?"

"You wizard?" the barbarian asked once more, exactly as before.

An uneasiness came over Kedrigern. It was not at the barbarian's great size and ugliness, nor even at his sudden appearance here in this isolated retreat where Kedrigern had withdrawn from worldly affairs to concentrate on his studies and enjoy Princess' companionship. It was intangible, a sense of wrong presence. He had the eerie sensation that a member of his brotherhood was near, and that was manifestly absurd. This creature was no wizard.

"It's interesting that you should ask," said Kedrigern thoughtfully. "It suggests an inquiring turn of mind not immediately evident in your manner and appearance." As he spoke, he slipped his hand behind him to work the figures necessary to a spell for the deflection of edged weapons. "Most people expect a wizard to go about in a long robe covered with cabalistic symbols, and wear a conical cap, and have a long white beard flapping down around his knees. I, as you can see, am plainly dressed in good homespun tunic and trousers, wear no headgear of any kind, and am clean-shaven. Consequently, a casual passerby might easily assume that I am some honest tradesman or artisan who has chosen to live apart from his fellows when I am in fact an adept in the rare and gentle arts." He hoped earnestly that this great brute would not decide to smash him flat with a club before he could proceed to a further protective spell. Even with the assistance of magic, it was difficult to be prepared for all contingencies when dealing with people such as this.

The barbarian's tiny black eyes, set closely on either side of a shapeless smudge of nose, peered at Kedrigern from behind a fringe of lank, greasy hair. In those eyes shone no glimmer of understanding.

"You wizard?" he repeated.

"Me wizard," Kedrigern said resignedly. "Who you?"

"Me Buroc," said the barbarian, thumping his chest proudly.

"Oh, dear me," Kedrigern murmured.

Buroc was the barbarian's barbarian. He was known throughout the land as Buroc the Depraved and had added to his name such epithets as Flayer of God's Earth, Fist of Satan, and Torch of Judgment, as well as other titles emblematic of mayhem and savagery. It was said of Buroc that he had divided the human race into two parts: enemies and victims. Enemies he slew at once. Victims he slew when he had no further use for them. He recognized no third category.

Looking into that flat expressionless face crisscrossed with pale scars, Kedrigern believed all he had ever heard of Buroc. The barbarian's face reminded him of a cheap clay vessel shattered to bits and hastily glued together. The chief difference, in Kedrigern's estimation, was that the vessel of clay would radiate a higher spirituality.

"You come with Buroc," said the barbarian.

"Oh, I think not. The offer raises some unusual possibilities, but I'm afraid murder, rape and pillage aren't my line of work, Buroc. I'm more the bookish sort. And I'm not so nimble as I used to be. Thoughtful of you to ask, though. Now it might be best if you were running along," Kedrigern said as he hurried through a backup spell against indeterminate violence. With that done, he felt secure against any of Buroc's bloodthirsty caprices.

"Buroc find golden mountain. Need wizard."

"Oh?"

"Mountain of gold. Spell hide mountain. You break spell. Split forty-forty," said Buroc in an outburst of eloquence.

"Fifty-fifty," Kedrigern corrected him.

Buroc's eyes glazed, and for a moment he seemed immobilized. Then he nodded his tiny head and repeated, "Fifty-fifty."

"Where is this golden mountain, Buroc?" Kedrigern asked, spacing his words and enunciating carefully.

Again the barbarian's eyes glazed over, and Kedrigern realized with a start that this was evidence of a reasoning process going on in the recesses of that little head. "You come. Me show."

"Is it far away?"

After a time, Buroc said, "Sun. Sun. Golden mountain."

"Three days from here, I take it. Not bad. Not bad at all," said Kedrigern, his interest growing.

This was a rare opportunity. It would set the alchemists on their ears and put them in their proper place once and for all. Let them stink up the countryside with their furnaces and fill the peaceful silence with their babble of Philosopher's Egg and Emerald Table and such pseudo-magical rot in their feeble attempts to create a pinch of third-rate gold dust. Kedrigern, using only his magic, would possess a golden mountain. Well, half a golden mountain. Whatever the dangers, magical or physical, this was too good to let pass.

"You're not the ideal client, Buroc, nor are you my first choice as a partner. And I'm sure that somewhere in that miniature sconce of yours lurks an inchoate notion of mincing me small once we've achieved our goal . . . but I can't resist your offer," he said.

"You come?"

"I come."

At this moment Princess made her appearance, approaching on delicate and silent feet. She bore a silver tray on which stood a frosty pitcher, two gleaming silver mugs, a fist-sized chunk of golden cheese, and a loaf of pale brown bread. Seeing Buroc, she stopped abruptly.

Princess was a woman of spectacular beauty, with a tumble of glistening raven hair cascading to her hips, eyes the colour of a midday August sky, and sculpture-perfect features. Her dress of emerald green clung to her slender form, and a circlet of gold ringed her brow. Buroc's eyes gleamed at the sight of

her, with a light that betokened single-minded lust. She
moved close to Kedrigern and glanced at him, wide-eyed,
in frightened appeal.

Inwardly, Kedrigern cursed Spot and promised the troll a
sound thrashing at the earliest opportunity. He did not like the
idea of Princess' being ogled by this brute, nor did he anticipate pleasant consequences from Buroc's all too patent interest. But what was done could not be undone, except at the cost
of more magic than he could presently spare.

"No need to be nervous, Princess. This fellow and I have
business," he said.

"Brereep," she replied softly.

"Lady talk funny," Buroc said.

"Spoken like a true connoisseur of linguistic elegance. Carp
if you will, Buroc, I'm very fond of Princess," Kedrigern said,
extending his hand to her. She set the tray down. He took her
hand and raised it to his lips, and she blushed prettily. "I know
that somewhere out in the ponds and marshes I was bound to
find her. They couldn't *all* be enchanted princes. But I
certainly wasn't going to go around kissing every toad I
saw. Time-consuming, for one thing, and not my idea of a
good time, for another. So I used my magic. About ninety-
eight percent successful, I'd say. Princess has been a charming
companion, and I'm very fond of her. Very fond, indeed."

"Brereep," Princess said, with a shy smile.

"Talk like frog," Buroc said, obviously disapproving.

Princess looked hurt. She pouted in a most fetching way.
Kedrigern squeezed her hand and said, "Not that it's any of
your business, Buroc; but we manage to communicate quite
effectively. Don't we, Princess?"

She raised a hand to stroke his cheek and murmured,
"Brereep."

"Sweet of you to say so," he responded. Turning to the
barbarian, he said, "I think Princess, by her very presence,
attests to my abilities. Now, do you have horses for us?"

"Lady come?"

Kedrigern weighed that for a moment. He could leave her
here, protected by a spell. But if anything befell him, Princess
would be alone and helpless, and unaware of her helplessness.

That was unthinkable. Much as he disliked subjecting her to Buroc's hungry eyes, he felt it the better course.

"The lady comes," he said.

Buroc's eyes again glazed over in thought, then he lifted one columnar arm and pointed down the road. "Horses wait."

"We'll pack some food and be with you shortly," Kedrigern said. His glance lighted on the tray Princess had brought. "Meanwhile, be my guest. Eat. Drink," he said, presenting the tray.

Impressed by the speed with which bread, cheese and ale vanished, Kedrigern decided to use Buroc in an experiment. Leaving Princess to pack the food for the journey, he filled a sack with objects captured in one of his blind gropings into the future. They were small cylindrical things of bright metal wound in bands of coloured paper marked with symbols and pictures. At first he had assumed that they were talismans of some unintelligible magic, but he had learned, quite by accident, that they were actually foodstuffs, protected by a near-impenetrable metal shell. He could not imagine how this had been done, or why, nor could he conceive of who, or what, would eat such things, or how they might go about it. If Buroc could manage to deal with the cylinders, that might explain something about them.

Kedrigern glanced about his study. It was cluttered with paraphernalia retrieved in the course of his temporal magic exercises, which had linked him with a remote future age. He had learned very little about that age so far, aside from the fact that it contained a great variety of mysterious metal objects and was very noisy. But his investigations were still in their infancy.

Outside, he pulled a metal cylinder from his bag and tossed it to Buroc. "Food, Buroc. Good. Eat," he said, rubbing his stomach in illustrative gesture.

Buroc bit down on the cylinder, frowned, and took it from his mouth. After staring at it for a time, he laid it on a stump, drew a huge, heavy dagger, and brought the blade down hard, splitting the object in two. He picked up one half, sucked at it, tossed it aside, and did the same with the other half. "More," he said.

Kedrigern tossed him the sack, and Buroc treated himself to a dozen more, leaving the dooryard littered with glinting metal and shreds of coloured paper. "Skin tough. Meat good," the barbarian said.

So that was how one enjoyed the contents of those metal cylinders. A dark thought came to Kedrigern. This remote age into which his magic had extended might be peopled by barbarians like Buroc. He pictured a landscape littered from horizon to horizon with shards of scrapped metal trodden by huge barbarian feet, and shuddered. Perhaps it was a sign that the alchemists would triumph in the end. That was the kind of world that would gladden their tiny hearts.

Buroc led the way to where two shaggy horses stood tethered, grazing complacently on the spring grass. He mounted the larger one, leaving the smaller for the wizard and the lady. Kedrigern mounted and reached down to swing Princess up before him. The saddle was quite roomy enough for the two of them.

They travelled in silence for some time. Kedrigern was absorbed in his troubled speculations, Princess was fascinated by the unfamiliar sights and sounds, and Buroc was completely occupied with keeping to the trail. The way led through open countryside for a time, across flowery meadows and down a fragrant woodland trail, then through a wide valley to the outskirts of a cathedral town. Kedrigern, still deep in thought, grunted in surprise as Princess squeezed his waist tightly and clung to him.

The town was a grisly scene. Smoke hung in the air, rank and sickly-smelling, only now beginning to dissipate on a gentle breeze. Doorways and windows gaped, and the great cathedral was open to the skies. Above wheeled flights of crows, and Kedrigern saw a wolf start from their path. When he saw the first bodies, he raised his hand to caress Princess' head, buried in his shoulder, and worked a small concealing magic to hide the carnage from her. He could feel her trembling.

"It's all right now, Princess," he whispered. "We're out in a meadow covered with flowers. Daffodils, as far as the eye can see."

"Brereep," she said faintly, not moving her head.

Buroc reined his mount to a halt and made a sweeping gesture that encompassed the scene. "Buroc do all," he announced.

"Why?"

The barbarian turned his little eyes on the wizard, held his gaze for a long moment, then pointed to the ruins of the cathedral. "Me burn." Swinging his hand to indicate a heap of sprawled corpses, he said, "Me kill." Jerking his horse's head aside, he rode on, erect and proud in the saddle.

At the sound of Buroc's voice, Princess clung more tightly to Kedrigern. "Odd, how barbarians seem to have no knowledge whatsoever of the nominative singular pronoun, Princess," he said by way of diversion. "It's always *me* this and *me* that, particularly when they're being boastful. Your typical barbarian's grasp of syntax seems to be on a par with his grasp of other people's rights to life and property."

"Brereep," Princess said softly.

"Well, yes, I know that your acquaintance with barbarians is slight, my dear. One would hardly expect a well-bred lady to mingle with the likes of Buroc, much less chat with him. You'll just have to take my word for it. I do, though, sometimes wonder if it's all an affectation."

"Brereep?"

"No, truly I do," Kedrigern said. He fell silent for a time, then smiled, then laughed softly to himself. "Can't you just picture them, off by themselves somewhere, hairy and rank, dropping all pretence and cutting loose with compound-complex sentences and sophisticated constructions in the subjective?"

She laughed at the suggestion, and from time to time, as they went on, she glanced at Buroc, then at Kedrigern, and the two of them smothered laughter as children do at a solemn ceremony. They passed no further scenes of devastation and Princess showed no further signs of fear.

Kedrigern relaxed somewhat in his concern for Princess, but he saw much to cause him concern about other matters. He had travelled not at all in recent years, content to live on his quiet hillside with Princess and his magic and loyal Spot to wait on them. The world he saw now was a far worse place than the world he had forsaken. Nature was as lovely as ever; but where the hand of man had fallen, all was blight and death and ruin. The barbarians were overrunning everything. What little they left intact, the alchemists pounded, and boiled, and burned in their hunger for gold.

He became increasingly certain that the alchemists were going to triumph in the end. They would persist until they had turned every bit of lead into gold, and their work would precipitate an age of chaos. The future world that Kedrigern had reached with his magic might well be a place of horrors, if he read the indications correctly. It was a troubling prospect, and he sank into gloom.

Their journey was relatively quiet. They passed three villages which lay in ruins, and at each one, Buroc stopped to point out the carnage and destruction and loudly claim credit for it. He evidenced a growing attentiveness to Princess' reaction, and that disturbed Kedrigern. But at night, when they camped, the barbarian behaved himself. All the same, Kedrigern cast a protective spell around the tent which he and Princess shared.

They came on the third day to a sunless valley where nothing grew. Carrion birds watched with interest from the twisted white limbs of dead trees as the riders picked their way across this place of muck and stone toward a low hill that rose in its centre. Only as they approached did Kedrigern determine that the bristling outline of the hill was not caused by the remains of a forest but by bare poles thrust into the ground at disturbing angles. He felt the tingling of magic in the air, and reined in his horse, calling sharply to Buroc.

"No further! That place is protected!"

Buroc jerked his horse to a halt and turned to face the wizard. "Golden mountain," he said.

Kedrigern was annoyed with himself. He should have known. There were few better ways to keep people far distant than to give a place the appearance of a burying ground of the Old Race. He dismounted, and cautioning Princess to stay behind with the restless horse, he walked closer. The sensation of enchantment grew.

With his back to Buroc, he reached into his tunic and drew out a silver disc about a hand's breadth in diameter which hung on a chain about his neck. It was the medallion of his brotherhood and contained great virtue. Running his first two fingers over certain of the symbols inscribed thereon, he raised the medallion to his eye and sighted through the tiny aperture at its centre.

Before him rose a mound of gold. It was not a mountain, not even a fair-sized hill. But it would do. It was pure, glittering gold, flooding the gloomy valley with its light.

Kedrigern slipped the medallion inside his tunic and rubbed his eyes wearily; using the aperture of true vision was a strain. When he looked again, the mound rose as before, like the trodden corpse of a giant hedgehog. He turned in time to see a flash of silver in Buroc's hand, which the barbarian quickly removed from before his eye and dropped inside his furs. Kedrigern recognized the silver object, and a chill went through him.

"How did you learn about the golden mountain, Buroc?" he asked off-handedly.

"Man tell Buroc."

"Freely and cheerfully, I'm sure. Did the man give you anything?"

The barbarian paused before replying, "Do magic. Buroc share gold."

"There's no hurry, Buroc. Did you take anything from this helpful man?"

"Do magic," Buroc said, and his voice was hard.

"Just now, I don't want gold. I want the silver medallion that's hanging around your filthy neck. You took it from a brother wizard."

The barbarian reached inside his fur tunic. He hesitated, then he withdrew his empty hand. "Wizard give to Buroc. Mine."

"No wizard gives away his medallion. You came upon a brother when his force was spent, and you killed him. That's how you found the golden mountain. But you don't know how to penetrate the enchantment, and you never will." Kedrigern folded his arms and gazed scornfully up at the mounted barbarian. "So, you great greasy heap of ignorant boastful brutality, you can look until your greedy heart consumes itself, but you can never possess."

With an angry growl, Buroc dropped to the ground, drawing his long curving sword with smooth and practised swiftness and charging at Kedrigern. The wizard stood his ground. The blade hummed down, then rebounded with the sharp crack of splintering crystal. Fragments of glinting steel spun through the air, and Buroc howled in pain and wrung his hands.

Kedrigern moved his lips silently, extending his hands before him. With a shout, he flung a bolt of shrivelling force at the raging barbarian. It struck, and burst in a shower of light, and it was Kedrigern's turn to cry out and nurse his hands. But worse than the pain of rebounded magic was the shock of realization – the power that protected him from Buroc, protected the barbarian from him.

The medallion had a twofold purpose: to signify fellowship in the company of wizards, and to protect whoever wore it against unfriendly magic. It knew no loyalty but to its current wearer.

They faced one another, Kedrigern standing his ground, Buroc circling warily, each eager to strike but cautious from the first shock. Buroc, snarling like a hungry dog, wrenched a jagged stone the size of a cauldron from the muddy ground. Raising it high overhead, he flung it squarely at the wizard's chest. It shattered into gravel and fell like hard rain around them.

"No use, Buroc. You can't hurt me."

The barbarian, panting as much with rage as with exertion, glared at him, motionless, eyes glazing in a furious attempt at thought. After a time, a malicious grin cut across his face.

"Buroc no hurt wizard. Wizard no hurt Buroc. No can hurt."

"I'll think of something."

"Wizard not hurt Buroc!" the barbarian repeated triumphantly.

"Don't gloat. You'll only make it worse for yourself."

With unnerving speed, Buroc turned and raced to Princess' side. He seized her wrist in one huge hand and clutched her hair with the other. "Buroc hurt lady!" he roared. "Wizard no hurt Buroc, and Buroc hurt lady!"

Kedrigern felt his stomach flutter at the thought of Princess in Buroc's hands. In desperation, he aimed a bolt at the barbarian's tiny head. The recoiling force staggered him, and he heard Buroc's laughter through a haze of pain. Princess's shriek brought him to his senses.

"I can't reach him, Princess!" he cried. "The medallion protects him, just as it protects me. I'm helpless!"

She turned her terrified eyes on him. Buroc forced her head around, to confront his ugly face.

One recourse remained. His magic was useless against the barbarian, but it would work on Princess. It was dangerous for anyone to be subjected a second time to shape-changing enchantment, but anything was better than ravishment and mutilation at Buroc's hands. She would understand, he was certain.

"Be brave, Princess. There's still a chance," he said. And shaking his head to clear it, Kedrigern began to recite the necessary words, spurred by the sight of Princess's vain struggle.

Buroc pulled her to him. She clawed at his face, and he struck her hands aside. She tore at his tunic, while he laughed and lifted her off her feet. Still she clawed at him. Then, with a bright flash, the silver medallion flew through the air.

Kedrigern broke off his spell to dash forward and snatch the medallion before it touched the ground. He dangled it by its broken chain, then swung it around his head, laughing aloud.

"Come, Buroc. Fetch," he said.

Buroc did not hesitate. He flung Princess aside and hurled himself at the wizard, clawing for the medallion. Kedrigern raised a hand, and Buroc froze in mid air, then crashed to the ground with a loud *splap* and a splash of mud. He was rigid as stone.

Kedrigern ran to Princess, raised her up and held her tightly in his arms, speaking soft consoling words until she had stopped shaking. He led her, half carrying her, to the horse and drew from the saddlebag a heavy cloak, which he threw over her shoulders.

"You're a brave woman, Princess. And quicker with your wits than either of us. Buroc never knew what you were up to," he said appreciatively.

"Brereep?" she asked timidly.

He glanced at Buroc. Already, the clarity of his outline was fading and greying as the petrifaction spell did its work. Soon the Flayer of God's Earth would be no more than a curiously formed pile of stone. The general barbarity would, no doubt, continue; but Buroc's contribution would be missing.

"Quick and painless, Princess," said Kedrigern. "Better than he deserved, but under the circumstances I wanted something quick and dependable. Anything more appropriate would have required more time than either of us could spare." A glint of gold caught his eye. He stooped and took up the golden circlet, wiping it free of mud before placing it on her brows. "We'll leave with no more gold than we brought, if you have no objection, Princess."

"Brereep," she said decisively.

"I didn't think you would." He gestured vaguely toward the bristling gravemound. "We know how to get back, and I doubt that anyone will stumble on this and carry it off in the meantime. I'd like to give this whole affair some thought," he said, swinging her up into the saddle.

He mounted Buroc's horse, and side by side they started back. He was silent for a time, deeply preoccupied, but when he became aware of her curious gaze on him, he explained himself.

"I might as well tell you now, Princess," he said, sighing, "that pile of gold is probably close to worthless. Well, maybe not completely worthless. Not just yet. But by the time we get all the wagons we need, and undo the enchantment that's been placed on it – a mighty powerful one – and get it all to a trustworthy buyer, it's sure to be too late. It's all these alchemists, you see. They're frauds, and charlatans, a pack of jargon-spouting pseudo-magicians, I know all that, but they're always *busy*, and there are so *many* of them . . ." He sighed again, and shook his head sadly. "They're bound to find what they're after. And once they can turn lead into gold, our golden mountain will be worthless. They'll turn all the lead in the world into gold. There'll be gold everywhere."

She laid her hand on his, to console him. He smiled bravely, but could not keep up a facade. Twice that day she heard him murmur, "All the lead into gold," and sigh, and say no more. At night, he said it in his sleep, and gnashed his teeth.

The second day he was silent. On the third morning, he said, "It's not as if I sought it out. I mean, it was just handed to me, and to have it taken away before we even have a chance . . . it isn't fair, Princess." He moped along for a time, then turned his mind to sending orders ahead to Spot. He wanted the house tidy and dinner ready for their return, and that required concentration. When instructing Spot, one had to be precise. Spot could not be left any margin for initiative. Telling him to prepare dinner meant risking the sight of a heap of dead moles on one's platter.

When they reached the foot of the trail to Silent Thunder Peak, Kedrigern, who had been leading his horse, gazing dejectedly on the ground, let out a sudden yell of exultation. He clapped his hands and shouted for joy. Princess, unable to resist his gaiety, laughed along with him, but looked at him in silent appeal.

"I've solved it, Princess! We'll beat those alchemists at their own game!" he cried, beaming. "Once they've turned all the lead into gold, lead will be rare and precious. So –" and he stopped to laugh and clap his hands and cut a caper on the path " – we'll turn the golden mountain into lead! It's a brilliant idea. Brilliant! Isn't it, my love?"

"Brereep," she said.

A SLOW DAY IN HELL

Julia S. Mandala

A lawyer by training, Julia Mandala is now a full-time writer since she sold her first story to Marion Zimmer Bradley in 1993. She used her background for a later story, "Dracula's Lawyer" (1995). The following shows her more anarchic side.

Satan, Prince of Darkness and Lord of All Evil, sipped a frozen margarita and stared out the window of his air-conditioned office at the writhing, moaning masses in the fiery pits below. Not that Satan cared a jot for temperature. Nor did he particularly like margaritas. He preferred a nice, woody Chardonnay, but no beverage aroused howling misery quite like a frosty frozen drink. On slow days, he was forced to resort to these petty tortures until something better occurred to him.

Screeching fingernails clawed the office door. Satan turned from his tormenting and called, "Come in, Meph." No one but Mephistopheles could achieve that particular grating noise – one that made skin crawl, ears cringe and hairs stand on end.

Mephistopheles, Greatest of Demons and Satan's Left-

Hand Man, ushered in a short, pudgy imp, who cowered in flatteringly appropriate fear and awe. "I have brought Cyril, O Evil One," said Mephistopheles, winking at Satan over the imp's head.

"Leave us, then."

Cyril's face showed utter panic at the prospect of being left alone with the Lord of All Evil.

Mephistopheles gave him a pitying look. "Ah, well," he sighed, leaving the imp to his fate.

Satan fixed fiery red eyes on the tiny imp and waited. Cyril's shaking worsened. He began to blubber and drool. He wrung his claws, carelessly slicing through his leathery hide. Still, Satan said nothing, but continued to pin Cyril with his gaze. Finally, the imp could take it no longer.

"Pleeeeeze, your worship, forgive my clumsiness," he sobbed, collapsing to the floor in a quivering mass. "How was I to know the man enjoyed being beaten?"

"His bio materials clearly stated he was a masochist," said Satan. "Didn't you read them?"

"I thought that meant he went to Catholic Church," sniffled Cyril.

The Prince of Darkness waved his arm dismissively. "I ought to consign you to the common pit."

"Noooooo! Not the pit! You know what the masses do to imps who are stripped of their powers."

"All the vile, evil, horrible things you did to them, I suppose," Satan said in a bored tone.

"Please, O Great Evil One, give Cyril another chance," the imp begged. "Cyril can be evil. Cyril can cause great misery. Yes. Yes, he can."

Satan despised those who spoke of themselves in the third person and was sorely tempted to cast Cyril into the pit and be done with it. But . . . it was a slow afternoon. "Very well. I have a borderline case for you. Break her spirit and she will be consigned to the pits in your place."

"Oh, thank you, thank you." Cyril grabbed Satan's sleeve and kissed it in gratitude.

The Lord of All Evil was less than moved by the gesture. Cyril's drool left stains on the fine material. "Get on with it!"

Satan shook the imp off with such force that Cyril crashed through the door with a splintering bang, leaving behind an imp-shaped hole.

"Sorry!" came Cyril's voice.

What a pickle I've gotten myself into, thought the imp as he waddled on stubby legs along the rutted, dusty path. It didn't have to be a dusty path. Oh no. Hell was limited only by the vision of the imps and demons inhabiting it. But therein lay the problem. No one could say Cyril wasn't an enthusiastic imp; he delighted in inflicting pain and misery as much as anyone in Hell. But even Cyril had finally come to realize he was slow of reasoning and limited in imagination.

"I'll show them this time," he vowed, swiping his keycard through the security access scanner that opened the holding area gate. "I'll make this woman shriek and howl in despair." But how?

The file the bored receptionist handed him was labelled "Marjorie Mornington". A glance through the material showed little. Housewife. Died in a fire. An optimist? He wondered why they bothered to mention it. Near-sightedness and other physical deformities vanished after death.

Cyril opened the door to the holding area. Seated on the moulded plastic bench, straight-backed, ankles crossed, Marjorie Mornington looked like anybody's middle-aged mother – immaculately coiffed hair dyed an artificial dark brown, bright blue duster dotted with cheery yellow daisies masking her plumpness, and blue terry house slippers that just matched her eyes. Cyril rubbed his hands and licked his cracked lips. Easy pickings.

"Mornington!" he barked, though only she and he graced the room.

Marjorie waved and smiled. "Here I am!"

He gave her his most ominous glare. "I am Cyril, your worst nightmare."

"Aren't you the cutest little thing!" She patted him on his remaining tuft of hair, which sprouted from the centre of his forehead. "Is this Hell?" Without waiting for an answer or his instruction, she stepped out of Receiving and into Hell proper. "My, it's nice and warm here. I can't tolerate the cold. I used to beg Bob (that's my husband) to turn up the heat in the winter, but he would just grumble about the gas bill and ignore me." She stretched luxuriantly and sighed. "That's what brought me here in the end."

She giggled – not a hideous, disgusting imp giggle, but the pleasant, childlike giggle of one who has done a naughty thing and been caught by an indulgent parent. "This winter was particularly cold and in late February, I just snapped. I asked Bob one last time to turn up the heat. That's what I said. 'Bob, for the last time, please turn up the darned heat." I figured when I *swore* like that, he'd know I meant business. But he just kept reading his paper and muttered, "I'm glad it's the last time." Well, he wasn't so glad after I blew out the pilot light, waited a few minutes and struck a match." She sighed again. "The blaze was so nice and warm."

Cyril scratched his head, forgetting until too late that his claws would rake bloody furrows into his scalp. This was going to be harder than he'd thought. Ideally, her personal hell should be colder than Antarctica in the dead of winter. But there hadn't been a Cold Day in Hell for centuries, and Cyril didn't have the faintest idea how to bring about another one, let alone an eternity of Cold Days. He racked his meagre brain cells. What did sweet, middle-aged ladies hate? Cyril got an impish grin on his impish face.

"Come with me," he said in a sticky-sweet voice. "I have just the place where you'll feel comfortable."

They meandered through the corridors of Hell, Marjorie chattering all the way, until they reached the door Cyril was searching for. He opened it with a grand, sweeping gesture, his eyes glued to Marjorie so he could get a good look at the horror on her face.

"Oooh!" she squealed. But instead of shrinking in fear, she lit up with delight. "Cute, fuzzy mice."

"They're *rats!*"

"Well, so they are." She squatted and reached out to one of the rodents. "Come here, little fellah. Don't be afraid."

To Cyril's surprise, the creature did not snap off a finger. It cautiously sniffed at Marjorie, then nuzzled her hand like a kitten. Cooing and smiling, she stroked its fur. "My father always said I'd make a pet out of anything. These little guys remind me of the bats I kept as a girl. They lived in our barn, and —"

"Out!" ordered Cyril.

"But I thought you said —"

"Out!"

Marjorie gave the rodent one final pat, then reluctantly rose to follow the imp. Cyril set his brain to churning again. Creatures were out. What, then? Suddenly, he got a Sly Idea.

"Now, you've already told me you hate the cold," he said solicitously. "Is there anything else that really gets to you? I mean, we wouldn't want to put you someplace where you'd be unhappy."

"Oh, I'm sure whatever you choose will be fine with me."

"Come on," cajoled Cyril. "There must be something."

"Well," Marjorie confided, "I'm not very fond of heights."

Aha! Cyril led the way, strutting with confidence that victory was near and an eternity of torture in the pits avoided. When they reached their next destination, he flung open the door and shoved a surprised Marjorie into the waiting arms of two demons. One restrained her while the other strapped a harness over her blue and yellow duster. Bungee cords dangled ominously from the back.

"Oh, my!" she exclaimed in dismay. Her face froze into a pleasing mask of horror as she peered over the edge of a platform into a seemingly bottomless pit.

"Cyril?" She stared in shock at his betrayal.

The two demons exchanged demonic grins. "Did you remember to shorten the cords?" asked one. "I don't want to clean up another smashed body."

"Oops, I forgot," said the other, simultaneously giving Marjorie a hard shove.

She stumbled off the platform and plunged toward the darkness. Bungee cords whipped from their coils. "My wooorrr—" Her voice faded. Half an hour later, the last of the cord unwound. The two bands stretched tight, paused, then began bunching together again. Cyril wriggled in antici- pation of Marjorie's blood-curdling screams on her journey up. He caught her voice, faint, but growing louder and louder. Instead of curdling, his blood froze. It couldn't be!

"Wheeee!" shouted Marjorie as she flew upward.

"Hey, imp," snarled one demon while the other rolled in the bungee cords. "What are you doing bringing us someone who *likes* to bungee jump?"

"But she said –" Cyril clamped his mouth shut before he said something he might regret. It never paid to piss off a demon.

"Whew!" gasped Marjorie. The demons roughly tore off the bungee harness and thrust them both out the door. She put her hands on her hips. "I ought to be mad as heck about that trick you played on me, but it worked. I'm completely cured of my fear of heights. Thank you!" She leaned down and gathered Cyril into a big hug.

His blood boiled inside his impish breast. Jerking away, Cyril tugged on his tuft and hopped from foot to foot, height increasing until he was bouncing off the ceiling and walls.

"My word," said Marjorie, clapping her hands in delighted rhythm. "What an interesting little dance. Could you teach me the steps? I want to fit in down here –"

"No!"

"Then I'll teach you a dance I know. Do-do-do-di-do-di-do-do-do, do-do-do-di-do-di-do-do-do."

Cyril watched in stunned fury as Marjorie Mornington began to disco, sing-songing an insipid seventies melody all the while. "C'mon, Cyril. Don't be a stick in the mud. Do the Hustle! Do-do-do-di-do-di-do-do-do, do-do-do-di-do-di-do-do-do."

Seething, he scratched "Boogie Wonderland" from his list of places to try on Marjorie. In Boogie Wonderland, the damned – usually aficionados of rock and roll or classical music – danced to an endless stream of disco songs, cleverly mixed by Hell's finest DJ so that it was impossible to tell where one song ended and the next began and no one ever got a chance to leave the dance floor. The pounding beat drowned out the wailing of "Disco sucks!" and the gnashing of teeth as tortured souls boogied for all eternity to the stylings of Donna Summer and the Bee Gees.

With moves that would make Travolta proud, Marjorie added the pointing fingers to her routine. "Aaargh!" wailed Cyril, yanking at his tuft again. His eyes widened in horrified disbelief as his fist came away with his last surviving strands of hair. "Oooh! If you weren't already dead, I'd kill you!"

"Lighten up, Cyril. Do-do-do-di-do-di-do-do-do." Marjorie's plump hips swayed in perfect rhythm.

"NO DANCING!"

"Oh, all right." As suddenly as she had begun, she stopped. "My, that was fun. I haven't danced in years. Bob had two left feet. You know, I'll bet they don't disco in Heaven. You're making me glad I ended up down here."

Steam poured from the imp's ears.

"What a neat trick," said Marjorie. "I wonder if I can do that." She screwed shut her eyes, face set in deep concentration. Steam trickled from her ears. Then, the trickle became a torrent. Then, steam turned to flames.

"H-how'd you do that?"

Marjorie opened her innocent blue eyes. "I'm not sure. But it *does* feel good to blow off steam, doesn't it?"

Cyril was beginning to suspect if he locked Marjorie Mornington in a room full of manure and gave her a shovel, she would find a pony.

"What's next?" she asked. "Though I suppose it's rude of me to assume you'll keep being so nice about showing me around and getting me settled in. I'll bet you have all kinds of things you need to be doing."

"Oh, no," he said with a hysterical edge like broken glass. "This is what I do. I'm an official greeter."

"Just like those elderly people at WalMart," Marjorie said. "You know, Hell's a much friendlier place than they lead you to believe down at the Baptist Church."

Cyril began to giggle uncontrollably – not a pleasant, child-like giggle, or even a hideous, disgusting imp giggle. It was the crazed giggle of someone who finally got the joke and realized it was a particularly cruel and nasty joke and that the joke was on him.

Marjorie beamed benevolently at him. "That's better, Cyril. You're learning to relax."

"Hee-hee! Hoo-hoo!" he giggled, rocking from side to side, drool spilling from the corners of his mouth, tears spilling from the corners of his eyes. Cyril was still hee-heeing and hoo-hooing when the demons dragged him off to the pit.

"My word," Marjorie said to the two new imps that flanked her. "He was an odd little fellow."

The imp guards glowered and motioned for her to walk between them. They soon arrived at the office of the Big Boss. A new door gleamed in the red firelight.

"Now you'll find out what Hell's really all about," growled one.

"Another tour?" asked Marjorie. "Splendid. I love seeing new sights. Bob never liked to go anywhere."

The imp snorted and knocked. "ENTER!" a deep voice called.

The imps opened the door, thrust Marjorie through, and pulled it shut behind her with a thud. Satan, Prince of Darkness and Lord of All Evil, regarded her with flaming eyes. "Well, Ms Mornington, you've had quite a first day in Hell." He grinned satanically as Marjorie's face melted and ran together. Her body shifted and flowed until she was a nauseating mass of moving flesh. Gradually, all the parts settled into the form of Mephistopheles.

Satan clapped him on the back. "Meph, you're a genius. You sure know how to liven up a dull day."

Mephistopheles bowed his head modestly and poured a couple of margaritas. Staring in satisfaction through the plate-glass window at the tormented souls languishing in the pit, they finally spotted Cyril. The imp alternately giggled hysterically and writhed in agony as those he had tormented took their revenge. Satan and his minion exchanged a high five. The Lord of All Evil's laughter boomed across the vast expanse of Hell. "Is this a great job or what?"

Two Tall Tales

HOW I GOT
THREE ZIP CODES

Gene Wolfe

Gene Wolfe (b. 1931) is one of the premier writers of science fiction and fantasy. He is probably best known for his novel sequence The Book of the New Sun, *which began with* The Shadow of the Torturer *(1980), but he has written much else besides. Amongst his most thought-provoking fantasy novels are* There are Doors *(1988),* Castleview *(1990) and* Soldier of the Mist *(1986). The complexity of these novels may make it seem surprising that Wolfe could produce any light-hearted fantasies. However, one of his very earliest stories, "Trip, Trap" (1967), was a clever variation on the troll-under-the-bridge tale, and anyone who can entitle a collection of his stories* The Island of Doctor Death and Other Stories and Other Stories *(1980) has to have his tongue planted firmly in his cheek. It's that side of Gene Wolfe we see here in a brand new story that begins our sequence of two "Tall Tales".*

The sun was sinking slowly in the Gulf, having been torpedoed by a Nazi sub.

"Thar's three ways ta start any artycle," the old man said, and spat brown and viscid juice like a grasshopper. "Or catch a catfish, if'n ya'd druther. 'Bout the same either way."

I deafened my ears to the faint despairing cries of the doomed crew. It's too hot anyway, I thought. Aloud I said, "You mean like with a dramatic incident?"

"Shore! Catch ya a frog. Not no big eatin' frog like ya'd gig. Understand? One a them li'l spotty 'uns, mebbe. There's lots that'll run their hook through the top lip *an'* the bottom 'un too. Don't make no sense a-tall, do it?"

Not to the frog, I supposed.

"No, siree!" The old man spat again, narrowly missing a herring gull that shrieked and fled. "How's he s'posed ta holler, down there under the water, after ya *hooked* his Li'l flytrap up like that? Then too, s'pose he's got a sinus condition? Huh! Got ta breath through his mouth, don't he? Why, with both lips hooked up together like that, he can't breath in, nor out neither. Some folks don't think. I seen a man down in Sonora got his head cut clean off with a machete. This's in a saloon. A cantina, they calls it."

I said, "I thought we were sitting on this pier."

He had not heard me. "Head cut clean off. Bounced on that sawdust floor and spun 'round three times spurting blood all over. Damnedest thing I ever seen. Well, his body now, it *couldn't* think, could it? Didn't have no brains, did it?"

"Some people never do," I reminded him gently, still wondering how to begin this article.

"Only it could be scared. And 'twuz, ya bet. Fear ain't in yor head nohow, sorta behind yor belt buckle. That body run right outa that there cantina and down the street ta the next 'un. Warn't much more'un half a block. Now ya'd think a body'd *know* it didn't have no head. And it would, too, if'n it'd thought about it. Only it never did. It'd jest got paid, ya see, and it wuz bound ta spend it all 'fore it died. I follered it, and it bellied up ta the bar an' sez gimme a slug a the best rotgut ya kin lay yor hands on in this here godfersaken hellhole. Couldn't talk, a-course, didn't have no mouth, but ya could see from the expression a its shirt buttons that wuz what it meant."

A vagrant breeze whisked sand across my notepad, and I sneezed.

"The barkeep, he knowed right away an' poured a shot. Well, sir! That wuz the funniest thing I ever did see! That body picked it up like ta drink it, see? Wasn't till it had it up about so high, it happened ta think it didn't have no mouth. I mozied up ta it and I sez ya ain't got no mouth, ya damn fool. Ya carry that shot back ta the other place, 'cuz that's where yor mouth is. Only it couldn't hear me 'cuz it didn't have no ears."

"I see," I said. I had lost interest already, and was wondering what had become of the girl I had observed removing a yellow bathing suit behind the creosote tree to my left. A girl like that, I mused . . .

"Put salt on it," the old man told me. "Don't ya lay it on no windersill, neither, if'n ya sees no doctor. Did I say how that head *ate* ever' crumb a sawdust it could reach? With its tongue, ya know?"

"Certainly," I lied.

"So what the *body* done wuz pour that shot inta its shirt pocket, jest 'fore it fell down dead. A story like that'n, right up front, mind, is bound ta take the eye a *any* catfish. Same thing with the frog. Ya got him thrashing around down there an' screamin' his li'l lungs out, why, ya could catch *The Reader's Digest* with him."

Already day was drawing to a close. Staring up at the darkening sky, I traced the letters HOW I GOT THREE ZIP CODES, an inkier black against the cloud-tossed sky. "This wasn't in Mexico," I told the old man. "It was in Chicago."

He levelled his forefinger. "Don't a one a them zip codes a yors start six-ought-six?"

I shook my head. "The little bubble in that gadget can't possibly tell you that."

"Stop rattlin' like that," he ordered me. "It's real destractin', but I'll have me a pair a Genes anyhow."

I waited for him to add on rye toast and hold the mayo. He did not.

"Didn't ya shake yor head like that before, back there 'bout a page?"

"I don't think so," I said.

"Mebbe that wuz a real snake, then. Better have another drink."

"I was going to tell you about my zip codes – how I came to be Sweet One Oh Three in Lake Zurich, Illinois; but you said something that interests me. You said that editors and catfish are much alike. It would seem to me to be somewhat in error, since editors have scales of payment, while catfish have no scales at all. How do you resolve the contradiction?"

"How much Leah payin' ya for this?"

"I stand corrected. My zip codes, I was about to say, are sixty thousand and ten, sixty thousand and eleven, and sixty thousand and forty-seven. Their sum is one hundred and eighty thousand and sixty-eight."

"An' what's their product, boy?"

"My calculator is not capable of expressing a number so large. I would have to resort to logarithms."

"I tol' yor ma ya wouldn't be normal. How 'bout the cube root?"

"Sixty thousand and twenty-two and two thirds, more or less."

"Reckon folks could write ya with that?"

"I don't see why not."

"Figured ya wouldn't. How 'bout the average?"

"The same."

"Always said ya wuz weird."

"Not really. You see, the numbers are large and differ by small amounts, and in such cases –"

"How big? Write 'em down fer me."

I moistened my forefinger (receiving a poignant reminder of the nightcrawlers with which I had baited my hook earlier) and wrote them out on the salt-rimed boards: 60010, 60011, 60047.

"Them's not so big." The old man gestured toward the gull-smeared sky. "Take a look at that three up there. Must be a half-mile high. Six long if'n it's a inch. That right thar's what *I* call a big number. Mebbe ya don't think so. Mebbe ya seen bigger'n that over ta Switzerland, but that 'un's big enough fer *me*."

"Sixty thousand and forty-seven isn't in Switzerland, it's in Lake Zurich –"

"Near 'nuf."

"You see, people don't use the United States Mail much any more."

"Whar do they stick their stamps, then?" the old man inquired.

"Don't tempt me like that, Grandfather. Mailing's too easy, I suppose. There are mail boxes on every corner, post offices everywhere, and so on."

"Always closed, though." The old man scratched the ankle of his wooden leg reflectively.

"I suppose that may be the reason. Our post office in Barrington opens at nine-forty-five and closes at four-thirty, and at noon Saturday. Naturally it's closed all day Sunday and on every conceivable and inconceivable holiday."

"That ain't no way ta catch a catfish!"

"I know. That's why I waited until this page."

"That place over to Switzerland –?"

"Mail Boxes She's Us. It's open a lot more, and the guy there gave me a key to the front door, as well as the key to Sweet 103."

"Ya mean box, don't ya, boy?"

"Yes, but you have to say *sweet*, it's a tradition. Write me at 830 West Main, Sweet 103. Or send me packages O.O.P.S., Fed X –"

"That one a them monster books yor always readin'?"

"Close enough. But the rest are worse, really. Some time ago, an editor in England told me he was going to send me a manuscript for checking via International Soup-Or-Swift. It would be in my hands in six hours. About a week later I got a postcard from Soup-Or-Swift saying it didn't deliver to my area. I could pick up my package at their head-quarters on Two Hundred and Seventy-Sixth Street. I live northwest of Chicago. That address is on the far south side."

"How fer?"

"Kentucky. Anyway Fed X, O.O.P.S. and the rest can deliver to Sweet 103."

"Ya could have 'em come ta yor house, boy. That first zip ya told about."

"I've tried that. I've had packages left next door and down the block and a whole lot one street over."

"I see what ya mean."

"I'm not through yet. In fact, I'm not anywhere close to it. I've had packages left in cars in my driveway. Half a dozen wedding presents were left in our garage and found before the wedding only by accident. An envelope containing ten thousand dollars in cheques was left on the stoop in the rain."

The old man was no longer listening. Shading his eyes to scan the lightless horizon, he muttered, "Ya think mebbe some a them solar sailors got off in the lifeboats?"

"I doubt it. That's a Leslie Fish album." I stepped from the dock. "I'd better be getting home."

Looking down into the dark and swirling waters of the bay, the old man grunted, "Huh! Which 'un, boy?"

THE FAILURE
OF HOPE & WANDEL

Ambrose Bierce

*These days the work of Ambrose Bierce (1842–?1914) seems to be
unjustly forgotten. If he's remembered at all it is either because of
his cynical observations on life collected as* The Devil's Dic-
tionary *(1911) or because of the nature of his disappearance. At
the age of seventy he decided to go and report upon the Mexican
revolution and was never seen again. A few years later another
person called Ambrose, Ambrose Small, also disappeared, causing
Charles Fort to comment "Maybe someone is collecting Am-
broses." Gregory Peck portrayed Bierce in the film* Old Gringo
*(1989), based on the book by Carlos Fuentes. Bierce was a writer
and journalist for over forty years, producing some of the best
horror stories of the late nineteenth century. Many of them were
written with a sardonic eye since he had little patience or time for
people and definitely suffered no fools. The following piece is one
of his more light-hearted ones.*

From Mr Jabez Hope, in Chicago, to Mr Pike Wandel, of New Orleans, 2 December 1877.

I will not bore you, my dear fellow, with a narrative of my journey from New Orleans to this polar region. It is cold in Chicago, believe me, and the Southron who comes here, as I did, without a relay of noses and ears will have reason to regret his mistaken economy in arranging his outfit.

To business. Lake Michigan is frozen stiff. Fancy, O child of a torrid clime, a sheet of anybody's ice, three hundred miles long, forty broad, and six feet thick! It sounds like a lie, Pikey dear, but your partner in the firm of Hope & Wandel, Wholesale Boots and Shoes, New Orleans, is never known to fib. My plan is to collar that ice. Wind up the present business and send on the money at once. I'll put up a warehouse as big as the Capitol at Washington, store it full and ship to your orders as the Southern market may require. I can send it in planks for skating floors, in statuettes for the mantel, in shavings for juleps, or in solution for ice cream and general purposes. It is a big thing!

I inclose a thin slip as a sample. Did you ever see such charming ice?

From Mr Pike Wandel, of New Orleans, to Mr Jabez Hope, in Chicago, 24 December 1877.

Your letter was so abominably defaced by blotting and blurring that it was entirely illegible. It must have come all the way by water. By the aid of chemicals and photography, however, I have made it out. But you forgot to inclose the sample of ice.

I have sold off everything (at an alarming sacrifice, I am sorry to say) and inclose draft for net amount. Shall begin to spar for orders at once. I trust everything to you – but, I say, has anybody tried to grow ice in *this* vicinity? There is Lake Ponchartrain, you know.

From Mr Jabez Hope, in Chicago, to Mr Pike Wandel, of New Orleans, 27 February 1878.

Wannie dear, it would do you good to see our new warehouse for the ice. Though made of boards, and run up rather hastily, it is as pretty as a picture, and cost a deal of money, though I pay no ground rent. It is about as big as the Capitol at Washington. Do you think it ought to have a steeple? I have it nearly filled – fifty men cutting and storing, day and night – awful cold work! By the way, the ice, which when I wrote you last was ten feet thick, is now thinner. But don't you worry; there is plenty.

Our warehouse is eight or ten miles out of town, so I am not much bothered by visitors, which is a relief. Such a giggling, sniggering lot you never saw!

It seems almost too absurdly incredible, Wannie, but do you know I believe this ice of ours gains in coldness as the warm weather comes on! I do, indeed, and you may mention the fact in the advertisements.

From Mr Pike Wandel, of New Orleans, to Mr Jabez Hope, in Chicago, 7 March 1878.

All goes well. I get hundreds of orders. We shall do a roaring trade as "The New Orleans and Chicago Semperfrigid Ice Company". But you have not told me whether the ice is fresh or salt. If it is fresh it won't do for cooking, and if it is salt it will spoil the mint juleps.

Is it as cold in the middle as the outside cuts are?

From Mr Jabez Hope, from Chicago, to Mr Pike Wandel, of New Orleans, 3 April 1878.

Navigation on the Lakes is now open, and ships are thick as ducks. I'm afloat, *en route* for Buffalo, with the assets of the New Orleans and Chicago Semperfrigid Ice Company in my vest pocket. We are busted out, my poor Pikey – we are to fortune and to fame unknown. Arrange a meeting of the creditors and don't attend.

Last night a schooner from Milwaukee was smashed into matchwood on an enormous mass of floating ice – the first berg ever seen in these waters. It is described by the survivors as being about as big as the Capitol of Washington. One-half of that iceberg belongs to you, Pikey.

The melancholy fact is, I built our warehouse on an unfavourable site, about a mile out from the shore (on the ice, you understand), and when the thaw came – O my God, Wannie, it was the saddest thing you ever saw in all your life! You will be *so* glad to know I was not in it at the time.

What a ridiculous question you ask me. My poor partner, you don't seem to know very much about the ice business.

THE BIRTHDAY GIFT

Elisabeth Waters

Elisabeth Waters is the author of dozens of short stories plus the novel Changing Fate *(1994). She has also collaborated with her cousin, Marion Zimmer Bradley, on the Lythande novel* The Gratitude of Kings *(1997) and assists Bradley with* Marion Zimmer Bradley's Fantasy Magazine.

"Aunt Frideswide, how could you?" Princess Rowena glared at the diminutive figure in the sorceress' robes across the amethyst, emerald, topaz, ruby and daisy that had dropped from her lips as she spoke.

Frideswide winced. *Oh, that voice! How could such a small girl have such a loud, shrill voice?* "Rowena, dear, remember your manners! Aren't you even going to say good morning? And do, please, moderate your voice."

"I can still say 'morning'," Rowena growled, "but I'm deleting the other word from my vocabulary. Rose thorns *hurt* when they scrape across your lips." The pile of precious stones and flowers on the table in front of her grew. "Why did you do it?"

"But my darling child, it was always your favourite fairy tale – it seemed the perfect gift for your fourteenth birthday, and besides it will add to the value of your dowry, now that you've reached marriageable age. I know your father was worried about that." *Really*, Frideswide thought to herself, *what's the matter with the girl? It's an elegant solution to all of our problems, and she's behaving like a sulky brat.*

"Oh, I see." Rowena's dark eyes blazed. "You think this will make a prospective husband willing to overlook my dreadful voice. You'll buy me a prince – but I have to do the suffering to earn him! Well, I don't want a prince, I don't want a husband, and I'd rather take a vow of silence than go around like this! Take this spell off me! Now!!" Her voice had risen almost two octaves above her usual piercing treble during this speech, and a beaker on the top shelf shattered on the last word.

"But, Rowena, dear," Frideswide protested, moving to the other side of the table to stir nervously the contents of her big cauldron, "I'm afraid I can't do that. I don't know the counterspell – indeed, I had difficulty enough getting the spell in the first place."

"No," Rowena said grimly, "not difficulty enough. I'm going to lock myself in my room, and I'm not coming out until you find a way to take this spell off me!"

A soft tap on the door was followed by a maidservant carrying Frideswide's breakfast tray. She dropped a curtsy when she saw Rowena. "Happy birthday, Your Royal Highness."

Rowena rushed past her and out of the room without replying. The maid stared after her in bewilderment, for Rowena was normally one of the friendliest people in the castle.

"She's overtired," Frideswide said hastily. *What a lame excuse; it is only breakfast time* "All the excitement of her birthday."

"I hope she'll be recovered in time for the party this afternoon," the girl remarked. "I hear all the princes of the Five Kingdoms will be there."

"I hope so, too," Frideswide said fervently, stepping in front of the pile of jewels on the table. "Put the tray on the end of my workbench, please, and then you may go."

When the girl had left, she sat on the stool at the end of the bench and took the cover off the tray. Immediately there was a scrabbling sound, and a dark-green newt appeared from among the clutter on the workbench to collect his share of the food. The newt had only one eye, the other having been sacrificed to a charm some time back. Frideswide also had a pet frog who was missing one toe, but that had not been one of her more successful charms, so she had not repeated it.

"Well, what do you think?"

The newt chewed several times and swallowed before answering. "*I* think she's an ungrateful brat. When I think of the trouble I took researching the spell, visiting that old dragon and bargaining – I could have been flambéed, and all she says is 'take it off'! It's a beautiful spell, one of the best you've ever cast, and it will make her rich and buy her a good husband and all she can do is yell and complain." He took another mouthful and paused to swallow it. "Why, with that spell, her husband wouldn't mind if she nagged at him day and night!"

Frideswide, however, was beginning to have second thoughts. "Maybe I *shouldn't* have done it. It was such a beautiful fairy tale – but I never thought about the practical aspects, like whether the roses would have thorns and exactly where they would come from. And what if she talks in her sleep and chokes on a ruby or something?"

The newt shrugged. "Then we wouldn't have to listen to her any more. Her speaking voice is bad enough – but why, in the name of all the gods and goddesses, does she have to love to sing?"

"Be fair; at least she goes deep into the forest to do it."

"Which is probably exactly why King Mark wants to marry her off – he hasn't been able to get any decent hunting for ten years." He snagged another mouthful off the plate, chewed, and swallowed. "Though part of that can be blamed on our Lady Dragon."

"Speaking of our Lady Dragon," Frideswide began hopefully.

"Absolutely not!" The newt's reply was emphatic. "I went
last time. If you really want to take this spell off Rowena, *you*
go ask the dragon for the counterspell." He ran down the
bench and disappeared through the crack in the wall that led to
the ledge. He'd lie there all morning, happily sunning himself
and carefully deaf to any pleas.

Frideswide gathered the spilled jewels into her belt pouch,
swung her cloak around her shoulders, and set off for the
dragon's lair.

The dragon looked impressed when the stones were set in
front of her. "So you did manage to work the spell." She
looked consideringly at Frideswide. "But obviously something went wrong, or you wouldn't be here. So what is
it?"

"I'm afraid that Rowena isn't taking it at all well. She made
a dreadful scene, saying that we had done this to buy her a
husband, and she didn't want one anyway, and –"

The dragon chuckled. "I can fill in the rest. My daughter
was like that for a time, too. Don't worry, they grow out of it in
a few centuries."

"We don't *have* a few centuries!" Frideswide protested.
"She's locked herself in her room, and she says she won't come
out until I take the spell off, and what her father will do if she
doesn't appear for her party this afternoon I don't even want to
consider!" She stopped for breath, and the dragon shook her
head.

"You mortals. Always frantic, always needing everything
done *now*. When will you learn to relax and take the long
view?"

"Doubtless when our lives are as long as yours, my
Lady Dragon," Frideswide snapped. "But at present, our
time moves more quickly. Do you have any *useful* suggestions?"

The dragon leaned back and blew a small gust of flame
toward the roof of the cavern. "I shall ponder this matter. In
the meantime, I suggest that you go home and try to reason

with your wayward child. Is there anyone she might listen to –
a playmate, perhaps a sweetheart? Think on that."

Frideswide got up and reached for the pile of jewels. A thin
stream of flame missed her hand by half a hand's span and the
heat made her jerk away.

"You can leave those." The dragon, damn her, sounded
amused. Frideswide seethed all the way home.

By evening, she had gone from seething to near explosion,
and so had King Mark. In his usual heavy-handed fashion, he
had ordered Rowena's door broken down when she refused to
come out. Rowena had fled to the balcony, whence the
dragon had neatly picked her up and carried her off. All
that was left was the pearl that had dropped when Rowena
screamed. Frideswide quickly pocketed it before anyone else
saw it.

With a castle full of princes (there were six of them still
there even after the party was cancelled – five visiting from
neighbouring kingdoms plus King Mark's son Eric), there
was, of course, an immediate proposal that someone should
go kill the dragon and rescue the princess. After all, it *was*
the proper princely thing to do. *But hardly*, Frideswide
thought, *proper mealtime conversation*, particularly when
Prince Eric described, in graphic detail, what the corpses
of the last few knights to challenge the dragon had looked
like after she had dealt with them. (The dragon, who valued
her privacy, had a habit of depositing the body of any knight
who disturbed it in the middle of the market place, in a
generally successful manoeuvre to discourage future attempts on her life. It was obvious that Eric, at least, wasn't
planning to make one.)

"But don't you feel honour-bound to rescue your sister?"
one of the other princes asked.

"And leave me without an heir and my kingdom open to
invasion or civil war?" King Mark inquired acidly. "Is that
what you would like to see? We've no way of knowing that
the girl is even still alive, and I forbid my son to embark
upon such a dangerous and unprofitable venture. And," he
added, looking around the table, "I forbid anyone else to

disturb the dragon – just in case one of you feels superfluous and suicidal enough to try. The dragon gets very annoyed when some idiot tries to kill her, and it will be my land and my people that she vents her annoyance on and *I won't have it!*" He glared menacingly around the table. "Is that *quite* clear, gentlemen?" The princes all nodded, looking relieved. They had all seen – and heard – Rowena, and while rescuing her could certainly have been considered the duty of any knight or prince, in the face of a clear prohibition from the king no one could expect them to attempt it. The wine flowed, and the conversation turned to hawking and tourneys.

"But I do wonder why the dragon carried off my daughter," King Mark said to Frideswide as they left the table.

Frideswide tensed. *Did someone tell him about the spell? If anything could make him want Rowena back . . .*

Apparently he didn't know, for he continued calmly, "You're the sorceress in the family, Frideswide. Find out what happened to my daughter – and why." He started to leave her, then turned back. "But don't upset the dragon while you're finding out!"

Doesn't want much, does he? Frideswide thought. *Oh, well, at least he isn't demanding Rowena's immediate safe return. And I am curious as to what the dragon has done with Rowena anyway.* She got her cloak, checked the sky – full moon and no clouds, plenty of light – and headed up the trail to the dragon's lair for the second time that day.

As she approached it, she could hear the most awful sounds; part rumbling, part screeching and part twanging, as if someone were plucking at random on the strings of a very badly tuned harp. She edged cautiously up to the cave entrance and peered inside.

There was a fire in the firepit, and the dragon was stretched out by it. Rowena was leaning back, propped against the dragon's side, plucking at a harp held loosely between her knees. The rest of the noise was coming from the dragon and Rowena, and presumably both of them would call it singing. Frideswide, not being tone-deaf, would not.

The dragon saw her first. "Come in, Frideswide." She

sounded amused. "Have you come to check on Rowena's welfare or demand her return?"

Rowena jumped to her feet, dropping the harp with a clang that made Frideswide wince, and dashed to the dragon's far side, peering at her aunt over the dragon's shoulder. "I won't go back!" she declared hysterically. "I like it here, and I want to stay here!" Jewels fell from her lips, bounced off the dragon's shoulder blade, and slid down her scales.

"But Rowena," Frideswide began.

"I won't go back there! Nobody there likes me, nobody listens to me – at least here the dragon likes my singing."

"And what am I supposed to tell your father?"

"Tell him I'm dead," Rowena said flatly. "I'm not going back there. Never."

"Are you sure that's what you want?" Rowena nodded. "What if you change your mind later?"

The dragon said lazily, "Rowena is free to come and go as she chooses, but nobody is going to take her from here as long as she wishes to stay. Do you have a problem with that, Frideswide?"

"Not in the slightest, Lady Dragon," Frideswide said calmly. "Although if Rowena truly wishes to stay here, it might be best to say that she's dead."

"True," the dragon agreed. "Knights intent on 'rescuing a captive princess' *are* a nuisance."

"King Mark has already forbidden the lot currently at the castle to bother you."

The dragon grinned, exposing rows of long sharp teeth. "I'm sure he has."

"He did, however, ask me to find out what had become of his daughter – and why."

"He doesn't know?" the dragon said in surprise. She twisted her head to look at Rowena. "Since your aunt does not appear determined to drag you away, child, you may as well sit down and be comfortable." Rowena returned to the fire and leaned back against the dragon's flank. At a nod from the dragon, Frideswide dragged a stool near the fire and sat down, too, shedding her cloak. It was certainly warm enough here, a nice change from the castle, where even the tapestries on the stone walls didn't keep the cold out. *Perhaps Rowena would be happier here. She's right in thinking that her father and brother don't care for her, poor child. She's always been rather plain, and between that and her voice, she wouldn't have much choice in a husband unless her father was willing to give her a large dowry, which he's not . . . and then I, with the best intentions, finished the process of turning her into a freak.* It was a sobering realization.

"Are you saying," the dragon asked, "that King Mark doesn't know about the birthday present you gave his daughter?"

"I really don't think he does," Frideswide said.

"Nobody knows," Rowena said. "Nobody except the three of us."

"Are you sure?" Frideswide and the dragon asked in chorus.

"Absolutely."

"Well, that frees us from any necessity to conform to the truth," Frideswide said, turning to the dragon, "so why did you carry off and kill the king's daughter?"

The dragon thought for a moment. "Tell him it was a dietary imbalance – that every few centuries a dragon has to eat a virgin. Tell him I would have warned him and given him time for a sacrificial lottery and all that nonsense, but the need came upon me suddenly. Convey my sympathy for his grief, and," the prehensile tail reached out, snagged a golden goblet heavily encrusted with precious stones, and dropped it in Frideswide's lap, "give him that as his daughter's blood price. Will that serve, do you think?" She looked at Frideswide, but it was Rowena who answered.

"He'll love it," she assured the dragon. "That goblet's much more to his taste than I am."

Frideswide nodded. "Mark doesn't want you upset," she told the dragon, "so he'll swallow any halfway plausible story, and yours is quite plausible." She stood up to go, then remembered something Rowena had said that morning. "Rowena, are you sure no one else knows? You said 'good morning' to someone; who was it?"

Rowena looked at her blankly. "I didn't talk to anyone but you all morning, Aunt Frideswide."

"You told me you were deleting the word 'good' from your vocabulary because the rose thorns hurt your lips."

"Oh, that." Rowena giggled. "I was talking to myself in the mirror. I *told* you no one ever listens to me at the castle." She laughed, and jewels fell from her lips and piled up in her lap.

CAPTAIN HONARIO HARPPLAYER, R.N.

Harry Harrison

It was Harry Harrison (b. 1925) who first made me realize that comic science fiction and fantasy could be good. His stories about criminal-turned-law-enforcer Slippery Jim DiGriz first began to appear in Astounding SF *in 1957 with "The Stainless Steel Rat" and are still entertaining readers today. His novel* Bill, the Galactic Hero *(1965) remains to this day one of the cleverest spoofs on science fiction. The following is not only an obvious parody of C. S. Forester's Hornblower stories but turns on its head the alien-invasion theme.*

Captain Honario Harpplayer was pacing the tiny quarterdeck of the *HMS Redundant*, hands clasped behind his back, teeth clamped in impotent fury. Ahead of him the battered French fleet limped towards port, torn sails flapping and spars trailing overside in the water, splintered hulls agape where his broadsides had gone thundering through their fragile wooden sides.

"Send two hands for'ard, if you please, Mr Shrub," he said, "and have them throw water on the mainsail. Wet sails will add an eighth of a knot to our speed and we may overtake those cowardly frogs yet."

"B-but, sir," the stolid first mate Shrub stammered, quailing before the thought of disagreeing with his beloved captain. "If we take any more hands off the pumps we'll sink. We're holed in thirteen places below the waterline, and . . ."

"Damn your eyes, sir! I issued an order, not a request for a debate. Do as you were told."

"Aye aye, sir," Shrub mumbled, humbled, knuckling a tear from one moist spaniel eye.

Water splashed onto the sails and the *Redundant* instantly sank lower in the water. Harpplayer clasped his hands behind his back and hated himself for this display of unwarranted temper towards the faithful Shrub. Yet he had to keep up this pose of strict disciplinarian before the crew, the sweepings and dregs of a thousand waterfronts, just as he had to wear a girdle to keep up his own front and a truss to keep up his hernia. He had to keep up a good front because he was the captain of this ship, the smallest ship in the blockading fleet to bear a post captain, yet still an important part of the fleet that lay like a strangling noose around Europe, locking in the mad tyrant Napoleon whose dreams of conquest could never extend to England whilst these tiny wooden ships stood in the way.

"Give us a prayer, cap'n, to speed us on our way to 'eaven cause we're sinkin'!" a voice called from the crowd of seamen at the pumps.

"I'll have that man's name, Mr Dogleg," Harpplayer called to the midshipman, a mere child of seven or eight, who commanded the detail. "No rum for him for a week."

"Aye aye, sir," piped Mr Dogleg, who was just learning to talk.

The ship was sinking, the fact was inescapable. Rats were running on deck, ignoring the cursing, stamping sailors, and hurling themselves into the sea. Ahead the French fleet had reached the safety of the shore batteries on Cape Pietfieux and the gaping mouths of these guns were turned towards the

Redundant, ready to spout fire and death when the fragile ship came within range.

"Be ready to drop sail, Mr Shrub," Harpplayer said, then raised his voice so all the crew could hear. "Those cowardly Frenchies have run away and cheated us of a million pounds in prize money."

A growl went up from the crew who, next to a love for rum, loved the pounds, shillings and pence with which they could buy the rum. The growl was suddenly cut off in muffled howls of pain as the mainmast, weakened by the badly aimed French cannon, fell onto the mass of labouring men.

"No need to drop sail, Mr Shrub, the slaves of our friend Boney have done it for us," Harpplayer said, forcing himself to make one of his rare jests so loved by the crew. He hated himself for the falseness of his feelings, ingratiating himself into the sympathies of these illiterate men by such means, but it was his duty to keep a taut ship. Besides, if he didn't make any jokes the men would hate him for the slave-driving, cold-blooded, chance-taking master that he was. They still hated him, of course, but they laughed while they did it.

They were laughing now as they cut away the tangle of rigging and dragged out the bodies to lay them in neat rows upon the deck. The ship sank lower in the water.

"Avast that body dragging," he ordered, "and man the pumps, or we'll have our dinners on the bottom of the sea."

The men laughed a ragged laugh again and hurried to their tasks.

They were easy to please, and Harpplayer envied them their simple lives. Even with the heavy work, bad water and an occasional touch of the cat, their existence was better than his tortured life on the lonely pinnacle of command. The decisions were all his to make, and to a man of his morbid and paranoic nature this made life a living hell. His officers, who all hated him, were incompetents. Even Shrub, faithful, long-suffering, loyal Shrub, had his weakness: namely the fact that he had an IQ of about 60 which, combined with his low birth, meant he could never rise above the rank of rear-admiral.

While he considered the varied events of the day Harpplayer began his compulsive pacing on the tiny quarterdeck, and its other occupants huddled against the starboard side where they wouldn't be in his way. Four paces in one direction, turn, then three-and-a-half paces back with his knee bringing up with a shuddering crack against the port carronade. Yet Harpplayer did not feel this, his cardplayer's brain was whirling with thoughts, evaluating and weighing plans, rejecting those that held a modicum of sanity and only considering those that sounded too insane to be practical. No wonder he was called "Sapsucker Harpy" throughout the fleet and held in awe as a man who could always pull victory from the jaws of defeat, and always at an immense cost in lives. But that was war. You gave your commands and good men died, and that was what the press gangs on shore were for. It had been a long and trying day, yet he still would not permit himself to relax. Tension and the agony of apprehension had seized him in the relentless grip of a Cerberus ever since soon after dawn that morning when the lookout had announced the discovery of sails on the horizon. There had been only ten of them, Frenchy ships of the line, and before the morning fog had cleared the vengeful form of the *Redundant* had been upon them, like a wolf among the sheep. Broadside after broadside had roared out from the precisely serviced English guns, ten balls for every one that popped out of the French cannon, manned by cowardly sweepings of the eighth and ninth classes of 1812, grey-bearded patriarchs and diapered infants who only wished they were back in the familial vineyards instead of here, fighting for the Tyrant, facing up to the wrath of the death-dealing cannon of their island enemy, the tiny country left to fight alone against the might of an entire continent. It had been a relentless stern chase, and only the succour of the French port had prevented the destruction of the entire squadron. As it was, four of them lay among the conger eels on the bottom of the ocean and the remaining six would need a complete refitting before they were fit to leave port and once more dare the retributive might of the ships that ringed their shores.

Harpplayer knew what he had to do.

"If you please, Mr Shrub, have the hose rigged. I feel it is time for a bath."

A ragged cheer broke from the toiling sailors, since they knew what to expect. In the coldest northern waters or in the dead of winter Harpplayer insisted on this routine of the bath. The hoses were quickly attached to the labouring pumps and soon columns of icy water were jetting across the deck.

"In we go!" shouted Harpplayer, and stepped back well out of the way of any chance droplets, at the same time scratching with a long index finger at the skin of his side, unwashed since the previous summer. He smiled at the childish antics of Shrub and the other officers prancing nude in the water, and only signalled for the pumps to cease their work when all of the white skins had turned a nice cerulean.

There was a rumble, not unlike distant thunder yet sharper and louder, from the northern horizon. Harpplayer turned and for a long instant saw a streak of fire painted against the dark clouds, before it died from the sky, leaving only an after-image in his eyes. He shook his head to clear it, and blinked rapidly a few times. For an instant there he could have sworn that the streak of light had come down, instead of going up, but that was manifestly impossible. Too many late nights playing boston with his officers, no wonder his eyesight was going.

"What was that, Captain?" Lieutenant Shrub asked, his words scarcely audible through the chattering of his teeth.

"A signal rocket – or perhaps one of those newfangled Congreve war rockets. There's trouble over there and we're going to find out just what it is. Send the hands to the braces, if you please, fill the main-tops'l and lay her on the starboard tack."

"Can I put my pants on first?"

"No impertinence, sir, or I'll have you in irons!"

Shrub bellowed the orders through the speaking trumpet and all the hands laughed at his shaking naked legs. Yet in a few seconds the well-trained crew, who not six days before had been wenching and drinking ashore on civvy street, never dreaming that the wide-sweeping press gangs would round them up and send them to sea, leapt to the braces, hurled the broken spars and cordage overside, sealed the shot holes, buried the dead, drank their grog and still had enough energy left over for a few of their number to do a gay hornpipe. The ship heeled as she turned, water creamed under her bows and then she was on the new tack, reaching out from the shore, investigating this new occurrence, making her presence felt as the representative of the mightiest blockading fleet the world, at that time, had ever known.

"A ship ahead, sir," the masthead lookout called. "Two points off the starboard bow."

"Beat to quarters," Harpplayer ordered.

Through the heavy roll of the drum and the slap of the sailors' bare horny feet on the deck, the voice of the lookout could be barely heard.

"No sails nor spars, sir. She's about the size of our long-boat."

"Belay that last order. And when that lookout comes off duty I want him to recite five hundred times, a boat is something that's picked up and put on a ship."

Pressed on by the freshing land breeze, the *Redundant* closed rapidly on the boat until it could be made out clearly from the deck.

"No masts, no spars, no sails – what makes it move?" Lieutenant Shrub asked with gape-mouthed puzzlement.

"There is no point in speculation in advance, Mr Shrub. This craft may be French or a neutral so I'll take no chances. Let us have the carronades loaded and run out. And I want the Marines in the futtock-shrouds, with their pieces on the half-cock, if you please. I want no one to fire until they receive my command, and I'll have anyone who does boiled in oil and served for breakfast."

"You are the card, sir!"

"Am I? Remember the cox'in who got his orders mixed yesterday?"

"Very gamey, sir, if I say so," Shrub said, picking a bit of gristle from between his teeth. "I'll issue the orders, sir."

The strange craft was like nothing Harpplayer had ever seen before. It advanced without visible motive power and he thought of hidden rowers with underwater oars, but they would have to be midgets to fit in the boat. It was decked over and appeared to be covered with a glass hutment of some kind. All in all a strange device, and certainly not French. The unwilling slaves of the Octopus in Paris would never master the precise techniques to construct a diadem of the sea such as this. No, this was from some alien land, perhaps from beyond China or the mysterious islands of the east. There was a man seated in the craft and he touched a lever that rolled back the top window. He stood then and waved to them. A concerted gasp ran through the watchers, for every eye in the ship was fastened on this strange occurrence.

"What is this, Mr Shrub," Harpplayer shouted. "Are we at a fun fair or a Christmas pantomime? Discipline, sir!"

"B-but, sir," the faithful Shrub stammered, suddenly at a loss for words. "That man, sir – he's *green!*"

"I want none of your damn nonsense, sir," Harpplayer snapped irritably, annoyed as he always was when people babbled about their imagined "colours". Paintings, and sunsets and such tripe. Nonsense. The world was made up of healthy shades of grey and that was that. Some fool of a Harley Street quack had once mentioned an imaginary malady which he termed "colour blindness" but had desisted with his tomfoolery when Harpplayer had mentioned the choice of seconds.

"Green, pink or purple, I don't care what shade of grey the fellow is. Throw him a line and have him up here where we can hear his story."

The line was dropped and after securing it to a ring on his boat the stranger touched a lever that closed the glass cabin once more, then climbed easily to the deck above.

"Green fur . . ." Shrub said, then clamped his mouth shut under Harpplayer's fierce glare.

"Enough of that, Mr Shrub. He's a foreigner and we will treat him with respect, at least until we find out what class he is from. He is a bit hairy, I admit, but certain races in the north of the Nipponese Isles are that way – perhaps he comes from there. I bid you welcome, sir," he said, addressing the man. "I am Captain Honario Harpplayer, commander of His Majesty's ship, *Redundant.*"

"*Kwl-kkle-wrrl-kl . . . !*"

"Not French," Harpplayer muttered, "nor Latin nor Greek I warrant. Perhaps one of those barbaric Baltic tongues, I'll try him on German. *Ich rate Ihnen, Reiseschecks mitzunehmen*? Or an Italian dialect? *E proibito; però qui si vendono cartoline ricordo*."

The stranger responded by springing up and down excitedly, then pointing to the sun, making circular motions around his head, pointing to the clouds, making falling motions with his hands, and shrilly shouting "*M'ku, m'ku!*"

"Feller's barmy," the Marine officer said, "and besides, he got too many fingers."

"I can count to seven without your help," Shrub told him angrily, "I think he's trying to tell us it's going to rain."

"He may be a metereologist in his own land," Harpplayer said safely, "but here he is just another alien."

The officers nodded agreement, and this motion seemed to excite the stranger for he sprang forward shouting his unintelligible gibberish. The alert Marine guard caught him in the back of the head with the butt of his Tower musket and the hairy man fell to the deck.

"Tried to attack you, Captain," the Marine officer said. "Shall we keel-haul him, sir?"

"No, poor chap is a long way from home, may be worried. We must allow for the language barrier. Just read him the Articles of War and impress him into the service. We're short of hands after that last encounter."

"You are of a very forgiving nature, sir, and an example for us all. What shall we do with his ship?"

"I'll examine it. There may be some principle of operation here that would be of interest to Whitehall. Drop a ladder; I'll have a look myself."

After some fumbling Harpplayer found the lever that moved the glass cabin, and when it slid aside he dropped into the cockpit that it covered. A comfortable divan faced a board covered with a strange collection of handles, buttons and divers machines concealed beneath crystal covers. It was a perfect example of the decadence of the east, excessive decoration and ornamentation where a panel of good English oak would have done as well, and a simple pivoted bar to carry the instructions to the slaves that rowed the boat. Or perhaps there was an animal concealed behind the panel – he heard a deep roar when he touched a certain lever. This evidently signalled the galley slave – or animal – to begin his labours, since the little craft was now rushing through the water at a good pace. Spray was slapping into the cockpit so Harpplayer closed the cover, which was a good thing. Another button must have tilted a concealed rudder because the boat suddenly plunged its nose down and sank, the water rising up until it washed over the top of the glass. Luckily, the craft was stoutly made and did not leak, and another button caused the boat to surface again.

It was at that instant that Harpplayer had the idea. He sat as one paralyzed, while his rapid thoughts ran through the possibilities. Yes, it might work – it *would* work! He smacked his fist into his open palm and only then realized that the tiny craft had turned while he had been thinking and was about to ram into the *Redundant*, whose rail was lined with frighten-eyed faces. With a skilful touch he signalled the animal (or slave) to stop and there was only the slightest bump as the vessels touched.

"Mr Shrub," he called.

"Sir?"

"I want a hammer, six nails, six kegs of gunpowder each with a two-minute fuse and a looped rope attached, and a dark lantern."

"But, sir – what for?" For once the startled Shrub forgot himself enough to question his captain.

The plan had so cheered Harpplayer that he took no umbrage at this sudden familiarity. In fact he even smiled into his cuff, the expression hidden by the failing light.

"Why – six barrels because there are six ships," he said with unaccustomed coyness. "Now, carry on."

The gunner and his mates quickly completed their task and the barrels were lowered in a sling. They completely filled the tiny cockpit, barely leaving room for Harpplayer to sit. In fact there was no room for the hammer and he had to hold it between his teeth.

"Mither Thrub," he said indistinctly around the hammer, suddenly depressed as he realized that in a few moments he would be pitting his own frail body against the hordes of the usurper who cracked the whip over a continent of oppressed slaves. He quailed at his temerity at thus facing the Tyrant of Europe, then quailed before his own disgust at his frailty. The men must never know that he had these thoughts, that he was the weakest of them. "Mr Shrub," he called again, and there was no sound of his feelings in his voice. "If I do not return by dawn you are in command of this ship and will make a full report. Goodbye. In triplicate, mind."

"Oh, sir —" Shrub began, but his words were cut off as the glass cover sprang shut and the tiny craft hurled itself against all the power of a continent.

Afterwards Harpplayer was to laugh at his first weakness. Truly, the escapade was as simple as strolling down Fleet Street on a Sunday morning. The foreign ship sank beneath the surface and slipped past the batteries on Cape Pietfieux, that the English sailors called Cape Pitfix, and into the guarded waters of Cienfique. No guard noticed the slight roiling of the waters of the bay and no human eye saw the dim shape that surfaced next to the high wooden wall that was the hull of the French ship of the line. Two sharp blows of the hammer secured the first keg of gunpowder and a brief flash of light came from the dark lantern as the fuse was lit. Before the puzzled sentries on the deck above could reach the rail the mysterious visitor was gone, and they could not see the telltale fuse sputtering away, concealed by the barrel of death that it crept slowly toward. Five times Harpplayer repeated this simple, yet deadly, activity, and as he was driving the last nail there was a muffled explosion from the first ship. Hutment closed, he made his way from the harbour, and behind him six ships, the pride of the Tyrant's navy, burnt in pillars of flame until all that was left were the charred hulls, settling to the ocean floor.

Captain Harpplayer opened the glass hutment when he was past the shore batteries, and looked back with satisfaction at the burning ships. He had done his duty and his small part towards ending this awful war that had devastated a continent and would, in the course of a few years, kill so many of the finest Frenchmen that the height of the entire French race would be reduced by an average of more than five inches. The last pyre died down and, feeling a twinge of regret, since they had been fine ships, though in fief to the Madman in Paris, he turned the bow of his craft towards the *Redundant*.

It was dawn when he reached the ship, and exhaustion tugged at him. He grabbed the ladder lowered for him and painfully climbed to the deck. The drums whirred and the sideboys saluted; the bos'uns' pipes trilled.

"Well done, sir, oh well done," Shrub exclaimed, rushing forward to take his hand. "We could see them burning from here."

Behind them, in the water, there was a deep burbling, like the water running from the tub when the plug is pulled, and Harpplayer turned just in time to see the strange craft sinking into the sea and vanishing from sight.

"Damn silly of me," he muttered. "Forgot to close the hatch. Running quite a sea, must have washed in."

His ruminations were sharply cut through by a sudden scream. He turned just in time to see the hairy stranger run to the rail and stare, horrified, at the vanishing craft. Then the man, obviously bereaved, screamed horribly and tore great handfuls of hair from his head, a relatively easy task since he had so much. Then, before anyone could think to stop him, he had mounted to the rail and plunged headfirst into the sea. He sank like a rock, and either could not swim, or did not want to; he seemed strangely attached to his craft, since he did not return to the surface.

"Poor chap," Harpplayer said with the compassion of a sensitive man, "to be alone, and so far from home. Perhaps he is happier dead."

"Aye, perhaps," the stolid Shrub muttered, "but he had the makings of a good topman in him, sir. Could run right out on the spars he could, held on very well he did, what with those long toenails of his that bit right into the wood. Had another toe in his heel that helped him hold on."

"I'll ask you not to discuss the deformities of the dead. We'll list him in the report as Lost Overboard. What was his name?"

"Wouldn't tell us, sir, but we carry him in the books as Mr Green."

"Fair enough. Though foreign-born, he would be proud to

know that he died bearing a good English name." Then, curtly dismissing the faithful and stupid Shrub, Harpplayer resumed walking the quarterdeck, filled with the silent agony which was his and his alone, and would be until the guns of the Corsican Ogre were spiked forever.

THE ALIENS WHO KNEW, I MEAN, *EVERYTHING*

George Alec Effinger

Long before the film Mars Attacks!, *there were many stories about seemingly helpful aliens who become a menace to human-kind. Jack Williamson did this brilliantly in the serious sf novel* The Humanoids *(1949), whilst in the following story George Alec Effinger has rather more fun with the idea.*

Effinger (b. 1947) has produced some of the most challenging sf and fantasy of the last twenty-five years. Some of the best will be found in the collections Mixed Feelings *(1974),* Irrational Numbers *(1976),* Dirty Tricks *(1978) and* Idle Pleasures *(1983), as well as the novels* What Entropy Means to Me *(1972) and* When Gravity Fails *(1987). The following story was nominated for both a Hugo and a Nebula award in 1985.*

I was sitting at my desk, reading a report on the brown pelican situation, when the secretary of state burst in. "Mr President," he said, his eyes wide, "the aliens are here!" Just like that. "The aliens are here!" As if I had any idea what to do about them.

"I see," I said. I learned early in my first term that "I see" was one of the safest and most useful comments I could possibly make in any situation. When I said "I see", it indicated that I had digested the news and was waiting intelligently and calmly for further data. That knocked the ball back into my advisers' court. I looked at the secretary of state expectantly. I was all prepared with my next utterance, in the event that he had nothing further to add. My next utterance would be "Well?" That would indicate that I was on top of the problem, but that I couldn't be expected to make an executive decision without sufficient information, and that he should have known better than to burst into the Oval Office unless he had that information. That's why we had protocol; that's why we had proper channels; that's why I had advisers. The voters out there didn't want me to make decisions without sufficient information. If the secretary didn't have anything more to tell me, he shouldn't have burst in in the first place. I looked at him awhile longer. "Well?" I asked at last.

"That's about all we have at the moment," he said uncomfortably. I looked at him sternly for a few seconds, scoring a couple of points while he stood there all flustered. I turned back to the pelican report, dismissing him. I certainly wasn't going to get all flustered. I could think of only one president in recent memory who was ever flustered in office, and we all know what happened to him. As the secretary of state closed the door to my office behind him, I smiled. The aliens were probably going to be a bitch of a problem eventually, but it wasn't my problem yet. I had a little time.

But I found that I couldn't really keep my mind on the pelican question. Even the president of the United States has *some* imagination, and if the secretary of state was correct, I was going to have to confront these aliens pretty damn soon. I'd read stories about aliens when I was a kid, I'd seen all sorts of aliens in movies and television, but these were the first aliens who'd actually stopped by for a chat. Well, I wasn't going to be the first American president to make a fool of himself in front of visitors from another world. I was going to be briefed. I telephoned the secretary of defence. "We must have some contingency plans drawn up for this," I told him. "We have plans for every other possible situation." This was true; the Defence Department has scenarios for such bizarre events as the rise of an imperialist fascist regime in Liechtenstein or the spontaneous depletion of all the world's selenium.

"Just a second, Mr President," said the secretary. I could hear him muttering to someone else. I held the phone and stared out the window. There were crowds of people running around hysterically out there. Probably because of the aliens. "Mr President?" came the voice of the secretary of defence. "I have one of the aliens here, and he suggests that we use the same plan that President Eisenhower used."

I closed my eyes and sighed. I hated it when they said stuff like that. I wanted information, and they told me these things knowing that I would have to ask four or five more questions just to understand the answer to the first one. "You have an alien with you?" I said in a pleasant enough voice.

"Yes, sir. They prefer not to be called 'aliens'. He tells me he's a 'nuhp'."

"Thank you, Luis. Tell me, why do you have an al– Why do you have a nuhp and I don't?"

Luis muttered the question to his nuhp. "He says it's because they wanted to go through proper channels. They learned about all that from President Eisenhower."

"Very good, Luis." This was going to take all day, I could see that; and I had a photo session with Mick Jagger's granddaughter. "My second question, Luis, is what the hell does he mean by 'the same plan that President Eisenhower used'?"

Another muffled consultation. "He says that this isn't the first time that the nuhp have landed on Earth. A scout ship with two nuhp aboard landed at Edwards Air Force Base in 1954. The two nuhp met with President Eisenhower. It was apparently a very cordial occasion, and President Eisenhower impressed the nuhp as a warm and sincere old gentleman. They've been planning to return to Earth ever since, but they've been very busy, what with one thing and another. President Eisenhower requested that the nuhp not reveal themselves to the people of Earth in general, until our government decided how to control the inevitable hysteria. My guess is that the government never got around to that, and when the nuhp departed, the matter was studied and then shelved. As the years passed, few people were even aware that the first meeting ever occurred. The nuhp have returned now in great numbers, expecting that we'd have prepared the populace by now. It's not their fault that we haven't. They just sort of took it for granted that they'd be welcome."

"Uh-huh," I said. That was my usual utterance when I didn't know what the hell else to say. "Assure them that they are, indeed, welcome. I don't suppose the study they did during the Eisenhower administration was ever completed. I don't suppose there really is a plan to break the news to the public."

"Unfortunately, Mr President, that seems to be the case."

"Uh-huh." That's Republicans for you, I thought. "Ask your nuhp something for me, Luis. Ask him if he knows what they told Eisenhower. They must be full of outer-space wisdom. Maybe they have some ideas about how we should deal with this."

There was yet another pause. "Mr President, he says all they discussed with Mr Eisenhower was his golf game. They helped to correct his putting stroke. But they are definitely full of wisdom. They know all sorts of things. My nuhp – that is, his name is Hurv – anyway, he says that they'd be happy to give you some advice."

"Tell him that I'm grateful, Luis. Can they have someone meet with me in, say, half an hour?"

"There are three nuhp on their way to the Oval Office at this moment. One of them is the leader of their expedition, and one of the others is the commander of their mother ship."

"Mother ship?" I asked.

"You haven't seen it? It's tethered on the Mall. They're real sorry about what they did to the Washington Monument. They say they can take care of it tomorrow."

I just shuddered and hung up the phone. I called my secretary. "There are going to be three –"

"They're here now, Mr President."

I sighed. "Send them in." And that's how I met the nuhp. Just as President Eisenhower had.

They were handsome people. Likable, too. They smiled and shook hands and suggested that photographs be taken of the historic moment, so we called in the media; and then I had to sort of wing the most important diplomatic meeting of my entire political career. I welcomed the nuhp to Earth. "Welcome to Earth," I said, "and welcome to the United States."

"Thank you," said the nuhp I would come to know as Pleen. "We're glad to be here."

"How long do you plan to be with us?" I hated myself when I said that, in front of the Associated Press and UPI and all the network news people. I sounded like a room clerk at a Holiday Inn.

"We don't know, exactly," said Pleen. "We don't have to be back to work until a week from Monday."

"Uh-huh," I said. Then I just posed for pictures and kept my mouth shut. I wasn't going to say or do another goddamn thing until my advisers showed up and started advising.

Well, of course, the people panicked. Pleen told me to expect that, but I had figured it out for myself. We've seen too many movies about visitors from space. Sometimes they come with a message of peace and universal brotherhood and just the inside information mankind has been needing for thousands of years. More often, though, the aliens come to enslave and murder us because the visual effects are better, and so when the nuhp arrived, everyone was all prepared to hate them. People didn't trust their good looks. People were suspicious of their nice manners and their quietly tasteful clothing. When the nuhp offered to solve all our problems for us, we all said, sure, solve our problems – *but at what cost?*

That first week, Pleen and I spent a lot of time together, just getting to know one another and trying to understand what the other one wanted. I invited him and Commander Toag and the other nuhp bigwigs to a reception at the White House. We had a church choir from Alabama singing gospel music, and a high school band from Michigan playing a medley of favourite collegiate fight songs, and talented clones of the original stars nostalgically re-creating the Steve and Eydie Experience, and an improvisational comedy troupe from Los Angeles or someplace, and the New York Philharmonic under the baton of a twelve-year-old girl genius. They played Beethoven's Ninth Symphony in an attempt to impress the nuhp with how marvellous Earth culture was.

Pleen enjoyed it all very much. "Men are as varied in their expressions of joy as we nuhp," he said, applauding vigorously. "We are all very fond of human music. We think Beethoven composed some of the most beautiful melodies we've ever heard, anywhere in our galactic travels."

I smiled. "I'm sure we are all pleased to hear that," I said.

"Although the Ninth Symphony is certainly not the best of his work."

I faltered in my clapping. "Excuse me?" I said.

Pleen gave me a gracious smile. "It is well known among us that Beethoven's finest composition is his Piano Concerto No. 5 in E flat major."

I let out my breath. "Of course, that's a matter of opinion. Perhaps the standards of the nuhp—"

"Oh, no," Pleen hastened to assure me, "taste does not enter into it at all. The Concerto No. 5 is Beethoven's best, according to very rigorous and definite critical principles. And even that lovely piece is by no means the best music ever produced by mankind."

I felt just a trifle annoyed. What could this nuhp, who came from some weirdo planet God alone knows how far away, from some society with not the slightest connection to our heritage and culture, what could this nuhp know of what Beethoven's Ninth Symphony aroused in our human souls? "Tell me, then, Pleen," I said in my ominously soft voice, "what *is* the best human musical composition?"

"The score from the motion picture *Ben-Hur*, by Miklós Rózsa," he said simply. What could I do but nod my head in silence? It wasn't worth starting an interplanetary incident over.

So from fear our reaction to the nuhp changed to distrust. We kept waiting for them to reveal their real selves; we waited for the pleasant masks to slip off and show us the true nightmarish faces we all suspected lurked beneath. The nuhp did not go home a week from Monday, after all. They liked Earth, and they liked us. They decided to stay a little longer. We told them about ourselves and our centuries of trouble; and they mentioned, in an offhand nuhp way, that they could take care of a few little things, make some small adjustments, and life would be a whole lot better for everybody on Earth. They didn't want anything in return. They wanted to give us these things in gratitude for our hospitality: for letting them park their mother ship on the Mall and for all the free refills of coffee they were getting all around the world. We hesitated, but our vanity and our greed won out. "Go ahead," we said, "make our deserts bloom. Go ahead, end war and poverty and disease. Show us twenty exciting new things to do with leftovers. Call us when you're done."

The fear changed to distrust, but soon the distrust changed to hope. The nuhp made the deserts bloom, all right. They asked for four months. We were perfectly willing to let them have all the time they needed. They put a tall fence all around the Namib and wouldn't let anyone in to watch what they were doing. Four months later, they had a big cocktail party and invited the whole world to see what they'd accomplished. I sent the secretary of state as my personal representative. He brought back some wonderful slides: the vast desert had been turned into a botanical miracle. There were miles and miles of flowering plants now, instead of the monotonous dead sand and gravel sea. Of course, the immense garden contained nothing but hollyhocks, many millions of hollyhocks. I mentioned to Pleen that the people of Earth had been hoping for a little more in the way of variety, and something just a trifle more practical, too.

"What do you mean, 'practical'?" he asked.

"You know," I said, "food."

"Don't worry about food," said Pleen. "We're going to take care of hunger pretty soon."

"Good, good. But hollyhocks?"

"What's wrong with hollyhocks?"

"Nothing," I admitted.

"Hollyhocks are the single prettiest flower grown on Earth."

"Some people like orchids," I said. "Some people like roses."

"No," said Pleen firmly. "Hollyhocks are it. I wouldn't kid you."

So we thanked the nuhp for a Namibia full of hollyhocks and stopped them before they did the same thing to the Sahara, the Mojave, and the Gobi.

On the whole, everyone began to like the nuhp, although they took just a little getting used to. They had very definite opinions about everything, and they wouldn't admit that what they had were *opinions*. To hear a nuhp talk, he had a direct line to some categorical imperative that spelled everything out in terms that were unflinchingly black and white. Hollyhocks were the best flowers. Alexandre Dumas was the greatest novelist. Powder blue was the prettiest colour. Melancholy was the most ennobling emotion. *Grand Hotel* was the finest movie. The best car ever built was the 1956 Chevy Bel Air, but it had to be aqua and white. And there just wasn't room for discussion: the nuhp made these pronouncements with the force of divine revelation.

I asked Pleen once about the American presidency. I asked him who the nuhp thought was the best president in our history. I felt sort of like the Wicked Queen in "Snow White". Mirror, mirror, on the wall. I didn't really believe Pleen would tell me that I was the best president, but my heart pounded while I waited for his answer; you never know, right? To tell the truth, I expected him to say Washington, Lincoln, Roosevelt, or Akiwara. His answer surprised me: James K. Polk.

"Polk?" I asked. I wasn't even sure I could recognize Polk's portrait.

"He's not the most familiar," said Pleen, "but he was an honest if unexciting president. He fought the Mexican War and added a great amount of territory to the United States. He saw every bit of his platform become law. He was a good, hard-working man who deserves a better reputation."

"What about Thomas Jefferson?" I asked.

Pleen just shrugged. "He was OK, too, but he was no James Polk."

My wife, the First Lady, became very good friends with the wife of Commander Toag, whose name was Doim. They often went shopping together, and Doim would make suggestions to the First Lady about fashion and hair care. Doim told my wife which rooms in the White House needed redecoration, and which charities were worthy of official support. It was Doim who negotiated the First Lady's recording contract, and it was Doim who introduced her to the Philadelphia cheese steak, one of the nuhp's favourite treats (although they asserted that the best cuisine on Earth was Tex-Mex).

One day, Doim and my wife were having lunch. They sat at a small table in a chic Washington restaurant, with a couple of dozen Secret Service people and nuhp security agents disguised elsewhere among the patrons. "I've noticed that there seem to be more nuhp here in Washington every week," said the First Lady.

"Yes," said Doim, "new mother ships arrive daily. We think Earth is one of the most pleasant planets we've ever visited."

"We're glad to have you, of course," said my wife, "and it seems that our people have gotten over their initial fears."

"The hollyhocks did the trick," said Doim.

"I guess so. How many nuhp are there on Earth now?"

"About five or six million, I'd say."

The First Lady was startled. "I didn't think it would be that many."

Doim laughed. "We're not just here in America, you know. We're all over. We really like Earth. Although, of course, Earth isn't absolutely the best planet. Our own home, Nupworld, is still Number One; but Earth would certainly be on any Top Ten list."

"Uh-huh." (My wife has learned many important oratorical tricks from me.)

"That's why we're so glad to help you beautify and modernize your world."

"The hollyhocks were nice," said the First Lady. "But when are you going to tackle the really vital questions?"

"Don't worry about that," said Doim, turning her attention to her cottage cheese salad.

"When are you going to take care of world hunger?"

"Pretty soon. Don't worry."

"Urban blight?"

"Pretty soon."

"Man's inhumanity to man?"

Doim gave my wife an impatient look. "We haven't even been here for six months yet. What do you want, miracles? We've already done more than your husband accomplished in his entire first term."

"Hollyhocks," muttered the First Lady.

"I heard that," said Doim. "The rest of the universe absolutely *adores* hollyhocks. We can't help it if humans have no taste."

They finished their lunch in silence, and my wife came back to the White House fuming.

That same week, one of my advisers showed me a letter that had been sent by a young man in New Mexico. Several nuhp had moved into a condo next door to him and had begun advising him about the best investment possibilities (urban respiratory spas), the best fabrics and colours to wear to show off his colouring, the best holo system on the market (the Esmeraldas F-64 with hex-phased Libertad screens and a Ruy Challenger argon solipsizer), the best place to watch sunsets (the revolving restaurant on top of the Weyerhauser Building in Yellowstone City), the best wines to go with everything (too numerous to mention – send SAE for list), and which of the two women he was dating to marry (Candi Marie Esterhazy). "Mr President," said the bewildered young man, "I realize that we must be gracious hosts to our benefactors from space, but I am having some difficulty keeping my temper. The nuhp are certainly knowledgeable and willing to share the benefits of their wisdom, but they don't even wait to be asked. If they were people, regular human beings who lived next door, I would have punched their lights out by now. Please advise. And hurry: they are taking me downtown next Friday to pick out an engagement ring and new living room furniture. I don't even *want* new living room furniture!"

Luis, my secretary of defence, talked to Hurv about the ultimate goals of the nuhp. "We don't have any goals," he said. "We're just taking it easy."

"Then why did you come to Earth?" asked Luis.

"Why do you go bowling?"

"I don't go bowling."

"You should," said Hurv. "Bowling is the most enjoyable thing a person can do."

"What about sex?"

"Bowling *is* sex. Bowling is a symbolic form of inter-course, except you don't have to bother about the feelings of some other person. Bowling is sex without guilt. Bowling is what people have wanted down through all the millennia: sex without the slightest responsibility. It's the very dis-tillation of the essence of sex. Bowling is sex without fear and shame."

"Bowling is sex without pleasure," said Luis.

There was a brief silence. "You mean," said Hurv, "that when you put that ball right into the pocket and see those pins explode off the alley, you don't have an orgasm?"

"Nope," said Luis.

"*That's* your problem, then. I can't help you there, you'll have to see some kind of therapist. It's obvious this subject embarrasses you. Let's talk about something else."

"Fine with me," said Luis moodily. "When are we going to receive the real benefits of your technological superiority? When are you going to unlock the final secrets of the atom? When are you going to free mankind from drudgery?"

"What do you mean, 'technological superiority'?" asked Hurv.

"There must be scientific wonders beyond our imagining aboard your mother ships."

"Not so's you'd notice. We're not even so advanced as you people here on Earth. We've learned all sorts of wonderful things since we've been here."

"What?" Luis couldn't imagine what Hurv was trying to say.

"We don't have anything like your astonishing bubble memories or silicon chips. We never invented anything comparable to the transistor, even. You know why the mother ships are so big?"

"My God."

"That's right," said Hurv, "vacuum tubes. All our spacecraft operate on vacuum tubes. They take up a hell of a lot of space. And they burn out. Do you know how long it takes to find the goddamn tube when it burns out? Remember how people used to take bags of vacuum tubes from their television sets down to the drugstore to use the tube tester? Think of doing that with something the size of our mother ships. And we can't just zip off into space when we feel like it. We have to let a mother ship warm up first. You have to turn the key and let the thing warm up for a couple of minutes, *then* you can zip off into space. It's a goddamn pain in the neck."

"I don't understand," said Luis, stunned. "If your technology is so primitive, how did you come here? If we're so far ahead of you, we should have discovered your planet, instead the other way around."

Hurv gave a gentle laugh. "Don't pat yourself on the back, Luis. Just because your electronics are better than ours, you aren't necessarily superior in any way. Look, imagine that you humans are a man in Los Angeles with a brand-new Trujillo and we are a nuhp in New York with a beat-up old Ford. The two fellows start driving toward St Louis. Now, the guy in the Trujillo is doing 120 on the interstates, and the guy in the Ford is putting along at 55; but the human in the Trujillo stops in Vegas and puts all of his gas money down the hole of a blackjack table, and the determined little nuhp cruises along for days until at last he reaches his goal. It's all a matter of superior intellect and the will to succeed. Your people talk a lot about going to the stars, but you just keep putting your money into other projects, like war and popular music and international athletic events and resurrecting the fashions of previous decades. If you wanted to go into space, you would have."

"But we *do* want to go."

"Then we'll help you. We'll give you the secrets. And you can explain your electronics to our engineers, and together we'll build wonderful new mother ships that will open the universe to both humans and nuhp."

Luis let out his breath. "Sounds good to me," he said.

Everyone agreed that this looked better than hollyhocks. We all hoped that we could keep from kicking their collective asses long enough to collect on that promise.

When I was in college, my roommate in my sophomore year was a tall, skinny guy named Barry Rintz. Barry had wild, wavy black hair and a sharp face that looked like a handsome, normal face that had been sat on and folded in the middle. He squinted a lot, not because he had any defect in his eyesight, but because he wanted to give the impression that he was constantly evaluating the world. This was true. Barry could tell you the actual and market values of any object you happened to come across.

We had a double date one football weekend with two girls from another college in the same city. Before the game, we met the girls and took them to the university's art museum, which was pretty large and owned an impressive collection. My date, a pretty, elementary ed. major named Brigid, and I wandered from gallery to gallery, remarking that our tastes in art were very similar. We both liked the Impressionists, and we both liked Surrealism. There were a couple of little Renoirs that we admired for almost half an hour, and then we made a lot of silly sophomore jokes about what was happening in the Magritte and Dali and de Chirico paintings.

Barry and his date, Dixie, ran across us by accident as all four of us passed through the sculpture gallery. "There's a terrific Seurat down there," Brigid told her girlfriend.

"Seurat," Barry said. There was a lot of amused disbelief in his voice.

"I like Seurat," said Dixie.

"Well, of course," said Barry, "there's nothing really *wrong* with Seurat."

"What do you mean by that?"

"Do you know F. E. Church?" he asked.

"Who?" I said.

"Come here." He practically dragged us to a gallery of American paintings. F. E. Church was a remarkable American landscape painter (1826–1900) who achieved an astonishing

and lovely luminance in his works. "Look at that light!" cried
Barry. "Look at that space! Look at that air!"

Brigid glanced at Dixie. "Look at that air?" she whispered.

It was a fine painting and we all said so, but Barry was
insistent. F. E. Church was the greatest artist in American
history, and one of the best the world has ever known. "I'd put
him right up there with Van Dyck and Canaletto."

"Canaletto?" said Dixie. "The one who did all those pictures of Venice?"

"Those skies!" murmured Barry ecstatically. He wore the
drunken expression of the satisfied voluptuary.

"Some people like paintings of puppies or naked women," I
offered. "Barry likes light and air."

We left the museum and had lunch. Barry told us which
things on the menu were worth ordering, and which things
were an abomination. He made us all drink an obscure imported beer from Ecuador. To Barry, the world was divided
up into masterpieces and abominations. It made life so much
simpler for him, except that he never understood why his
friends could never tell one from the other.

At the football game, Barry compared our school's quarter-
back to Y. A. Tittle. He compared the other team's punter to
Ngoc Van Vinh. He compared the halftime show to the Ohio
State band's Script Ohio formation. Before the end of the
third quarter, it was very obvious to me that Barry was going
to have absolutely no luck at all with Dixie. Before the clock
ran out in the fourth quarter, Brigid and I had made whispered
plans to dump the other two as soon as possible and sneak
away by ourselves. Dixie would probably find an excuse to
ride the bus back to her dorm before suppertime. Barry, as
usual, would spend the evening in our room, reading *The
Making of the President 1996*.

On other occasions Barry would lecture me about subjects
as diverse as American Literature (the best poet was Edwin
Arlington Robinson, the best novelist James T. Farrell),
animals (the only correct pet was the golden retriever), clothing (in anything other than a navy blue jacket and grey slacks a
man was just asking for trouble), and even hobbies (Barry
collected military decorations of czarist Imperial Russia. He

wouldn't talk to me for days after I told him my father collected barbed wire).

Barry was a wealth of information. He was the campus arbiter of good taste. Everyone knew that Barry was the man to ask.

But no one ever did. We all hated his guts. I moved out of our dorm room before the end of the fall semester. Shunned, lonely and bitter Barry Rintz wound up as a guidance counsellor in a high school in Ames, Iowa. The job was absolutely perfect for him; few people are so lucky in finding a career.

If I didn't know better, I might have believed that Barry was the original advance spy for the nuhp.

When the nuhp had been on Earth for a full year, they gave us the gift of interstellar travel. It was surprisingly inexpensive. The nuhp explained their propulsion system, which was cheap and safe and adaptable to all sorts of other earthbound applications. The revelations opened up an entirely new area of scientific speculation. Then the nuhp taught us their navigational methods, and about the "shortcuts" they had discovered in space. People called them space warps, although technically speaking, the shortcuts had nothing to do with Einsteinian theory or curved space or anything like that. Not many humans understood what the nuhp were talking about, but that didn't make very much difference. The nuhp didn't understand the shortcuts, either; they just used them. The matter was presented to us like a Thanksgiving turkey on a platter. We bypassed the whole business of cautious scientific experimentation and leapt right into commercial exploitation. Mitsubishi of La Paz and Martin Marietta used nuhp schematics to begin construction of three luxury passenger ships, each capable of transporting a thousand tourists anywhere in our galaxy. Although man had yet to set foot on the moons of Jupiter, certain selected travel agencies began booking passage for a grand tour of the dozen nearest inhabited worlds.

Yes, it seemed that space was teeming with life, humanoid life on planets circling half the G-type stars in the heavens. "We've been trying to communicate with extraterrestrial intelligence for decades," complained one Soviet scientist. "Why haven't they responded?"

A friendly nuhp merely shrugged. "Everybody's trying to communicate out there," he said. "Your messages are like Publishers Clearing House mail to them." At first, that was a blow to our racial pride, but we got over it. As soon as we joined the interstellar community, they'd begin to take us more seriously. And the nuhp had made that possible.

We were grateful to the nuhp, but that didn't make them any easier to live with. They were still insufferable. As my second term as president came to an end, Pleen began to advise me about my future career. "Don't write a book," he told me (after I had already written the first two hundred pages of a *A President Remembers*). "If you want to be an elder statesman, fine; but keep a low profile and wait for the people to come to you."

"What am I supposed to do with my time, then?" I asked.

"Choose a new career," Pleen said. "You're not all that old. Lots of people do it. Have you considered starting a mail-order business? You can operate it from your home. Or go back to school and take courses in some subject that's always interested you. Or become active in church or civic projects. Find a new hobby: raising hollyhocks or collecting military decorations."

"Pleen," I begged, "just leave me alone."

He seemed hurt. "Sure, if that's what you want." I regretted my harsh words.

All over the country, all over the world, everyone was having the same trouble with the nuhp. It seemed that so many of them had come to Earth, every human had his own personal nuhp to make endless suggestions. There hadn't been so much tension in the world since the 1992 Miss Universe contest, when the most votes went to No Award.

That's why it didn't surprise me very much when the first of our own mother ships returned from its 28-day voyage among the stars with only 276 of its 1,000 passengers still aboard. The other 724 had remained behind on one lush, exciting, exotic, friendly world or another. These planets had one thing in common: they were all populated by charming, warm, intelligent, humanlike people who had left their own home worlds after being discovered by the nuhp. Many races lived together in peace and harmony on these planets, in spacious cities newly built to house the fed-up expatriates. Perhaps these alien races had experienced the same internal jealousies and hatreds we human beings had known for so long, but no more. Coming together from many planets throughout our galaxy, these various peoples dwelt contentedly beside each other, united by a single common adversion: their dislike for the nuhp.

Within a year of the launching of our first interstellar ship, the population of Earth had declined by 0.5 per cent. Within two years, the population had fallen by almost 14 million. The nuhp were too sincere and too eager and too sympathetic to fight with. That didn't make them any less tedious. Rather than make a scene, most people just upped and left. There were plenty of really lovely worlds to visit, and it didn't cost very much, and the opportunities in space were unlimited. Many people who were frustrated and disappointed on Earth were able to build new and fulfilling lives for themselves on planets that, until the nuhp arrived, we didn't even know existed.

The nuhp knew this would happen. It had already happened dozens, hundreds of times in the past, wherever their mother ships touched down. They had made promises to us and they had kept them, although we couldn't have guessed just how things would turn out.

Our cities were no longer decaying warrens imprisoning the impoverished masses. The few people who remained behind could pick and choose among the best housing. Landlords were forced to reduce rents and keep properties in perfect repair just to attract tenants.

Hunger was ended when the ratio of consumers to food producers dropped drastically. Within ten years, the population of Earth was cut in half, and was still falling.

For the same reason, poverty began to disappear. There were plenty of jobs for everyone. When it became apparent that the nuhp weren't going to compete for those jobs, there were more opportunities than people to take advantage of them.

Discrimination and prejudice vanished almost overnight.

Everyone cooperated to keep things running smoothly despite the large-scale emigration. The good life was available to everyone, and so resentments melted away. Then, too, whatever enmity people still felt could be focused solely on the nuhp; the nuhp didn't mind, either. They were oblivious to it all.

I am now the mayor and postmaster of the small human community of New Dallas, here on Thir, the fourth planet of a star known in our old catalogue as Struve 2398. The various alien races we encountered here call the star by another name, which translates into "God's Pineal". All the aliens here are extremely helpful and charitable, and there are few nuhp.

All through the galaxy, the nuhp are considered the messengers of peace. Their mission is to travel from planet to planet, bringing reconciliation, prosperity, and true civilization. There isn't an intelligent race in the galaxy that doesn't love the nuhp. We all recognize what they've done and what they've given us.

But if the nuhp started moving in down the block, we'd be packed and on our way somewhere else by morning.

HISTORY BOOK

A Thog the Mighty Text

John Grant

John Grant is the pseudonym of Scottish writer Paul Barnett (b. 1949), long resident in England and recently moved to American shores. He has written several comprehensive books on paranormal phenomena, including The Directory of Possibilities *(1981) with Colin Wilson, and* A Directory of Discarded Ideas *(1981). Amongst his fiction two titles particularly relevant to devotees of comic fantasy are* Sex Secrets of Ancient Atlantis *(1985) and* The Truth About the Flaming Ghoulies *(1984). He also wrote a parody of the disaster novel,* Earthdoom! *(1987) with David Langford (whom you'll find elsewhere in this anthology). In addition, he has written a long series of novels known as the* Legends of the Lone Wolf. *The following, originally written as a separate story, was subsequently incorporated into the last Lone Wolf book,* The Rotting Land *(1994), but the author has resurrected it and extensively revised it for publication here.*

I Faded Lesa

There is a tale told of how – some time around the 5000th year
before the Fragmentation of The World into The Empire and
The Dross – the House of the Ellonia came to the throne of
Harmadree. Whether it is true or not is a matter beyond human
judgment, but it is believed by the common folk of the Dour
Mountains region of that land, and it is as likely as many of the
other histories of the early days of The World. Besides, it has the
feel of truth, and that must surely count for as much as any more
objective reckonings of historical accuracy.

The tale goes maybe like this:

The arms of death had almost completely embraced the old
chieftain – everyone knew it, including himself. For days he
had been confined to his tent, lying abed and cursing steadily,
but steadily more weakly. His face was a grey, putty-like mask,
the skin hanging in wrinkles from the all-too-visible bones.
Sometimes his eyes showed the clear blueness they had possessed of old, but more often the light in them shone but dimly
– unless, as sometimes happened, his wrath rose and his eyes
blazed briefly with the glare of madness.

It had been his own fault: that was why he was so unremit-
tingly furious with his shamans, his nurses and his wife, Lesa
the Faded. None of them could legitimately be blamed for the
fact that, despite all their chidings, he had insisted – at his age!
– in going out on a storgh hunt with the younger warriors of
the tribe. He *did* blame them, of course, nonetheless – he
blamed them for not being legitimately blamable, although
that was only among the more minor of their many offences.
Much worse was the fact that nobody had thought to tell him
that marrowsuckers had become stronger, wilier, more vicious
and more swift-moving during the years since last he had
hunted one. The blasted reptile had taken a fist-sized hunk out
of his left calf muscle: a lesser man might have screamed and
fainted; the old chieftain, made of sterner stuff, had merely
fainted. The next he had known he had been back here in his
tent, struggling to avoid drowning in the many poultices and
potions his shamans had insisted on thrusting at or into him.

That was the shamans' major crime. Had he not had to waste so much energy in fighting off their attentions he might have been able to concentrate his venerable mind on the more important matter of curing his wound. As it was, the exposed flesh had been allowed to rot. The rot had been eating him up these past three weeks, and now he knew it was encroaching close upon his heart, the seat of his emotions and all his higher mental functions.

The crime of his nurses was that of being nurses. A traditionalist, he detested nurses as much as the illnesses which they feigned to tend. In the early days after his injury he'd been able to strike out at them with something like full force, squashing noses and breaking the occasional satisfyingly important bone, but now he was reduced to impotence as they bathed him in their fresh, bright and – worst of all – irremediably *cheerful* smiles. There was no escaping their merry cries of "Good morning, Overlord of the Sky and All That Depends Therefrom, and how are we feeling today?" or, most loathsome of all, "Have we moved our bowels this morning?", followed by an ignominious wrestling behind him with the bedclothes and an icily cold chamber pot.

Ach! Were he fit enough he'd pronounce a mandatory sentence of death, throughout the Universe, on all the craven scum who pretended to the profession of nursehood.

But their crimes – nurses and shamans alike – were as nothing compared with the vile sin committed against him by his Lesa the Faded.

Deliberately, purely in order to spite him for his quite accidental liaison with a visiting Sanjranian priestess, his vixen of a wife had *borne his two sons in the wrong order*!

To call the elder, Ellonium, a milksop would have been to invite protests from all the milksops of the region. A lanky vegetarian youth with a thin face and a pimply nose, Ellonium was at his happiest when going for – very short – country rambles with his mother in order to gather nosegays with which he might bedeck his tent. The old chieftain had first begun to suspect the feeble-mindedness of his firstborn when the youth had been only six or seven, and his father had discovered him tickling a kitten rather than pulling its legs off,

like any self-respecting future warlord. Now, though Ellonium had been informally banished forever from his father's
sight, the old man could still sometimes hear him, when the
wind blew southward across the camp, singing lullabies to the
flowers in his tent.

Thog, now – ah, Thog, the younger boy, was something
different. Stockily built and steadfastly unimaginative, Thog
was a lad after his father's heart. Undisputed champion for
several years now in the tribe's annual wrestling and gouging
contests, he was a master of every weapon except the sword, a
childhood misapprehension concerning the use of which had
cost him the first two fingers of his right hand. Thog the
Squat, as the tribesmen affectionately called him, looked less
like a human being than like a shaved grizzly bear, but he was
the apple of his father's eye for all that.

Yet, by every law known to humankind – and the old
chieftain should know, being the hereditary Overlord of the
Sky and All That Depends Therefrom – it would be Ellonium,
not Thog, who would succeed to the Mandrake Chair in a few
days' time. How the dying man cursed his own procrastination
of early years! Often enough he'd decided that his elder son
should encounter some inexplicable but heartwarmingly fatal
accident, but always he'd put off the execution of the deed,
preferring to prolong the thrill of anticipation . . . and now,
now he lay on his deathbed and it was too late to thwart Lesa
the Faded's malicious designs!

Or was it?

Thought did not come easy to the old chieftain. He tried to
wrinkle yet further his already entangledly wrinkled brow.
There was something he'd once heard about . . . Perhaps there
was a way in which he might leave at least a part of his territory
to his favoured son . . .

In a weak voice he called for his chief henchman. "Mikra-
Maus! Mikra-Maus!"

Four burly warriors carried the old chieftain out into the weak
sunlight for what everybody knew was to be the last time. Lesa
the Faded wept copiously – and probably falsely – by the side
of his rude stretcher while his elder son, Ellonium, simpered

nearby. With some difficulty Thog was lured away from a particularly exciting stomach-punching contest in which he had been engaged.

The light in the old man's blue eyes waxed to a feverish brightness as Mikra-Maus reverentially placed the ancestral longbow and the ancestral arrow across the shrunken chest. The chieftain's claw-like fingers scrabbled at the haft.

"It is the rule of our people," wheezed the old warrior, "that on the death of a leader his eldest son should succeed him as ruler. However," he improvised frantically, "it is permitted that the father should also make provision for his younger offspring, and this I choose to do. Thog, my lad, come close to me."

"Why?" said Thog blankly. It was dawning on him that the old codger looked a bit peaky this morning – had been for the past few days, in fact. Must have been one heck of a binge . . .

"Never mind that now, my boy," croaked the chieftain. "I bequeath to you as much of my territory as will lie outside a circle around this spot, a circle of radius as great as the distance that you can shoot the ancestral arrow. Here, fine fellow – take the bow, and loose the arrow!"

Thog looked momentarily confused – geometry had never been his strong point – but he accepted the intricately carved weapon eagerly enough. Firing arrows was something he understood. The longbow seemed like a living, throbbing creature in his hands as he nocked the obscenely wrought arrow – point foremost, as he had been laboriously taught – to the singing ancestral string.

The surrounding warriors backed off warily.

"Do not loose your shaft in the direction of the morning sun," hissed Mikra-Maus. His wizened eyes narrowed. "There's someone over there."

Thog, distracted by the partly heard whisper, stared in the appropriate direction. There was indeed someone there, about a hundred metres off – just within arrow-range – and walking through the mud away from the little gathering. It was difficult at first to tell whether the skinny figure was male or female, for it was clad in a long, rust-brown cloak that reached down almost as far as its naked ankles. He squinted.

Above the neckline of the cloak was a head of scruffily cropped copper-coloured hair. A boy, he decided. He didn't like boys. He didn't like girls, either, which made his decision all the easier.

He tensed the bow.

"And do not fire your arrow too far," added Mikra-Maus. "Your father wished me to tell you that."

Thog scowled at him. It seemed clear the henchman was trying to bamboozle him. The tribal territory was huge, as everyone knew – at least five bowshots across – so clearly Thog's best plan was to fire the arrow as far as possible. He wrinkled his nose, suddenly doubtful about this. He was better at geometry than he was at arithmetic.

"Father!" said Ellonium suddenly, seemingly at his mother's prompting. "Father, stop this!"

The old chieftain growled threateningly.

"Don't you see how *unfair* it is, Father?" Ellonium's voice was close to cracking. "Nasty Thog could simply let the arrow fall to his feet, and there'd I'd be, disinherited, the heir to none of your land at all!"

"That's what I . . ." the chieftain began, but then thought better of it. "What do you propose instead, you pathetic young whelp?"

"I propose that *I* be the one that fires the arrow," said Ellonium after a few seconds' hasty consultation with Lesa the Faded, "and that I fall heir to all the ground that lies within the circle described by the place where the arrow should fall." This would still leave his brother with the lion's share of the inheritance, of course, but most of the tribal lands outside this immediate area were worthless bog anyway. Ellonium produced as much of a beaming grin as his ferret-like features could manage.

Thog looked at his brother. His puddle-coloured eyes crossed as he tried to follow the reasoning. If one of them didn't hurry up and fire an arrow, the brown-cloaked target would squelch out of range. At last he shrugged reluctantly and passed the ceremonial bow over to Ellonium, followed by the blackened, phallus-encrusted arrow.

"Do your worst with it, brother," he said.

Ellonium examined the bow curiously, then turned to gaze at Lesa the Faded. With a few movements of her eloquent fingers she mimed what he must do. As he nocked the arrow in an even clumsier parody of what Thog had done scant moments before, there came a weary whisper in his ear.

"As I told your brother," said Mikra-Maus, "take care not to loose your missile towards the morning sun. The stranger still walks there."

"Aw, come off it, ol' bozo," growled Thog. "Ain't you got no sense of fun? Let Ellonium try to spit the lad an' we can all have a bit of a laugh. 'Specially if – fat chance for such a skinny limpwrist – he succeeds."

Ellonium shrugged and turned deliberately away from the morning sun. Ahead of him the bogland stretched away greasily and emptily. He raised the bow high in front of him and drew back the string as far as it would go, the haft of the arrow feeling incongruous between his fingers. He tried to breathe steadily and easily.

From the outset it was obvious that the shot was poor. The arrow seemed to flutter and waddle in the air as it struggled through the first part of a feeble parabola. But then something – the wind perhaps? – seemed to catch it. To Ellonium and the others it was as if the arrow had suddenly been given a fresh injection of strength, shrugged its shoulders and decided to persevere. In a slow graceful arc it began, paradoxically, to rise higher above the fetid, moss-greened ground. Then the wind must have taken it again, for at ever-increasing speed it curved up and high over their heads, so that the little party, mouths hanging open, had to turn on their heels to watch its flight.

Straight as – well, straight as an arrow, actually, it whistled and whooped directly towards the caped figure, now further than two hundred metres away.

With a firm *choccckkk!* – like the sound of an axe slammed into a ripe cantaloupe, mused Ellonium – it slammed into the stranger's back, neatly between the shoulder blades.

Ellonium closed his eyes in misery. That he, a lifelong pacifist and vegetarian, should inadvertently have caused the death of a fellow human being. His gorge rose. It had been a long time – weeks and weeks, for sure – since he'd last had an accident like this, but age hadn't made his anguish seem any easier to bear.

"Look," said his mother's voice. "It's a miracle."

Reluctantly he prised one eye open.

The stranger still stood – no, more than that: the stranger was still walking unconcernedly away from them, despite the evil-looking arrow protruding jauntily behind.

"Armour," said Mikra-Maus in wondering tones. "The boy must be wearing thick leather armour under that cape of his. That's the only possible explanation. But even then the impact should've knocked him flat on his . . ."

The old man's words died away into a mumble.

"To horse!" cried Thog gleefully. "I'll deal with this!"

Obediently a couple of warriors fetched the tribal horse. Thog took its reins and began to check his weaponry: swords, daggers, axes, spears, morning stars, maces . . .

"No!" shrieked Lesa the Faded when she saw what was up. "That person is a stranger and therefore our guest. Fetch him back here so that we may extend our hospitality to him, and tend any wound that he might have."

Thog looked confused.

"Kill 'im," grunted the old chieftain. "The way I see it, he's a trespasser on our land. Quartering's the only language trespassers understand."

"No, father," said Ellonium pluckily, finding his voice at last. "I shall pursue the lad myself and bid him share our supper while mother draws the arrow from him and bathes his wound."

"Beware the Swamp of Thomasina!" cried Lesa the Faded, her hands wringing at her ample bosom. "The Mutant Hordes of the Dark Masters who dwell there would eat you as soon as look at you! And you know how poorly you can become if you get your feet wet."

The old man humphed and grumphed, but there was nothing he could do from his bed. Finding courage from who knows where, Ellonium shouldered aside his younger brother. Scrambling into the saddle in a flurry of limbs, he spurred the ancestral horse, and soon had left the very different cries of his mother and brother behind.

*   *   *

The day grew hot, and still Ellonium rode in pursuit of the
stranger. The horse was old and overweight, but this hardly
explained the fact that, however much he raked at the beast's
barrel with his spurs, the rust-caped youth remained a couple
of hundred metres ahead of him. To add to his perplexity, the
slight figure seemed to be doing no more than ambling along,
and once or twice even paused for a moment to regard
solemnly a clump of sphagnum. He wondered if the stranger
might be a chimera, a spectre sent by the Gods to test his
valour and stamina so that they might be assured of his
suitability to inherit a parcel of his father's land.

It came to him suddenly that the relevant parcel had already
become an extremely big one, and was growing even more so
by the minute. Twisting in the saddle, he stared back the way
he had come and realized that he had already crossed two
broad tracts of bogland, not to mention the range of rolling
hills between them. Very soon, he reckoned, he and the
enigmatic youth whom he was so doggedly following would
reach the shores of the vile Swamp of – there was a loud splash
and the ancestral horse lurched beneath him – Thomasina.

As he struggled to pull the beast back ashore, he saw out of
the corner of his eye that the object of his pursuit was standing
not ten metres away, watching him soberly. Even that swift
glance was enough to tell him that this was no boy, as he'd
thought, but a young woman.

Once he and the horse were safely back on dry land he took
another look. The woman was unlike any other that he'd seen
before. In the light of the afternoon sun her short frondy hair
looked as if it had been blown from copper. Her hands and her
feet were small and pale; her body seemed to him so slight that
a gust of wind might bear her away. She stared at him frankly,
her air one of complete composure, and he realized that her
eyes, the yellow-green of a cat's eyes, were as large as all The
World. The dully feathered shaft of the ancestral arrow
peeped at him over her shoulder, but he barely noticed.

"Hurry up and get yourself riding again," she said. "We've
got a long way to go before this day is done."

"I came to apologize . . ." he began. His throat seemed full
of treacle. He tried again. "Stranger lady," he said, "you . . ."

"Stranger than whom?"

"Stranger than . . . No! That's not what I meant. No, you seem perfectly normal to . . ."

Two pink spots appeared abruptly on the woman's face, one at the tip of each cheekbone. " 'Strange' I can cope with," she said sourly, "but continents have been sunk for less than a 'perfectly normal'."

"That's not what I . . ." Ellonium began again, tumbling eagerly from the saddle. "Let me offer you my horse, so that you may rest your . . ."

I'm in love! he thought through the clamour of his heart's singing. *I, who never thought that such a pure and wondrous emotion dwelt within me – except towards my mother, of course, but that's different – I, Ellonium, heir to the tribal bogland: I – AM – IN – LOVE.*

"I often have that effect on men," said the woman coolly, the temper fading from her face as rapidly as it had appeared, "but it's nice to know that I haven't lost my touch. Life begins at a couple of billion, say I." She looked distractedly at her fingernails; her smile told him that she judged them perfect. "Now saddle yourself up, my boy, and carry on following me. We've got to go all the way round the Swamp of Thomasina before nightfall – I've no fancy to travel in the dark, have you? Come on! Bat away the twenty bluebirds and the little pink puffy hearts from around your head and let's get moving."

She turned away suddenly, and immediately she was once more a couple of hundred metres away. She stood impatiently by the swampside as he clambered back into the saddle.

Love! he thought anew once the ancestral horse was again jogging arhythmically beneath him. *Isn't love a marvellous thing? Already I feel like a new man – twice as strong, twice as intelligent, twice as . . . twice as* well hung *as ever I was before!*

In the distance, he could see the shoulders of his adored one shake, and for just a moment he feared that she might be in some distress. He relaxed in the saddle as she continued to walk steadily away from him.

Poetry! he thought. *Yes!* That's *what impassioned young swains are supposed to compose for the objects of their adorations. I have it! I have it! I'll form an epic ballad, stuffed with heroic*

couplings and stanzas by the fathom, entwining the two driving
ardours of my existence – vegetarianism and my yearnings for the
affections of this fair lady! She'll like that: it'll win her for me,
for sure! It's the next best thing I can offer her aside from dying of
unrequited passion. "She's the apple of my eye" – yes, that's good,
that's good! "A bright marrow hath piercèd my heart" – yea: the
words are singing within me! Now, if I can only find a rhyme for
"kumquat" . . .

II   Lesa Fading

Darkness was falling by the time the young woman strolled
back into the tribe's camp. Catching up with her at last,
Ellonium was certain that darkness really should have fallen
some considerable while before – about a week and a half, at a
guess – but he saw no reason to complain. Thanks to his
father's idiosyncratic injunction and the short-haired lady's
incomparable walking skills, he was now the ordained ruler of
a territory larger than any that the tribe had ever envisaged in
even their wildest dreams. From today he, Ellonium, could
proudly boast, as his father had never been able to do, that he
was in truth the undisputed Overlord of the Sky and All That
Depends Therefrom! Moreover, he was four hundred and
thirty-eight stanzas into what he had come to recognize was
already a veritable lyrical bonanza.

The old chieftain took one baleful look at the slender woman
and another at his elder son, who'd got his foot tangled in his
stirrup while attempting to dismount. Then he died.

The tribesmen, awed, fell to their knees. "Our leader is
dead. Long live Ellonium," intoned Mikra-Maus, speaking
for all of them.

"Yes," said the strange woman quietly, standing off to one
side, forgotten by everyone else there except the new Overlord
of the Sky and All That Depends Therefrom, "long live
Ellonium indeed."

Later that night, once the perfunctory funeral was over and
the under-provisioned celebrations were in the fullest swing
they were likely to manage, Ellonium, somewhat tiddly on his

mother's sweet-rosehip pick-me-up, sought out the woman who had, quite literally, led him to his position of pre-eminence. She was sitting cross-legged in the flickering shadows well away from the roaring campfire and the banquet table, humming an atonal tune to herself. In the muted light her strange eyes seemed to glow.

"I must proffer you my thanks, fair lady," said Ellonium, bowing lankly.

"Consider them proffered," she said. "Come here. Sit down beside me." She patted a miraculously dry piece of ground next to her. "You'll be wondering what you can offer me in return for the tremendous favour I've done you. Well, wonder no more: I've taken the burden of decision off your shoulders. You can marry me."

Ellonium stared at her, speechless. He had loved her – yea, passionately and true – for the whole of a livelong day, which was longer than he could remember having felt any strong emotion about anything before, unless you counted his mother. And, come to think of it, her spinach bake. But marriage – *that* was something he had never contemplated. According to all that he had read, and all that he had heard from the troubadours who occasionally passed hastily through these lands, the next steps along the path of true love consisted of silent yearnings, unspoken glances, insuperable obstacles, broken trysts, cureless afflictions, ashen countenances and, after a decorous period of pining, a mordant death. There seemed to him something vaguely improper about the prospect of marriage to the woman of his dreams. But then he thought of his ballad, and of how he might be able to recite it to her in its entirety rather than merely having to smuggle her the occasional stanza or two in the guise of a laundry list.

His mouth snapped shut and his jaw adopted a new resolve.

"Right willingly shall I take you to my heart, fair lady," he said grandly, sweeping his arm around as if to embrace the Sky and All That Depended Therefrom, as he now had every right to do. "To my heart and to my bed, and everything that I have I shall share with you."

"We can discuss the 'bed' part of that later, and probably acrimoniously," said the woman. More loudly she said: "I accept your proposal, King Ellonium – 'King', for that is what people shall come to call you. There's no need for us to bother with a long engagement, don't you think? We can just hop over and tell your mother and that'll be that."

She pulled herself to her feet, brushed off her cape – even though, for some unaccountable reason, the mud and slime that adhered immovably to everything else seemed to shun her and her clothing – and led him by the hand towards the campfire.

"Er, what's your name?" he stuttered as they picked their way.

"You may choose the name by which you call me," she said.

"Lesa?"

"Apart from that."

He tripped over a root and swore.

"That's a nice name," she said brightly. "You may call me Maglittle."

III Lesa, Faded

Ellonium was weeping. Two years had passed since his nuptial night, and the tiny tribal territory that his father had ruled was now the core of a large nation bordering the Swamp of Thomasina. On that bizarrely long day when he had pursued Maglittle wherever she might lead him, he had unknowingly tracked out a colossal area of bogland and jungle, much of it poor but also much of it, especially along the river valleys and in the open land around the north of the swamp, fertile and rich. The minor tribes that had inhabited those regions in the old chieftain's day had, with various degrees of gratitude, conceded Ellonium's rule over them, and he in return had brought to them a hitherto unthought-of prosperity. Even the Kindelwuersten Kindlybears, the gentle folk who dwelt along the fringes of the Swamp of Thomasina, had drawn themselves from their contemplations of the goodnesses of Nature long enough to acknowledge a truce between themselves and his people; Ellonium even had hopes, never mentioned to his wife, that one day the ancient Temple of Ascidian, built at the swamp's heart by a race of people who had been long gone from this land before history had begun, would come under his sway. But that was to look far ahead. In the meantime, the threat from the Mutant Hordes of the swamp had been at least temporarily contained: some of the gloomier of his shamans predicted that the foul beasts would soon erupt from their heartland and reclaim the territory they regarded as theirs, but for the moment that hazard seemed as far distant as the incorporation of the Temple of Ascidian into his realm, and the recently designed banners of the Dour Mountains of Harmadree fluttered carelessly above the turrets of Thog City (pop. 1706), the capital which Ellonium had founded on the shore due south of his father's old camp, and which he had so named in a not-so-subtle but apparently successful attempt to quell any rebellious thoughts that his brother might nurture.

The sun shone each day brightly on the Dour Mountains of Harmadree, as if it would do so for all the rest of eternity.

And yet Ellonium wept.

His brother looked at him unsympathetically. They were in the regal apartments in the North Tower of Castle Thog – a building only somewhat less grand than its name. Sunlight beamed in through the narrow windows and played across the crudely tiled floor. From outside there were the faint sounds of the city going about its work. The wind, blowing today from the north, brought with it the sweet scents of rotting vegetation and fresh woodsmoke.

"You got everything," said Thog roughly. "You got the kingdom. You got the power. You got the doxy, for what the scrawny midget's worth. You got no cause to go blubbing your eyes out, like *girls* do."

"I've got everything but the thing I want," sobbed Ellonium.

"Wossat?" Thog's brows, undecided as to whether to knit or beetle, wrestled furiously.

"The 'doxy', as you call her. Maglittle!"

The right eyebrow seemed to have the left in an armlock, but the contest was clearly far from over.

"But you and her, you tied the knot, di'n you? Spliced the mainbrace? I thought you was as close as chalk and cheese. What you mean you ain't got the doxy?" Thog picked up a jug of mead from a jewel-encrusted table and drained it at a draught. Smacking his lips, he picked up another.

Ellonium plucked at the hem of his lavishly embroidered robe, staring beyond it to the floor. His brother was coarse of locution, yet Ellonium recoiled from the prospect of expressing himself in the same vulgar terms. *How to explain to him in a way that he'll understand?* he thought. As ever, his roving mind fell upon its eld-loved topic.

He imagined himself to be in a market place. All around him were stalls displaying the ripest and richest products of the farms and fields of the Dour Mountains. But, to Ellonium's mind's eye, the brightly coloured fruits and vegetables of the displays had an additional, fresh meaning: they were also similes and metaphors rendered into physical form, so that he could pick and choose among them as he wished. He felt his inner face wrinkle with indecision as he approached the first stall. The stall-holder beamed ruddily at him.

Melons. Perhaps, in the circumstances, not. Nodding politely to the now disappointed countryman, Ellonium moved slowly away towards the next display. Maybe pawpaws weren't what he was looking for, either.

He controlled his breathing, forcing himself not to panic. The market was huge: he was aware without having to look that it stretched for hundreds of metres, if not hundreds of kilometres, to every side of him. Unfortunately, however, he appeared to be the solitary customer, which meant that the fruit- and vegetable-sellers were eagerly watching his every move, hoping that their monarch would choose to purchase their products, and theirs alone. He felt as if he were at the focal point of a lens, his skin in danger of frazzling in the hot sunlight of their stares.

Shiftily he continued to browse. Leeks were out, obviously, as were bananas and corn on the cob and especially aubergines. He gave the strawberries barely a glance, puzzled over a pair of Brussels sprouts and a stick of rhubarb before hastily rejecting them – likewise the gherkins and the courgettes – and regarded the mangoes, figs, peaches, nectarines, apricots, cherries, oyster plants and walnuts in frank dismay. A towering heap of passion fruit made him shudder audibly.

Celery, carrots, parsnips, plums, fennel, runner beans, gooseberries, jackfruits . . . the nightmare continued. By now Ellonium was sprinting in full hysteria up and down the aisles of his vast mental market place, seeing the strongly coloured displays as little more than blurs of light as he sped past them. The expressions on the faces of the stall-holders merged into a single, tooth-packed, kilometres-long leer. Chicory, chickpeas, chard, chives, checkerberries, cherimoyas and chillies smeared past him in a kaleidoscopic cornucopia. Lingonberries, lychees, loquats, limes and loganberries – a thin scream was trickling from the sides of his mouth – tangelos, tangerines, tamarinds, turnips and tomatoes. A plantain cackled at him, a jaboticaba hooted, an olive ogled, a horseradish whinnied and he was perfectly certain he heard a boysenberry belch. Huckleberries snapped at his heels like crazed terriers, while sapodillas spat and scallions scowled. His breath was coming in cruel, choking whoops as he pounded onwards, the thunder of the pursuing produce – a mountain of tumbling fruits and vegetables dwarfing him as it trundled menacingly after him – seeming to echo at him from the very walls of The World.

With one last despairing scream he found himself back on the wooden throne of his kingly apartments. Thog was eyeing him alarmedly.

"What you bin doing?"

"Trying to think of a way to explain my problem to you," gasped Ellonium. Cold sweat was pouring from his forehead and down the concavity of his chest. "It's a bit . . . well, personal."

"Just say it, man!" Thog hurled another empty jug towards the pile in the corner. "Say it straight out! I can take it. I'm a warrior."

"Well, you know what . . . er . . . kohlrabi is."

"Greens, right?"

"Yes, that's it. And . . . um . . . guavas. And custard apples and persimmon. Not to mention grapes."

"Yes. Girls' stuff."

"Well, Maglittle isn't letting me make a fruit salad out of those."

Thog blanched. "I say, that's a bit close to the knuckle, brother!"

"I couldn't think of a more refined way to put it. I . . ."

"Yes, but – what if *Mother* had heard you?"

The two men looked guiltily around the room's gilded walls, as if Lesa the Faded might at any moment spring from behind a panel and swoon at them. Reassured, they nevertheless moved closer to each other and began to speak in quieter, more urgent tones.

"Right from the outset she's been the same," said Ellonium. "The very night of our marriage, when I was expecting . . . well, not much, because I'd been drinking a lot, but at least a bit of a squash, or maybe even an endive . . ."

"A cuddle, you mean?"

"Yes, if you have to put it as crudely as that. But she said no way, not ever, that wasn't what she'd married me for. What she'd married me for was to install me as ruler over the Dour Mountains of Harmadree for as long as we both should live – which, she hinted darkly, would be a very long time indeed, or else."

"Glug," went Thog's throat as another pint of mead disappeared. "Couldn't you have, er, truffled?"

"I truffled to the point of mushrooming!" exclaimed Ellonium, slapping his thigh to emphasize the point. " 'Honeydew,' I said to her, as civil as you'd wish, 'honeydew, my sweet mamey apple, a married man needs his lentils, his okra and his onions. To deny him those is to deny the dictates of his inmost gumbo.' But all she said was: 'Hagberries!' I didn't know what she meant then, but" – he began to sob afresh – "I do now."

"Well, I still don't." Thog's right eyebrow had been thrown right out of the ring, but was gamely crawling back in.

"That first night, I tried to follow her into our tent. The very moment I crossed the threshold she . . . changed. It was hideous – hideous!"

Thog said nothing, just stared glumly at the last jug of mead. He had the feeling that courtesy dictated he should leave it for his brother, but he also had the feeling that courtesy was nothing but a blasted nuisance. He reached for it.

"There, in the moonlight," Ellonium was continuing, "she

altered from the trim young bunch of spring greens I'd been
following all day into . . . into a *crab apple*! She looked as
ancient as if she'd been in her grave six weeks. Her head was
shiny – not a hair on it – but her nostrils more than compen-
sated for that. Dewlaps . . . pimples . . . boils . . . She gave me
a terrible toothless smile, and just then her glass eye dropped
out. I . . . I'm not ashamed to admit, brother, that I fainted."

"Sissy."

"And it was the same every night after that, until finally I
couldn't take it any more, and gave up. Since then I've been
perfecting my epic ballad, born out of my ardour for her, but
she refuses to listen to me declaim it. What can I *do*?"

His final wail was truly piteous. He threw his face down
onto his forearms and whimpered.

Courtesy be damned: Thog drained the final dregs of the
mead.

"You've thought of getting yourself a bit of asparagus on the
side?" he said to his brother's convulsing shoulders. "I know a
perky little slice of civet fruit as'll give a man . . ."

"It's no *use*! It's *her* that I want – not some *substitute*! Oh,
woe . . ."

Thog shifted in his seat uneasily. After a last exchange of
forearm smashes his brows declared a truce. "Well, brother,"
he said ponderously, "not to set too fine a point on it, you
could always just put out the lights. As the old tribal saying
goes, in the night all manzanillas are . . . well, whatever colour
manzanillas are. As of this moment I can't rightly recollect.
But you get my dri–"

"You fool!" bleated Ellonium, wrenching at the cloth of his
robe and staring viciously at his brother through bloodshot
eyes. "That's no help at all!"

"Why ever not?"

"Because she *glows in the dark*!"

IV   Stainless Alyss

She's got to sleep sometime, thought Thog grimly as he
prowled the castle that night, sharpening the blade of his
favourite sword. *My brother may not be much, but I owe him*

something – didn't he go and name a whole city (pop. 1706) in my honour, after all? I'll rid him of his soursop, and then perhaps he can find himself a complaisant jujube and reign happily ever after.

The queen, who never slept any time, smiled as she listened to his thoughts. Thog didn't know it yet, but he was going to have tremendous difficulty tonight – and any other night – finding his way through the castle's maze of corridors. The very next door he charged through should land him in – yes, the swearing had started – the castle midden.

Leaving him to his fate, she thought for a few seconds longer of the more important problems that faced her: Ellonium, and his happiness. She had really grown unconscionably fond of the gawky youth – as fond as she could ever be of a mere mortal – and she had no wish to hurt him unnecessarily. The thought of succumbing to his blandishments was momentarily appealing – she liked a good laugh – but only momentarily. No, far better to tell him at last of the reasons that had brought her here and had led her to create the nation of which he was now monarch. And, too, she should inform him of her plans for his future.

She issued a silent summons, and felt Ellonium, in his own bedchamber, suddenly jerk out of his fitful sleep. Half a minute later he was at her door.

He was staring at her, aghast, his knees beginning to fold beneath him . . .

"Oh," she said, "silly me. Sorry about that. Just habit." She swiftly readjusted the pimpled, dewlapped image of herself that she had projected into his mind. "There, is that better?"

His eyes told her that it was. Sitting in the middle of her bed, she looked to him as she always did during the day – like a slim, wiry but somehow very feminine woman, dressed in incongruously boyish clothes. She ran her fingers through her hair absently, smiling affectionately at him.

"It's time that you and I had a talk," she said. "But you'd better keep your distance."

"A talk about what?"

"About the future we're going to share, you and I."

"Together?"

"Together. Not all of the time, and not quite in the way you might think, but together."

"Maglittle . . ."

"For a start, you should know that my real name is Alyss. 'Maglittle' is the name that you gave to me, and I'm happy enough to live with it. But Alyss is the name by which I've been known since time began – and it's *my* name for myself, also. You presumably know it well." She preened.

"Er . . . no," said Ellonium. "Now look here, Maglittle, you once said that we'd rule the Dour Mountains of Harmadree together for a very long time. Just quite how long did you mean by that?"

"For a few thousand years." Pouting, she ignored his open mouth. "About three and a half thousand, to be exact. At least. After that, if you still want to, you can carry on ruling in my absence. But I need to be here, as the long-established queen of the Dour Mountains, in the year BF 1500."

"You're immortal?" he said at last, wondering what "BF" stood for. Not what it normally meant amid the ribald badinage of his infantry, he assumed.

"I'm surprised it surprises you," she said calmly. "You must have noticed that I am not . . . not as other women."

He looked at her dumbly, and she abruptly realized that he had had little to compare her with except his mother. Which meant that . . . It struck her that she'd been being crueller to him than she'd intended, these past two years. "I mean," she said gently, "mortal women don't shapeshift at will. They can't fly. They can't walk faster than a speeding horse, or make a single day endure for weeks."

She read in his face that this was all news to him. His *mother* couldn't do any of these things, of course, but obviously it had never dawned on him that his mother was a woman. She brushed his mind lightly and discovered that yes, indeed, he'd concluded that women were all magical, strange supernatural beings like herself. Except that other women grew old and eventually died. She wondered how he'd been able to derive some of the more fevered images involving herself that were currently clogging his mind.

"I'm not really a woman at all," she breathed. "I'm female,

I think, inasmuch as that term has any meaning when applied
to me, but it's only an illusion that I'm a woman. I've deceived
you – and I apologize for that: it's been a necessary deceit.
With your collusion, I propose to continue that sham." She
thought it best not to add that it would be pifflingly easy for
her to enforce his cooperation – enforce it in such a way that he
would never even be aware that she had done so. She would
rather that he be her willing partner in this enterprise.

"Why?"

"I told you. I need to be the queen here in the year BF
5070, when a certain individual will come to Harmadree on a
particularly important quest – one that is so important that I
don't exaggerate if I say that the future of The World hinges
on it. Moreover, I need, with your help, to have guided the
history of this nation in such a way that the conditions here
are just right for that individual to have the best possible
chances of attaining his goal and escaping afterwards with his
life."

Unspoken questions were making a battleground of Ellonium's face. Again she brushed his mind, extracting from it a
list.

She held up the little finger of her left hand, resting the
index finger of her right hand on its tip. "One," she said. "No,
I have no objections to your taking up with an occasional perky
little slice of civet fruit on the side, as your brother so
eloquently put it, so long as you're discreet in doing so. I
think it would be good for you if you did. Indeed, as part of my
plan you will spend extended periods away from the capital, so
you may well wish to have a succession of families quite
independent of your relationship with me.

"Two," – she adjusted her fingers accordingly – "if you
value your good looks, such as they are, you won't even
think the part about 'if she's not really a woman then –
yippee! – doesn't that mean our marriage is null and void?',
because that would be to cast a slur upon my form and my
personality, which are perfect the way they are. As you can
imagine, I can be very dangerous if someone makes me
petulant."

Ellonium cowered. The sight cheered her up, and her voice

was bubbling as she continued. "Three, in order that the people of our domains don't eventually rebel against what they might come to regard as our necromantic reign, we will perform a simple charade, whereby we will seem to grow old and die, to be succeeded on the throne by our children, who will of course look remarkably like us as they slowly grow old and die, to be succeeded by – you follow my meaning?"

He nodded.

"Sometimes we'll rule together, sometimes singly. Your 'son', Ellonium II, for example, will be a fearless fighter, and will drive back into the Swamp of Thomasina the Mutant Hordes that I, in my weakness as your empty-headed widow, will have allowed to terrorize the countryside in the years after Ellonium I's 'death'."

She grinned at him. "Four – gosh, Ellonium, this is a silly question. Of course I can confer immortality on you. Don't regard it as an unmixed blessing, though. You've got only a mortal's brain, with all the limitations of potential which that implies, so in due course you'll become bored by the vistas of eternity – they'll be largely beyond your comprehension. By the time Jol . . . by the time the individual I was talking about has come and gone, and me with him, it's my guess you'll be keen enough to be allowed to die. But it'll be your decision.

"Five – no, I'm not a God. If I were, things would be run a little differently around here. There'd be no need for all these quests and subterfuges. Unfortunately the Gods insist on running their Universes their own ways, and in this particular one the Gods are very keen on allowing the free will of mortals to have full rein – twerps. All I can do is influence outcomes a little, in the same way that a teacher can help children understand things but can't actually do the understanding for them.

"Six – it's a very flattering idea, but I thought I'd made my feelings on that issue crystal-clear. At least for the next couple of thousand years. If that offends you, then just tell yourself that one of the disadvantages of immortality is that a woman's headaches tend to persist for an awfully long time."

She touched his mind once more, and discovered that a

seventh and an eighth and a ninth question had come shuffling to the fore.

"Yes, I did say 'Universes' in the plural. The reason that I'm in this one at the moment is that I'm in *all* of them at the moment. And no, I'm not making your mother immortal as well – she'll just have to take her chances like the rest of them."

He stared at her. Most men would have fled for the refuge of insanity long before, but with part of her attention she'd been redecorating his mind so that it seemed to him far too alluring an environment to leave.

"Why," he said at last, "why do you wish this individual to succeed in his quest?"

"Because otherwise Evil will swamp The World – and in due course the whole of your Universe. He is an important factor in the maintenance of Good and the eventual Fragmentation."

"But why –?" He broke off, and she watched him fondly as he fumbled to find the words. "Why are you on the side of Good? Why does it make any difference to you whether Good or Evil comes to rule the Universe, or if this Fragmentation you talk about comes to pass?"

She smiled at him. "I could tell you that it's because I'm so inherently Good myself – although I doubt you'd believe that. There are qualities within me that roughly correspond to what you mean by the word "Good", but they're not the same, and I know that by their very nature they'd be incomprehensible to you. Or I could tell you that it's because the God of the Temple – Ascidian – begged me to come here to this rather poxy little Universe. But that wouldn't be true, either: that would be to impute to me a motivation greater than whim, which is the most I ever feel."

Her smile deepened. "You know something, Ellonium, my dear, dear Ellonium?"

"What, my love?"

She giggled.

"You know something *terrible*? And be assured that you would get the same answer to your question from any of the Gods who purport to wave the flag of virtue and benevolence, and indeed if you asked any Dark Master or even the

Devil himself why he was so eager to perpetrate Evil throughout The World. So let me be as honest with you as ever I will be.

"The truth of the matter – the ultimate truth for me as much as for any of the demons or deities who dwell in the infinite Universes that comprise the polycosmos . . .

"The terrible truth is that I *don't know* why."

ELIJAH P. JOPP
AND THE DRAGON

Archibald Marshall

One of the many pleasures in editing this anthology is being able to find rare and long-forgotten comic fantasy. I'm sure that some people believe that comic fantasy only emerged about ten or fifteen years ago and forget the rich heritage of such fiction that we have. In the first volume I reprinted some classic work by Lewis Carroll and Edward Lear, to all intents the real founding fathers, and in this volume I have a few other old-timers dotted around. Archibald Marshall (1866–1934) is one such, largely forgotten today. Even in his day, at the start of the twentieth century, he was only mildly well known. His best work was certainly his humorous novels with their pointed jabs at society. The best of these was his fantasy Upsidonia (1915), but also of note were his Wodehousian Peter Binney, Undergraduate *(1905) and* Richard Baldock *(1906). The following story was first published in* The Royal Magazine *in 1898 and, so far as I can tell, has never been reprinted since.*

I

Elijah P. Jopp was an American from "way down" some-where, but exactly where doesn't matter. He was in the show line, and had got hold of a real paying freak. This was nothing less than a dragon; not a crocodile, nor an alligator faked up with green paint and gilding, but a genuine medieval, fire-breathing, princessivorous dragon, with a voice that could be heard ten miles off when it wasn't muzzled, and an appetite like a Gatling gun.

Elijah P. Jopp had found a curious-looking egg one morning when he was prospecting for gold in an unknown part of the country. He would have been better pleased if he had found a nugget, but, if he had only known it, that egg was going to prove worth fifty nuggets to him. He was at first minded to throw it away, but his lucky star saved him, and he put it in his pocket. He knew nothing about eggs, or he would not have done what he did next; but here, again, his lucky star stood him in good stead, for, when he returned home a few months later in a very bad temper, owing to his not having found the gold mine for which he had been looking, he put the egg in an incubator.

He had carried it in his pocket for four months. For all he knew, it had been lying where he found it for four months before that, though, as a matter of fact, it had been lying there for rather more than a thousand years. The chances were against the incubator making anything of a job of the hatching, but, what with Elijah knowing nothing about incubators, and the incubator being equally ignorant on the subject of dragons' eggs, the experiment was successful, and in due time the egg was hatched.

Its first meal was off its fellow lodgers in the incubator; it then burnt its way through the inflammable part of its foster mother and was free. Elijah was at first inclined to administer capital punishment for these offences, and would have done so if he had known how to set to work. He did make an attempt with a hatchet, but the infant dragon blew its nose and Elijah retired with his trousers singed and his legs scorched. He judged it wiser not to come to close quarters after that, but retired into the house and fetched his revolver. The first bullet flattened itself on the dragon's steely hide, the second glanced off and found a billet in the eye of Elijah's cow. He then decided to forgive the dragon, which bore no offence, and indeed liked its owner none the worse, imagining that Elijah's attempts on its life with his hatchet and revolver were intended simply as an amusement for its unoccupied hours.

It soon became tame and followed him about like a dog. He did not let it eat out of his hand, for it would probably have made a meal off that member in more senses than one, and besides, it always cooked its food by breathing on it before satisfying its appetite, which caused Elijah to become proficient in throwing, as he found it advisable to make a habit of feeding his pet at a range of about fifty yards.

It was fortunate that the dragon attached itself to Elijah, or trouble might have ensued, but it had a soft and engaging disposition, and after a time he could do anything with it, and even punished it by means of a crowbar when the infant mortality of the village began to attract the attention of the Insurance offices. This was in the dragon's early days. By the time that Elijah had got it sufficiently under control to join a travelling circus at a large salary, it had settled down into quite a respectable member of the animal world and was content to accept whatever sustenance was offered to it instead of helping itself.

Elijah toured with the circus in his native country for some time, and made quite a nice little sum of money. Finally the concern was broken up by the disappearance of the proprietor. There was nothing to account for it. Business had been good, and domestic relations all that could be desired. The theory of suicide was scouted on all sides; besides, where was the body? Elijah's dragon showed its grief at the untimely occurrence by refusing all food and going to sleep for two days. Then the proprietor's watch and chain were found in a corner of its cage, and spiteful things were said and regrettable accusations made against it. Elijah, on behalf of the dragon, was very much hurt, and told the widow that unless she withdrew her insinuations he should go away and start a little circus of his own. The widow refused to withdraw, so Elijah did, and made more money as his own manager than he had ever made in his life before.

About five years after the dragon was hatched, Elijah P. Jopp found himself making an extended tour through the Continent of Europe and drawing crowded houses at whatever place he and the dragon went through their performance. The dragon was Elijah's best friend now, and had been trained to do a lot of showy tricks. Elijah would fill his pipe and the dragon would light it for him. Elijah would then take a piece of iron, hold it in the dragon's breath until it became red hot and hammer it into a horseshoe, using the dragon's back as an anvil. A live sheep was brought onto the stage, there was a strong smell of small houses at dinner time, and the sheep had disappeared. The dragon would finish up the entertainment by roaring (by kind permission of the Mayor and Corporation), and the local aurist would retire to a villa in the country in less than a twelvemonth.

Elijah and the dragon were very happy together, and were simply coining money, when one fine morning, after a successful performance in a little town in the Black Forest, which they reached by this time, Elijah woke up to find that the dragon had disappeared. He ran round the little town ringing his hands, and the crier did the same with a bell, but nobody had seen or heard anything of the dragon. One of the burgomasters had missed his wife, but that was all. He behaved in a gentlemanly manner about it and made no fuss, but even if he had claimed damages, there was nothing to connect the dragon with the mishap. No tidings came from the country round. The dragon had simply disappeared.

Elijah was a very unhappy man. It was not so much the loss of his income that troubled him, for by the help of the dragon he had already made his pile. It was the loss of his friend, his constant companion, his fireside, so to speak, and all that made life worth living to him. With the indomitable will of his countrymen he set out on a search for his dragon, but he went with a heavy heart, for sharper than its own teeth was the pang that its desertion had caused him.

II

The dragon, in the meantime, travelling by easy stages and picking up a fair living by the way, had arrived at the kingdom of Dummeleutia and set up house in a convenient swamp a few miles from the royal city of Putzenheim. Its presence in the neighborhood soon began to be felt, and the land in the vicinity of the swamp began to lose value as a site for building purposes. The dragon, freed from its civilizing intercourse with Elijah, reverted to the habits of its ancestors and mopped up the surplus population of the kingdom of Dummeleutia with surprising celerity. It had entirely lost the popularity which it had gained under the wise control of its master, and was now looked upon as something little better than an embarrassment. As a freak in a museum it had been a decided success. As a fatal indisposition and a cemetery rolled into one, it overdid the business.

When it had been settled near Putzenheim for a week the inhabitants of the city were publicly warned against going near the swamp. When it had been there a fortnight they were encouraged to do so, for the dragon, becoming lonely through lack of society, made an expedition, and saved one or two worthy citizens the expense of a funeral. After a month's experience of its healthy appetite matters became serious, and the standing army of Dummeleutia was sent out to engage the monster. They marched away from Putzenheim one summer's morning, banners flying and trumpets braying, and by dint of forced marches arrived at the swamp about teatime. The dragon was delighted. It had been left so much to itself that it was quite down in the mouth. By nightfall half the brave and gallant army of Dummeleutia were down in the mouth, too, and the other six had returned to Putzenheim to resign their commissions.

Then the king took counsel of his advisers, and issued the following proclamation:

WANTED!
A ST GEORGE to slay the DRAGON.

REWARD
As Usual: Daughter's Hand and Half Kingdom.

FERDINAND R.

The neighbouring kingdoms were thrown into great excitement by this proclamation, which was spread far and wide. Princes by the score came thronging into the royal city of Putzenheim and were entertained night after night with costly banquets by the king. But by the end of the month the palace had settled down again to its usual state of meat teas and board wages. Some of the princes had seen the dragon, others had seen the princess. In either case the result was the same. Not one of them had got any further than a nodding acquaintance with the redoubtable beast. They had lost interest in its habits after that, and had either run away or else tried to. The princes had failed.

Then came the turn of the cranks. They didn't want royal banquets and were not so expensive to entertain in other ways. One said he was a magician and could exorcise the dragon. No one knew quite what he meant, but it was generally agreed afterwards that the dragon had done most of the exorcising. Another said he could charm it out of the kingdom by his flute-playing. He might have succeeded with the dragon, but as he insisted on practising beforehand, the inhabitants saved him the trouble of trying and deprived the brute of a meal at the same time.

The enterprising vendor of a patent rat poison then tried his hand. He waived his claim to the princess, having a wife on hand already, but said he could make use of the other part of the reward. He was willing to supply the goods required gratis, as an advertisement. He sent one of his travellers to start operations with a hundred tins. The traveller saturated a sheep and left it near the dragon's home in the swamp. The dragon had been a trifle indisposed for a few days, but managed to make away with the sheep. The poison seemed to revive it, much to the chagrin of the traveller, and it became more of a nuisance than before. The traveller wired to headquarters for a thousand tins, and dressed an ox with the condiment. The dragon swallowed the spiced beef with avidity, and found out who was responsible for the treat, the traveller having waited to see the effect of the dose. An advertisement was put into the papers by the firm for a pushing agent to take the traveller's place, and the cost of eleven hundred tins, with a small pension for his widow, was written off the books. The cranks had failed.

Another meeting of the council was called. "We can't go on like this," said the Lord Chamberlain. "Half the army is gone, and the factories are being closed. Your Majesty must act, and act promptly."

"We *have* acted," said the king, "and nothing has come of it. We have offered a very large reward – our daughter and the half of our kingdom. We have done all we can." The king always spoke of himself in the plural. He thought it very fine.

"There is one thing that is always done in these cases that has *not* been done," said the Lord Chamberlain.

"What is it?" asked the king.

"The princess must be sacrificed."

The king grew thoughtful. "Do you really think so?" he asked.

"It is the only course left to us."

"It doesn't seem a bad idea," said the king. "But we are not quite sure how Her Royal Highness might take it."

"Your Majesty can command."

"Yes – there is that. We can command – of course. We say, Sploschstein, just come here a minute. *You'll* break it to her, won't you?"

"Well, Your Majesty, it would come better from you, I think."

"Oh, Sploschstein, just think of a father's feelings."

"If the worst came to the worst, we could mobilize the army to take her along, couldn't we?"

"Do you think there is enough of it left?"

"What, six brawny men – the gallant army of Dummeleutia not enough to take one old –"

"We beg your pardon?"

"I mean one simple maiden a couple of miles?"

"Well, we should think it might do, perhaps. You arrange it all, Sploschstein, just as you think best. We must be off now. We've just to go round the corner to see a man about a dog. Goodbye."

The Lord Chamberlain pulled himself together and went to interview the princess. She tumbled to the idea directly, much to his relief. She liked the idea of the white robe, and the flowers, and the weeping maidens, and being allowed to choose what she liked for breakfast; she was a sentimental woman, and had little doubt that a St George would turn up in the nick of time to save her from the dragon and marry her afterwards. They had no trouble with her at all.

The king objected at first to having to fall on her neck before leaving her to the dragon – he wanted the whole thing over as quickly as possible – but it was pointed out to him that if he didn't do his part he would spoil the whole performance, so he consented.

The ceremony went off very well. The stage manager of the Royal Opera House arranged the details and was congratulated on his success by the whole of the Press. They got together a dozen virgins to strew flowers in the way, and the stationmaster's little daughter offered the princess a magnificent bouquet of choice hothouse blooms. There was a band, but the less said about that the better. The princess enjoyed herself thoroughly.

She was more popular than she had ever been in her life. The whole population of Putzenheim turned out to see the last of her, but the concourse thinned off a bit as they neared the swamp. However, nothing was seen of the dragon.

The proceedings were a little hurried when they reached the margin of the swamp, but the princess was duly chained to a tree – she would have preferred a rock if there had been one – and then the king tucked up his robes and scuttled back to his royal city as fast as his legs would carry him, followed by the Lord Chamberlain and the rest of the cast.

III

The king reached the palace first and went in by the back door, as his feet were rather muddy. As he passed through the kitchen the servant told him that a man was waiting to see him in the passage by the umbrella stand.

"What is his name?" asked the king.

The servant wiped her hand on her apron and produced a card. On it was printed: "ST GEORGE".

"He has come," said the king. "We knew he would. Show him into the best parlour and light the stove."

The king went upstairs to change his boots, and then went down into the parlour to receive his honoured guest.

"Saint George, we believe," he said politely, as he entered the room.

"That's so," said the stranger. He was a tall, thin man with a goatee beard. He was dressed in a suit of broadcloth and had deposited a stovepipe hat on the table by his side.

"You have called, we believe, about that little matter of the dragon."

"I guess you've about figured it out correct."

"You are prepared to rid our kingdom of this pestilent monster?"

"I'm prepared to do it right now, terms being satisfactory."

"You insist on the reward, do you?"

"You bet."

"I thought, perhaps, being in that line of business –"

"Won't do, Ferdy. Where's the gal?"

"Well, unfortunately, we have just led her out to die, but –"

"You have, have you? That's mighty awkward for her. What's the poor girl been doing?"

"She hasn't been doing anything. She's a sacrifice for the dragon. We thought, perhaps, if we gave her up it might be satisfied and go home."

"Well, I guess it won't be the dragon that's gone home. We shall see what's happened when I get there."

"Yes, and there's no particular hurry, is there?"

"Depends. Got a map of her face?"

"We have a photograph taken by a travelling artist a month ago."

"Bring it right here."

The king left the room to comply with the saint's request, and returned with a carte-de-visite of the princess.

The saint took it. A spasm of pain passed across his face and he grew pale.

"So that's the princess, is it? No, I guess old fire-bellows can wait till tomorrow. Now what about the kingdom? Got the books handy?"

"The Accountant-General has them," said the king. "He will be happy to show them to you, we have no doubt. You will find them all right, we think."

"I guess I'll just step round and see the gentleman," said St George. "There's no hurry. If everything's satisfactory, I'll sail in and settle old blowhard tomorrow, and take over half the concern then."

The king had no objection. He directed the saint to the Accountant-General's house. "Sauerkrautstrasse," he said, "the third house. It's called 'Braeside'."

"It would be," said the saint. He put on his hat and the king let him out by the front door.

The Accountant-General was pleased to see his distinguished visitor. He had kept the books of the kingdom for many years, and had everything in apple-pie order. St George was the first of the applicants for the reward who had taken the precaution to form an estimate of what it might tot up to in pounds, shillings, and pence. He was closeted with the Accountant-General until late at night and went into every detail.

"Well," he said when the scrutiny was finished, "I guess there's money in it. It ain't been worked proper. That's going to begin tomorrow. What the firm wants is push, and I'm the man to make things hum."

He said good-night to the Accountant-General and went back to his hotel. He had declined the king's offer of a bed in the palace, thinking it as well not to make himself too cheap.

The next morning he unpacked a suit of armour and put it on. The livery stable supplied him with a charger at half a crown the first hour and two shillings an hour after that. The populace turned out to see him off, but he declined all offers of company and rode towards the swamp alone.

"I guess I'll give the old beast something for clearing out like that," he said to himself as he rode along. "But he'll be pleased to see his old master again. Kill him? Not quite. But I'll see that he don't break out again."

As he neared the swamp he caught sight of one solitary, blasted tree. It was the one to which the princess had been tied. Of her there was no sign, but at the foot of the tree was stretched the glittering form of the dragon.

Elijah P. Jopp, for St George was no other than that intrepid American, approached it with a beating heart, calling out the many endearing names he had given to his pet during the time of their companionship. The dragon slowly moved its scaly tail, but did not bound towards him as he had expected. Elijah's heart sank, and putting spurs to his horse he galloped up and dismounted at the foot of the tree. The dragon turned a fast-glazing eye upon him, and would have licked his hand if it had not been trained never to do so. It was plain that it would not live many minutes. Elijah threw himself on the ground in a passion of grief, and took its heavy head onto his lap.

Over that last harrowing scene a veil must be drawn. In a quarter of an hour Elijah rose again, and wiping away his tears mounted his horse and rode slowly back to Putzenheim, leaving the dragon dead on the grass. The poor beast had eaten the princess, and, in spite of its iron constitution, had succumbed to a severe fit of indigestion.

There was great rejoicing when St George rode into the city in all his glittering, bright array, and announced that the scourge of Dummeleutia had been slain by his hand. Nobody suspected the truth, and nobody grumbled because he had come too late to save the princess. She had not been popular, and all the eligible bachelors had gone about in fear and trembling as long as she was alive. Now they breathed freely. The deed of partnership between Elijah and the king was drawn up and signed the next day.

THE DRAGON DOCTOR'S APPRENTICE

Charles Partington

Charles Partington (b. 1940) has been involved in various aspects of science fiction and fantasy for nearly forty years. In 1963 he and Harry Nadler started an amateur magazine, Alien, *which, in 1966, they tried to convert into a professional publication,* Alien Worlds. *Lack of finances made it impossible to continue, although Partington had another attempt in 1980 with* Something Else, *a rather anarchic magazine that tried to pursue the revolution that Michael Moorcock had started in* New Worlds *some years earlier. By profession, Partington is a printer, but in the 1980s had success with developing new computer games. He has also sold several science fiction and horror stories, starting with "The Manterfield Inheritance" in 1971. The following story was specially written for this anthology.*

Kell was convinced that things couldn't get much worse. They were hurrying along a narrow ledge, with a dizzying descent down a snow-covered incline on one side and a steep wall of rock on the other. Behind them the howling of wolves was growing ever closer. At any moment the ravenous pack would be upon them.

Then Liss gasped in horror and came to a sudden halt. "Look!" She pointed at a set of huge footprints stamped deeply into the snow further along the ledge. The imprints of long flesh-rending claws could clearly be seen.

"What is it?" Tullo gasped, peering anxiously over the woman's shoulder.

"A Fo-Go," she said, trembling.

Tullo peered at her with that blank look so common amongst his family. "A what?"

"A Fo-Go . . . a Yeti!"

Kell, who was more worried about the wolves, pleaded with them to push on, but it was already too late. At that moment a nightmare creature came shambling around the corner.

The Fo-Go. It was at least nine feet tall. Its massive ape-like frame was covered in bristling white fur, but its hairless, wart-covered head, bulging eyes and horny-ridged slitted mouth called to mind a giant toad. Kell imagined he could see some kind of family resemblance to Tullo.

The Fo-Go lifted its powerful arms high above its head and let out a series of blaring croaks that grated on the freezing air. Behind Kell there was a slithering of paws in the snow and plaintive whimperings as the wolves came to a sudden halt. Hackles raised in fright, the entire pack instantly turned tail. Clambering over each other in their desperation to escape the Fo-Go, they fled, howling miserably, back along the path and out of sight.

The Fo-Go honked again, lowered its arm and reached out for Liss.

Suddenly aware that he was next in line, Tullo moaned and, in a fit of panic, turned and tried to scramble past Kell. Unfortunately the ledge was too narrow and the snow was inveterately slippy. Tullo lost his footing. Swaying out over the abyss, he grabbed hold of Kell and tried to regain his balance, clinging on for dear life. Kell struggled, but his feet went from under him and, entangled together, they slithered off the ledge.

"No!" Tullo screamed.

Liss opened her mouth to scream. They were all roped together and now she was about to be dragged down the incline with them.

But at that moment, the Fo-Go stamped a massive foot onto the unravelling rope. Tullo and Kell's slide was brought to a sudden bone-jarring halt. Liss heaved a sigh of relief.

Reaching down, the creature grasped the rope in its clawed hands and began hauling the man and boy back up to the ledge as easily as if they were no more than two sacks of feathers.

Blubbering like a child, Tullo gazed up at the Fo-Go. Kell fancied he could see a smile in its grimacing, pop-eyed face, though all Tullo focused on was the slobbering jaws. Before Kell could utter a protest the horrified man had whipped out a knife from his belt and slashed through the rope. In a glittering cloud of snow, the two of them started sliding and skidding helplessly down the incline. Down they went, picking up speed all the time, sometimes on their backs, sometimes face down, sometimes spinning round and round. As they dropped further into the valley and the fog thinned, Kell could see they were slithering down a snow-choked ravine, travelling as fast as if they had been riding toboggans.

Tullo was waving his arms so much he looked as if he was trying to fly. Kell was only too aware of the massive tree trunks and razor-edged rocks that whizzed past them on either side, threatening a fate worse than death. Kell kept his legs together just in case. It was then that the rope holding them together snagged on something sharp and parted with a musical twang. They shot over a rise and the ground dropped away beneath them. Kell closed his eyes as the branches of a tree came hurtling towards him. There was a furious snapping and cracking as twigs tore his clothes, and he came to rest twenty feet above the ground, clinging to a dipping and swaying branch, while flakes of powdery snow drifted down all around him. Then the branch snapped under his weight, depositing him comparatively gently on the mossy forest floor. Gingerly, Kell climbed to his feet, relieved to find that, apart from a few superficial scratches, he was okay. No bones were broken.

Liss was waiting for him.

He stared at her, amazed. "How did you get here?" he asked.

"The Fo-Go brought me," she told him.

"What?"

She smiled. "Yes. It can run as fast as the wind. We got here before you did. The creature's very friendly." She smiled as if in fond remembrance. "It only wanted to help. That's why it scared the wolves away. It couldn't understand why Tullo cut through the rope when it was about to pull you both to safety."

Kell raised his eyes to heaven but, still uncertain, looked around nervously. "Where is it now?" he asked.

Liss looked behind her. "Oh," she said, rather dejectedly. "It's gone. That's a shame. It was such a warm, cuddly creature. Maybe it's taken a dislike to Tullo."

"Where is Tullo?" Kell asked, wondering slightly at the look of carefree bliss that had passed over Liss's face.

She pointed to a deep snowdrift. Two furiously wriggling feet were sticking out of the top. Tullo was wedged in real tight. "There he is," she said.

Kell stared at the ludicrous sight and began laughing so hard he could barely get his breath. The boy's laughter was contagious and Liss couldn't help but join in. It was several minutes before they even thought about pulling him out.

Of course, Tullo was in a foul mood. He barely spoke, trudging along and simmering with pent-up violence. But even he became more animated when they emerged from the trees at the outskirts of a small town surrounded by a patchwork of neatly laid-out fields. To Tullo the lights spoke of only one thing.

"Taverns!" the big man muttered, licking his dribbling lips. "I can smell the beer already." Then he groaned. "We've no money!" Inevitably, as he always did, he took his frustration out on Kell. Without warning, he lashed out, sending the boy sprawling in the gutter. The dirty strips of cloth tied around Kell's head slipped down, revealing his eyes.

"Look," Tullo growled, nursing his knuckles, "that's the *real* reason we were thrown out of Albor; your sister's aberrant son. Pity he wasn't delivered dead so we could've buried 'im with his mother. Saved us a lot o' trouble, it would."

Liss sighed helplessly and helped the boy back to his feet. "You were equally to blame for us being driven out, Tullo," she reminded him. "All that drunken brawling and thieving. I warned you it would happen one day."

Tullo cursed and raised a fist to strike the woman, but something caught his eye. Instead of hitting her, he grabbed her by the arm and pulled her over to the front door of a house that was partly built into the hillside. A notice was pinned to the door. "Wot does that piece o' paper say, woman?" he demanded.

Liss shook herself free. She leaned closer in the dim light, frowning with difficulty as she struggled with some of the strange words.

Apprentice Required Urgently!
Young man to assist Dr Augustus Vem with the
Remedial Treatment of Helminthic, Ophiomorphic and
Reptant Forms. (Applicant must be fit and quick on his feet.)
Apply Within.
30 Crowns.

"Thirty crowns!" Tullo gasped. "Why, that's near enough a year's wages!" He wagged a finger at Kell. " 'Ere's your chance to learn a trade, young man, and earn me and the Missus a few coins in the process. Now cover your eyes again and stand up straight boy. I want you to make a good impression."

Sensing he was about to be sold into some kind of slavery, Kell began to back away, horrified, but Tullo grabbed him tightly by the ear and banged loudly on the door with his free hand.

After a couple of minutes a tall thin man opened the door and peered out. He had a long goatee beard and shoulder-length white hair and he seemed to be dressed entirely in black. "Yes?" he snapped, peering at them through a pair of wire-framed, thick-lensed spectacles, "What do you want?"

"Doctor Augustus Vem, is it?" Tullo asked, feigning respect.

"Yes . . . Yes. I'm Doctor Vem." He glared at them. "What do you want?"

"I've got that assistant you've been advertising for, sir," Tullo said, grinning. "Smart young lad. Ever so willin'. Ever so quick to learn, 'e is."

The old man peered out into the night, squinting myopically through his spectacles. "Assistant? Where? Not that scrawny little runt, is it?"

"Oh, very deceptive is our Kell, sir," Tullo snivelled. "Not much fat on 'im I'll agree, but the young lad's as 'ard as nails."

"Take him away, you fool. I can't use him."

"But sir . . . !"

"Goodnight!"

Tullo rammed his boot in the door as Dr Vem tried to slam it shut. "Wot if we were to say, p'r'aps, fifteen crowns?"

"I beg your pardon?" Dr Vem expostulated.

"Ten, then?" Tullo suggested, getting desperate. "I'll take ten at a push."

Dr Vem glared disbelievingly at the ragged, smelling figure hovering expectantly outside his front door. "You want *me* to pay *you*?"

"Well . . ." Tullo sniffed. "Your advert did say thirty crowns, sir."

"Fool! That's what *you* have to pay *me*. It's a charge against the assistant's education and upkeep. Boys do eat, don't they? Now, get your foot out of my door so I can get back to my work."

Tullo groaned. A year of utter paradise, just drinking and loafing around, had been snatched away from him. His face crumpled in despair and, he turned to glare at his wife. "This boy's bad luck, Liss. We should never have brought 'im with us. 'E's a jinx, that's wot 'e is! A bloody jinx!" He gave Kell another heavy-handed smack across the head that sent him staggering to his knees in the road. Again the rags slipped down from his eyes and the boy lay sprawled in the mud, staring mutely up at him.

Dr Vem gasped. "The boy's eyes . . ." he murmured incredulously.

"Yes," Tullo said dispiritedly. "Awful innit. 'E must be

some kind o' throwback. Bad blood in that side of the family if you ask me. I mean, 'ave you ever seen anything like it? One eye red and the other green. And look, sir, they glow in the dark. Work of the Devil. Has to be."

But Dr Vem was digging frantically in his coat pockets. He pulled out a fistful of heavy gold coins. "Here!" he snapped. "Take that. All of it. There must be at least sixty crowns there."

"What?" Tullo's expression was one of total amazement. "You *still* want the boy?"

"Yes!" Augustus Vem barked, thrusting the coins into Tullo's filthy hands. "Sixty crowns! Is that enough? Have we got a deal?"

"A deal?" A bemused grin slowly began to spread across Tullo's heavy-jowled, unshaven face. "Oh, that we 'ave, sir. That we 'ave indeed."

"No!" Liss protested angrily. "It's not fair! Give him the money back, you beast!"

But before Kell properly understood what was happening, Dr Vem had grabbed him by the wrist, dragged the sack off his shoulders and pulled him inside the house. The sound of the door slamming shut behind them reverberated like distant thunder and the piece of paper advertising for an assistant fluttered unnoticed to the ground.

When the front door banged shut, Kell recovered his wits sufficiently to start yelling blue murder. Kicking and scratching, he tried to wriggle out of Dr Vem's grasp, but it proved impossible. Though his will was still strong, Kell's muscles had no strength left in them after being half-frozen and all but starved of food for days during their debilitating march across the mountains.

Dr Vem dragged him across a wide hallway lit by the guttering flames of oil-lamps. Unlocking another door, he thrust Kell into a small room, then closed and locked the door again, before limping away without uttering another word.

Kell surveyed his prison, for that's what it was. He could see immediately that escape was impossible. The heavy door was securely locked, the walls were built of solid stone, and what little light there was came filtering dimly into the room through a series of small holes high up in the walls. Even if he could reach them they were too small for him to wriggle through. The only item of furniture was a straw-filled mattress covered by rough woollen blankets.

Kell slumped down on the mattress, struggling to fight off the waves of self-pity and desperation that were threatening to overwhelm him. It wasn't that difficult. All his short life he had been subjected to abuse and ill-treatment. He'd had no real friends in Albor. The village adults had shunned him and the kids of his own age either taunted him mercilessly or ganged up on him to give him a beating. As a result, Kell had become solitary by nature. He had learned to endure, to expect only the worst from life and everyone around him. Only Liss had ever shown him friendship and compassion. She was the one person in his wretched life he'd been able to depend on. Now even she was gone and Tullo had sold him into servitude. His future looked bleaker than ever.

A great sob convulsed his shoulders and his lower lip trembled. But he refused to cry. Tears had never got him anywhere. He lay down on the mattress and closed his eyes. Almost immediately, waves of tiredness began to wash over him.

But before sleep could claim him, there was a loud rattle of bolts, the door was thrown open, and Dr Vem entered. The room was suddenly filled with a delicious mouth-watering aroma. "I thought you might be hungry," he said. He stooped over and placed a wooden tray beside the mattress. "A bowl of stew and a crust of bread."

Kell nodded silently.

After Dr Vem had left again, Kell sat up and began wolfing down the food, burning his lips on the hot stew, tearing at the bread with trembling fingers. He ate every scrap and drop. Then, sinking his head back onto the mattress, he wriggled into the warm blankets. A few minutes later, as he hovered, half-dreaming on the edge of sleep, he thought he heard a series of terrible echoing roars emanating from somewhere deep within the earth, the cries and wailings of unimaginable beasts. Kell shivered, turned over, then slept.

Before dawn, Dr Vem quietly opened the door and poked his head into the room. He could just make out the shape of his new charge snoring soundly on the mattress. But the boy was no longer alone. Snuggled beside him were four small dragons. They lifted their scaly heads to survey the doctor, flapped their tiny wings and hissed out warnings. Their green and red eyes gleamed luminously in the dimness of the room.

Dr Augustus Vem quietly closed the door.

"Well I'll be damned," he said, chuckling.

Kell had no idea how long he had slept but it felt like many hours. He struggled to sit up, stretching his arms and legs with difficulty, groaning as his stiff joints cracked and his muscles protested. Suddenly his eyes jerked open and his body became bathed in a cold sweat of fear.

Now he knew what had awakened him. Something was in the bed with him.

Rats? Kell almost let out a betraying scream. Instinctively he drew his knees up under his chin, shivering with alarm as he saw a hump moving about under the disarrayed blankets. His eyes bulged. Three or four shapes were crawling about down there. The heat of his sleeping body must have attracted them.

Kell had an understandable hatred of rats. At certain times of the year, Albor became infested with hundreds of the disease-carrying creatures, rats as big as small dogs and fearlessly aggressive. They killed chickens and piglets, even calves. Children were often attacked by the swarming rodents if left unattended. And once bitten, it was not uncommon for death to follow within hours.

Kell knew that any sudden movement could provoke the rats. He looked for something to defend himself with as the bumps crawled closer to his tucked-in feet. All he could see was the empty metal dish Dr Vem had brought the soup in. As he slowly reached out to pick it up he saw a blur of movement as two of the creatures emerged from under the blankets and went scuttling across the floor and up the wall, disappearing through one of the apertures. So that was how they'd got in.

Taking hold of the heavy soup dish, Kell raised it high above his head, intently following the motion of the remaining creatures as they burrowed through the bedclothes, emitting curious whistling and chattering cries. When they came to a momentary halt, Kell got ready to bring the dish crashing down on them with all the strength he could muster!

It was then that Dr Vem opened the door and came limping into the room. A look of anguish contorted his dour aesthetic face when he saw what Kell was preparing to do. "No!" he cried. "In the name of the Triple Suns, put the dish down, boy!"

"But the rats!" Kell exclaimed.

"Rats?" Augustus Vem echoed, puzzled. "Where?"

"There!" Kell said, pointing to the shape that had started humping about again.

Dr Vem grabbed a corner of the blankets, dragging them off the bed with a mighty heave. "Not rats, boy," he yelled. "Dragons!"

Kell's jaw dropped open in amazement. He couldn't believe what he was looking at. There, cowering at the bottom of the straw mattress, were two small, incredible creatures.

Kell had never seen anything like them before. The bigger of the two creatures was about nine inches long from the tip of its tapering snout to the end of its furiously lashing barbed tail. The smaller animal was less than half that size. They were both covered in overlapping greenish iridescent scales. They had four legs that ended in clawed feet, bat-like leathery wings and heads that reminded Kell of the grass lizards and terrapins that baked themselves on the rocks in high summer back in Albor. Then Kell noticed their eyes; and this was what really shocked him. Both of the creatures had one red eye and one green eye, just like his. And, he observed, nictitating membranes that wiped sideways across the eyeball – again, just like his.

Dragons?

The soup dish fell from his nerveless fingers with a loud clatter onto the stone floor and the tiny creatures leapt off the mattress and scampered across the floor. Chittering in alarm, they raced up the wall and vanished through one of the barred apertures.

"Dragons," Augustus Vem repeated. He coughed. "Am I to understand that you, of all people, have never seen such creatures before?"

The expression of bewilderment on Kell's face was sufficient answer.

"I see . . ." It was Dr Vem's turn to look puzzled. "Can you tell me something about your parents, Kell?" he asked.

Pain flooded across the boy's face. "I never knew my mother," he answered reluctantly. "She died shortly after I was born. My aunt Liss, who brought me up, told me she was very beautiful . . ."

Dr Vem nodded. "What about your father?"

Kell was silent for a moment. "I never knew him. And Liss never talked about him. But the villagers said . . ." The boy looked suddenly uncomfortable.

"Said what, Kell?"

"That my father was some kind of monster – that he was different from ordinary men. They said that his eyes were like mine but that he was different in other ways too."

Dr Vem waited for a moment; then he said, "One last question?"

The boy shrugged.

"Did the villagers know where your father came from?" the doctor asked.

Kell's shoulders slumped. "My father lives in the sky. Everyone in Albor knows that."

Dr Vem's bushy eyebrows arched in surprise and he nodded sagely. Then, placing a bundle of clothes on the bed, he said, "I've brought these for you, Kell. They belonged to Jed. Nothing special, but better than the rags you're wearing."

Kell stared at them suspiciously. "Who's Jed?" he asked.

"Well." Dr Vem coughed. "Jed used to be my apprentice. A very strong-willed boy he was, always teasing the dragons, always playing what he called his little tricks on them. I warned him to stop. I was afraid something bad would come of it. But he just grinned and persisted . . ."

"What happened to him?"

Dr Vem looked decidedly embarrassed. "I'm afraid that one of the larger dragons . . . how shall I put it . . . ate him."

"What?"

The doctor nodded. "It was dreadful. Heaven knows what his parents will say if they ever come back. But I don't think they will. They were glad enough to have Jed indentured. I don't think there was much love lost between them." Dr Vem placed the bundle of clothes on the mattress. "You may as well make use of them. He certainly won't be needing them any more." He paused for a moment before shutting the door. "I'll be in my workroom at the end of the corridor. When you're ready I'll show you around the place and explain some of your new duties."

Kell didn't move for a minute or two after the doctor left. A boy had been eaten! That was terrible. What kind of place was this? A distant spine-tingling roar came echoing through the apertures. Kell glanced up and shivered. He was going to escape from this madhouse at the first opportunity he got.

Jed's clothes were warm and serviceable if a bit too loose around the waist. Kell tightened the leather belt to its last notch before opening the door and peering up and down the corridor. To his right was the locked and bolted front door, to his left was the open door of Dr Vem's workroom. Kell stepped out into the hall and began to creep towards the front door. If he could just reach it, maybe somehow he could get it open, and . . .

"Ah, there you are, Kell!" Dr Vem was standing behind him, beckoning with a crooked finger. "Ready to get started . . . ?"

That first morning Kell got only a vague impression of how far into the hillside Dr Vem's house extended. The neat corridor of richly carved wooden panelling quickly became a dark damp tunnel, hewn out of the solid rock, along which a faint breeze was blowing. Kell tried to remember everything he saw, every turning, every junction, in the hope that it would aid any attempt at escape he made.

Dr Vem seemed to be able to read his thoughts. "I wouldn't advise you to go wandering about on your own down here, young man. It's easy to get lost. And there's the dragons . . ."

A number of times, Kell thought he had sensed things go rushing past in the shadows, accompanied by the furious beating of leathery wings. They even whizzed around his head several times before shooting off again.

"Just some of the small dragons," Dr Vem explained. "They appear to have taken quite an interest in you. Word of your arrival will be spreading like wildfire amongst the swarm." He brandished the torch higher, illuminating a series of gloomy openings in the tunnel walls, the entrances to large cells. "Here we are, Kell. Time to start work."

"What?" Kell grimaced doubtfully.

"Oh, there's no need to worry," Dr Vem chuckled. "None of these pens are occupied at the moment. My patients are in another wing. But these do badly need mucking out. You can do that for me, can't you?"

"Mucking out . . . ?" Kell questioned.

"That's right." The doctor thrust a rusty shovel into his hands. "You can make a start filling those . . ."

Kell stared. Dr Vem was pointing at a large mound of empty sacks piled up in a rickety wooden wheelbarrow. Stepping carefully into the cell, the doctor took down a lantern hanging from a wall bracket. The damp wick fizzed and crackled when he lit it. The scene brightened considerably as the flame steadied. "There, plenty of light now," he said, placing it back on its hook.

Kell peered uncertainly into the echoing gloom. After the cramped, low-roofed tunnel, the cell seemed enormous. Shimmering spears of translucent stone dripped a slow rain from the high ceiling. The floor was buried in a thick, putrid black ooze. Everywhere, blurred and overlapping sets of clawed footprints were stamped deeply in this foul-smelling dung. Here and there a series of sharp furrows revealed where a heavy spiked tail had rested.

Glancing from the clawed footprints to his own feet, Kell tried to calculate the difference. He began to feel uneasy. "How big do these dragons grow?" he asked at last.

"Oh, quite big . . ." the doctor conceded.

"Very big?" Kell pressed.

Dr Vem nodded. "Yes . . . very big." He began limping back down the tunnel. "I'll see you in an hour."

"An hour?" Kell groaned.

"Not long enough?" the doctor asked, completely misinterpreting Kell's complaint. "I suppose you're right – that muck must be a couple of feet deep. I'll make it three hours, then."

As the doctor's footsteps grew fainter, Kell sighed and tentatively pressed the tip of his shovel through the hard crust that had formed on the manure. A stench of epic intensity assailed the boy's nostrils. Coughing and retching, he backed away, appalled. Tears streamed from his eyes. Even the flame in the lantern flared up, momentarily changing colour to a sickly blue. Kell threw down the shovel. Right, he decided, that was enough. That was all the digging he was going to do! Dr Vem may have decided that he was here to work – Kell's only priority was finding a way out of this unpleasant place.

Just a few steps away from the lantern's glow, the tunnel was inky black. Rather than run the risk of bumping into Dr Vem again, Kell decided to explore the sloping tunnel in the other direction. As the darkness closed in around him, he kept the fingers of his outstretched hands in contact with both sides of the narrow tunnel. He had covered only a few paces, when the hairs began to rise up on the back of his neck. Intuitively he sensed danger, sensed that something was blocking the tunnel ahead. Something was waiting, crouched in the darkness. Now he could hear its slow, bellows-like breathing. Then two eyes opened, eyes as big as dinner plates, one red, the other green. A dragon. Its jaws gaped in the gloom, its glistening fangs reflected faint glimmers of light from the distant lantern. Then it roared a warning.

In the confined space the noise was deafening. Kell let out a shriek of pain, clapped both hands over his ears, then fled, terrified, back up the tunnel as the creature lurched after him. The pounding of its feet seemed to shake the tunnel walls and Kell expected at any moment to feel its immense jaws ripping his flesh as it gulped him down.

Knowing that he couldn't hope to outrun the dragon for long, Kell ducked back inside the cell, hoping desperately that the creature's momentum would carry it on past. No such luck. The dragon dug its claws in and came to a slithering halt right outside the entrance.

Knowing he was well and truly trapped, and fearing that his end had come, Kell retreated through the stinking ooze to the far wall. But the dragon stayed outside the cell. With a grunt, it sank belly down, lowering its lizard-like head between its outstretched claws, watching him as carefully as a collie watches an errant sheep or a lion surveys its shivering prey. Every time Kell even threatened to make a move towards the entrance, the dragon lifted its head and let out a low rumbling growl of displeasure, exposing its fearsome teeth in a menacing grin.

Kell got the message.

This dragon wasn't going to let him go anywhere.

Always pragmatic, Kell probed resignedly around in the muck until his fingers closed around the shaft of the shovel. He pulled it out and started work. The stench was appalling. The dragon half-closed its eyes and began making contented, low rumbling sounds. Kell could have sworn the beast was purring . . .

When Augustus Vem returned several hours later, Kell had got the cell cleaned out, right down to the hard stone floor. In the process he had become thoroughly caked and spattered with the foul stuff. He looked a truly sorry sight. Sacks filled with the wet dung were piled up in one corner three or four high.

Dr Vem scratched the dragon behind its ears before shooing it out of the way. He smiled at the bedraggled boy.

"Right, come on, Kell," he said, grinning. "We'd better get you cleaned up now."

"Where are we going?" Kell asked tiredly.

"Just follow me and I'll show you." The doctor placed a handkerchief over his nose. "But Kell: not *too* closely, please?"

They set off down the tunnel with the dragon ambling behind.

As they followed the twisting tunnel deeper into the hillside, a confused babble of noise, at first not much louder than a whisper, grew into a tumult. The noise reached its zenith after they negotiated a sharp corner and emerged suddenly into a large cavern. The roof of this natural chamber rose up more than a thousand feet and a small central opening allowed a view of the sky and a sprinkle of distant stars. Stretching out before them, beyond a strip of rocky beach, was a lake of continually agitated water. Bubbles of hot gases both large and small were constantly rising to the surface of the churning water. Out near the middle of the lake, directly beneath the opening, hissing tongues of fire erupted from deep in the boiling submarine depths, giving off brilliant flashes and sparks and sending up dense columns of writhing smoke.

But as strange and unexpected as this subterranean volcanic lake was, Kell's astonished eyes were focused on the many dragons swimming or just floating lazily in the heated waters of the chemical lake. More dragons were lounging on the salt-encrusted shore. Apparently unaffected by the gouting flames or the near-boiling water, four massive beasts floated serenely out in the middle. When one of them slowly stretched its wings, Kell's mouth fell open in disbelief. There were many small dragons too, skimming this way and that like kingfishers above the waves. Kell could see that the dragons fell into several distinct types. Some seemed more related to wriggling winged snakes, others were massively muscled and heavy of body with powerful claws and terrible fangs. Some had brightly coloured scales, while others were monotonous shades of drab grey or green. Kell even saw a dragon that was a dazzling translucent white. But every dragon he saw had the same eye colourings: one red, the other green. Just like him.

Two of the smaller dragons, about the size of magpies, came swooping over to look at Kell, setting up an excited screeching as they flashed past on thrumming wings only inches from his nose. Then, excitedly, they darted back out across the lake again to communicate the news of their discovery to the rest of the dragons. The water now swelled in waves as the larger creatures came swimming towards the narrow strip of beach where Kell and Dr Vem were standing and the air swirled in mini-vortices as the rest came winging in. Within a few minutes almost all of the dragons had gathered on the beach, straining and jostling to get as close to Kell as possible. Fearing he was about to get crushed in the stampede, the boy tried to back away, but Dr Vem grabbed him by the shoulders.

"It's all right, Kell," he shouted. "They're just curious. They won't harm you. It's your eyes; they're as puzzled about you as I am!"

The four largest dragons had remained floating out in the centre of the lake, as if disdaining to take part in the flurry of interest surrounding the arrival of Kell. Now, suddenly, they began flapping their immense wings while running across the water in the fashion of geese or swans, struggling to get their heavy bodies airborne. Finally making the transition to effortless skimming flight, all four went soaring upward in slow circles towards the opening high above. One of them turned its head and looked down, emitting a haunting reverberating call.

Immediately, the dragons clustering ever closer around Kell jerked their heads upwards, responding in a medley of excited whoops and whistles, before launching themselves into the air like a flock of startled birds. Within seconds they were disappearing through the opening.

But one dragon was left standing disconsolately on the rocky shore, shaking its ancient leathery head from side to side, while staring mournfully up into the empty air. Kell recognized it immediately. It was the same dragon that had watched over him all morning.

"Why does he not fly with the others?" the boy asked, feeling a sudden pang of pity for the sorrowful beast.

"He cannot," Dr Vem answered. "Olm came to me with torn wing ligaments more than two years ago now. I repaired the physical damage but, for some reason, he has been unwilling even to attempt to fly. I'm beginning to suspect that he may never use his wings again."

"The others will come back?" Kell asked, glancing up at the opening in the rocks.

Dr Vem nodded. "When they are ready. Though some never return, newcomers always take their place."

"Where do they fly to?" the boy wondered out loud.

"That's enough chattering for one day, Kell," the doctor snapped abrasively. "I've got work to do. Olm will look after you while you're here, but a word of warning. When you enter the water stay close to the edge. Further out, both the temperature and the mineral concentrations can rise to dangerously high levels. So be careful. Olm will let you know when it's time to start back."

Kell waited until Dr Vem had limped back into the shadows of the tunnel before walking down to the water's edge. Kicking off his shoes, he waded out a few steps. The water *was* warm. Very warm. It had been days since he'd last bathed and that had been in a near-freezing river up in the mountains. By contrast, this felt wonderful. When the water reached up to his chest, Kell spread his arms and just floated. The water tingled, sending pleasant little shocks through his skin. The fatigue in his muscles was gradually massaged away by the swirling, bubbling currents, replaced by a sense of glowing well-being. Olm surfaced beside him, water streaming from his lizard head, blinking his enigmatic eyes and wiggling his rudimentary ears. Then he rolled his great body and submerged again, coming up playfully beneath the boy and lifting him clear of the water. Kell yelled in delight. For a while they cavorted and plunged around, then, growing tired, Kell left the water and found a shelf of rock overgrown by a carpet of soft moss. After laying his clothes out to dry, he stretched out on the ledge and rested. Within minutes he was asleep.

Some time later he was nudged into a state of surprised wakefulness by Olm, whose energetic proddings with his scaly nose almost shoved the boy right off the ledge. "Hey, lay off there!" Kell complained sleepily. The dragon opened its jaws and deposited the boy's clothes at his feet. The message was obvious. It was time to go.

After Kell had dressed, Olm anxiously herded the boy back up the tunnel, snorting and exposing its fangs whenever Kell tried to explore any of the side tunnels they frequently encountered. A bobbing light advancing towards them eventually turned out to be Dr Vem carrying a lantern.

"Where *have* you been, Kell? I was beginning to suspect something had gone wrong . . ." Obviously irritated, Dr Vem reached out and gave Olm a painful rap on his tapering snout. The dragon hissed threateningly and made the faintest of lunges towards the doctor. Then it spun around, squeezing Kell up against the hard tunnel wall as it slithered past him on its way back to the lake.

Dr Vem was unmoved. "Right, follow me, Kell, we've got work to do."

"What kind of work?" the boy asked, struggling to get his breath back.

"A little case of infestation control," the doctor responded tetchily.

Kell heard a plaintive roaring up ahead. "I thought all the dragons, apart from Olm, had flown away," Kell said.

"Several remain," Augustus Vem answered. "Those most in need of treatment."

In a circular cell with a sunken stone floor, a miserable-looking dragon was waiting for them. Its wedge-shaped head drooped listlessly and its forked stubby tail writhed despairingly from side to side. As Kell watched, the dragon started scratching. In fact, it never really stopped scratching. The rattling of its claws through its scales sounded like hail bouncing off the leaves of a ticcari tree.

"What's wrong with it?" the boy asked.

"Fleas," Dr Vem answered. "Dragon fleas. It's your job to get rid of them."

"How do I do that?"

"First," the doctor said, moving his lantern close to something that looked like a collection of fishing nets hanging from a hook on the wall, "you put these on."

"What for?" A perplexed expression haunted the boy's face.

"Your protection," Augustus Vem responded.

The fishing nets turned out to be a pair of leggings, a long-sleeved jerkin, a pair of boots and a helmet all woven out of stiff wire, the loops of which were so small that the point of a sharp knife could not have been inserted through them.

Reluctantly, Kell pulled them on. Even through his thick woollen trousers and shirt, the heavy metal garments chafed and nipped his skin. Kell was less than impressed. "Are these *really* necessary, Doctor?" he asked, sighing.

Dr Vem nodded. "You do want to live, don't you?"

A rusting, broad-bladed knife that resembled a machete, and an iron lever, curved at one end, hung from another hook. Dr Vem lifted them down, then handed the machete to Kell. Approaching the dragon, which was watching all this with long-suffering, dull eyes, the doctor said, "Now get ready with that blade, Kell!"

"Why, what's going to happen?" Kell asked.

"You'll see." Approaching the dragon's flank, the doctor inserted the curved tip of the lever under the rear edge of one of its scales. He applied pressure and slowly the scale lifted. Nothing else happened for a second or two, then something about the size of a fat cockroach but with more legs scurried out from underneath the scale.

"Kill it!" Dr Vem yelled.

Kell whacked the flat side of the blade down onto the parasite. Blood and matter spurted out from the bloated insect.

"Hey," Kell beamed, pleased with himself and staring at the remains of the squashed corpse, "that wasn't so bad."

"*That*," Dr Vem cautioned with a shake of his head, "was a little one . . ."

"A little one?" Kell said disbelievingly.

The doctor nodded. "The biggest can reach the size of a chicken. You've got to watch all of them, regardless of size, but the big ones are the worst. Vicious as small tigers they are, more cunning than weasels, faster than hares. Got to watch out you don't get bitten. Those devils can suck a couple of pints of blood out of you in as many seconds. Drain you dry in a minute."

He handed Kell the iron lever.

"Right, there'll be a meal waiting for you when you've finished here. So don't take too long." He turned to leave.

Kell took a deep breath. He wasn't at all happy about this. "How will I know when I've finished?" he asked. "There must be hundreds of scales on this dragon – if I have to look under every one, I'll be down here for days."

Dr Vem nodded reassuringly. "The dragon will let you know when your work is done. Just check beneath the scales he scratches; that's where the most irritating areas of infestation are. The smaller fleas don't seem to worry them."

After Dr Vem left, Kell just stood around sulking. Mucking out the slurry had been bad enough, but at least that stuff had only smelled bad. This job sounded as if it was going to be physically dangerous. Avoiding contact with the dragon's tortured gaze, Kell slowly began to slink out of the cell. He didn't get very far. Olm had returned. He had hunkered down right across the only way out.

Kell laboured at this awful task for nearly all of that afternoon. Most times it was the smaller varieties of fleas he disturbed. Usually five or six of the little wretches would go scurrying off in various directions, looking to re-establish themselves under the nearest suitable scale. Kell could never get all of them, but three or four would end up as messy stains beneath the flat of his blade. Yes, he thought, he was getting the hang of this quite nicely. It appeared that Dr Vem's warning to be careful had been somewhat exaggerated. There was really nothing to this business.

Then he encountered one of the larger specimens.

The creature came out in a mad rush, totally surprising Kell. Making a prodigious jump, the insect clamped itself around his left ankle. The boy felt a stab of pain as the insect inserted its proboscis into his skin, penetrating deep into his flesh. Immediately the revolting creature started sucking and Kell could feel the blood being drawn out of his flesh. He screamed in revulsion and reduced the flea to a shapeless, pulped mush with a single swing of the heavy lever.

Handling one of the chicken-sized fleas was difficult enough, but Kell got himself in really deep trouble when suddenly he was faced with trying to dispose of five of the larger parasites. To save time and effort, Kell had adopted the practice of sliding the iron bar under several of the dragon's scales, flipping them all open with one movement of the bar. It appeared that Kell had uncovered a nest of the fleas on one of the dragon's flanks, for suddenly maybe a dozen of the little parasites were dashing away in all directions. More worrying were the creatures that emerged after them. Kell's jaw dropped when he saw them and a little bit of panic set in. These appeared to be fleas of a different type. They had alternating bands of yellow and black running around their swollen bodies and intense staring eyes on the ends of constantly quivering stalks. They were obviously irritated about being disturbed and he soon learned that their intelligence matched their ferocity. They headed straight for him, leaping out and scuttling across the stone floor of the cell as Kell instinctively backed away. Olm's snoozing bulk was blocking the only way out of the cell, and the dragon he was de-fleaing looked at him with dull cow-like eyes, offering no help at all. He ran around to the other side of the dragon, hoping that maybe, if the fleas lost sight of him, like goldfish they'd immediately forget all about him. But they were far too smart for that. Warbling angrily, all five of them set off in pursuit. Running flat out, Kell could just about stay ahead of them. The iron bar was still wedged under the dragon's scales and the machete went spinning out of his fingers when he almost tripped headlong over the dragon's tail on his sixth circuit of the cell. He didn't dare slow down to try and retrieve it. Every time he passed Olm, he gave the beast a kick and yelled loudly, trying to wake him up but the dragon's upper lip just curled slightly and he carried on snoring.

Leaning up against the back wall were two wooden brooms. Kell grabbed them as he ran past and, one in each hand, he began flailing them around and beating madly at the fleas, which curled up like hedgehogs and rolled away, only to come charging back at him. He was horrified when a flea leapt onto one of the brooms and started chewing its way up the handle to reach him, splintering the wood as if it had been a matchstick. Kell dropped both of the brooms with a shriek and turned to run again, but by then a flea had circled round the back and attacked him from behind. Its proboscis was wedged firmly in the rear of the boy's wire leggings. Unable to either drag itself free or stab through to his skin, the insect was screaming with frustration as it was dragged along behind him.

Then, as the largest of the fleas made a prodigious leap straight at Kell's head, a stream of something wet and sticky jetted past the boy, splattering the insect and knocking it out of the air. Covered in a phlegm-like liquid that hissed like acid on the stone floor, the insect dropped to the floor and lay writhing on its back, piping piteously. Within seconds it was dead.

Kell turned his head to see where this jet of burning liquid had come from. Olm was awake and had seen the danger he was in. He had to duck his head hurriedly to avoid being doused by a second glob of projectile saliva.

Thrown into a frenzy of terror by this occurrence, the remaining fleas fled in all directions, scrabbling up the walls and even running across the ceiling, desperately searching for a way out. But to no avail. More jets of the acid spit arced through the air. Splat! Splat! Splat! Within seconds all the fleas were lying on the floor, dead or dying, even the one stuck in Kell's wire leggings. Its body had shrivelled up and fallen away, leaving the horny proboscis dangling uselessly. Kell picked up the machete and sliced it free, kicking it into a corner with a shudder. He glanced at Olm. His guardian seemed to be sleeping again, though perhaps the lid covering its green eye was not quite fully closed.

Eventually, the dragon that had been infested with fleas seemed happy enough with Kell's efforts. It was no longer scratching any of its scales and had perked up considerably. Swinging its head round on its long neck, the creature nuzzled him playfully then opened its jaws. Something that gleamed a rich yellow in the lamplight dropped into the boy's hand. Kell stared at the object in amazement: it was a heavy gold ring of exquisite workmanship. Kell had seen nothing like it, not even on the fingers of Sagg, Albor's headman. It had to be worth a small fortune. The boy shrugged and slipped it into his pocket. He'd tell Dr Vem about it, of course, though he wished he could offer it to Liss as a present. She'd never had anything valuable to call her own.

Kell took the opportunity to sneak out of the cell unobserved while Olm and the other dragon were conversing in a mixture of highly stylized head movements and low grunts and growls. As he stepped into the corridor that led to the hall, the boy's heart leapt excitedly. The entrance door to the street was standing ajar. Sunlight came streaming in and a breeze of fresh air, wonderful after the musty stench of the tunnels, wafted gently towards him. Kell could scarcely believe his luck. With all his thoughts focused on escape, he took a deep breath and started to run.

Five paces he completed. Then something large, powerful and growling went hurtling past him so fast that it was just a blur of motion. Kell was jostled to the ground. Rubbing a cracked elbow, the boy looked up.

Olm was crouched in front of the open door, his eyes glittering, his mouth agape and drooling. Warning growls rumbled deep within its throat. Kell's shoulders slumped in despair. Sighing in resignation, he walked back along the corridor and knocked on Dr Vem's workroom door. There was no answer but the door swung open on squealing hinges. Kell looked inside.

Why, not even the theurgist's hut in Albor, with all its weird talismans and amulets, compared with this! The walls were lined from floor to ceiling with strong wooden shelving. Heavy tables took up most of the available floor space. Bottles, jars and ceramic pots of all shapes and sizes were stacked haphazardly on the stained racking. Some contained unidentifiable liquids, several were filled with coloured powders, others had residues of glittering crystals or sticky waxes in them. Kell tried to read the faded, badly scribbled labels: banewort, larkspur, anion, spruce oil, corn crackle, jequirity, glycerine. He frowned. Some he recognized as poisons, others as physics. There was collyrium, luminal and ptisan; many preparations he'd never even heard of, but whose scents and odours seemed oddly familiar. One section was entirely taken up with randomly stacked boxes and cartons of pills and tablets. Heaped on the tables and across the floor were carboys, ewers, metal pails and wooden flasks filled with exotic chemicals and fluids. Kell sniffed cautiously at one of these, only to recoil, spluttering and gasping for breath.

At the back of this cluttered workroom was another door that led into a well-lit, comfortable study: a room with elaborately carved bookcases filled with ancient books, manuscripts, enchiridions and bound volumes of incunabula. Clay tablets impressed with cuneiform text and papyrus leaves

decorated with hieroglyphics hung on the walls next to imaginative maps and projections of the Unexplored Regions. It
was a scholar's room. And Kell was impressed. Not with the
books and the maps, but with the platters and trays of cold
meats, cheeses, slices of rich black bread, cakes and sweetmeats laid out on a central table. But then he hadn't eaten all
day and Dr Vem had told him a meal would be ready. Kell was
salivating furiously at the sight of this tempting feast. Perhaps
he could try just a small slice of that delicious ham or a crumb
of cheese while he was waiting? Maybe even a morsel of
chicken? Kell immediately started shovelling food into his
mouth with the wild abandon of a starving man, and gulping
down draughts of strong red wine from the silver-chased
decanters.

Then the door was thrown open and Augustus Vem limped
into the room.

Kell, his cheeks bulging like a hamster's, spun round,
coughing and blushing guiltily.

"Started eating already, have we, young man?" the doctor
observed dryly.

Kell's mouth was so full he could only manage a few
incoherent grunts.

"No matter!" The doctor disposed of the episode with a
casual wave of his hands. "It's sensible to keep your strength
up. We've still got a couple of tasks to complete before I leave
for Zellusar, tonight . . ."

"What's the matter with you, boy, are you going deaf? Yes,
that's exactly what I said, we're going to extract a dragon's
tooth!"

"What?" Kell was now more convinced than ever that
Augustus Vem was quite mad. He tried to back away, but
succeeded only in colliding with a rickety section of shelving.
Pots wobbled and threatened to fall. Dust descended in
clouds.

"Oh, come come!" Dr Vem chided with exasperation. "It's
a minor medical procedure with very little risk attached to it.
I don't know what you're getting so worked up about." The
doctor consulted a list he was carrying. "Now, what else do

we need? Of course! Grab that jack over by the wall, will you?"

"Jack?" Kell repeated, looking around him, dumbfounded.

"Don't tell me you don't know what a jack is? How primitive *was* your village?" Augustus Vem sent a mute prayer skywards. "Look, that's a jack there, see, that geared rack and pinion device, the thing with wheels and little steps cut into them. Even nominally advanced societies use them for lifting heavy weights . . ." The doctor shook his head. He could see he was wasting his breath.

"Oh, you mean this thing!" Kell picked up the strange mechanical device, adding it to the coiled length of sisal and the large pair of pliers he was carrying.

"That's it, Kell," the doctor muttered with a sigh. "Now one final item, then we've got everything." Moving further along the racking, he paused opposite a shelf of narrow-necked bottles labelled "SOMNIFICS".

Carefully he ran his index finger along the bottles. "Morphine? Laudanum? No . . . Extract of lotus? Well perhaps . . . Kef? Hmm . . . not strong enough, I fear." He selected a small purple bottle, shook it and held it closer to the lamp. "Yes, here we are, essence of nepthene. That should do the trick." Heading towards the door, he turned and said, "Now come along, Kell, this shouldn't take long . . ."

The dragon was big. *Very* big.

Its mouth was enormous.

Its teeth were gigantic.

And it was obviously in a lot of pain.

"It's only noise, Kell," Augustus Vem told the trembling boy after a second spate of agonized roaring had echoed into silence off the damp stone walls. "This dragon's a big softie. Most of the larger dragons are carnivores. They're easy to identify. They have sharp spines growing along their tails, triangular helmet crests and huge central and lateral incisors; makes them really fierce-looking. This specimen's definitely a herbivore. Nothing for you to worry about at all."

"What's a herbivore?" Kell asked, wondering if there was a way out that wasn't guarded by Olm.

"A herbivore is a plant-eater, a very placid type of dragon. They don't eat meat, any kind of meat, *especially* not people. So you see, there's really nothing to worry about. What can go wrong?"

Kell stared at him, concerned. That was the second time the doctor had told him there was no need for him to worry. And that was worrying.

Dr Vem calmly took the bottle of nepthene out of his coat pocket, unscrewed the cap, walked close to the dragon's snout, and emptied half the contents onto the end of its flickering forked tongue. "Now get ready with that jack, Kell. We're going to need it in . . ." he glanced at his pocket watch, ". . . three and a half minutes."

They waited.

In two minutes the dragon yawned sleepily for the first time.

By the end of the third minute it had yawned a second time. Its movements were becoming sluggish, its great head lolled and its eyes were closing fast.

"Quickly, Kell," Dr Vem urged quietly, "pass me that jack!" The doctor was now so close to the beast that his frayed black coat was flapping uncontrollably in the breeze streaming from the beast's vibrating nostrils. Kell stepped forward and placed the jack in the doctor's hands.

Exactly on three and a half minutes, so close to sleep that rumbling snores were beginning to vibrate every stone in the cell and every bone in Kell's body, the dragon yawned again. And as its massive snout gaped, Dr Vem reached forward and rammed the jack inside the dragon's mouth. Hurriedly, he started pumping a wooden lever attached to the side of the instrument up and down. The jaws tried to close. But the jack held them open, and with every downward stroke of the lever, the head of the jack ratcheted further up and the jaws were forced further and further apart. Within just a few seconds, the jaws of the now totally comatose dragon were gaping wide open.

Augustus Vem stepped back to admire his work. "Good! That's the hardest part done. Now climb in there, lad, and find the tooth that's troubling the poor beast." The doctor locked his hands together ready to give the boy a shimmy up.

"*What?*" Kell began to back away, his voice a strangled groan of disbelief. "Climb in there? You don't expect me to get into its mouth, do you?"

"Of course," the doctor answered, puzzled. "You have to go inside in order to pull the bad tooth out. It can't be done from down here, and I can't get up there, not with this bad leg of mine. It'll only take you five minutes, Kell." Augustus Vem put on his most reassuring voice. "Look, it's a herbivore, its jaws are propped firmly open *and* it's unconscious. Now what possible harm can come to you? You'll be quite safe. I absolutely guarantee it . . ." Dr Vem smiled helpfully and locked his hands together again. "Now quick, before the nepthene starts to wear off."

Not believing what he was doing, Kell crawled carefully up and over the dragon's huge lower grinding molars until he stood, slightly crouched, inside the open jaws. Now he was surrounded by two long curving rows of glistening teeth, each at least half as tall as a man. The fang-like incisors hovered like waiting swords. He looked down the creature's windpipe, watching the slow opening and closing of the epiglottis and the surging of phlegmy liquids. Overhead was the arching, concave palate, from which threads of sticky saliva dripped on and around him. Under his feet, the creature's soft, blue-veined and constantly trembling forked tongue shifted un-easily. Kell realized, wincing, that he was standing in the veritable mouth of hell.

Dr Vem's anxious voice called up to him. "Kell, the tooth we're looking for is probably a badly chipped or fractured lower molar. Should be easy enough to identify."

Kell shook himself. The sooner he was out of here the better. "What kind of tooth?" he shouted.

"One of the broad grinding teeth somewhere on your left. It'll probably be rotted or partly discoloured."

Kell worked his way along the line. He noticed something white lodged firmly between two of the teeth. He pulled it free and stared at it, horrified, then threw it down to the doctor. "Is that what I think it is?" he asked.

The doctor examined it with a baffled expression. "It appears to be a gnawed ungulate tibia," the doctor suggested.

"A what?" Kell yelled.

"A half-eaten antelope bone."

Kell groaned. "But you assured me this dragon was a plant-eater!"

"I . . . er, thought it was," Dr Vem admitted lamely.

"I'm coming down, I'm getting out of here, now!" Kell cried, starting to scramble over the nearest tooth. As he placed his weight on it, the tooth swayed away from him. Kell looked closer. A jagged hole punctured the enamel from the crown to the half-exposed root. Most of the inside face was rotten with decay. He reached out and pulled it back to the upright position. There was very little resistance. Throwing his arms around it, the boy heaved with all his strength. He could clearly hear a soft sucking sound as the damaged molar lifted slightly out of its socket. "Doctor!" he cried excitedly, his worries momentarily forgotten. "I've found the bad tooth. It's so loose, it waggles!"

"Excellent!" Dr Vem shouted. "We'll have it out in no time! Catch this and fasten it around the tooth." He threw up one end of the rope. Kell grabbed it and saw that it had already been tied in a noose. He slipped it over the tooth, then yanked it tight.

"Right!" he yelled. "Pull!"

"Not yet!" Dr Vem warned. "I want you to help by levering the tooth out while I heave on the rope." He held up a long iron bar.

Kell slipped the bar halfway down the molar. Then, using the crown of the next tooth along as a fulcrum, he began leaning on the other end of the bar. "Right, Doctor," he cried. "Pull!"

Augustus Vem spat on his hands and pulled.

Almost immediately the damaged molar, to the accompaniment of disgusting sucking and plopping noises, began to rise out of its socket.

"It's coming!" Kell screamed. "Keep pulling, Doctor." Below the tooth's yellowed base, the three fang-like roots appeared, smeared with blood and lymph. Strands of flesh shredded and parted. Then, as Kell applied all his body weight to the bar, the molar suddenly eased free and popped out. Down below, Dr Vem threw himself to one side as the dental mass came crashing down almost on top of him. Up in the dragon's jaws, a powerful jet of black blood welled up out of the empty socket and started cascading down its throat. Kell lost his footing on the slippery tongue as this sanguinary flood surged around his knees. Thrown backwards by the pressure of the bloody tide, Kell, his arms waving wildly, screamed in horror as he was washed head-first down the dragon's gaping gullet.

A suffocating darkness closed around him as the muscles of the oesophagus squeezed the breath from his lungs and clamped tightly around his body. Even the slightest movement was impossible, only the slow remorseless slippage as he dropped further and further down the dragon's long distended throat . . .

Dr Vem raised his hands in abject horror. "Oh my goodness!" he muttered, hopping from one foot to the other and remembering what had happened to Jed only the week before. "Not another one, surely?" Reaching up, he grasped hold of the dragon's teeth, pulling himself up until he could peer inside its open jaws. Fearing the worst, he looked down the blood-streaked gullet. "Are you there, Kell?" he cried in a faltering voice.

"Of course I'm here!" Kell answered, his voice muffled and echoey. "Where the hell do you think I am?" There was the sound of struggling. "Now will you please . . . please! . . . get me out of here?"

"Yes," the doctor assured him. "Right away. Just close your eyes and hold your nose!"

"Why?"

"Just do it, Kell!" Augustus Vem ordered. "Now!"

Kell took a deep breath and did as he was told.

Suddenly the dragon started retching and almost before Kell realized what was happening, he was spewed out of the dragon's mouth onto the cell floor. He lay there, blinking and coughing, struggling to get his breath back in a spreading pool of bile.

"You're alive!" Dr Vem yelled.

"No thanks to you," the boy complained, wiping streaks of the foul liquid from his face and out of his hair.

"No thanks to me?" Augustus Vem was mortified. "You forget, young man; if I hadn't made the dragon regurgitate you, you'd be a shapeless lump of fat dissolving in a pool of digestive juices by now."

Kell shook his head disbelievingly. "If it wasn't for you, I wouldn't have been in the dragon's mouth in the first place," he said bitterly, trying to stand up.

Dr Vem held the boy's arm, steadying him. "Well . . . perhaps you're right, Kell," he accepted gruffly. "But then we shouldn't fall out over an unforeseen little accident, should we?"

Kell rolled his eyes.

"Come on," Dr Vem suggested. "Let's get out of here. You need a wash and a complete change of clothes."

Behind them, the dragon, recovering from the effects of the nepthene, roared groggily and brought its jaws snapping together with such force that the jack was reduced to splinters.

"Another unforeseen little accident?" Kell asked.

Dr Vem looked aghast. "But I was *sure* the jack was strong enough!" he insisted. "Oh, just think what might have happened if the dragon had woken up a little earlier . . ."

Kell didn't want to think about it.

Two hours later, after Kell had washed and dressed in more of his unfortunate predecessor's clothes and eaten so many hot sausages he was convinced his stomach was about to burst, he remembered the ring. He dug it out of the pocket of his discarded trousers and handed it to Dr Vem.

"You can keep it, Kell," the doctor said. "Over the years the dragons have made me a rich man with the gifts they bring as payment for the medical aid I offer them. I'll be retiring soon. During the few years I have left I'd like to concentrate exclusively on certain scientific problems I've become aware of. That's why I need an apprentice – to take over my duties here. You too can end up rich, Kell; richer than you could ever imagine. This is a great opportunity."

Kell listened, but said nothing.

Twenty minutes later, the boy was parading up and down

the workroom wearing a mocked-up dragon suit Dr Vem had pulled out of an old box.

The disguise wasn't exactly convincing. A cracked full-length mirror revealed how ridiculous the boy looked. The suit comprised a pair of wings fastened to his arms, whose tips drooped to the floor, three-toed shoes equipped with long claws, a one-piece body-jerkin covered in glittering scales and a red-crested head-dress with a snout.

"Why do I have to wear this?" Kell asked, feeling thoroughly idiotic.

The doctor sighed patiently. "All I want you to do is parade up and down outside Yarb's cell," he explained.

Kell had heard rumours about Yarb. Dr Vem had earlier let it slip that this particular dragon was very moody and extremely short-tempered. "But what for?" Kell insisted on an answer.

"Well, I want you to entice him out of his cell," Dr Vem explained. "He's not even stuck his head out for at least five days and I'm getting worried about him. I thought that if he saw a lady dragon walking past his entrance, he might get interested enough to come out."

"Lady dragon?" Kell dragged off the head-dress. "This is supposed to make me look like a female?"

"To another dragon, yes . . ."

"And when you say it might get Yarb interested enough . . ." Kell's eyes widened. "You mean that he might want to . . . ?"

"That's the general idea," the doctor agreed.

Kell spun round, colliding with the shelves. Bottles went flying. "No! I refuse!" the boy said. "You're even crazier than I'd imagined."

Augustus Vem tutted pompously. "There's no need for that, now, Kell. And you don't need to worry. You won't be in any danger. As soon as Yarb pokes his head out, I'll knock him unconscious with this . . ." He held up a heavy wooden club studded with lead nails.

"But what if you miss?" Kell groaned.

"Miss?" Dr Vem snorted. "Me, miss? How ridiculous. I won't miss. I've got everything worked out exactly. But even if I did, you can run, can't you?"

Kell could run. And this time, even encumbered with the dragon suit, he was faster than Olm. Just faster. He'd reached his room and slammed and wedged the door shut behind him just before the flightless dragon collided with the heavy timbered frame. The door shook violently under the impact, but held. The dragon snorted and clawed furiously. The timber shredded but held. Olm sank down on his haunches, waiting.

Dr Vem appeared after a few minutes. He weighed up the situation, glanced impatiently at his pocket watch, then knocked on the door. "Kell?" he said. "Can I talk to you?"

"I'm not opening the door," the boy warned.

"All right, I understand, and I'm not annoyed with you," Dr Vem told him. "We can talk about the Yarb situation when I get back. I'm leaving for Zellusar in less than an hour, but I'll be away no longer than two days. You'll be all right till then? I've left plenty of food on a trolley here in the hall." He glanced down at the dragon. "Olm will look after you."

"I'll be fine." Kell knew that the dragon was never going to let him out of its sight.

He waited then, listening patiently for the sound of the front door slamming behind Augustus Vem. When the distinctive crash echoed through the house, followed by the clanking of the doctor's heavy brass keys turning in the triple locks, Kell could control himself no longer. From his pocket he pulled out a half-full bottle labelled "ESSENCE OF NEPTHENE" that he'd snatched from under Dr Vem's nose when he deliberately slipped against the workroom shelves. Clutching the bottle tightly, he jigged around the room. Glee overwhelmed him and he burst out laughing.

Kell waited for just a little longer, then opened the door and stepped into the hall. Olm immediately backed away, placing himself before the front door. A low warning rumble came from the dragon's throat, its neck arched and its wings fluttered stiffly. Kell walked right up to it and reached out with his left hand as if to touch the door. Immediately, Olm's head snapped forward and the dragon's jaws fastened securely around Kell's arm. In his other hand, Kell had the bottle of nepthene ready. He flicked out the cork stopper with his thumb and poured the contents between the dragon's teeth. There was a gargling sound as the liquid ran down its throat. Kell watched and waited. The dragon licked bubbles of froth from its lips. Its eyes became glassy and unfocused. It blinked foolishly. As its head drooped, the grip on his arm relaxed. The dragon's legs splayed outwards and it slumped from a sitting position into a slouch. In less than two minutes it was completely unconscious and snoring. Kell patted Olm's warty, ridged head and allowed the last few drops from the bottle to fall on the dragon's quivering tongue.

Kell looked up. Above the front door was a fanlight window. It was at least eight feet high, too high to reach normally, but by climbing up onto the sleeping dragon's back, he could just get his fingers over the edge of the lintel. The glass was badly cracked and looked like it should break easily. Kell pulled himself up and banged on the dust-streaked pane with the edge of his fist. The glass fell outwards, shattering on the cobbles below. Taking a deep breath, he heaved himself up and wriggled through the empty frame, dropping down into the street. He was out! He was free!

But even before he could run away, a sharp pang of regret gripped him. And a question formed in Kell's mind. Was he *really* doing the right thing, returning to all the hatred and distrust shown to him in the world of men? And what about the dragons? He had begun to feel a growing affinity towards them, an understanding he found impossible to put into words. Apart from Liss, everyone and everything he had encountered in his short life had seemed alien to him. It began to dawn on Kell that in the company of the dragons he no longer felt like an outcast. At last, he had found somewhere he belonged. It would be an act of stupidity to abandon it all now.

He glanced up at the fanlight. It shouldn't be too difficult to climb back in. If he grabbed hold of the ivy growing down the wall and placed one foot on the doorknob . . .

A heavy hand grabbed him by the shoulder and an all too familiar voice bellowed out, "Well oo'd a thought it, fellas! If it isn't just the young man we've been lookin' for!"

Kell's heart sank. It was Tullo. And he wasn't alone. He was accompanied by two unshaven and ill-kempt accomplices. All three were so drunk that they could barely stand up straight. But Tullo's grip on the boy was like iron. The big man belched. "You've saved us the problem of breakin' in, 'asn't he, fellas!" He thrust his unshaven face close to Kell's. "It appears that I sold you too cheaply to old Doctor Vem. Seems that a boy with dragon eyes, – 'cause that's what you've got, innit? – is 'ighly valued by some individuals in this part of the world."

Kell wriggled furiously, kicking out, trying to break free. But Tullo just smirked and held him even tighter. "I've got a customer waiting oo's willing to pay a small fortune for a boy cursed with one red and one green eye!"

Kell didn't remember much more. Something hit him hard on the back of his head. Stars exploded painfully inside his skull and he slumped towards the cobbles. Kell knew that he must have been slipping in and out of consciousness, for he had confused recollections of being bound and gagged and forced into a filthy sack. He was carried somewhere, he was sure about that, then left alone for a long time. His head was throbbing and his hair was matted with dried blood. He felt like being sick. He passed out again.

Later still the sound of voices roused him. He recognised Tullo's voice but none of the others. There was much arguing, apparently about money. Kell heard his name mentioned a number of times. He could hear the banging of bottles, the tinkling of glasses, curses and rough laughter. How long would it be before they reached an agreement, he wondered?

His headache had eased a little and now a dim light filtered down through the bars of a rusty iron grating. In the feeble light he could see that he was lying in a dirt-strewn cellar. His bound limbs had lost nearly all their feeling. He tried to cry out, but only a muffled moan of distress came from his gagged mouth.

Lying on the edge of waking and dreaming, he was jerked back into full consciousness by the sound of scratching up on the grating. He looked up. Several small shapes, silhouetted against the pre-dawn sky, were trying to squeeze through the bars. Rats! It must be! Kell was horrified. Beads of cold sweat ran down his forehead. He knew such vermin ran in packs. Two or three would quickly become a ravening horde. They'd rip him to shreds in minutes! It would be a dreadful death and there was nothing he could do about it. Then one of them wriggled through and dropped to the cellar floor. No, not dropped; it extended a small pair of wings and fluttered down. Another followed quickly behind it. Kell heard a familiar whistling and chittering as the creatures surveyed him with glowing eyes of red and green. They were dragons. And they'd come to rescue him.

Within seconds they'd gnawed through the ropes binding his legs and wrists. Kell suppressed a groan as the agonies of cramp began surging through his limbs. Aware that he had no time to lose, he crawled towards the steps leading up out of the cellar, clinging to the handrail and desperately trying not to make a noise as he pulled himself up one step at a time. As the blood started flowing again his strength slowly returned. The little dragons fluttered around him, urging him on with soft piping calls.

At the top of the steps was a wooden door. Shafts of lamplight from the room beyond streamed through chinks in the rough planking. Kell peered through one of the cracks. Four men were sprawled in chairs around a table littered with empty wine bottles. Tullo and a bald-headed man were drunkenly counting through a large pile of coins on the wine-stained table. The other men seemed to have passed out. A hissing oil-lamp was the only source of illumination. Away from the table, the rest of the room was in deep shadow. With infinite care, Kell swung the cellar door open just enough so he could ease his way past it. Then, with his heart pounding in his ribs, he began crawling silently across the floor towards another door, badly hung and partly ajar, that led onto the street.

Kell was halfway across the room when his hand brushed against something. A discarded wine bottle. Alarmed, the boy reached out to grab it, but the bottle rolled out of reach across the floor with a series of musical clinks and tinklings.

"Wot?" Tullo rasped thickly, halting in mid-count. " 'Ere, wot's that noise?" The bottle came to rest against one of his mud-stained boots. Confused, he looked down, then up, straight into the eyes of Kell.

"Grab 'im, Blant!" he yelled. "The boy's loose! Don't let 'im escape!"

The table went flying as he stood up. Coins and bottles cascaded across the floor and the sleeping men were thrown backwards as their chairs tipped over. The lamp hit the floor and went out. Blackness engulfed the room. Kell leapt to his feet and dived for the door, reaching it just ahead of Blant's wildly grasping hands. There was a flurry of disturbed air as the little dragons swooped out to join him. In the alley, with dawn just breaking overhead, Kell started running – running as if his life depended on it. And from behind him came the curses and yells of Tullo, Blant and the others. The pounding of their boots filled the alley as they raced in pursuit.

Kell knew he couldn't run far. His legs were trembling and the cold air burned like liquid fire in his lungs. But maybe he could find somewhere to hide. Behind him the little dragons were doing their best to delay his pursuers, swooping into their faces, scratching with their claws and nipping at the men's heels with their sharp little teeth, screeching and squealing and making nuisances of themselves. The men cursed, waving their arms and kicking out angrily at their agile and persistent tormentors.

With almost the last of his strength, Kell struggled over a low stone wall and through a thick hedge. He was in a cemetery. Ancient, untended gravestones adorned with hideous gargoyles leaned at crazy angles in the weed-choked black earth. He stumbled over a partly buried slab, skinning his knees, and picked himself up with difficulty. With a sinking heart he realized that there was no place of concealment here. And behind him, the men were already emerging from the hedge.

Then a huge shadow surrounded Kell as something descended out of the air on strongly beating, leathery wings. He glanced up as a pair of three-toed, powerfully taloned feet grabbed the collar of his jerkin, preparing to haul him up into the air. Kell sensed the massive shape of one of the large dragons hovering above him. Then a familiar ridged and warty head on the end of a scaly neck descended to look at him. The dragon's jaws opened in a parody of a smile. It was Olm! Somehow he had regained the use of his wings!

As Kell's feet left the ground there was a startled cry from the hedge, followed by the sound of running feet. Tullo's anguished voice could be heard shouting: "You won't get away from me that easy, boy!"

Kell twisted around in the dragon's grip. To his horror he saw that Tullo had grabbed the dragon's tail and was hanging on for dear life while Olm struggled to gain height. As they crossed an ornamental lake, the desperate beating of Olm's vast leathery wings kept Kell just above the lily-pads, but the dragon's tail, drooping under Tullo's excessive weight, trailed in the icy water, soaking him to the skin and throwing up a wake of glittering bubbles.

Tullo spluttered, coughing up mouthfuls of water, but he refused to release his grip. As they flew across the cemetery grounds, heading towards the nearest of the houses, Tullo was kicking and struggling so violently that he was hindering the dragon's ability to fly straight. Olm was zooming erratically, first this way, then that, and it seemed that a collision was inevitable. Kell closed his eyes and waited, but with a rush of air, the dragon swooped over the house-top with only inches to spare. Tullo let out an agonized shriek as he was dragged into a row of darkened chimney pots which were sent crashing into the deserted street below. A flock of pigeons, roosting under the overhanging eaves, took to the air in panic, leaving feathers swirling behind them in the undertow.

Tullo's grip was slipping, but he hung on desperately, screaming and raising his knees to his chin, just avoiding a wickedly pointed compass arrow on a revolving weathervane. Kell couldn't help but grin as, looking back, he saw Tullo's blanched and horror-stricken face.

Kell recognized his surroundings now. They were heading back to Dr Vem's house. As Olm flew down a long narrow alley, Tullo became entangled in layers of washing hanging on lines stretched between the buildings. Damp sheets, dripping shirts, blouses and socks were plastered to him, trailing from his threshing body like spectral shrouds. One of the lines snagged firmly on his belt buckle. It stretched taut, tensioned like a bow-string. It twanged; Tullo was dragged away from the dragon's tail and left dangling helplessly, bound up in the washing, while on each side, windows were thrown open and irate women began screaming at him.

Olm's wings were beating more strongly. Kell stared mesmerized as the hill loomed massively above them. Any moment now, the dragon would start gaining height to reach the summit so it could swoop down through the opening into the volcanic lake. Kell would be back where he started.

Then a chill gripped his heart as an awful sound came. The tearing of cloth reached his ears, the relentless plunk, plunk, plunk of snapping stitches. The collar of his tunic, held fast in Olm's claws, was ripping away. The material was separating under his weight!

"No!" he screamed, as his collar and his tunic parted company completely. Then he was falling helplessly, down through the cold air, down towards the rooftops of Dr Augustus Vem's house . . .

. . . straight into a chimney flue.

Yelling helplessly, Kell plummeted down the fire-blackened stack, banging and bouncing off the sides of the slowly curving chimney, dislodging years of accreted soot and carbon until, coughing and spluttering, he ended up sprawled out full length, in a spreading cloud of smoke dust, on the fireside carpet back in Dr Vem's study.

At that exact moment the door opened and the doctor appeared. "What in Hades is going on here, Kell?" he demanded, his expression a thunderous mixture of anger and disbelief.

"I can explain, Doctor," Kell stammered, rubbing his eyes and sneezing uncontrollably.

"Well I hope you can, young man! This is not how I expected to find things when I returned from collecting my niece from college. If you want to continue in my employment, you'll have to perk up your ideas a bit. Indeed you will!"

Kell blinked as his vision returned. Standing beside Dr Vem was a beautiful young girl with long dark hair, radiant blue eyes, satin-smooth skin and lustrous red lips.

"Your niece, sir?" Kell could feel his pulse racing and his heart melting.

"Yes," the doctor answered tetchily. "Lucinda always comes home at half-term. Now, Kell, your explanation. And I hope you can make it good!"

Lucinda gave Dr Vem's arm a sympathetic squeeze, then she smiled shyly but encouragingly at Kell. "Oh, I'm *sure* he can, Uncle. And as for this mess, why, it's nothing. You just go and lie down, rest your feet. We'll have this cleared up in no time, won't we, Kell?"

Kell nodded, utterly speechless. His heart was soaring with possibilities. He was now surer than ever that he was in no rush to leave this House of Dragons. In fact, despite all the mishaps and calamities he'd suffered recently, he was quite looking forward to the rest of his apprenticeship.

RULES OF ENGAGEMENT

Molly Brown

Although born in Chicago, Molly Brown is now resident in London and is perhaps best known for her historical mystery novel Invitation to a Funeral *(1995). Research for this made her something of an expert on Restoration London and she has developed a website at www.okima.com. She has also written a novelization of the TV series* Cracker – To Say I Love You. *A feature film, based on her award-winning story "Bad Timing" (1991), is currently in development at Twentieth Century Fox. In the previous volume I reprinted one of Molly's stories about the petulant Queen Ruella. Here's another one.*

Ruella, fifteen-year-old Queen of Tanalor, slouched back on her throne, a dwarf in a jester's costume massaging her bare feet. A herald came into the throne room. "Your Majesty," he said, kneeling before her with his head bowed.

"Yeah?"

"A messenger from the kingdom of Hala awaits without for your pleasure."

"Work, work, work. All right, send him in."

A young man with flowing black hair, large dark eyes, and extremely tight tights entered and knelt before her. She quickly straightened her back, sucked in her stomach, and kicked the dwarf out of the way.

"Arise, sir," she said, sliding her feet into a pair of jewel-encrusted slippers. "Welcome to our fair kingdom."

"Truly thy kingdom is fair, lady, but I must say without fear of contradiction that the fairness of thy kingdom is nothing compared to the fairness of its Queen."

Ruella lowered her head slightly and raised one finger to her lips, regarding the young messenger with half-closed eyes. "So what can I do you for?"

"I bear tidings of great joy. My lord, the King of Hala, hearing of your great beauty and wit . . ."

" . . Wants me to marry his son," Ruella interrupted, rolling her eyes. "I get these proposals every day."

"If I may be so bold as to correct you, Your Majesty, the King of Hala does not wish you to marry his son. He requests your hand in marriage for himself."

"This is King Reynard of Hala you're talking about, right?"

"Yes, my lady."

"Seventy-five years old, no teeth, bad breath, with hair growing out of his ears?"

"Your description is cruel, but I cannot deny its accuracy."

"And this is your idea of joyful tidings? Well, tell your King this for me. I'm not going to marry him because A: he's an ugly old man; and B: with an A like that, who needs a B?"

"My lady," the messenger said, looking her in the eye, "I would urge you to reconsider. My sire, King Reynard of Hala, is a man of enormous wealth; wealth beyond any your poor tiny kingdom can imagine. He can offer you a life of luxury beyond anything you could dream."

"Let me guess the next bit. All I have to do is give up control of my own tiny kingdom?"

The messenger shrugged. "And you'd have to sleep with him at least once."

Ruella burst out laughing. It amazed her that she had ever found this idiot attractive. "Get out of my sight," she said.

"One more thing, my lady," the messenger said. "I must warn you that if you refuse, your kingdom and even your fair self may be destroyed."

"I bet you say that to all the girls."

The messenger lowered his voice. "I must tell you my lord is a master of darkness."

"A what?"

"He has power over things that are not of this earth."

Ruella made a face. "I'm impressed."

"I warn you, lady, my father will not take kindly to your attitude."

Ruella raised one eyebrow. He'd said "my father". So this was Prince Merriller, heir to the Halan throne and inestimable wealth. On second thoughts, maybe he was kind of cute after all. "I pray you will forgive my hasty speech, Prince Merriller, but I didn't know who you were. I mean, it isn't every day a girl gets a proposal of marriage . . ."

"I thought you said it was," the prince interrupted.

"I was about to say from such a fine man as your father."

She clapped her hands, and two guards appeared. "Show Prince Merriller to suitable quarters. He's going to be our guest for a while."

"But . . ." the prince protested as the guards carried him away.

In a cavern far below the palace, a hooded figure stood bent over a cauldron. It looked up as Ruella entered. "I've been doing a little checking on your latest suitor," it rasped.

"Oh yeah?"

"Yeah." It poured a vial of brightly coloured liquid into the cauldron, stirring it slowly, then dipped a fleshless finger into the bubbling mixture. "Needs more salt," it muttered.

Ruella reached for a container on a shelf. "So what did you find out?" she asked, handing it over.

The hooded figure tossed a pinch of salt over its shoulder. "Since when is Queen Know-It-All interested in what I have to say?"

Ruella rolled her eyes. "Try me."

The hooded figure dipped another finger into the boiling

liquid. "Perfect," it said, removing the cauldron from the heat before crossing over to the shelves to dust its collection of jars labelled "POISON".

"It seems King Reynard started out with a little kingdom, not much bigger than this one. Then he married a neighbouring princess. Her father died shortly after the wedding, in mysterious and unexplained circumstances. A week after his new wife was crowned queen, she died, also in mysterious circumstances. Then he married another neighbouring princess, who died soon after in . . . guess what?"

Ruella made a face. "Mysterious circumstances?"

The hooded figure nodded. "He's done it five times. In five marriages – not one lasting longer than a year – he's managed to quintuple his lands, his power base, and his treasury." It picked up a jar of dead toads, gently polishing the glass. "So what do you think he wants with you?"

Ruella laughed.

"I told you you wouldn't be interested," the hooded figure said, putting back the jar.

"No," Ruella protested, giggling. "It's just that I know all this already. I've been studying up on Reynard for months, and I think it's about time someone beat him at his own game, don't you? It wouldn't be the first time a seventy-five-year-old man died on his wedding night. Nobody would suspect a thing, and Hala is so-o-o wealthy." She tilted her head to one side, licking her lips. "Who do you think sent him my portrait in the first place?"

"You shouldn't do things like that without telling me first," the hooded figure rasped in disapproval. "Some of these local sorcerers can be dangerous."

She waved her hand in dismissal. "Anything they can do, I can do better. Watch this."

She stood in the middle of the cavern, a look of concentration on her face. A pillar of flame shot from her fingers. "How's that?"

The other pulled back its hood, scratching a bare skull crawling with worms. "All right for a party trick. Next you'll be pulling rabbits out of hats."

"How about this, then?" She closed her eyes, intoning a

series of strange harsh syllables. The ground below them
began to shake. The rock walls of the cavern dripped blood.
There was a sound of weeping and then a roar of fury. The
air around them swirled into a red mist, reeking of sulphur.
Ruella opened her eyes. The cavern split in two as the earth
cracked open, spewing forth its dead. Ruella, breathing fire,
grew impossibly large as a legion of corpses, soldiers of
darkness ready to die and die again, bowed down before
her.

"Better," the hooded figure rasped.

Prince Merriller stormed into the throne room. "You are
foiled, lady!" he shouted.

In unison, without turning to look at him, the Queen, her
guards, and each member of her court raised one finger to their
lips and shushed him. Every eye was focused on a stage erected
in the middle of the room, every ear was straining to listen.
The prince tried to speak again. A guard placed one hand
firmly over the prince's mouth.

On the stage, an actor and an actress were looking at each
other intensely. "What is thy problem?" the actor said. "Thou
knowest I need my space."

"Truly I know this, and have agreed on this basis to an open
relationship," the actress replied, "but woe is me and triple
times woe! For I fear I am great with child."

There was a dramatic musical chord. The actor turned to
face the audience, looking startled.

The candles surrounding the stage were extinguished, plunging the actors into darkness. A chorus of singers began the
theme: "Peasants, everybody needs good peasants . . ."

The prince broke free of the guard who was holding him.
"Ruella!"

She shrugged, looking sheepish. "I know it's crap. But I'm
hooked."

"You can keep me prisoner here no longer," Prince Merriller announced, thrusting his jaw forward in defiance.

"Why not?" she asked, yawning.

"While your guards were down here watching this . . ." he
gestured towards the stage, ". . . mindless rubbish, I made my

way to the castle roof. From there, I saw the Halan army approaching, my father the King leading them to my rescue."

The Queen jumped up excitedly. "King Reynard's on his way? That's wonderful!"

"When I tell him the things I have witnessed and heard, how you have held me here against my will, how you cavort with undead skeletons . . ."

"Oh, shut up!" She moved closer to him, lowering her voice so that only he could hear. "Who do you think he's going to believe? You? Or me, when I tell him how you came to my chamber in the middle of the night, vowing to kill your father, take his throne, and marry me yourself?"

The prince's eyes nearly popped out of his head. He shook all over as he sputtered, "But, I didn't! I never . . . !"

Ruella winked and gave him a gentle nudge with her elbow. "I'll keep quiet if you will."

The chorus was still singing the theme from *Peasants*. "Will you guys clam up already?" They were silent. "And you can take tomorrow off. I'm getting married!"

Ruella giggled as she put on her wedding dress. She was already thinking about her second husband. And her third. But *they* would have to wait for the sequel.

THE TRIUMPH OF VICE

W. S. Gilbert

*It's easy to forget that William Schwenck Gilbert (1836–1911) –
the librettist half of Gilbert and Sullivan – was one of the best comic
writers of the late nineteenth century. Several of the light operas
that he wrote with Sullivan are fantasies –* Thespis *(1871),* The
Sorcerer *(1877),* Iolanthe *(1882) and* Ruddigore *(1887). Gilbert had been writing witty poems, ballads and articles for the
Victorian periodicals since 1863. He became a regular contributor
to* Fun *– indeed, he contributed to it at the same time as Ambrose
Bierce, who will be found elsewhere in this book. He also wrote
several stage plays, many of which are comic fantasies, including
his first,* Dulcamara, or The Little Duck and the Great Quack
*(1866). Gilbert always valued his short stories above his light
operas and it is such a shame that they have been overlooked. Most
of them appeared either as small chapbooks or in magazines and the
only collection published during his life was* Foggerty's Fairy and
Other Tales *(1890). Peter Haining did a sterling job in resurrecting many of these stories in* The Lost Stories of W.S. Gilbert
(1982), from which the following story is taken.

The wealthiest in the matter of charms, and the poorest in the matter of money of all the well-born maidens of Tackleschlosstein, was the Lady Bertha von Klauffenbach. Her papa, the Baron, was indeed the fortunate possessor of a big castle on the top of a perpendicular rock, but his estate was deeply mortgaged, and there was not the smallest probability of its ever being free from the influence of the local money-lender. Indeed, if it comes to that, I may be permitted to say that even in the event of that wildly improbable state of things having come to pass, the amount realized by the sale of the castle and perpendicular rock would not have exceeded one hundred and eighty pounds sterling, all told. So the Baron von Klauffenbach did not even wear the outward show of being a wealthy man.

The perpendicular rock being singularly arid and unproductive even for a rock, and the Baron being remarkably penniless even for a Baron, it became necessary that he should adopt some decided course by which a sufficiency of bread, milk, and sauerkraut might be provided to satisfy the natural cravings of the Baron von Klauffenbach, and that fine growing girl Bertha, his daughter. So the poor old gentleman was only too glad to let down his drawbridge every morning, and sally forth from his stronghold, to occupy a scrivener's stool in the office of the local money-lender to whom I have already alluded. In short, the Baron von Klauffenbach was a usurer's clerk.

But it is not so much with the Baron von Klauffenbach as with his beautiful daughter Bertha that I have to do. I must describe her. She was a magnificent animal. She was six feet in height, and splendidly proportioned. She had a queenly face, set in masses of wonderful yellow hair; big blue eyes, and curly little mouth (but with thick firm lips), and a nose which, in the mercantile phraseology of the period, defied competition. Her figure was grandly, heroically outlined, firm as marble to the look, but elastically yielding to the touch. Bertha had but one fault – she was astonishingly vain of her magnificent proportions, and held in the utmost contempt anybody, man or woman, who fell short of her in that respect. She was the toast of all the young clerks of Tackleschlosstein; but the

young clerks of Tackleschlosstein were to the Lady Bertha as
so many midges to a giantess. They annoyed her, but they
were not worth the trouble of deliberate annihilation. So they
went on toasting her, and she went on scorning them.

Indeed, the Lady Bertha had but one lover whose chance of
success was worth the ghost of a halfpenny – and he was the
Count von Krappentrapp. The Count von Krappentrapp had
these pulls over the gay young clerks of Tackleschlosstein –
that he was constantly in her society, and was of noble birth.
That he was constantly in her society came to pass in this wise.
The Baron von Klauffenbach, casting about him for a means
of increasing – or rather of laying the first stone towards the
erection of – his income, published this manifesto on the walls
of Tackleschlosstein:

> A nobleman and his daughter, having larger premises
> than they require, will be happy to receive into their
> circle a young gentleman engaged in the village during
> the day. Society musical. Terms insignificant. Apply to
> the Baron von K., Post Office, Tackleschlosstein.

The only reply to this intimation came from the Count von
Krappentrapp; and the only objection to the Count von
Krappentrapp was that he was not engaged in the village
during the day. But this objection was eventually overruled
by the Count's giving the Baron, in the handsomest manner in
the world, his note of hand for ten pounds at six months' date,
which was immediately discounted by the Baron's employer. I
am afraid that the Baron and the Count got dreadfully tipsy
that evening. I know that they amused themselves all night by
shying ink-bottles from the battlements at the heads of the
people in the village below.

It will easily be foreseen that the Count von Krappentrapp
soon fell hopelessly in love with Bertha; and those of my
readers who are accustomed to the unravelling of German
legendary lore will long ere this have made up their minds that
Bertha fell equally hopelessly in love with the Count von
Krappentrapp. But in this last particular they will be entirely
in error. Far from encouraging the gay young Count, she

regarded him with feelings of the most profound contempt. Indeed, truth compels me to admit that the Count was repulsive. His head was enormous, and his legs insignificant. He was short in stature, squat in figure, and utterly detestable in every respect, except in this, that he was always ready to put his hand to a bill for the advantage of the worthy old Baron. And whenever he obliged the Baron in this respect, he and the old gentleman used to get dreadfully tipsy, and always spent the night on the battlements throwing ink-bottles on the people in the village below. And whenever the Baron's tradespeople in the village found themselves visited by a shower of ink-bottles, they knew that there was temporary corn in Egypt, and they lost no time in climbing up the perpendicular rock with their little red books with the gilt letters in their hands, ready for immediate settlement.

It was not long after the Count von Krappentrapp came to lodge with the Baron von Klauffenbach, that the Count proposed to the Baron's daughter, and in about a quarter of a minute after he had proposed to her, he was by her most unequivocally rejected. Then he slunk off to his chamber, muttering and mouthing in a manner which occasioned the utmost consternation in the mind of Gretchen, the castle maid-of-all-work, who met him on his way. So she offered him a bottle of cheap scent, and some peppermint-drops, but he danced at her in such a reckless manner when she suggested these humble refreshments, that she went to the Baron, and gave him a month's warning on the spot.

Everything went wrong with the Count that day. The window-blinds wouldn't pull up, the door wouldn't close, the chairs broke when he sat on them, and before half his annoyances had ceased, he had expended all the bad language he knew.

The Count was conscientious in one matter only, and that was in the matter of bad language. He made it a point of honour not to use the same expletive twice in the same day. So when he found that he had exhausted his stock of swearing, and that, at the moment of exhaustion, the chimney began to smoke, he simply sat down and cried feebly.

But he soon sprang to his feet, for in the midst of an
unusually large puff of smoke, he saw the most extraordinary
individual he had ever beheld. He was about two feet high, and
his head was as long as his body and legs put together. He had
an antiquated appearance about him; but excepting that he
wore a long stiff tail, with a spear-point at the end of it, there
was nothing absolutely unearthly about him. His hair, which
resembled the crest or comb of a cock in its arrangement,
terminated in a curious little queue, which turned up at the
end and was fastened with a bow of blue ribbon. He wore
mutton-chop whiskers and a big flat collar, and his body and
misshapen legs were covered with a horny incrustation, which
suggested black beetles. On his crest he wore a three-cornered
hat – anticipating the invention of that article of costume by
about three hundred years.

"I beg your pardon," said this phenomenon, "but can I
speak to you?"

"Evidently you can," replied the Count, whose confidence
had returned to him.

"I know: but what I mean is, will you listen to me for ten
minutes?"

"That depends very much upon what you talk about. Who
are you?" asked the Count.

"I'm a sort of gnome."

"A gnome?"

"A sort of gnome; I won't enter into particulars, because
they won't interest you."

The apparition hesitated, evidently hoping the Count would
assure him that any particulars of the gnome's private life
would interest him deeply; but he only said –

"Not the least bit in the world."

"You are poor," said the gnome.

"Very," replied the Count.

"Ha!" said he, "some people are. Now I am rich."

"*Are* you?" asked the Count, beginning to take an interest in
the matter.

"I am, and would make you rich too; only you must help me
to a wife."

"What! Repay good for evil? Never!"

He didn't mean this, only he thought it was a smart thing to say.

"Not exactly," said the gnome; "I shan't give you the gold until you have found me the wife; so that I shall be repaying evil with good."

"Yes," said the Count musingly: "I didn't look at it in that light at all. I see it quite from your point of view. But why don't you find a wife for yourself?"

"Well," said the gnome diffidently, "I'm not exactly – you know – I'm – that is – I want a word!"

"Extremely ugly?" suggested the Count.

"Ye-e-es," said the gnome (rather taken aback); "something of that sort. *You* know."

"Yes, I know," said the Count; "but how am I to help you? I can't make you pretty."

"No; but I have the power of transforming myself three times during my gnome existence into a magnificent young man."

"O-h-h-h!" said the Count slyly.

"Exactly. Well, I've done that twice, but without success as far as regards getting a wife. This is my last chance."

"But how can I help you? You say you can change yourself into a magnificent young man; then why not plead your own case? I, for my part, am rather – a—"

"Repulsive?" suggested the gnome, thinking he had him there.

"Plain," said the Count.

"Well," replied the gnome, "there's an unfortunate fact connected with my human existence."

"Out with it. Don't stand on ceremony."

"Well, then, it's this. I begin as a magnificent young man, six feet high, but I diminish imperceptibly day by day, whenever I wash myself, until I shrink into the – a – the—"

"Contemptible abortion?"

"A – yes – thank you – you behold. Well, I've tried it twice, and found on each occasion a lovely girl who was willing and ready to marry me; but during the month or so that elapsed between each engagement and the day appointed for the wedding, I shrunk so perceptibly (one is obliged, you know, to wash one's face during courtship), that my bride-elect became frightened and cried off. Now, I have seen the Lady Bertha, and I am determined to marry her."

"You? Ha, ha! Excuse me, but – Ha, ha!"

"Yes, I. But you will see that it is essential that as little time as possible should elapse between my introduction to her and our marriage."

"Of course; and you want me to prepare her to receive you, and marry you there and then without delay."

"Exactly; and if you consent, I will give you several gold mines, and as many diamonds as you can carry."

"You will? My dear sir, say no more! 'Revenge! Revenge! Revenge! Timotheus cried,' " (quoting a popular comic song of the day). "But how do you effect the necessary transformation?"

"Here is a ring which gives me the power of assuming human form once more during my existence. I have only to put it on my middle finger, and the transformation is complete."

"I see – but – couldn't you oblige me with a few thalers on account?"

"Um," said the gnome; "it's irregular: but here are two."

"Right," said the Count, biting them; "I'll do it. Come the day after tomorrow."

"At this time?" said the gnome.

"At this time."

"Good-night."

"Good-night."

And the gnome disappeared up the chimney.

The Count von Krappentrapp hurried off without loss of time to communicate to the lovely Bertha the splendid fate in store for her.

"Lady Bertha," said he, "I come to you with a magnificent proposal."

"Now, Krappentrapp," said Bertha, "don't be a donkey. Once and for all, I *will* NOT have you."

"I am not alluding to myself; I am speaking on behalf of a friend."

"Oh, any friend of yours, I'm sure," began Bertha politely.

"Thanks very much."

"Would be open to the same objection as yourself. He would be repulsive."

"But he is magnificent!"

"He would be vicious."

"But he is virtuous!"

"He would be insignificant in rank and stature."

"He is a prince of unexampled proportions!"

"He would be absurdly poor."

"He is fabulously wealthy!"

"Indeed?" said Bertha; "your story interests me." (She was intimately acquainted with German melodrama.) "Proceed."

"This prince," said Krappentrapp, "has heard of you, has seen you, and consequently has fallen in love with you."

"Oh, g'long," said Bertha, giggling and nudging him with her extraordinarily moulded elbow.

"Fact. He proposes to settle on you Africa, the Crystal Palace, several solar systems, the Rhine, and Rosherville. The place," added he, musingly, "to spend a happy, happy day."

"Are you in earnest, or" (baring her right arm to the shoulder) "is this some of your nonsense?"

"Upon my honour, I am in earnest. He will be here the day after tomorrow at this time to claim you, if you consent to have him. He will carry you away with him alone to his own province, and there will marry you."

"Go away alone with him? I wouldn't think of such a thing!" said Bertha, who was a model of propriety.

"H'm!" said the Count. "That is awkward certainly. Ha! A thought! You shall marry him first, and start afterwards, only as he has to leave in two days, the wedding must take place without a moment's delay."

You see, if he had suggested this in the first instance, she would have indignantly rejected the notion, on principle. As it was she jumped at it, and, as a token of peace, let down her sleeve.

"I can provide my trousseau in two days. I will marry him the day he arrives, if he turns out to be all you have represented him. But if he does not –" And she again bared her arm, significantly, to the shoulder.

That night, the Baron von Klauffenbach and the Count von Krappentrapp kept it up right merrily on the two thalers which the Count had procured from the gnome. The Baron was overjoyed at the prospect of a princely son-in-law; and the shower of ink-bottles from the battlements was heavier than ever.

The second day after this the gnome appeared to Count Krappentrapp.

"How do you do?" said the Count.

"Thank you," said the gnome; "I'm pretty well. It's an awful thing being married."

"Oh, no. Don't be dispirited."

"Ah, it's all very well for you to say that, but – Is the lady ready?" said he, changing the subject abruptly.

"Ready, I should think so. She's sitting in the banqueting hall in full bridal array, panting for your arrival."

"Oh! Do I look nervous?"

"Well, candidly, you do," said the Count.

"I'm afraid I do. Is everything prepared?"

"The preparations," said the Count, "are on the most magnificent scale. Half buns and cut oranges are scattered over the place in luxurious profusion, and there is enough gingerbierheimer and currantweinmilch on tap to float the Rob Roy canoe. Gretchen is engaged, as I speak, in cutting hamsandwiches recklessly in the kitchen; and the Baron has taken down the 'Apartments furnished', which has hung for ages in the stained-glass windows of the banqueting hall."

"I see," said the gnome, "to give a tone to the thing."

"Just so. Altogether it will be the completest thing you ever saw."

"Well," said the gnome, "then I think I'll dress."

For he had not yet taken his human form.

So he slipped a big carbuncle ring onto the middle finger of his right hand. Immediately the room was filled with a puff of smoke from the chimney, and when it had cleared away, the Count saw, to his astonishment, a magnificent young man in the place where the gnome had stood.

"There is no deception," said the gnome.

"Bravo! Very good indeed! Very neat!" said the Count, applauding.

"Clever thing, isn't it?" said the gnome.

"Capital; most ingenious. But now – what's your name?"

"It's an odd name. Prince Pooh."

"Prince Pooh? Pooh! Pooh? You're joking."

"Now, take my advice, and never try to pun upon a fellow's name; you may be sure that, however ingenious the joke may be, it's certain to have been done before over and over again to his face. Your own particular joke is precisely the joke every fool makes when he first hears my name."

"I beg your pardon – it *was* weak. Now, if you'll come with me to the Baron, you and he can settle preliminaries."

So they went to the Baron, who was charmed with his son-in-law elect. Prince Pooh settled on Bertha the whole of Africa, the Crystal Palace, several solar systems, the Rhine, and Rosherville, and made the Baron a present of Siberia and Vesuvius; after that they all went down to the banqueting hall, where Bertha and the priest were awaiting their arrival.

"Allow me," said the Baron. "Bertha, my dear, Prince Pooh – who has behaved *most handsomely*" (this in a whisper). "Prince Pooh – my daughter Bertha. Pardon a father if he is for a moment unmanned."

And the Baron wept over Bertha, while Prince Pooh mingled his tears with those of Count Krappentrapp, and the priest with those of Gretchen, who had finished cutting the sandwiches. The ceremony was then gone into with much zeal on all sides, and on its conclusion the party sat down to the elegant collation already referred to. The Prince declared that the Baron was the best fellow he had ever met, and the Baron assured the Prince that words failed him when he endeavoured to express the joy he felt at an alliance with so unexceptionable a Serene Highness.

The Prince and his bride started in a carriage and twenty-seven for his country seat, which was only fifty miles from Tackleschlosstein, and that night the Baron and the Count kept it up harder than ever. They went down to the local silversmith to buy up all the presentation inkstands in his stock; and the shower of inkstands from the castle battlements on the heads of the villagers below that night is probably without precedent or imitation in the chronicles of revelry.

Bertha and Prince Pooh spent a happy honeymoon: Bertha had one, and only one cause of complaint against Prince Pooh, and that was an insignificant one – do all she could, she couldn't persuade him to wash his face more than once a week. Bertha was a clean girl for a German, and had acquired a habit of performing ablutions three or even four times a week; consequently her husband's annoying peculiarity irritated her more than it would have irritated most of the young damsels of Tackleschlosstein. So she would contrive, when he was asleep, to go over his features with a damp towel; and whenever he went out for a walk she hid his umbrella, in order that, if it chanced to rain, he might get a providential and sanitary wetting.

This sort of thing went on for about two months, and at the end of that period Bertha began to observe an extraordinary change not only in her husband's appearance, but also in her own. To her horror she found that both she and her husband were shrinking rapidly! On the day of their marriage each of them was six feet high, and now her husband was only five feet nine, while she had diminished to five feet six – owing to her more frequent use of water. Her dresses were too long and too wide for her. Tucks had to be run in everything to which tucks were applicable, and breadths and gores taken out of all garments which were susceptible of these modifications. She spent a small fortune in heels, and even then had to walk about on tiptoe in order to escape remark. Nor was Prince Pooh a whit more easy in his mind than was his wife. He wore the tallest hats with the biggest feathers, and the most preposterous heels to his boots that ever were seen. Each seemed afraid to allude to these extraordinary modifications to each other, and a gentle melancholy took the place of the hilarious jollity which had characterized their proceedings hitherto.

At length matters came to a crisis. The Prince went out hunting one day, and fell into the Rhine from the top of a high rock. He was an excellent swimmer, and he had to remain about two hours, swimming against a powerful tide, before assistance arrived. The consequence was that when he was taken out he had shrunk so considerably that his attendants hardly knew him. He was reduced, in fact, to four feet nine.

On his return to his castle he dressed himself in his tallest hat and highest heels, and, warming his chilly body at the fire, he nervously awaited the arrival of his wife from a shopping expedition in the neighbourhood.

"Charles," said she, "further disguise were worse than useless. It is impossible for me to conceal from myself the extremely unpleasant fact that we are both of us rapidly shrinking. Two months since you were a fine man, and I was one of the most magnificent women of this or any other time. Now *I* am only middle-sized, and you have suddenly become contemptibly small. What does this mean?"

"A husband is often made to look small in the eyes of his wife," said Prince Charles Pooh, attempting to turn it off with a feeble joke.

"Yes, but a wife don't mean to stand being made to look small in the eyes of her husband."

"It's only fancy, my dear. You are as fine a woman as ever."

"Nonsense, Charles. Gores, Gussets and Tucks are Solemn Things," said Bertha, speaking in capitals; "they are Stubborn Facts which there is No Denying, and I Insist on an Explanation."

"I'm very sorry," said Prince Pooh, "but I can't account for it." And, suddenly remembering that his horse was still in the Rhine, he ran off as hard as he could to get it out.

Bertha was evidently vexed. She began to suspect that she had married the Fiend, and the consideration annoyed her much. So she determined to write to her father, and ask him what she had better do.

Now, Prince Pooh had behaved most shabbily to his friend Count Krappentrapp. Instead of giving him the gold mines and diamonds which he had promised him he sent him nothing at all but a bill for twenty pounds at six months, a few old masters, a dozen or so of cheap hock, and a few hundred paving stones, which were wholly inadequate to the satisfaction of the Count and the Baron's new-born craving for silver inkstands. So the Count von Krappentrapp determined to avenge himself on the Prince at the very earliest opportunity; and in Bertha's letter the opportunity presented itself.

He saddled the castle donkey, and started for Poohberg, the

Prince's seat. In two days he arrived there, and sent up his card to Bertha. Bertha admitted him; and he then told the Prince's real character, and the horrible fate that was in store for her if she continued to be his wife.

"But what am I to do?" said she.

"If you were single again, whom would you marry?" said he with much sly emphasis.

"Oh," said the Princess, "you, of course."

"You would."

"Undoubtedly. Here it is in writing."

And she gave him a written promise to marry him if anything ever happened to the Prince her husband.

"But," said the Count, "can you reconcile yourself to the fact that my proportions are insignificant?"

"Compared with me, as I now am, you are gigantic," said Bertha. "I am cured of my pride in my own splendid stature."

"Good," said the Count. "You have noticed the carbuncle that your husband (husband! ha! ha! but no matter) wears on his middle finger?"

"I have."

"In that rests his charm. Remove it while he sleeps; he will vanish, and you will be a free woman."

That night as the clock struck twelve, the Princess removed the ring from the right-hand middle finger of Prince Pooh. He gave a fearful shriek; the room was filled with smoke; and on its clearing off, the body of the gnome in its original form lay dead upon the bed, charred to ashes!

The castle of Poohberg, however, remained, and all that was in it. The ashes of the monster were buried in the back garden, and a horrible leafless shrub, encrusted with a black, shiny, horny bark, that suggested black beetles, grew out of the grave with astounding rapidity. It grew, and grew, and grew, but never put forth a leaf; and as often as it was cut down it grew again. So when Bertha (who never recovered her original proportions) married Count Krappentrapp, it became necessary to shut up the back garden altogether, and to put ground-glass panes into the windows which commanded it. And they took the dear old Baron to live with them, and the Count and he spent a jolly time of it. The Count laid in a stock of inkstands which would last out the old man's life, and many a merry hour they spent on the hoary battlements of Poohberg. Bertha and her husband lived to a good old age, and died full of years and of honours.

THE TOP 50 THINGS I'D DO IF I EVER BECAME AN EVIL OVERLORD

Peter Anspach

Have you ever read a fantasy novel or watched a film and wondered why the villain is so stupid? Peter Anspach certainly has. A few years ago he began to compile a list of these stupid things on his website, The Evil Overlord, *and before long others were contributing to it. If you have access to the Internet and want to see the full list, then dial up www.eviloverlord.com, but for now here's a selection of the top fifty!*

Being an Evil Overlord seems to be a good career choice. It pays well, there are all sorts of perks and you can set your own hours. However, every Evil Overlord I've read about in books or seen in movies invariably gets overthrown and destroyed in the end. I've noticed that, no matter whether they are barbarian lords, deranged wizards, mad scientists or alien invaders, they always seem to make the same basic mistakes every single time. With that in mind, allow me to present:

THE TOP 50 THINGS I'D DO IF I EVER BECAME AN EVIL OVERLORD

1 My Legions of Terror will have helmets with clear plexiglass visors, not face-concealing ones.

2 My ventilation ducts will be too small to crawl through.

3 My noble half-brother, whose throne I usurped, will be killed, not kept anonymously imprisoned in a forgotten cell of my dungeon.

4 Shooting is *not* too good for my enemies.

5 The artifact which is the source of my power will not be kept on the Mountain of Despair beyond the River of Fire guarded by the Dragons of Eternity. It will be in my safe-deposit box. (The same applies to the object that is my one weakness.)

6 I will not gloat over my enemies' predicament before killing them.

7 When I've captured my adversary and he says, "Look, before you kill me, will you at least tell me what this is all about?" I'll say, "No," and shoot him. No, on second thoughts, I'll shoot him and then say "No."

8 I will not include a self-destruct mechanism unless absolutely necessary. If it is necessary, it will not be a big red button labelled "DANGER: DO NOT PUSH". The big red button marked "DO NOT PUSH" will instead trigger a spray of bullets on anyone stupid enough to disregard it. Similarly, the ON/OFF switch will not be clearly labelled as such.

9 All slain enemies will be cremated, or at least have several rounds of ammunition emptied into them – not left for dead at the bottom of the cliff.

10 The hero is not entitled to a last kiss, a last cigarette, or any other last request.

11 I will never employ any device with a digital countdown. If I find that such a device is absolutely unavoidable, I will set it to activate when the counter reaches 117 and the hero is just putting his plan into operation.

12 I will never utter the sentence, "Before I kill you, there's just one thing I want to know."

13 When I employ people as advisers, I will occasionally listen to their advice. One of my advisers will be an average five-year-old child. Any flaws in my plan that he is able to spot will be corrected before implementation.

14 Despite its proven stress-relieving effect, I will not indulge in maniacal laughter. When so occupied, it's too easy to miss unexpected developments that a more attentive individual could adjust to accordingly.

15 I will hire a talented fashion designer to create original uniforms for my Legions of Terror, as opposed to some cheap knock-offs that make them look like Nazi storm troopers, Roman foot soldiers or savage Mongol hordes. All were eventually defeated and I want my troops to have a more positive mindset.

16 I will keep a special cache of low-tech weapons and train my troops in their use. That way, even if the heroes manage to neutralize my power generator or render the standard-issue energy weapons useless, my troops will not be overrun by a handful of savages armed with spears and rocks.

17 No matter how well it would perform, I will never construct any sort of machinery that is completely indestructible, except for one small and virtually inaccessible vulnerable spot.

18 I will never build only one of anything important. All important systems will have redundant control panels and power supplies. For the same reason I will always carry at least two fully loaded weapons at all times.

19 My pet monster will be kept in a secure cage from which it cannot escape and into which I could not accidentally stumble.

20 I will dress in bright and cheery colours and so throw my enemies into confusion.

21 All bumbling conjurers, clumsy squires, talentless bards and cowardly thieves in the land will be pre-emptively put to death. My foes will surely give up and abandon their quest if they have no source of comic relief.

22 I will not fly into a rage and kill a messenger who brings me bad news just to illustrate how evil I really am. Good messengers are hard to come by.

23 I will not turn into a snake. It never helps.

24 If I absolutely must ride into battle, I will certainly not ride at the forefront of my Legions of Terror, nor will I seek out my opposite number among his army.

25 When I capture the hero, I will make sure I also get his dog, monkey, ferret or whatever sickeningly cute little animal capable of untying ropes and filching keys happens to follow him around.

26 If I learn the whereabouts of the one artifact that can destroy me, I will not send all my troops out to seize it. Instead I will send them out to seize something else and quietly put a Want-Ad in the local paper.

27 I will hire a team of board-certified architects and surveyors to examine my castle and inform me of any secret passages and abandoned tunnels that I might not know about.

28 If the beautiful princess that I capture says, "I'll never marry you! Never, do you hear me, NEVER!!!" I will say, "Oh well" and kill her.

29 My Legions of Terror will be trained in basic marksmanship. Any who cannot hit a man-sized target at ten metres will be used for target practice.

30 Before employing any captured artifacts or machinery, I will carefully read the owner's manual.

31 If it becomes necessary to escape, I will never stop to pose dramatically and toss off a one-liner.

32 I will never build a sentient computer smarter than I am.

33 I will see a competent psychiatrist and get cured of all extremely unusual phobias and bizarre compulsive habits that could prove to be a disadvantage.

34 When my guards split up to search for intruders, they will always travel in groups of at least two. They will be trained so that if one of them disappears mysteriously while on patrol, the other will immediately initiate an alert and call for backup instead of quizzically peering round a corner.

35 I will instruct my Legions of Terror to attack the hero en masse instead of standing around waiting while members break off and attack him one or two at a time.

36 If the hero runs up to my roof, I will not run up after him and struggle with him in an attempt to push him over the edge. I will also not engage him at the edge of a cliff. (In the middle of a rope-bridge over a river of molten lava is not even worth considering.)

37 If I am fighting with the hero atop a moving platform, have disarmed him and am about to finish him off, and he glances behind me and drops flat, I too will drop flat instead of quizzically turning round to find out what he saw.

38 I will not shoot at any of my enemies if they are standing in front of the crucial support beam to a heavy, dangerous, unbalanced structure.

39 If I'm eating dinner with the hero, put poison in his goblet, then have to leave the table for any reason, I will order new drinks for both of us instead of trying to decide whether or not to switch with him.

40 I will not have captives of one sex guarded by members of the opposite sex.

41 I will not use any plan in which the final step is horribly complicated, e.g. "Align the twelve stones of power on the sacred alter then activate the medallion at the moment of total eclipse." Instead it will be more along the lines of "Push the button."

42 My vats of hazardous chemicals will be covered when not in use. Also, I will not construct walkways above them.

43 If a group of henchmen fail miserably at a task, I will not berate them for incompetence and then send the same group out to try the task again.

44 I will not design my Main Control Room so that every workstation is facing away from the door.

45 If I decide to hold a double execution of the hero and an underling who failed or betrayed me, I will see to it that the hero is scheduled to go first.

46 When arresting prisoners, my guards will not allow them to stop and grab a useless trinket of purely sentimental value.

47 My dungeon will have its own qualified medical staff complete with bodyguards so that if a prisoner becomes sick and his cellmate tells the guard it's an emergency, the guard will fetch a trauma team instead of opening up the cell for a look.

48 My dungeon cells will not be furnished with objects that contain reflective surfaces or anything that can be unravelled.

49 Any data file of crucial importance will be padded to 1.45 MB in size.

50 Finally, to keep my subjects permanently locked in a mindless trance, I will provide each of them with free unlimited Internet access.

HOW TO BE FANTASTIC

Elizabeth Counihan

In the same vein as the previous item is the following clever piece about ways into and out of a fantasy story. Elizabeth Counihan is the publisher and editor of her own small-press magazine Scheherazade, *which has been appearing since 1991, and which specializes in fantasy and gothic fiction.*

You wake up. You are lying on the floor. It's hard and cold and there's straw. It's dark but there is some light coming in through a gothic-looking stained-glass window high above. The heraldic colours are shining right on you like a spotlight. You try to move. There's a clinking noise. Your hands are chained to the wall. Looks like you're in trouble. So where are you and who are you? Is this a dream? *Or are you part of someone's fantasy?*

How do you find out and are you going to live happily ever after? Are you going to live at all? Here are some tips.

First check your species. If you are a small furry animal or a cuddly alien, relax, someone will rescue you. No author would dare to let you die for fear of annihilation by animal rights campaigners.

Next check your gender. That should be easy even in these conditions. Shift yourself under the pretty lights and check out your shoe size. Obviously if you've got big, hairy legs and size twelves you aren't the heroine of this fantasy. If you can feel bulging biceps then you're laughing. With one bound you'll be free (see below).

So . . . you are female it seems. Are you old or young? Do a quick wrinkle count.

(a) No wrinkles: You are probably a child, which is nearly as safe as being furry/cuddly. If you are cute and American you are definitely not going to die (unless this is Literature, in which unlikely case – tough!).

(b) Lots of wrinkles: Bad news. You are either a wicked old witch and will die anyway or you are someone's old mother and therefore expendable.

(c) Nice legs: Ah! That's better. You just might be the heroine of this adventure but you need more information first.

What are you wearing? Shuffle yourself under the light again. It may be difficult to see the colour of your outfit, what with all that azure, vert, warm gules and so on, but persevere. It is an important prognosticator.

(a) You are in a white dress with a high neckline and a few tasteful rents in the hem: No problem unless you want excitement. You are the heroine, the damsel in distress, but you won't get any of the action. This is an old-fashioned story where you don't do anything except scream and get rescued.

(b) You are in scanty red rags with an amazing décolletage and tasteless rips at groin and cleavage: Well, you will probably die in the second to last chapter (or the last reel) but enjoy life while it lasts. You are already having your wicked way with the villain and if you play your cards right you have a good chance of seducing the hero as well before the villain finally tops you.

(c) You are wearing a short pleated tunic with a plunging
    neckline, leather wristbands and thigh length boots; you
    can see a short scabbard attached to your belt (they must
    have taken the weapon): Bingo! You are the all-action
    female hero who not only gets the fancy swordplay but
    ends up with the man, the money and the kingdom.

So what next? Somebody has captured you and chained you to
the wall of a ruined abbey (probably). How are you going to
escape and get down to the harbour, where, as you somehow
know, a tall ship will wait for you until high tide, but not a
minute longer?
   Do you have anything magical on your person? An amulet?
A precious jewel? Best of all, a ring? No? Never mind. Look
for a file.

(a) Forget it. The only use you have for a file is to do your
    nails. Your job is to look pathetic. You could try taming
    a mouse while you wait for the hero to come to the
    rescue.
(b) It will be tucked into your cleavage.
(c) It will be tucked into your boot.

As you are furiously sawing through your fetters, the file held
in your teeth, you hear the sinister sound of a creaking portal.
The portal slowly opens. (They don't have doors in this story.)
A man enters. In the light of his smoking torch (they don't
have electricity either) you see that he is tall, dark and looks
like Alan Rickman. He bows and says with an ironic smile and
an English accent:
   "Well, my fine proud lady, how are you enjoying the
hospitality of my humble abode?" You notice that he has
come without his cronies – obviously for a gloating session.
   You say:

(a) "I will never give you what you want – never!"
(b) You don't say anything. Just pout and stick your chest out.
(c) "Oh, so *you* live here. I thought I smelled a rat."

He strides forward and, bending down, holds the torch up to
your face. He strokes your (a) golden hair (b) dusky tresses (c)

dreadlocks, and then, with one eyebrow raised, holds you under the chin with a perfectly manicured hand and says:

"You know, you are a very beautiful woman,
(a) Princess Moonflower/Dawnblossom/Something-unpronoun-ceable-and-Celtic
(b) Delilah/Lolita/Magenta
(c) Red Sheila/Black Nina/Tonkawoman."

He laughs and then presses his lips to yours, kissing you savagely.
You:

(a) push him away and tearfully ask what has become of your beloved Conan/Prince Kevin/Gwyddion ap Llew Llaw Gyffup.
(b) almost tonsillectomize him with the enthusiasm of your return kiss.
(c) kick him in the groin. It's the least you can do after what he did to your family/your dog/your bike.

His mocking laughter echoes once more around the gothic vaulting. He slaps you across the face.
You:

(a) smile bravely through your tears.
(b) smile wantonly, and decide to bobbit him at the first opportunity.
(c) kick him in the groin, but harder this time. Then stun him with a well-practised head-butt, snatch his sword and . . . whoa! You can't kill him until the last chapter . . . only he knows the secret formula/whereabouts of your kid sister/spell which will free you from that terrible curse. Remember? But no time now, you have twenty-four hours to save the planet and you have to catch the tide. Just grab the keys and run for the exit. Follow the smell of rat.

Now let's go back to the beginning again. This time you have discovered that you have the hairy knees and the size twelves. Are you the hero or merely a shreddie, destined for extermination by Alan Rickman and the Forces of Darkness? As in real life you have a wider range of career choices than a female and are also more likely to get yourself prematurely dead. So how can you tell who you are?

Start with a style check.

(a) You have a white beard and are dressed in a grey robe, a long cloak and Doc Martens. You may also have a wide-brimmed hat, with or without a feather. With a bit of luck the guards have left you your staff. No? They must have been brighter than usual. Not to worry, take a quick swig from the flask in your hip pocket (labelled "for medicinal purposes only") to up the power a bit. Sketch a few runes in the air. Say something unintelligible in the Ancient Tongue. Shake the chains off and walk through the wall. The harbour is first on the right past the pub – I mean tavern.

(b) You are dressed in leather boots and a few thongs. You can't see over your pecs. Promising, but it doesn't necessarily mean that you are the hero – you could be the strong but stupid hired help and therefore at risk of dying a noble death. Try saying "Me Conan – you asshole." You sound like a psychiatrist with laryngitis? Fine – you are the hero and definitely invincible, so all you have to do now is break the chains, kick a hole in the wall and go off to find your magic sword (which you left in the umbrella stand at the Rover's Return). After that it should be dead simple to find the harbour. Even you can't miss it.

(c) You are wearing an old leather jerkin, dusty trousers and a travel-stained cloak. Oh yes – and boots – but then everyone wears boots around these parts. Your thews are not particularly mighty. Don't despair. If you are short and very young, try saying: "Blimey, guvnor. 'Ere's a go." Convincing? Then you are a thief and should do well. Simply slip your chains, pick the lock and escape through the sewer. This should lead you quite literally into the harbour. If you are older and taller you could still be the hero. But you are going to be the Lost King. That means you are tired, wise and perhaps a little cynical. You should possess some kind of talisman. It's probably in your scrip (whatever that is), or maybe stuck in your belt. A broken sword? One half of an amulet? You've got it? Good. All you have to do now is . . .

But wait! The portal is creaking again. It's that villainous Alan Rickman clone. This time he is accompanied by two guardsmen. He's come to gloat again, but isn't taking any chances with heroes.

He says:

(a) "You fools, you've let him escape! After him!" The guards try to run but are frozen in their tracks by the raw zap force. "__□○__◆◆__□●__" utters the A. R. clone, waving his arms about. When he sees that it is too late, instead of sending the guards on a how-to-resist-little-spells course, he stabs one of them with his dagger. (That's what guardsmen are for.)
(b) "You fools, he's escaping! After him!" The guards run clumsily after you and one of them aims his crossbow – and misses at point blank range. Instead of sending the guard on a brush-up-your-marksmanship course, the clone stabs him with his poniard. (Villains never learn.)
(c) "So . . . at last we meet, Stroller, or should I say King Edelweiss Bottelbier?"

You say:

(a) & (b) Nothing, obviously, as you've got clean away and are hot-footing it to the harbour.
(c) "Know, Servant of the Dark, that you will never prevail against the True King . . . Long has the way been and weary . . . At my right hand has been Hunger, Sorrow at my left . . . Bitter has been the struggle . . . But all roads must fail at last, etc., etc. . . . ." You break into the *Lay of the Token That Was Broken*, which was especially written for you by the Queen of the Faeries. But you needn't have bothered. Alan and his two hapless guardsmen are snoring gently on the straw.

You walk out. Just follow the smell of fish.

HERSHEY'S KISSES

Ron Goulart

Ron Goulart (b. 1993) has been producing ingenious and often humorous fantasies since 1952. I've lost track of his total output, since much has also appeared under pen names, but if you want to sample some of his way-out books, then try to find After Things Fell Apart *(1970),* What's Become of Screwloose? *(1971),* Ghost Breaker *(1971) and* Hello, Lemuria, Hello *(1979). In the previous volume I published one of his Max Kearny stories. This time I've selected something different, but just as crazy.*

It's too soon to tell if his reputation and his career have been seriously affected. Several million cable viewers witnessed some of what happened in that Manhattan penthouse bedroom, and as a result, Bob Hershey is enjoying considerable notoriety at the moment. His initial motive, the reason he got mixed up with sorcery and black magic at all, was nothing more than a perfectly natural desire for job security.

Bob Hershey was a medium-sized, slightly overweight man of thirty-six. His life began to change on a windy Friday morning late in the autumn of the year. His office, which was about eleven feet narrower than he would've liked it to be, was on the topmost of three floors occupied by the publishing firm of Ollendorf & Sons. Hershey had been an Associate Editor there for just under three years. Had things gone well, he'd have been promoted to Senior Editor in January, and the extra thirty-five hundred dollars in annual salary would have helped pull him back from the brink of financial ruin. Things hadn't gone well, however, and the company had been bought two months ago by Blitzgarten, the German conglomerate.

As Hershey sat at his desk, talking on the phone with his mechanic in Brimstone, Connecticut, he caught a glimpse of the former Editor-in-Chief, the woman who'd promised him the promotion, as she went trudging by in the hall with everything she'd accumulated in her office now stuffed into a cardboard carton that had *Macri Bros. Wines* lettered on its side. Not looking in his direction, she waved a forlorn farewell.

"What's that, Rosco? Sounded like you said my sports car is suffering from chronic melancholy."

"No, no, Mr Hershey . . ." Horns began honking again in the background. ". . . and general aphasia."

"I'm having trouble hearing you. Just tell me when it'll be ready."

"Better call me late next Tuesday afternoon."

"The damn car won't be ready until then?"

"I won't be able until then to tell you when it'll be ready."

A few seconds after Hershey hung up, his phone buzzed. "Yeah?"

"There's a Miss Bendix on the phone. She'd like –"

"Who are you? Where's my secretary, Rita?"

"Rita was let go, sir. I'm Nan, sir, filling in until –"

"Hey, I just talked to Rita fifteen minutes ago."

"It was a rather sudden dismissal, sir. This Miss Bendix is with the Pancho LasVegas office. You know: he hosts that cable show *Invasion of Privacy*, and they –"

"Nope, I don't have time to talk to them. Take a message."

Hanging up, Hershey sighed and turned to gaze out of his small window. Several crisp golden leaves went riding by on the sharp wind. That was odd, since there weren't, as far as he knew, any trees left in this stretch of New York City.

The phone buzzed again.

"Yeah?"

"A Mr Zipperly. He sounds almost hysterical, and perhaps you'd rather not –"

"He's one of my authors. Put him on."

Egon Zipperly actually sounded fairly calm, by Zipperly standards. "It's not me who's ticked off, Bob; it's Archie," he said. "Myself, hell, I'd let you miserable scummy bastards stall another month on the goddamn enormous royalties you owe me. Archie, as you know, is –"

"Archie is in a maximum-security prison in rural Kentucky. So he can't –"

"He escaped. Somehow he got hold of a knife. Cut up two guards, a visiting social worker, and somebody there's not enough left of to identify," explained the writer. "They think he's holed up in the Ozarks someplace now. Archie broke into a hardware store, slaughtered the owner and a man who came in to ask for change for a parking meter. He stole six of the largest axes they had in stock. You remember how Archie is about axes."

"Egon, Archie can't collect any royalties from the book. There's a law against that."

"No, no, Archie is concerned about *my* royalties and the fact that you slimy scumbags have been withholding them. The guy really identifies with me. Did I ever tell you what he did to my former agent?"

"Egon, everybody here at Ollendorf is really pleased with the way the new paperback edition of *Chop: Story of a Crazed Axe Murderer* has been selling," said Hershey soothingly. "But, as I've told you, since the Blitzgarten takeover, the Accounting Department has been really screwed up, and everybody is –"

"Do you know what Archie said when I told him that? 'Bullshit.' And then he made that funny noise he –"

"You're in communication with him?"

"Well, the poor guy calls me from pay phones now and then."

"But he's still down in the Ozarks someplace, hiding out?"

"Far as I know. Him and those half a dozen axes."

"I'll go in and talk to Accounting soon as I hang up," he promised, and hung up.

The phone buzzed.

"Miss Bendix says they're doing a programme on Janine Warbler, and since you and she were once a torrid item, would you —"

"Janine and I were never anything, least of all torrid. She merely thinks, since she's an absolute and total loon, that I . . . but never mind."

"I heard you'd planted some of those famous Hershey's kisses on her."

Hershey answered that with silence and put the phone down. "Ninety-two thousand, six hundred and six," he muttered. That was, approximately, how many times, since childhood, he'd been kidded because he had the same name as that of a famous chocolate concern.

"Got a minute?" Kevin Mulrooney was leaning in the open doorway, holding the rough layout for the cover of *Invasion of the Bioflavonoids*. He was tall, thin, and bald.

"Come on in." Hershey began rummaging through the assortment of folders, manuscripts, letters and sundries piled high atop his desk. "My sports car seems to have mental problems. A madman with an axe is unhappy with his royalty situation. This is not the life I envisioned when I graduated from finishing school."

"I always saw myself ending up as a distinguished gent with lots of white hair. What are you hunting for?"

"Here it is. A memo from Oskar Hitler, our new CEO."

"See? There are worse things to be named after than a candy bar."

"Ninety-two thousand, six hundred and seven," Hershey said. "This thing says — 'As of today, our entire sci-fi line is dead. All titles in production are to be suspended.' Thank you for your help, Oskar Hitler."

Mulrooney sank into the only other chair in the small office. "Shit."

"Exactly. I forgot to tell you when I got this damn memo yesterday afternoon."

Mulrooney leaned the layout, gently, against a filing cabinet. "You see so few Help Wanted ads asking for tall, skinny Art Directors with no hair," he explained. "That's the reason I don't quit."

"Things have been lousy since the takeover."

"Aw, you won't have to worry, Robert."

"Hum?"

"Your old true love is coming here to run the whole operation. Yeah, I heard that at a reliable cocktail party just last night."

Slowly, Hershey sat up very stiff and straight in his lopsided chair. "When you say my old true love, you mean my erstwhile wife? She isn't likely to run Ollendorf, since she's down in some tropic paradise, spending my alimony cheques on fripperies and —"

"I'm talking about Janine Warbler. The word is, she's leaving Mildmay Books to become Editor-in-Chief of our —"

"Oh my God." He pressed his hands to his chest. "My whole life is starting to pass before my eyes. I must be dying."

Mulrooney grinned. "I was under the impression, Robert, that you and Warbler were once quite close."

"Janine had me fired from Mildmay four years ago. She smeared my reputation, and I was out of work for nearly a year. If there hadn't been people here who loathed her as much as I do, I would probably never have worked in publishing again."

"You're telling me you and Warbler were never lovers?"

"OK, listen. There was a party. Five years ago in the Village. I did have a few drinks, but I never lost touch with reality. As I recall it, Janine and I had a short conversation in the kitchen — we were alone at the time, I admit — about the novels of Robert Musil and Joseph Roth. Janine claims, though, that I grabbed her, fondled her, and planted hot kisses on her face and body."

"She's not bad-looking, so it —"

"I never so much as touched the woman," swore Hershey. "But she became obsessed with the notion that I was a human beast, somebody who belongs in a book by Egon Zipperly. She got a job at Mildmay, and within two years, had worked up to a position of power. She'd been perfectly content at her other publishing house; she took the new editorial job only so she'd be at the same outfit with me. Then, when she was running things, she fired me."

"Why didn't you sit down and reason with her?"

"She's a very emotional woman." Hershey shook his head. "You don't reason with Janine."

"If she does come here to work as your boss, what'll you do?"

"Probably something violent," answered Hershey.

Although it was raining on Saturday, Hershey went hiking anyway. He'd found that solitary hiking in Witch's Wood, the thirty-acre nature preserve near his thoroughly mortgaged home in Brimstone, Connecticut, was conducive to brooding. Hands in pockets, collar of his down jacket turned up, old golf hat tugged down low on his forehead, he was trudging the winding, narrow trail that led to Suicide Pond.

The rain that was falling down through the grey afternoon was chill and hard, well on its way to becoming hail. It poked at Hershey's ears, prodding at his hunched shoulders. He'd been walking for over twenty minutes, and hadn't as yet encountered another human being. Off among the stiff, nearly leafless trees, some kind of angry-sounding birds were calling to each other.

Hershey had been thinking about his future, but found that too dismal a topic, and was now striving to make his mind an absolute and total blank.

"Excuse me, squire. Might I make what may initially sound like an odd and unusual request of you?"

Hershey, making a gasping noise, came to a sudden halt on the muddy pathway. Frowning, he glanced into the shadowy woods at his left and then at his right. He didn't see anyone.

"Next I'd like to ask you not to start screaming like a dozen blue devils when you first lay eyes on me. And, if you can, try not to go rushing away into the blinking dusk."

"If this is a practical joke, boy, have you picked the wrong target," he announced to the woodlands in general. "I recently edited a book about an axe murderer, and I picked up some useful tips on how –"

"If you could stroll over a mite closer to the maple tree, squire?"

"Which tree is that?"

"Mayhap you ought to see about editing a basic book of woodlore. You've been slogging through this blinking pre-serve for near to six years now, and you, apparently, don't yet know a maple from a poplar or an elm. OK. I'll make things easier for you and manifest myself. Stay put."

Brush near the tree that must have been the maple rattled. Then an unimpressive and woebegone raccoon came skittering into view, watching Hershey intently. "I had in mind a more impressive champion, but you'll have to do, I suppose," it said to him.

Taking a step back, Hershey took another look around. "OK, kids, this is sufficient. I'm not really in the mood for ventriloquism or hidden speakers."

"Do I look like a blooming trick? Do I appear to be dubbed?" The raccoon reared up on its hind legs, poking at its furry chest with a delicate forefinger. "Now, what say we get down to business? And, whilst I'm narrating my plight, try to keep an open mind."

Hershey gave the twilight woods a more careful scanning. "This must be one of those hidden-camera shows – *People Are Fools* or *America's Biggest Idiots*. Is it?"

"The way this works, alas, I can approach only one potential saviour per year. You seem to be it, and I ain't any happier about that than you."

The damn thing really did seem to be talking to him. It had a piping voice and a slightly British accent. "Of course, it may be that I've just gone completely round the bend," he told the raccoon. "This is a hallucination, and –"

"You're borderline bonkers at best, squire. This is really happening," the impatient animal assured him. "If you'd be so kind as to attend to me. You can save me from another full year of emotional trauma and foraging in garbage cans, simply by doing me a small – one might almost class it minute and minuscule – favour."

"Wait now." Moving closer, Hershey squatted, eyeing the raccoon. "You aren't going to tell me that you're under an enchantment?"

"Bingo. You got it first crack."

"Somebody's put a spell on you?"

"Right again. You're brighter than you look."

"If you're trying to wheedle a favour out of me, insults aren't going to help your cause much."

"True, forgive me, do." The raccoon gave a small, contrite shrug of its shaggy shoulders. "Very well, then, squire, here's the pitch. A rival sorcerer put this blinking spell on me back in 1979, and I've been trying ever since to –"

"Rival sorcerer? You're a sorcerer, too?"

"In my true human form, yes, I am. Right now, though, I'm without my full magical resources," it admitted. "The manner in which you have to break this particular spell may strike you as trite, but my arch-enemy wasn't an especially imaginative chap, and he had a perverse streak as well. I'm getting a weak message that you've also edited a book of folk tales, so you are probably aware that –"

"Whoa. No, nope. Absolutely not." Hershey stood up, took yet another glance around him. "Is this your idea, Mulrooney? Are you lurking in the trees someplace, chortling?" he asked the damp, darkened woods.

"Mulrooney's over in Jersey at the moment, in the sack with that new Assistant Editor in the Young Adult Department," the raccoon informed him. "OK, what you have to do is – well, kiss me."

"Sure this has to be a gag. Hershey's kisses again. Christ, that makes ninety-two thousand, six hundred and eleven times since the unfortunate day I was born that some wiseass has –"

"Look, Hershey, I don't make the rules. I had a spell put on me, and this is the way the damn thing works."

"How come you know my name?"

"You just blurted it out. Besides, it isn't much of a trick, even for someone running on diminished mystical powers, to guess some gink's name and occupation."

Hershey asked, "You're a guy sorcerer, a male?"

"I am not an enchanted princess. Sorry."

"I don't know; if it got around that I kissed a guy –"

"A raccoon. I'm a raccoon at the moment," the animal pointed out. "And who's to know? I'm not going to blab."

"I might get rabies."

"I can assure you I'm not suffering from rabies."

"So you say."

"You don't have to kiss me on the mouth. A simple peck on the noggin will do."

Hershey tugged at the soggy brim of his golf hat. "What's in it for me?"

"Doing a humane deed ought to be its own reward."

"I suppose so. But traditionally there are perks. A pot of gold, a cask of jewels, three wishes, marriage to a princess – things along that line."

"Tell you what, Hersh. You help me out, and I'll show you how to get the best of Janine Warbler."

"You know about her, too?"

"I've been getting faint glimmers from realms beyond."

Hershey took a last, careful look around. "OK." Leaning, he kissed the raccoon, gingerly, on its forehead.

The sorcerer was still there, sprawled in the big black leatherette armchair in the family room and gazing toward the television screen, when Hershey came home, weary, from work on Monday evening. "What are you up to, Runcible?" he inquired. "I still think that's a nitwit name, by the way."

"It was bestowed upon me. I've been playing video games, squire."

"I don't have a video-game setup."

"When one is a first-rate magician, one doesn't require the mundane paraphernalia of –"

"I thought you were going to use your powers to find yourself a place to live. A place other than mine."

Runcible had turned out to be a short, pudgy man with tight-curling white hair. He dressed in a rumpled, tweedy suit, a pink shirt, and a rainbow-pattern tie. Over that ensemble he wore a floor-length tan overcoat. He appeared to be in his middle sixties and never took off his frayed yellow gloves. "I'm still recuperating," he replied in his high-pitched voice.

"Being a blinking raccoon for lo these many years has taken its toll."

Hershey, hunched slightly, dropped his attaché case at the doorway and slouched over to the low white sofa. He sat facing the wizard. "About Janine Warbler," he said.

"In another few days at most, squire, I'll be strong enough to tackle your problem with that –"

"It's definite she's coming to Ollendorf. She's going to be Editor-in-Chief *and* Vice-President," he said, sagging. "My days there are numbered."

"Don't go fretting. I'll use my impressive talents as a warlock to –"

"As of the first of the month, Runcible, I'll be tossed out of there. All because Janine claims I kissed her that fateful night in –"

"Kisses." Runcible sat suddenly upright, his short legs kicking a few times. He gestured at the TV set, and it turned off. "Hush a minute, squire. I'm getting a flash." He thrust a gloved hand deep into one of the cluttered pockets of his lengthy overcoat. "I must consult my crystal."

When Runcible tugged the baseball-sized crystal from his pocket, a small lizard fell free and went scurrying across the peach-coloured rug and up the drapes.

"Is that your crystal ball? It looks scuffed and sticky."

"Maintain silence. This happens to be the Sacred Crystal of Sargon." After burnishing it on the left sleeve of his coat, Runcible brought the ball up near his face and squinted into it. The sphere commenced glowing with a faint green. "Janine Warbler . . . Yessir, I'm seeing an image of Janine Warbler. Goodness me, the lass is jaybird naked and about to step into her shower bath."

"Let's see." Hershey started to leave the sofa.

"Stay back; don't shatter the delicate spell." The sorcerer waved him away with his free hand. "Why, oh mystical guides from the spirit world, are you showing me a close-up of this bimbo's rear end? Ah, I see. I am to pay particular attention to the beetle."

"What beetle?" Hershey was poised on the edge of the sofa cushion.

"Ah, I see. Yes, the secret mark that is tattooed on her left buttock . . . sacred scarab of . . . Say again? I'm not getting this, fellows." He tightened his grip on the crystal ball. "How's that again? I missed part of it . . . He has to do what? He has to . . . Don't talk so fast. Ah yes. But what exactly will that accomplish? I see. It . . ." His body went slack.

Runcible slumped in the chair, his eyes falling shut. The fingers of his gloved right hand snapped open, and the crystal, no longer glowing green, dropped from his grasp, thunked onto the carpet, and rolled three and a half feet in the direction of the shallow fireplace.

Hershey rushed over to him. "Hey, are you OK?"

The wizard blinked. "It's exhausting work, this sorcery stuff. Especially when you're a touch rusty. If I'd been in peak form, I might've found out a lot more for you," he explained, wheezing some. "I may be able to contact them again, although most times –"

"What did you find out about Janine?"

Runcible stood up, brushed at his overcoat, sat back down. "Wellsir, I didn't pick up all this as clearly as I would've liked," he said, intertwining his gloved fingers. "The upshot, near as I can get it, is that the young woman has a special sort of mystical tattoo on her bum. It's magical in some way, but I didn't get all the details on that."

"How come I couldn't hear anything?"

Runcible tapped the side of his head. "My spirit guides communicate telepathically – and show me pictures in the crystal. Could you fetch it for me?"

Hershey walked to where it had rolled, then knelt and scooped up the globe. It was sticky. "What's this tattoo have to do with anything?"

"As I understand the situation, squire, you're going to have to . . . Thanks." He accepted the crystal ball, gave it a fond squeeze before dumping it back amidst the clutter of his overcoat pocket. "To gain some sort of control over the lady in question, you have to kiss the beetle tattoo. That –"

"More kissing."

"Kissing the beetle gives you power over Janine. I'm not exactly sure why. You have to buss it thrice, by the way."

Hershey sat down. "You're telling me that, based on information from your contacts in the mystic realms, I have to arrange things so that I can plant not one, but three kisses on Janine's bare backside? That's the only way I can hold on to my job?"

"That about sums it up, yep."

"I'd better start updating my résumé."

Thursday Afternoon, there were snow flurries. From his office window, Hershey could see swirls of snowflakes go flickering by. He turned away from the window, concentrating again on surveying the movable contents of his office. It was going to take more than one carton to haul all this crap out of here. Maybe he should simply leave it all and let them turn his office into a shrine.

Of course, it was still possible he wouldn't have to leave. Runcible kept assuring him, between protracted sessions of video gaming, that sorcery – with possibly a bit of black magic tossed in – was going to save him and his job. His sorcerer house guest hadn't as yet explained how that was going to work.

"Oy," Hershey remarked.

"Hitler hasn't cancelled this series, too, has he?" Mulrooney appeared in the doorway, holding up a cover rough for the latest novel in the Young Adult *Unwed Mothers Hospital* series. "It would actually come as a profound relief if he has."

"No such luck. What's that thing in the foreground?"

"An owl. This novel is the one where the owls in the woods behind the hospital are endangered, and Nurse Vicki and Intern Billy save them, remember?"

"Your owl looks like a watermelon with sunglasses." Hershey slouched in his chair. "But why should I care? I'll be given the heave-ho before the year runs out."

"Perhaps not." Mulrooney, tucking the drawing under his arm, came in and sat.

"What do you mean? Isn't Janine coming in to rule this place with an iron hand?"

"She's still scheduled to, yes," said Mulrooney, lowering

his voice and leaning forward. "However, I've gotten to know Miss Bendix, the one who's been trying to contact you. She's Pancho LasVegas's assistant, as you may recall, and she tells me they're planning an *Invasion of Privacy* show aimed at exposing Janine Warbler. Showing how she clawed her way to the top of publishing, how she –"

"There's nothing unusual or newsworthy about clawing your way to the top."

"Yeah, but they apparently have proof that she indulged in some shady practices to get her present exalted post. There are also hints of amorous adventures."

"What good is all this going to do me?"

"The show's set to air very soon. It could tarnish her reputation enough to cause Blitzgarten to have second thoughts about her."

"Naw, if Blitzgarten were the sort of outfit that ever had second thoughts, they wouldn't own us now."

"I think you ought to talk to Miss Bendix. She's got great legs, and *Invasion of Privacy* is, as I see it, on your side."

"Nope, pass."

"They may drop in on you anyway. The show is noted for busting in on people, walking into motels, breaking into meetings, doggedly pursuing the truth."

"I'm not interesting enough to be broken in on," he assured Mulrooney.

On Friday night at a few minutes past eleven, Hershey was standing in a New York City alley in the East Sixties. A light snow was falling, and, hands deep in the pockets of his down jacket, he was shivering and muttering. He'd been waiting here beside the Manhattan Museum of Folklore for seventeen minutes now.

"Eighteen," he corrected after tugging his hand out of his pocket and checking his wristwatch yet again.

"All set, squire." Runcible, his long overcoat buttoned up tight, appeared at the alley's mouth. "Come along."

"I thought your mystic powers could put anybody into a trance in less than –"

"Can I help it if the night watchman at this benighted

museum likes to nap on the job? Took awhile to awaken the coot out of his tipsy doze." He beckoned with a gloved hand. "We can now, I am pleased to announce, slip into the joint undetected."

"It took you eighteen minutes to wake this guy up?"

"You can't simply start putting a spell on someone the blinking second you meet him," explained the sorcerer as they hurried up the snow-covered stone steps of the darkened museum. "A certain amount of prelim chitchat is needed to get him in a relaxed and receptive mood; some cordial banter has to be exchanged."

"Eighteen minutes of banter is a lot of banter."

Runcible pushed at the wide metal door, and it swung open. "This particular watchman wasn't an ideal subject."

"That's why it took you so long?"

"That and tying and gagging the fellow."

They were in a shadowy corridor, which smelled strongly of dust, furniture polish, and time. "If he's in a trance, why was it necessary to tie –"

"In the end, squire, I had to bop him on the sconce."

Hershey halted next to a glass case full of beaded necklaces. "That's assault."

"Sometimes a nice, simple bit of assault works as well as wizardry."

"I don't know." Hershey shook his head. "This isn't going as smoothly as –"

"We'd best hurry along," advised the sorcerer. "The exhibit we seek lies through yonder door on your left."

"You're certain this is going to work?"

"The message came in loud and clear."

Hershey crossed the indicated threshold. "I've been thinking that if this Sacred Ring of Karnabahar actually had the magic powers your mystical advisers claim, it wouldn't be on display in this rinky-dink little museum."

"Many objects of extreme occult power lie hidden from the average gink," reminded the wizard. "We're on a tight schedule, so move along. There's the statue yonder." He pointed across the dim-lit room.

"That's Karnabahar?"

A large wooden effigy, about seven feet high and resembling a muscular man with the head of a dog, stood on a low pedestal near a high, thin window. "He was a highly thought-of deity in ancient Makkaristan. Virgins sacrificed annually, bullocks offered up once a month, the works."

"That was a long time ago, thousands of years. Could be the magic powers of the ring have worn out."

"Magic doesn't have to be recharged, squire. Shake a leg now and kiss the ring."

"That's something else that unsettles me," mentioned Hershey, halting next to the statue of the ancient god and gazing at it. "All this odd kissing I'm doing lately. This whole mess, after all, started when Janine thought –"

"The ring you want is the silver one with the fake ruby. Don't kiss the gold one with the fake emerald or that one made out of animal teeth. Smooch it right on the stone for the best results."

"How many times do I have to kiss it?"

"Just once, according to my information."

"And then I turn invisible?"

"So my mystical guides informed me when I asked them to suggest a foolproof way for you to sneak into Janine Warbler's boudoir undetected."

"It's a cold night."

"That it is, squire, but we can discuss the weather after you –"

"In order to take full advantage of being invisible, supposing that this thing actually works, I'm going to have to strip off my clothes."

"It will aid the effect, yes."

"Taking off all my clothes on a night like this, I'm going to freeze my ass."

"A frozen ass is better than a blighted career," the sorcerer pointed out. "Kiss the ring, Hersh. I think I hear the watchman groaning."

Hershey glanced around the dim room, eyeing the lurking glass cases and the dark statues. Nodding, he took a deep breath, stretched up, and kissed the ring.

*   *   *

"I'm getting goosebumps."

"They don't show."

Hershey was sitting on the chill passenger seat of his Zitrone 210S. "I'm going to have to take this car back to the shop and have them work on the heater," he said. He was naked and invisible.

The sorcerer was at the wheel of the sports car, rubbing at the steamy windshield with the heel of his left hand and the frayed cuff of his overcoat. "Ah yes, there's a space right up ahead."

"Janine's apartment is over on East Seventy-second; this is East Seventy-third." Hershey shivered and rubbed his unseen hands together, missing the first time he tried to bring them into contact. "I'd prefer not to trudge through the sleet and snow for a whole damn block."

"You still don't appreciate the fact, Hersh, that great deeds require great sacrifices. Once, for example –"

A loud scraping sound interrupted him.

Hershey said, "Damn, more bodywork."

Runcible succeeded finally, with only a little more banging and scraping, in getting the car parked. "There now, snug as a whistle."

"One wheel up on the curb, the fender pushed into a lamp-post – that's not my idea of snug."

"I'll escort you to the door of the building," said the sorcerer. "While I'm distracting the doorman, you slip into the building and scoot up to the lass's apartment." He opened the door, which let in a fiercely cold gust of night wind. Stepping to the street, Runcible wrapped his long, heavy overcoat tighter around him.

"She's probably not even home." Very carefully, Hershey stepped barefoot onto the snowy sidewalk. "Ow wow, this is cold."

"The lady is home, alone and sound asleep," said the sorcerer. "My mystical sources have already informed me of that."

"Her apartment will be locked up tighter than –"

"The crystal told us the door to her kitchen is unlocked. You're going to use that, remember?"

Hershey was starting to shiver violently; his invisible feet were turning numb. "I'm leaving footprints in the slush."

"Can't be helped. We'll cross the street here and head round the corner."

"Suppose Janine wakes up while I'm planting the kisses?"

"Won't matter."

"Why?"

"Because once you kiss the beetle mark three times, that'll give you, I suppose, some kind of control over her. We've already been over all the –"

"You suppose?"

"Some of the messages, as you recall, didn't come across clearly," said Runcible, halting on the snow-covered sidewalk. "Speaking of which, there's the possibility that you'll remain invisible for only an hour."

"Hey, you told me three. You swore that your magical correspondents guaranteed you that kissing that damn Sacred Ring of Karnabahar would make me completely and totally unseen for no less than three solid hours."

"Actually, that was one of the details that came across the void a bit blurred, squire," admitted the sorcerer. "Thinking about it now – well, I'm not all that confident they may not've been trying to say one hour rather than three hours."

"I kissed the thing twenty minutes ago, meaning I may have only –"

"Best not to dawdle here in idle chitchat," Runcible pointed out.

A dog lunged into the elevator a few seconds after the unseen Hershey had dived into the cage. A small pinkish poodle, it became immediately fascinated with him.

The weary grey-haired man who'd just come back from taking it for a walk tugged at the poodle's leash. "Knock it off, asshole," he advised the dog.

The poodle began sniffing vigorously at Hershey's invisible toes, making a perplexed growling sound in its tiny chest.

"C'mon, quiet down, putz." The weary man gave another tug of the leash.

Hershey stood stiffly, holding his breath, debating whether or not to give the hound an invisible kick.

The elevator shuddered to a stop at the tenth floor. The door whooshed open. The man, grabbing up the agitated poodle, took his leave.

Alone in the climbing cage, Hershey let out his breath in a long sigh. He noticed that the snow he picked up on his bare feet had melted and left a small puddle on the carpet.

Rattling, the elevator stopped again and opened its door. This was the thirteenth floor.

Hershey stumbled out into the corridor. He hadn't realized how much he looked down at his feet while walking. Not being able to do that now made moving somewhat difficult. He weaved some, staggered a little.

He was about fifteen feet from Janine's when an apartment door across the hall opened a few inches. Hershey had the impression someone was peeking out. The door shut quickly and quietly.

He hesitated, eyeing the door he wanted. After a few seconds, he started moving again. He found the kitchen door was indeed unlocked, but it produced an enormous rasping noise when he pulled it carefully open. The door across the way was opening again as Hershey slipped into Janine's kitchen. He shut the door, leaned against it.

There was a single light showing over the sink. The large white and yellow room smelled strongly of health foods.

Hershey paused at the sink. He had the sudden desire for a glass of water. Reaching out, he took hold of the faucet handle.

He was turning it gingerly, when he noticed fingers. Three at first, starting from the little finger. Next the thumb and forefinger appeared.

"Mother of Mercy," he muttered as he stood watching his entire right hand and then his wrist materialize.

He moved back, shaking his head forlornly, and sat on a white kitchen stool. In a little less than three minutes by the wall clock, he became entirely visible once more.

"So here I am, naked as a jaybird and perfectly visible, sitting smack in the middle of Janine's kitchen at six minutes before midnight," he said. "No wonder Karnabahar doesn't have any worshippers these days."

Getting clear of the apartment seemed the best thing to do, except that he was naked. To travel down thirteen floors in the elevator, cross the lobby, and walk out into the street was going to be difficult. What he'd have to do was borrow a raincoat or something similar out of Janine's closet.

Still, as long as he was going to prowl around, he might as well try to do what he'd come for. She was, according to Runcible's not-always-reliable sources, supposed to be sound asleep now in her bedroom. He might, with a little luck, be able to sneak in there unheard and kiss the tattoo.

He started to stand up, then sat quickly down. Hershey had heard some whispering and murmuring from out in the hall. Perched, very still, on the stool, he listened. A minute clicked by, during which he heard nothing further.

Leaving his perch, he pushed through the swinging door and into the large dining room. It was dark, and, staying close to one wall, he flatfooted across and into the living room. That was even bigger, and its high, wide window showed the snowy night outside and the apartment buildings that rose high all around.

He remained for a minute with his back to the fireplace. The last remnants of a fire still glowed, warming him some. The door to Janine's bedroom, according to Runcible, was the one immediately to the right of the ceiling-high bookcases. He made his way to that, took hold of the brass knob, and slowly turned it. The door opened quietly, and he crossed the shadowy threshold.

The bedroom was lit by a small globular night-light plugged in close to the floor near Janine's wide, low bed. Hershey remained, breath held, near the doorway.

Janine was in the bed, her long dark hair spilled across the pink pillow. She was breathing evenly, snoring in a quiet, purring way.

Moving very slowly and quietly, Hershey made his way over to the sleeping editor.

She was sleeping on her stomach, which would make accessing her backside easier. After risking a very cautious breath, Hershey took hold of the top of the quilt that covered Janine. As delicately and deftly as he could, he began peeling it away from her. Janine was, as the sorcerer had predicted, sleeping naked.

Bending closer, Hershey, with narrowed eyes, scrutinized Janine's left buttock. The beetle tattoo was just discernible in the yellowish glow of the night-light.

The young woman stirred, murmuring into her pillow.

Hershey straightened up, ready to retreat. He glanced around until he located the closet. But the sleeping editor didn't awaken.

After shrugging once, Hershey bent again. Very carefully, he rested both palms on the mattress. Then, slowly, he began lowering his head toward the vicinity of the dark tattoo.

He missed the first try, kissing instead her upper right thigh.

Now Janine started stirring, murmuring.

Hershey dived and planted the three requisite kisses, all on target.

She rolled over, sat up, gasped. "Oh, it's you, Bob," she said, recognizing him.

"Let me explain, Janine, what must appear at first glance, I have to admit, like a somewhat odd and unusual –"

"There's no need to apologize, Bob dear," she told him, smiling. "I was expecting you sooner or later. I knew that sooner or later you'd come to your senses about me."

"Come to *my* senses about *you*? Holy Hannah, for years it's been you who has persecuted me, vilified –"

"Only because you kept ignoring me. That's why I spread those stories about us initially. But instead of seeing more of me, you went and got married to somebody else. That really ticked me off, and I . . . well, I set out to get my revenge. Sometimes love and hate can be very close."

"Yeah, close."

She patted the bed beside her. "Sit here, darling," she invited. "First I have to confess something. It's really a very dreadful thing to have resorted to, and I really didn't even believe in it – but it does seem to have worked where nothing else would, doesn't it?"

"I don't think I'm following all this, Janine."

She took hold of his hand. "I must sound like a babbling idiot," she said apologetically. "Well, a week or so ago, after attending a party for one of our authors, I found myself down in the Village. I had, don't know why, a sudden impulse to get tattooed."

"Tattooed," he said slowly. "Then that beetle is new?"

"Yes, it was an impulse thing," she admitted. "Sometimes, when I've had more than two or three glasses of wine, I get impulses. The thing is, the tattoo artist sensed that I was unhappy, and he confided in me that he was a sorcerer. I've never fooled with anything like that previously, but he was extremely convincing. He persuaded me that, for a fee, a fairly stiff one, he would be able to help me get what I wanted in this world. Now that you're divorced, I thought it would be OK if I had him help me get you, and –"

"This sorcerer has grey curly hair?"

"Why, yes."

"Wears a long tan overcoat."

"Well, there was a long tan overcoat hanging on a peg in his tattoo parlour."

"Then it looks like we –"

It was at that point that Pancho Las Vegas and a camera crew from *Invasion of Privacy* burst into the bedroom and started taping.

ESCAPE FROM THE PLANET OF THE BEARS

Tom Holt

Tom Holt (b. 1961) has a remarkable capacity for producing an incredible diversity of humorous fantasy novels. Expecting Someone Taller *(1987) was the first, followed by* Who's Afraid of Beowulf? *(1988),* Flying Dutch *(1991),* Ye Gods *(1992),* Faust among Equals *(1994),* Djinn Rummy *(1995),* Paint Your Dragon *(1996),* Open Sesame *(1997),* Wish You Were Here *(1998),* Only Human *(1998) and many more. Comedy plays with the emotions, and some of the best comic writing often counterbalances humour with pathos. Despite the amusing premise of the following story I also found it remarkably poignant. See what you think.*

Not all the fearful monsters there need fill you full of dread;
The demon-flies speak English, and they love to scout
  ahead.
The mantacores will pull you through the swamp and
  through the mud —
But the little fuzzy animals will drink your blood.
                    — Frank Hayes, "Little Fuzzy Animals"

Captain's log, deep space exploratory vehicle Zarathustra. Date and location unknown.

Slade paused and looked back over his shoulder. Far behind him in the bay, the ship was sinking; only the engine nacelle was still visible through the cloud of swirling steam. He thought about the effect of seawater on a neutronium pulse reactor manifold, and scrambled behind a nearby rock.

Just in time. The ground shook like a laughing jelly, as most of the contents of the bay reared up into the air, hung for a moment and came down again in a hammer-heavy shower, drenching Slade to the skin. He'd been brought up in England, so he didn't mind that particularly; but the thought that the ship was gone for ever hit him so hard that he staggered and sat down hard on some unfamiliar species of jellyfish.

(And that was just the coffee machine. Just as well he'd had the wit to jettison the engine cores while they were still in orbit.)

Wherever this was, it had suddenly become home.

Pity about that.

He looked around. Seen from one perspective, it was fortuitous to say the least that he'd contrived to crash-land on a planet that was, at first sight, virtually indistinguishable from Earth. Most planets, he knew for a fact, weren't. Further, he had to admit that pitching on a planet that apparently teemed with organic life was a stroke of luck. The percentages were all against that; statistically, he ought to be either completely submerged in corrosive gases or standing on something that looked like post-industrial Cleveland. Instead — well, it could be a lot worse.

On the other hand . . .

Well, the ship was gone, and walking home from here wasn't a viable option. It was something that all spacefarers had nightmares about, usually after a late dinner of freeze-dried chicken korma – stranded on an alien world with nothing but an environment suit and an emergency toolkit. There had, of course, been a briefing about just such a set of circumstances at the Academy. He could remember the exact words.

Find a cliff and jump. You'll be better off.

Nothing if not succinct, those Academy briefings. But there didn't appear to be any cliffs in these parts, and besides, he wasn't quite ready to give up.

Captain's log, resumed, he dictated into the portable recorder. *Ship lost, am stranded on unknown planet. Rest of crew presumed dead. Unable to salvage anything from ship. Bummer. End log.*

The ground rose steadily in front of him, and on the crest of the rise was a wood. Shelter, he thought; probably food and building materials as well. Without looking back, he started to walk.

The trees looked for all the world like good old Earth pines, and the smell brought back a flood of childhood memories, most of them to do with rained-on picnics, arguing parents and getting lost in woods. Situated as he was, however, the concept of *lost* didn't have a whole lot of relevance; he couldn't bring himself to worry about it, in the same way that Joan of Arc, about to be roasted alive at the stake, probably wasn't too fussed about being out in the sun without a hat. He walked for about an hour, idly noticing that the wood seemed remarkably clear of brambles and undergrowth. As far as he could tell, it extended for at least a hundred acres. But it was unnaturally quiet; no birds sang, nothing moved except the tips of the branches as the soft breeze played around them. No beetles, even. Very strange.

Then he heard a woman scream.

He looked round, trying to gauge the direction; at which point, he saw her. She was human – also tall, young, blonde, dressed only in a few scanty rags. Although she was barefoot, she ran as if she was wearing three-inch heels. Her fingernails were that perfect elongated oval shape that usually only occurs in nature within walking distance of a beauty parlour. Once, she stopped to look over her shoulder; then she screamed again – "Eeek," she said, quite distinctly – and fell over a tree root.

Slade sat up on his heels. *I could get to like it here*, he thought. Obviously, evolution on this planet followed different rules – if he'd been a native of these parts, Charles Darwin would have given up on biology and gone into the tortoiseshell comb business – but who says things always have to be the same? In the country of the dumb, the half-witted man . . .

Then he heard another sound; faint and far away, but woodland acoustics are notoriously tricksy. It was like the distant popping of corks.

Way to go, Slade thought; he stood up and hurried toward the woman, noticing as he went that her hair was straight and looked as if she'd just spent three hours in a salon chair. "Excuse me, can I help . . ." he said, but she stood on one foot staring at him, her mouth open, a total lack of understanding behind her ocean-deep blue eyes.

Hey, Slade thought, *maybe this isn't a planet after all. Maybe I just died and went to California.*

The popping-corks noise was getting closer now; the woman heard it and went "Eeek" again. She tried to run, but her ankle was obviously giving her grief. "Here, let me give you a hand," Slade said, but she still didn't seem to understand; and it wasn't just the words, it was as if language itself wasn't something she was familiar with. *Not just California*, Slade muttered to himself. *A couple of specific square miles around Malibu.* He suppressed a big grin and started to walk forward –

– Just as a bunch of enormous bears appeared over the lip of a patch of dead ground, no more than twenty-five yards away. They were, to put it mildly, not like any other bears he'd seen before. For one thing, they were *big* – nine or ten feet tall – and they were standing upright, just like humans. Furthermore, they were wearing little short, tight red jackets (which reminded Slade of something he'd seen, years ago, but he couldn't quite think what) and they were carrying what looked like . . .

. . . Pop-guns. Yes, those little wooden tube things with a plunger in one end that fire corks. Slade stood and stared, rooted to the spot. Some party, even by Californian standards.

Then one of the bears saw him, raised his pop-gun to his shoulder and fired. Maybe he snatched the shot at the last moment; hard to say. At any rate, the cork missed Slade's head by the width of two fingers, whizzed past his ear and hit a tree; which sagged and fell over.

Some cork.

Slade had the wit to duck; just in time, because the other bears were shooting at him now. "Get him!" one of them roared, and three of the monsters lurched toward him, stuffing fresh corks into the muzzles of their weapons as they advanced. *Not Malibu, then,* Slade thought as he jumped up and started to run. *More like LA.* A cork hit the ground a foot or so in front of him, spraying him with shredded leaf-mould.

Fortunately, the bears couldn't manoeuvre very well among the trees, and he managed to lose them; or, at least, they got bored and gave up. When he was sure it was safe (relatively safe), he crept back to a high point overlooking the spot where he'd seen the girl, tucked himself in behind a tree-stump, and looked down.

The sight he saw was amazing: there was a whole mob of humans there now, all dressed in the same sort of rags, some of them screaming (but he couldn't make out any words; and then he remembered that he'd been able to understand the bears). They were being driven steadily inwards by a surrounding ring of the giant bears, who were shouting and firing their pop-guns in the air; others were cracking whips. It was like an armed uprising in Santa Claus' toy factory.

They were making the humans climb trees.

What the hell? Slade thought; and he noticed a low, ominous humming noise, like a giant underground generator – except that it seemed to be coming from high up in the treetops. Not a generator. Bees.

The humans had obviously done this before, although (equally obviously) they weren't enjoying it a bit. As they reached the upper branches, great clouds of bees sailed out like fleets of tiny nano-warships, completely enveloping the climbers. Slade could hear the screams, and the occasional thump as one of them lost hold and fell. The bears didn't seem in the least concerned about that; they were watching the climbers and grinning.

It was a matter of numbers; for every three climbers engulfed by bees, one made it through relatively unscathed to the

hives lodged in the high forks; long enough to tear a hive out
and drop it to the ground, where it cracked open. *Honey*, Slade
realized. *Why am I not surprised?*

He didn't stay to watch the end. It wasn't a pretty sight, and
he'd seen enough. Somehow, by God knows what freak of
natural selection, on this planet humans were the dumb beasts
and bears were the dominant species. Huge great big golden-
blond bears, in cute little red jackets.

What's more, they smelled awful. So, he realized, did the
whole planet; a foul stench of violets, lavender, rosewater and
forest-fresh pine needles. He shook his head, took one last look
at the red-coated, sleek-furred bears, and put his hand firmly
over his nose.

"Pooh," he said.

How long he wandered alone in the forest, he didn't know.
Since he had nowhere to go to, moving about was pointless in
any case – not to mention extremely dangerous, if there were
any more bear raiding-parties loose. But the thought of keeping still and hiding didn't appeal, somehow – maybe he was
still just human enough to retain a trace of hope, like the last
smear at the bottom of the honey-jar . . .

He didn't see the trap until it was too late, by which time the
rope had tightened around his ankle, the bent sapling had
straightened, and he was hanging upside down in the air.
Marvellous, he thought; and then the bushes parted, and two
creatures emerged. They were upright, about his own height,
bright pink, with perky little ears –

Piglets?

– Except that they were wearing clothes; bizarre outfits,
bright red, like body-length nappies. And they were talking, in
words he could understand.

"What an extraordinary specimen," one of them said.
"Look at the clothes it's wearing."

(*Gimme a break*, Slade thought.)

"And its eyes," said the other one, looking at him with its
head slightly on one side. "To look at it, you could almost
imagine it was sentient."

The other piglet laughed. "There you go again," it said.

"That silly sentimental streak of yours. Come on, I'll lower the rope while you get the tranquillizer ready."

"Hey!" Slade shouted. It was hard to sound authoritative when he was dangling in the air like a rep's jacket in the back of a Ford Orion, but he put a fair amount of effort into it. They were, after all, only piglets. Weren't they?

The taller piglet stopped. "Extraordinary," it said.

"I've always thought that some of them have the ability to mimic speech," the other one said. "I'm convinced that with a little patient training –"

"You two," Slade yelled. "Get me down out of this thing, will you?"

The two piglets stared at him as if he'd just jumped up out of a cake. "Amazing," the tall one said.

"I told you, didn't I?" the other one replied. "It's the eyes, you know."

"Will you two quit fooling about and –" Which was as far as he got, before he heard the faint hiss of the tranquillizer, and darkness came up all around him.

He was in a cage.

As cages went, it wasn't so bad. It was high enough to allow him to stand up straight. There was a large bowl of water in the corner, and plenty of space to walk about. Compared with, say, an apartment in Tokyo it was lavish.

But it was a cage, the sort of thing you'd keep a pet animal in. Or (Slade shuddered at the thought) a laboratory specimen.

"Hey!" he yelled.

The cage was in a cave, and the only other occupant was one of those damned bears, which lifted its head and stared at him. "Shuddup," it growled; then it went back to its mindless humming. There was, Slade noticed, a pop-gun lying across its knees.

"Excuse me," he said.

"Shuddup," the bear repeated, scowling. "Who said you could talk, anyways?"

Maybe it was the way it said it; definitely a hint. Something about the idea of a talking human obviously bothered the hell out of the bear. Even over on the other side of the cave, Slade could almost feel the tension. "Tweep," he said. "Tweep tweep. Eeek."

The bear relaxed a little, looked away and hummed a little louder (tumpty-tum-tum, tumpty-tum-tum, tumpty-tumpty-tumpty-tum-tum; at the back of Slade's mind, a minuscule tendril of memory stirred uneasily). Slade turned his back to the creature and sat perfectly still, studying the construction of the cage. It was made of massive logs crudely but efficiently lashed together with strips of pale yellow rawhide (best not to think about that); without tools –

Tools. He remembered.

The emergency toolkit had gone; the pocket was empty. That was seriously worrying, if the guard bear's attitude to an apparently sentient human was anything to go by. Even if he could somehow explain away a plasma cutter and a sonic wrench as primitive dress accessories, the mere act of explanation wasn't going to make things any better for him.

"Human."

Instinctively he swung round, remembering too late his resolution to act dumb. Oh well; no point now in pretending he couldn't understand.

It was the piglets, the ones who'd snared him.

"You can understand what I'm saying, can't you?" said the tall piglet.

"Tweep," Slade replied, but his heart wasn't in it. "Tweep. Eeek?"

The piglet frowned. "Human?"

Slade reached a decision. The thought that he might be able to communicate, something he felt a desperate need to do, outweighed the warnings his instincts were yelling at him. "Tweep," he said, nodding sideways in the direction of the guard. "Tweep *tweep*."

"What? Oh." The piglet nodded, its eyes full of wonder. "You there," it called out. "Why don't you take a long lunch? We can look after the specimen."

"Got my orders," the bear's voice growled.

"Well, I'm giving you some more." The piglet's tone of voice spoke volumes about social hierarchies; a command, but Slade could feel the apprehension. Obviously the piglets were nominally higher rank, but still afraid of the bears. "Go and get something to eat, take a stroll, whatever. We'll be fine."

Slade didn't look round, but he could hear the thump-thump-thump of the bear's heavy paws. Even at that moment he couldn't help thinking: *Bears don't move like that, they're gracefully efficient hunter-gatherers, their design honed down and streamlined by millions of years of trial and error.* These bears waddled, as if they were afraid that anything more energetic would split their seams.

"It's all right," the piglet said, "he's gone. Well, you really are an exceptional specimen, human. In all my years in the profession –"

"Slade. My name is Slade."

"Slade." The piglet thought about that. "That's not very cute," it said.

He felt as if he'd just been hit over the head with a fish. "Cute?" he repeated.

"Cute," the piglet said. "You do know what 'cute' means, don't you?" it continued, and its tone of voice suggested that it was dealing with a concept that was vital; perhaps even holy. Imagine an evangelist describing his god, or an accountant explaining the importance of keeping all the relevant receipts, and you'll get the idea.

"Yeah, I know what 'cute' means," Slade replied. "You're cute," he added, with a slight shudder. "Even the goddamn bears are cute. You make it sound like it's important."

The piglets looked at each other. They were – shocked.

"It's all right," said the short one, after a long moment of silence. "It's only a human, I don't suppose it really understands what it's saying."

"You're right. But you –" The piglet was scowling at him. "Don't you ever say anything like that again, do you hear? It's going to be hard enough to keep you alive as it is, a talking human and all. It's all right with us, we're scientists, but if you suddenly start blaspheming where other people can hear you –"

Slade nodded. "Sorry," he said.

"You should be." The piglet was wiping its dear little snout with its funny little paw. A million animators working together for a thousand years couldn't have contrived a sweeter, more touching gesture. Slade felt like he'd just eaten a whole jar of marshmallows.

"I didn't realize it'd upset you," he said. "You see –" (How to put it?) "You see, I'm not actually from round here. I'm –"

"I knew it," the other piglet interrupted excitedly. "Of course, it's from the Outlands. That's right, isn't it, human? From across the great desert? There is another country out there, and that's where you're from."

Shit, Slade thought. "In a manner of speaking," he said. "Look, guys, do you think you could possibly see your way to –?"

"Tell me." The piglet was gazing at him with a terrible urgency in its little button eyes. "Tell me, human; where you come from – are there mice there? Mice that talk?"

"And funny little baby deer," added the other piglet anxiously, "who slip on the ice and bump their noses?"

"And white dogs with black spots? And mermaids? And flying elephants with enormous ears?"

A very disturbing idea freed itself from the sludge at the bottom of Slade's subconscious mind and started to drift slowly towards the surface; but he forced himself to ignore it. "In a sense," he replied. "It's true, I have seen things like that. A long time ago," he added, with a slight shudder. "But that was in another country, and besides –"

The piglets were staring at each other. "I know it's a terrible risk," said the tall one, "but we can't keep this to ourselves."

"But what if the bears –?"

"I don't care," the tall one interrupted. "Don't you see? It's living proof, there really is life outside the valley; and once they see it for themselves, with their own eyes –"

The short piglet nodded, as if reaching a truly momentous, split-the-atom decision. "You're right," it said, "of course. We'll have to tell Professor Eeyore."

The old grey donkey stared at him through the bars, and he winced as if he'd been burned. The sheer malevolence of its unwavering stare reminded him uncomfortably of his ex-wife's lawyer.

"Remarkable," it said at last. "Who else have you told about this?"

"Nobody." The piglets couldn't bear to look the donkey in the eye. Slade could see their point. There was something extremely disconcerting about the creature; misery fermenting into insanity. Something about the name, too . . . It belonged somewhere back in time, along with the smell of the pine needles.

"And have you tested it yet?" The donkey's voice was low, almost feverish. "Does it float?"

The piglets looked at each other. "Actually, Professor," they said, "no, we haven't. We were more interested, actually, in this possible missing-link aspect; you know, the great desert, the possibility of there being somewhere else . . ."

They tailed off. The donkey's stare seemed to soak up words like absorbent kitchen towel.

"So you haven't tested it," the donkey said slowly, rolling its long, sad eyes. "Well, we'd better do it now, then, hadn't we? Of course, it's too much to expect that anybody else would think of a perfectly obvious thing like that."

There was terror in the piglets' eyes. "But Professor –"

"Now."

"Yes, Professor."

Slade watched anxiously as they unlocked the cage door. "What's he talking about, do I float?" he asked, but they shushed him.

"Just don't say anything, all right?" whispered the short piglet. "It's going to be all right. Potentially," it added. "I mean, who knows? Maybe you do float, at that."

Somehow those weren't the most reassuring words Slade had ever heard in his life; but it wasn't the time to argue the point. If they were opening the cage, he was getting out; and once they were outside the cave, if he couldn't give two piglets and a broken-down old donkey the slip, then he wasn't the man he thought he was.

(Although he wasn't sure about that. In fact, he wasn't sure he ever had been . . .)

The daylight nearly blinded him; and while he was still dazzled, he heard bear voices. "Chief," one of them grunted.

"You." No question about it, there was no hint of reservation or fear in the donkey's voice when he spoke to the bears. "Arrest these two. They're blasphemers and abominators. And put a set of chains on that human; I don't want it getting away."

There was nothing Slade could do. *Should've known better*, he rebuked himself, as the manacles snapped shut around his ankles and neck. They were as bright and shiny as a new pin, with specks of glitter on them. *Nothing I could've done, anyhow*.

The bears marched him through what he took to be some kind of settlement. At any rate, there were strange, rickety structures up in the branches, and some of the trees had little (cute little) painted wooden doors let into them (although the colours were— well, strange; bright reds and yellows and livid greens, and all so goddamn *shiny* . . . Even Lawrence Llewellyn-Bowen in his wrath never abused primary colours to quite such a ferocious extent). The clearing was crowded with animals; mostly bears, some lounging around aimlessly, others squatting on the ground with their muzzles buried in jars. Here and there he noticed a handful of rabbits – *huge* rabbits, with hoes and forks over their shoulders, talking at the tops of their high, folksy voices. At one point, he and his convoy were nearly trampled underfoot by something stripy and incredibly fast; but Slade didn't even want to think about what that might be.

It was a long, silent march, out of the forest into the encircling mountains beyond. The donkey led the way, setting a pace that the rest of the party were hard pressed to match. Both piglets radiated misery and doom, the bears were sullen and Slade knew better by now than to say anything. All in all, he hadn't been on a hike this depressing since his childhood holidays in Wales.

After climbing for an hour up a steep, rocky trail, they came to a deep gorge, at the bottom of which a river bounced and hissed through high, jagged rocks. A rope-bridge spanned the gorge, threadbare and crazy. The donkey stopped.

"Now we'll see," it said.

Even the bears looked nervous. "We going across that, chief?" one of them grunted.

The donkey grinned. "Only about half way," it replied.

It was at that point that the penny dropped in Slade's mind. It dropped down uncounted years, freefalling from generation to generation, from a time so far away as to be completely alien – more so than the talking donkey or the bears in red jackets who chased humans up trees. Slade was well aware that he didn't have a clue what it meant. It was like unearthing some incredibly ancient artifact whose purpose had been lost and could never be worked out from first principles. All he had was a word.

"Poohsticks," he said.

The donkey slowly lifted its head. "I was right, then," it said slowly. "It's true. You're the spawn of the Child. Do you understand what that means?" he asked of the two piglets, who huddled in quivering terror against the rock face behind them. "No, of course you don't. You call yourselves scientists, you conjured up such pretty dreams of a land far away across the burning sands; an enchanted place where a boy and his bear are forever playing." That was completely lost on the piglets – and Slade too, of course – but the donkey didn't seem particularly bothered. "A talking human, you thought," the donkey went on, its eyes fixed on the white spray lashing the rocks below, "how wonderful. Perhaps one day all humans can be taught to talk, and then they can take their place in a universal brotherhood of sentient species. Idiots," the donkey sighed, flexing its chest so much that a seam appeared between its neck and shoulder, from which poked out a tiny curl of white fluff. "Oh, you sneer at *them*" (with a nod toward the guards) "when you know they're not looking, you call them bears of very little brain and repeat the ancient slanders you learned at your grandfathers' trotters; but no bear ever dreamed of consorting with the spawn of the Child, or turning his back on Cute. Which is why I say," he added, his black button eyes suddenly hot with fury, "Cute may forgive you, but I never will."

"Excuse me," said Slade.

The donkey turned (a process involving a six-stage manoeuvre in the cramped confines of the bridgehead) "Well?"

"Sorry to be a pest," Slade said, "but would you mind

explaining all that? You see, I haven't got a clue what you're talking about."

The donkey stared at him, then started to laugh. "You know," it said, "I think I almost believe you. Now wouldn't that be a fine irony: for the spawn of the Child to have forgotten the Story. It's too good to be true, of course. And besides, you've already proved that you know the Word."

"You mean 'poohsticks'? Hey, I don't know why I even said that, really. In fact, it was more like a sneezing noise –"

"It's in your blood," the donkey replied solemnly. "You are what you are. But tell me, do you really not know the Story?"

"Once, long ago," said the donkey, "before the river gouged out the valley, even, there was another human who talked, just like you do. He was only a cub, a Child; but not only did the animals who lived in the wood spare him, they accepted him as one of their own, an equal. I know it's almost impossible to believe," the donkey added, as the bears made hostile noises, "but that's what the Story said. The Child talked; and not only that, the animals listened to what he said, because he taught them the word of Cute. He and no other.

"It was the Child who first dressed up the bear in his smart red jacket, ordained for the piglet that absolutely ridiculous outfit that you all wear today. He laid down that the Tigger shall bounce and the Rabbit shall upbraid him for it. He decided that the mother should be Kanga and the baby Roo. Everything we are, even the bear's love of honey and humming, we had from him. He was our god. He gave us the Cute.

"Because of him," the donkey went on, "everything we say, do and are is just ever so slightly wrong. Because of him, the owl can't spell its own name. Why? Because of him, we believe that the north pole is a piece of wood stuck in the ground – we know perfectly well what the north pole really is, but even so, we must believe or else die the hideous death of the heretic. Why? Because of him, we have to sit on chairs that don't fit us at tables that aren't suited for our anatomy; we have to wear clothes we don't need and eat food that slowly poisons us – have you any idea" (the donkey almost howled) "how *painful* it is to eat nothing but thistles? – and live all our lives in some kind of hideous mockery, all because of what he taught us; the Cute. That was the Child, the talking human. And that," concluded the donkey, staring at Slade with such raw hatred that he covered his face with his hands and looked away, "is why humans must never be allowed to talk again –

"Unless," it went on, its voice suddenly soft, "they float."

Slade uncovered his eyes. "Excuse me?" he said.

The donkey's sigh came right up from its fetlocks. "It was written," it said simply. "There was a time when the Child grew angry with the first donkey and hurled it from the bridge into the great chasm. But when the donkey hit the river, it didn't sink; instead it floated on its back under the bridge with its feet sticking up in the air, and the Child looked upon the face of the waters, and behold, it was very cute. So the Child spared the donkey, the first of my line; and ever since we have vowed that if ever the spawn of the Child comes into our hooves we would show it the same mercy, no more and no less."

"All right," Slade replied, glancing down at the deep pool directly under the bridge and thinking of the flotation control modules built into his environment suit. "I don't have a problem with that. Okay, how do we do this? Do you want me to jump, or would you rather push? Either way's cool with me, it's entirely up to –"

"No!" broke in the taller piglet. "We can't let you do this. It's a sentient creature, Professor; it has a mind, possibly even a soul. For all we know, all the humans have souls. You can't –".

"It's all right, really," Slade tried to say. "I honestly don't mind. In fact –"

"Blasphemer!" The donkey pawed at the rocky track with its paws. "How can you say such things? Can't you see this abomination for what it is?"

"It's not an abomination!" shouted the smaller piglet. "It's – dammit, I think it's *cute*! I mean," it added, as the other animals, including the other piglet, stared at it in dumbstruck horror, "look at its dear little face. And its funny little crinkly pink paws. And the adorable way its sweet little nose turns up at the end . . ."

"Enough!" The donkey was beside itself with fury now. "I won't hear another word of this. Bears, throw that – that *animal* off the bridge."

"No!"

"Oh, not you as well," groaned the donkey, as the taller piglet stationed itself between the bears and its diminutive colleague. "That one too, then. Both of them. In your own time," it added irritably, as the bears hesitated. "Go on, that's an order."

The bears were looking at the donkey. "But Chief . . ." one of them said.

"Well? What?"

"You can't throw piglets off cliffs, Chief. It ain't right."

"Piglets is cute too," the other bear pointed out. "Ac'shly, piglets is reely cute."

"Could I just mention here that I really don't mind –?" Slade tried to say; but they weren't listening.

The donkey was lashing its tail, which came loose. Quickly, a bear pinned it back on. "I think they's cute too," it mumbled.

"Listen to yourselves!" howled the donkey. "You heard what it said, the abominations it uttered. How can something like that be suffered to live? Off the cliff with it, right now, unless you two want to go the same way."

"How'd it be," Slade persisted, "if I jumped and the rest of you stayed here? That way –"

With a turn of speed Slade would never have thought it capable of, the donkey charged. With the first heady impetus of its charge it butted the tall piglet backwards over the bridgehead stay. With a chilling "Eeek!" it wavered and fell.

"Oh my God," howled its fellow, "you killed Piglet. You ba–"

The donkey charged again; but the piglet took precisely one step to the left, allowing the donkey to pass neatly under the rope and over the edge. Just as it was about to vanish from sight, however, it lashed out with its tail, entangled the other piglet's leg, and dragged it off the ledge. The two animals fell together, their screams mingling into one cry of terror and abruptly ceasing. The two bears, meanwhile, hurled themselves against the rope and leaned over, either making a last vain effort to catch them or getting a grandstand view – the outcome was the same, whatever their motivation; the bridge buckled and twisted under their considerable weight, and they slid under the rope and down into the chasm. A second later, Slade heard the splash.

He waited for the bridge to stop swaying; then he edged his way onto it and looked out over the other side, watching as the current swept the five animals away towards the grinding ferocity of the rapids. They were, he couldn't help noticing, all bobbing along on their backs with their paws in the air. They looked –

– Kinda cute.

He could have walked for a week, three weeks, three months; he neither knew nor cared. When he was hungry, there were nuts and berries. When he was thirsty, even in the middle of the great desert, he found convenient waterholes and oases, complete with modular palm trees of regulation height and shade diameter. He wasn't in the least surprised.

Beyond the desert was another country. He found talking animals there too, different in some respects but basically similar; all of them cuddly and furry, all of them cute. Beyond that country was another country, and another beyond that, all slightly different, all pretty much the same. He passed through a country where the animals sang as well as talked – there was a panther and a bear and a snake and lots of extremely irritating monkeys, and none of them was particularly pleased to see him. When at last he reached the sea, he met talking dolphins and talking whales and even a talking crab, which he managed to tread on before it got too painfully on his nerves. Everywhere he went, every damn thing talked, except the humans; and they were all dumb. Really, really dumb. And that, too, figured.

One day, months or years later, he walked along a beach in the bright sunlight. He was alone; not a talking seagull or chatty killer whale in sight. As the sun rose higher, he looked

around for somewhere to shelter from the heat, and happened
to notice a small, round knoll sticking out of the side of the
cliff. It was pleasantly cool under the lee of the mound, and
Slade lay on his back for a couple of hours, his eyes closed. He
drifted into a doze, until the sun moved down the sky and the
slight change in temperature suggested to him that it was time
to move on.

He opened his eyes; and for the first time noticed a shape.
Why it attracted his attention he wasn't quite sure; it was little
more than a vague, almost fractal suggestion of familiarity, but
once he'd noticed it, somehow he couldn't pass on without
investigating further. Picking up a piece of driftwood, he
began to pick away at the loose sand. After a while he stopped
and stared, then began shovelling madly, as if his life depended on it.

An hour later he stood in front of what he'd uncovered, the
driftwood forgotten in his hand. It was a statue; a huge black
plastic representation of a highly stylized mouse's head, with
round ears and eyes and nose, a perky, toothy grin on its
curved lips.

Thousands of years fell away, as if they'd never been.

Slade sank to his knees and began to sob uncontrollably. At
last, he slumped forward, covering up the shattered plaque, on
which he'd seen the words "WELCOME TO THE UNITED STATES
OF DISN—".

"You fools!" Slade shouted to the unheeding sky. "You did
it. You finally did it!"

He lay on his face in the sand, weeping like a child; while
above his head, the great plastic mouse smiled its implacable
smile.

QUEST

Sue Anderson

Sue Anderson (b. 1946) is a teacher by profession. She had long held the ambition to be a writer but it was only after she had married and raised a family that she turned her sights back to the goal, reaching the final of the Mail on Sunday *novel competition in 1991. Her first story, "Watched", appeared in 1994. The following was specially written for this anthology.*

There was a thunderous knocking and an unearthly howl which shook the house. "Who will that be, love?" asked Hendrath sleepily.

"Search me," said Cindramel, as she threw another pile of dung on the fire, "I haven't had time to read the droppings today." Great puffs of smoke billowed up the chimney and Cindramel reminded herself to use dry dung in future.

Another burst of knocking, even louder this time. "I expect it's those bloody dwarves again," said Cindramel, irritably. "They always turn up around teatime and set the Keeper off."

"Can you get it, sweetbreath?" Hendrath wriggled deeper into the rat-skin cushions. "Only I'm a bit busy."

Obviously he wasn't going to move. Cindramel sighed, put on her dragon-hide slippers, pulled the rat-fur robe tighter about her and made her way through the draughty hallway, trying not to stub her toes on the uneven floor. The candles had gone out again; rat fat was no good at all, in spite of the dwarf publicity.

The small spy-window was boarded up. Successive visitors battering on it with skull-headed sticks and dragon's-tooth clubs had cracked the crystal so badly it wasn't accurate any more, and was quite likely to give you a blurred picture of a magic duster salesman from last week. The Doorkeeper, an ugly-looking beast with six legs and a flat head, was bouncing up and down and dribbling. "Get down, Dog!" said Cindramel. She drew the rusty bolt and peered round the thick wooden door. A gust of wind blew into her face and she screwed her eyes up to see. The night was dark and starless, even at this early hour, and she could hardly make out the figure on the step. She could tell it was alone though, and far too tall for a dwarf.

There wasn't time to ask. The person swept past her, patted Dog on the head, which shocked him into silence, and hissed, "Bolt the door quickly. I fear I'm followed. There are dorcs about and I've seen at least one Geldorf on the road."

"But who . . ."

"Hurry up!"

A man, probably. Cindramel followed him through the hall, looping up a strand of hair which had escaped from the rat's-tooth comb. He seemed to know the way without asking.

He was dressed in a long blue cloak encrusted with silver stars and some strange curved symbols like toenail clippings. As he stalked into the sitting-room his tall pointed hat caught on the beam over the door and almost toppled, but righted itself in a mysterious way. Two clawed feet could be seen briefly underneath it. Cindramel was not impressed. Animated clothing was, well, rather old hat.

Hendrath had dragged himself off the couch and was standing in the corner of the room, staring thoughtfully at the magic mirror. It was on a rickety wooden stand under a rather indifferent print of a dorc-fight, and was showing some indistinct runic signs. Hendrath gave the stand a kick and it wobbled, but the mirror didn't clear.

"We've got a visitor," said Cindramel.

"Yes?" Hendrath turned, frowning. The tall person didn't look familiar. Probably somebody from the elves' new welfare programme checking up on him. He'd been claiming extra rations on account of health problems.

"It's me, Hen. I know we haven't met in an age, but surely you recognize an old friend."

"Well, the light's terrible in here, and that beard's a bit . . . Hang on!" Hendrath scrambled to his feet, beaming all over his grubby face, "It's never . . . It can't be . . ."

The mysterious person swept off his tall hat and bowed deeply. A small black crow flew out from under it and landed on the sideboard, where it began to peck at the remains of a roasted rat. "Alfred Gann. Electronics wizard. At your service."

"Alf, old mate. I didn't know you. You never had the robe and all that clobber before."

"I got promoted."

"Well, come and sit down. You're just the person I need. Cin, will you make us some dragon's-blood tea? There's a love."

Cindramel, muttering darkly, shuffled out of the room, swiping the crow off the sideboard as she went. It flew round a bit and perched on the mantelpiece.

"Excuse the mobile," said Alf. "He's a bit of a pain, but very good for emergency calls."

Hendrath was oblivious to anything but the joy of seeing Alf and went on about it for some time. "You couldn't do something with this steaming thing?" he said eventually, pointing to the mirror. "I've been trying to get the Carnage League tables up all afternoon and all it gives me is Monster ratings."

Alf threw the magic utensil a scornful glance. "No time for that now, mate. I'm on a Quest."

"A what?"

"You know," said Cindramel, reappearing with a loaded

tray, "Quests. They're on about them all the time. If it's not the mirror advertising for volunteers it's somebody coming round with envelopes for Quest contributions. Drives you crazy." She set down the tray with a crash and went out again.

"I know all about that. Give us a minute." Alf chose a stuffed balrog, one of the more solid pieces of furniture, sat down and took out from the folds of his robe a silver box from which he extracted the makings of a roll-up.

Hendrath looked on in fascination as the wizard struck sparks off his boot-heel with a sliver of wood dipped in some concoction and inhaled deeply. "This one's different though," said Alf. "Watch."

As he exhaled, coughing slightly, a cloud of blue smoke filled the room. Cindramel, coming in with the teapot, had to waft the air ahead of her. She was just about to make some pointed remark when the picture appeared.

Before their eyes the smoke cleared and they were looking at an unfamiliar scene. A group of people sat in a brightly lit room, with comfortable seats and polished tables. There were bowls of strange fruit and tempting sweetmeats dotted around. A warm, bright fire blazed on the hearth, with not a trace of noxious fug. In the centre of the room was a large black box with a huge bright window through which a man's face could be seen.

"They look so clean," whispered Cindramel, "and those curtains are really tasteful." She'd always had a hankering for the high life. She had turned down quite a good proposition from an elf in order to run off with Hendrath, and she never let him forget it. He had been so different in those days: short, but charming and full of plans and dreams. Now he just lay about the house all the time, putting on weight and complaining about his feet. Perhaps she had let herself go a little, but was there any wonder?

"They look so comfortable," breathed Hendrath. "And look at all that food." His stomach growled enviously. "What kind of place is it? One of those new holiday resorts? Can we go?"

"That," said Alf, taking another puff and coughing again, "that's the Quest."

Outside, the night was trying to darken still deeper. Huge creatures stirred in the blackness. A weremouse howled. Even the trees in the Old Forest were feeling the cold, and a group of them made plans to go south as soon as possible. A posse of dark riders had a cursory scout round, shrieked a bit and decided to go back to the tower for a hot toddy.

"Well basically," said Alf, after a couple of mugs of tea and a rat sandwich, "it's all down to this." He delved into yet another pocket and produced a small, gold object. "It's what they call a Wizards' Disc."

As if hypnotized, Cindramel and Hendrath leaned towards the shimmering thing. Hendrath's hand reached out of its own accord to touch it. Alf drew it back sharply. "Careful!" he said. "One fingerprint and it could be ruined. Besides, if it gets into the wrong hands it's bound to cause chaos." He assumed a dreamy expression and began to chant:

> "One year to start it all,
> One disc to stop it.
> Debug the program.
> Or we'll all cop it."

The crow flew round the room a few times, and sidled up to the rat carcass again. Nobody noticed.

"You see," said Alf, "once, long ago, in another place, there was a golden age when you could eat fish and chips, and watch the football on a Saturday. Womenfolk cleaned the house, and did the washing, without worrying about dragon-droppings and soothsaying, and went round the shops of an afternoon for the makings of delicious meals instead of bartering for rat steaks in the meat market. It was an age when a man was a man and didn't have to spend his time fending off monsters and sucking up to dwarves for a living."

Hendrath and Cindramel looked at him, bewildered. They didn't understand above half of what he said, but it stirred something deep inside Hendrath, like rat's-tail wine, only without the aftertaste.

"Then," Alf went on, "The people of that place started to meddle with time. They counted it, measured it, chopped it up and sorted it, in a way we know not in this world, where the hours are simply dark or light, and the only measure needed is a candle-length. They even formulated a theory which said that surviving a certain point in time was crucial, and that to prevent society collapsing they had to protect themselves by all sorts of dark devices. Wars and destruction were foretold. There was much talk about a New Age, and a Transition.

"One person, who thought himself a Lord of Time, resolved to use the chaos which would ensue as a means of taking over all the power. And so he fabricated ten golden discs, with which he would change that world at the crucial moment. For what he had realized, and what everyone else had forgotten, was that time is relative, just another dimension, the fourth in fact.

"He built a machine, a magic engine which would use the discs as fuel. And he hid it in the Darkest Cave, in the heart of the Blackest Mountain. And while everyone's mind was occupied with the fourth dimension, the world slid slowly through the fifth, sixth and seventh, and on into the dark."

Alf took a long swig at his mug of tea, wiped his lips with the sleeve of his robe, and continued before Hendrath and Cindramel could think of anything at all to say.

"It wasn't obvious at first how much things were changing. Little by little it happened. Suddenly fish and chips were unavailable and rats became the staple diet. Unaccountably, the shops disappeared one by one. And worst of all, men forgot the rules of football. Then the momentum increased, monsters walked the earth and the moon went out."

"The earth?" whispered Hendrath hoarsely. "So it was here, this place you're talking about?"

"In a manner of speaking," said Alf irritably. "Weren't you listening? I told you it was a different dimension. The point is," he paused significantly, "the point is that with this disc, which was lost long ages ago, and has now come into my hands, we can put ourselves back on track. It's part of the program. The other bits are missing or stolen, but this is the start-up disc, the one that rules them all." He stood up, flung wide his arms, dropping a few assorted items from his pockets, and announced: "That is the purpose of the Quest."

Cindramel looked doubtful. Hendrath looked stunned.

"Are you on, then?" asked Alf. "It will be a long hard road, but worth it."

"Sounds brilliant," whispered Hendrath. He didn't know what fish and chips were but it had to be an improvement on rat. And football, something told him, was magic. He was so enchanted he forgot all about his bad feet. "When do we start?"

"The company is assembling by the blasted oak as we speak. One or two people from the village seemed interested. I also have a dorc-fighter who took early retirement, a couple of dragon-trackers, the token dwarf and a mysterious bloke who says he's meant to be the Prime Minister of the New Age. Your mission, should you choose to accept it, is to be the disc-carrier. It will be kept in a special protective case, and when you reach the Darkest Cave in the Blackest Mountain you will have to insert it in the Deepest Slot."

"That doesn't sound so hard," said Hendrath. He sounded ten years younger already. But Alf was determined to impress him with the full gravity of the situation:

"You wait. These things are supposed to be indestructible but you have to look after them like babies."

Just at that moment the crow flew onto the wizard's shoulder and croaked into his ear.

"Must go," said Alf. "There's trouble brewing. Somebody's dug up a toaster and they're probably going to stick a knife in it. I'll catch you later." And with that mysterious statement he swept out.

Taking only the time to find his lucky socks and pick up the bag which Cindramel had packed for him, complete with guess-what sandwiches, Hendrath gave his wife a parting peck on the cheek and was gone.

At the corner of the road he paused for a moment and looked back at his little house, nestling deep into the hillside. It was shabby, but it was home. He wondered if he would ever see it, or his wife, again.

Cindramel sat with Dog before the dying embers of the fire, weeping softly. After a relatively short time, though, she got up, brushed herself down, pinned up her hair, sent Dog to fetch his lead and set off across the Foggy Hills to see Sharana, her old mate from soothsaying college. It was quite a long journey, but Cindramel was used to walking.

High on a ledge on the Blackest Mountain sparks of electricity bounced off the rocks, the thunder rolled, the mice howled and the weather was generally appalling. The dark riders had given up altogether after a warning from their air-traffic wizard, and gone home for the duration.

The journey had been long and hard, over mountain passes so high they made your teeth ache, through nightmare tunnels where giant garden-pests of the most repulsive kind lurked in evil-smelling holes. They had been harassed by bands of wild crystal salesmen and dispossessed sports fans. They had eaten in roadside hostelries where agonizing death lurked on the edge of your plate.

The small company was depleted by dorc-fights and dragon raids. Some of them had been killed in battle. Others had succumbed to temptation and accepted offers of hospitality from tree-dwellers and jobs in dwarf companies. One in particular had found the garden-pests more than he could cope with.

Now there were only two left, and they staggered along, battered and bruised, up the rocky ledge to the final goal. The wind buffeted them constantly, cold trickles of rain ran down their necks, Hendrath's very soul was weary with the weight of responsibility, and his feet were giving him hell.

"This cave here," he whispered to his companion, "this is where Alf said we had to go. There's a giant machine in there somewhere, with a huge black slot." The thought of Alf, lost days ago in the mines of Cole, almost made him weep, but he swallowed and carried on.

The cave was dark and deep. There was a dim, bluish light, which seemed to come from a large square panel on the back wall. Under the panel was a thin strip of black.

"Go on, then," said the companion to Hendrath, "do what you must. But before you put it in, let us touch it, just once for luck, my lovely."

He was a pathetic creature, pale and diseased from too much

exercise, whom Hendrath had found wandering in the wilderness. His name was Gloom. He had begged to see the disc before, but had been denied. Hendrath himself, heedful of Alf's warnings, had not dared even to open the case. "Not on your life, sunshine," he said. "Now where the dorcsbut did I . . . Oh here it is." He reached right down into the bottom of his bag and took out a square, flat box.

Gloom was weary and stressed. He had dreamed of this moment for years and could contain himself no longer. He lunged forward, eyes glazed with greed, and made a grab for the case.

Hendrath grabbed back and a fight ensued, which sent them rolling to the end of the cave. Biting and scratching, punching and kicking, they struggled for supremacy. Slowly, inch by inch, Gloom wormed his slimy fingers towards the case. His other hand was at Hendrath's neck, trying to squeeze the life from him. Hendrath was tired and weak; the sandwiches had run out long ago. This repulsive creature was used to starvation; he had spent ages in a secret underground gymnasium, stretching and torturing his body. He was going to win.

With a cry of despair, Hendrath watched the pale fingers prise open the case. They both peered inside. They both gasped.

"Oh bugger," said Gloom and Hendrath, at exactly the same moment.

Over a pot of tea and a plate of gingered rat's brains, Cindramel had brought her old friend up to date with the story of the Quest.

"What do you think?" she said. "Admittedly, some good's come out of it. It's got Hendrath back on his feet for a start but . . ."

Sharana twitched her long nose. "Typical men's stuff. Always something better round the corner. Basically for us, love, it's just cleaning, cooking and going to market same as usual, without a bit of light relief, because you can be sure the soothsaying will be out the window. Men, of course, don't see it that way. They neglect the important things. For instance, if we change dimensions, you can bet the names go all peculiar. I'll end up as Sharon, and you're bound to be called something like Cindy." She shuddered.

"That's what I thought," said Cindramel. "And that football thing sounds a bit suspect. You don't need a magic mirror to spot trouble coming there."

"I know what you mean, dear," Sharana said. "But what can you do?"

Cindramel fished in her rat-skin purse and brought out an object which glimmered in the firelight. "He left the packing to me as usual, and, well, I kind of forgot to put something in."

Sharana looked at it for a long moment. A whole new world.

"Chuck it in the fire, love," she said at last. "We're better off without it."

THE HILLS BEHIND HOLLYWOOD HIGH

Avram Davidson
and Grania Davis

Avram Davidson (1923–93) was one of the most idiosyncratic talents to write science fiction and fantasy. He was at his best writing short stories, and even his longer works have an episodic feel. Well worth tracking down are Peregrine: Primus *(1971) and its sequel* Peregrine: Secundus *(1981), plus the collection of stories about a wizard detective,* The Enquiries of Doctor Esterhazy *(1975). His best short fiction has been collected as* The Avram Davidson Treasury *(1998). With his wife, Grania Davis (b. 1943), he wrote* Marco Polo and the Sleeping Beauty *(1988). Grania Davis has been writing fantasy since 1972 and most of her books draw upon ancient myths and legends, as in* The Rainbow Annals *(1980) and* Moonbird *(1986). The following is a perfect example of their prodigious talents.*

That there *are* hills behind Hollywood – that is, behind Hollywood Boulevard and Hollywood High School – is perhaps not universally known. Smog often hides them, and tourists have no reason to look for, let alone explore, them. They remain unnoticed by the valley commuters who flood past them twice daily. Fish, it is said, do not see the water in which they swim, nor birds observe the winds which bear them.

In the late thirties, according to *Life* magazine, that omniscient observer of the world scene, the students of Hollywood High School were the most beautiful in the world, being the issue of beautiful young men and women who had come to Hollywood in the twenties seeking movie stardom and, although they had failed – *because* they had failed – stayed on in Hollywood doing Something Else, anything else.

Success would have removed them to Beverly Hills or Brentwood – failure prevented their return to Cowpat, Kansas; Absalom, Alabama; or Pretty Bird, Idaho. ("Diddunt *make* it in thuh pitchers, huh, Jeff? Huh, Jean? Huh huh haw!") So there they stayed, frying hamburgers on Hollywood Boulevard, pumping gas or sacking groceries on Vine. Marcelling waves or setting perms on Cahuenga, clipping hedges or mowing lawns on Selma. Or, if exceptionally lucky, working in studio jobs on the other side of the cameras.

Hollywood was their hometown now, just as Cowpat, Absalom, or Pretty Bird had been. No more profitable maybe, but lots more interesting. And the beautiful failures met and married other beautiful failures – and together begat beautiful babies, who their parents hoped *would* Make It In The Movies. Make It Big.

"*What?* Television, what is *that*?"

It was in the mid-fifties. The huge red juggernaut trolley cars still rolled down the alley right of way. Vibi's restaurant still advertised *Breakfast Served 24 Hours a Day*, but did not advertise the answer to the old-timers' eternal question: Was "Vibi" Vilma Bankey or was she not, and if not, who *was* she? Because the old-timers knew she was *some* movie star from the old days.

As to who was the little old lady in the short black velvet

tunic and the sandals cross-strapped halfway up her shrunk shanks, nobody had an answer, or knew why she carried a cane-length silver wand: an ancient fairy in the ancient meaning of the word, she stepped her light-fantastic way and bothered no one.

Dorothy, Angela and Luanne giggled when they saw her – but only after she had moved well on – as they giggled in confused respect when passing the old dark house smothered in foliage, which was the home of the ninety-odd-year-old widow of L. Frank Baum, the original Wizard of Oz. The original house where he had dreamed his strange – and strangely profitable – dreams.

Sometimes the three girls went to buy snacks at the all-night Ranch Market on Vine, and sometimes they went there just to stare at the odd types who went there to stare at the other odd types. Once they heard a squat woman who looked as though Central Casting had selected her as a Ma Kettle stand-in say to her equally typical Farmer-Husband: "Land sakes, Pa, what is *this*?" – holding up the scaly green fruit of the cherimoya tree – and Pa had said: "Looks like a armadillo egg to me, Ma!"

Past the Hollywood Hotel, which presumably dated from the Spanish *Conquista*, and near Grauman's Chinese Theatre, built like an oriental shrine with hand-and-foot-prints of the famous set into cement out front for the faithful pilgrims to worship, was the business place of Angelo, the dwarf newsvendor. Sometimes they would see Angelo darting across Hollywood Boulevard to pick up a bundle of papers while he meanwhile waved a large white sheet of cardboard as a signal to drivers that he was not merely a driven leaf. Angelo had been in the movies, too.

Side by side, waving and squealing, Dorothy, Angela and Luanne had seen *Robert Cummings* ride past in an open car with his family, and *Robert Cummings* had waved back and smiled widely – but did not squeal.

More than once they had clutched each other to see, walking on the sidewalk, just like anybody else, the movie-villainous *Porter Hall*, not looking the least villainous, looking dapper and rosy-cheeked – and *Porter Hall* had tipped his dapper hat and said: "Hello, lovely ladies!"

Lovely ladies!

As for names even more (well . . . much more) glamorous than Robert Cummings or Porter Hall – well, Dorothy, Angela and Luanne seldom saw *them* . . . in the flesh. Very seldom, though, at great and rare intervals, some of the Very Biggest Stars could be seen cruising majestically along at less than top speed. Showing the flag, as it were. Tyrone. Lana. Lauren and Bogie. Bette. Ava. Joan. Clark.

In a Company Town, people naturally hope to get jobs with The Company. In Hollywood there is no one company – there is The Industry. So, although none of their parents had ever become even minor stars, it remained the natural hope of Dorothy, Luanne and Angela that she . . . and she . . . and she . . . would nevertheless become Major Ones.

Outsiders, had they ever penetrated the neighbourhood of squat, scaly palm trees and pseudo-Spanish stucco houses in the Hollywood Foothills, where the smog meets the ocean breezes, might have seen merely three perfectly ordinary teenage girls – wearing fluffy bouffant felt skirts and fluffy bouffant hairdos, or pedal pushers and pageboys. One with large dark eyes and slight, skimpy figure (Dorothy), one a tall and narrow blonde with a face marked chiefly by freckles and zits (Angela), one with a lovely complexion and a lavish bosom, but stocky hips and legs (Luanne).

To themselves, however, they were far from ordinary. They were *Daughters of Hollywood*. Moviedom was their birthright; obstacles in the form of imperfectly good looks were merely temporary. Things to be overcome. They were still at Hollywood High School, yes, but they merely endured the boring academic routine. (Really! Classes in *English*! Like they were some kind of *foreigners*!) They saved all enthusiasm for their drama courses.

If there were diets, Luanne dieted them. If there were complexion creams, Angela creamed her complexion with them. If there were exercises, all three exercised them – Luanne for hips and legs, Angela and Dorothy for bosoms.

And – did it *help*?

Well.

Luanne at least obtained a one-shot modelling job, with her picture cut off above the hips.

Angela did get, once, an extra part in a scene at a youth rally. (Politics? Circa 1953? Bless your Adam's apple, *no!* The youths rallied for – in the film – a newer and larger football stadium.)

These opportunities never knocked again; even *so* –

But Dorothy got . . . nothing at all.

* *Sigh* *

The last straw was the sign in the storefront window: *Now Signing Up! For Open-Air Spectacular! WANTED One Hundred Teen-Aged GIRLS! GIRLS! GIRLS!* In she went. Surely, if a hundred were wanted, she –

"No."

"But why *not*?"

The woman at the table heaped with application forms said, "Because, honey, *who* goes to *see* these things? Men." She pronounced this last word as though she were pronouncing "pubic lice". And went on to explain, "My dear, the average American man has never been *weaned*. If a girl is not prominent in the mammary section, if she doesn't have what is called 'a full figure', though one might ask, 'full of *what*?' – well, Mr Average American John hasn't gotten his money's worth, the *fool*!"

Suddenly Dorothy realized three things: first, this woman was herself of slight and boyish figure; second, this woman had somehow taken hold of Dorothy's hand, and then of Dorothy's arm, and was steadily hauling in to take hold of more and more of Dorothy; third, that she desired to be out of the place – at once.

Which, in another moment, she was.

Perhaps she should have stayed? Only perhaps not.

What she *did* do, after getting the hell out, was to walk fast. Next to walk rapidly, and next to run. Then to stumble, then to halt. And then to start weeping. She didn't burst into tears, she just wept.

And cried.

At that moment, Dorothy caught sight of her slender, tiny little self reflected in a store window. Even amidst her grief and woe she realized that, if her life had been a movie, someone would have come up behind her and asked, "Why are you crying?"

At that moment someone came up behind her and asked, "Why are you crying?"

The moment was one of genuine thrill. Mingled with its pleasure, however, was an element of alarm. The voice wasn't that of a wholesome, handsome American Boy with a mouthful of large white teeth set in a cornflakes smile; *no*: it definitely had a Foreign Accent.

Dorothy looked up. Was the man who had spoken – *was* he tall, dark, and handsome? Truth to say – not altogether. He was rather short. He was kind of dark; sallow, one might say. He had large and shining eyes. Now there was nothing wrong with all of this, or with any of this. Dorothy had long ago learned that even the most wholesome-looking of American Boys was not above urging her into some rotten old Nash or Chevy or Studebaker, stinking of grease, and then trying to Get Fresh with her. She gave a cautious sniff: no auto grease. However: something else. What? Something odd. But something not unpleasant.

"Why are you crying?" the man repeated. Impossible to guess his age.

"It's my figure," she said mournfully. "It's too thin and skimpy."

This was the strange man's signal to say, "Nonsense, there's nothing wrong with your figure; it's all in your mind, you have a *lovely* figure." Which would be her signal to slip away and get going. Men and boys had lied to her before, and with what result? (Never mind.)

What the strange man did say was, "Hmm, yes, that is certainly true. It *is* too thin and skimpy. About that you should something do."

So right. "I need to see a doctor," she whimpered.

"*I* am a doctor," said the stranger. In his hand he held a small, wet-glistening bottle of a brown liquid, which he shifted to draw a wallet out, and out of the wallet a card. He handed the card to her. It read:

Songhabhongbhong Van Leeuwenhoek
Dr Philosof.   Batavia.

The word *Batavia* had been crossed out with a thin-point fountain pen and the word *Djakarta* written above. The word *Djakarta* had been scratched out with a thick-point fountain pen and the word *Hollywood* written beneath. In pencil.

"I have only come down to buy this bottle of celery tonic at the deli store. Of course you are familiar with it, an American drink. I wish to have it with my *Reistafel*. How. 'Rice Table,' you would say. It is mixed dish, such as me, self. Part Nederlandse, part Indonesian. Are you fond of?"

Dorothy had no idea if she was fond, or not fond of. She had a certain feeling that this doctor with the funny name was weird. *Weird*. But still there was the chance that he might be able to help her. If anything, it increased the chance, for everything normal had certainly failed.

"Is your office near here?" she asked.

It wasn't like other doctors' offices, for sure. It had funny things in it: skulls, stuffed things, carved things, things in bottles. *Other* doctors didn't give her a spicy meal. Was she fond of? Or not? Well, it was different.

So – "What kind of medicine do you think will help me?"

The doctor, who had been eyeing her intently, seemed surprised by the question. "What? Ah, the medicine. Oh, to sure be. Hmm!"

He got up and opened a few drawers, then took out a funny-looking bottle with a funny-looking powder in it. "In my native island Sumatra," he explained, "I was very interested in natural history and botany, zoology and pharmacology, also hunting and fishing. And so therefore. But. Details."

She eyed the powder. "Do I take it by the spoonful? Or in a capsule, Doctor?"

He was again staring at her with his odd and shining eyes. "Take – Oh, but first I must you examine," said he.

Well, what he did with Dorothy before, during, and after the examination was certainly no worse than what had been done with her by others, not that most of them had been

doctors, though *this* doctor used his *fingers* fairly freely. It was
. . . well . . . *int*eresting. And the couch was nicer than the
back seat of a tatty old jalopy, and the spices and incense
certainly smelled lots better than auto grease.

"Gnumph," he said, after helping her on with her clothes.
"You seem in excellent physical condition, exception of thin,
skimpy figure, of course. The medicine substance; it is a
glandular one which I prepared myself from – but details
you would not be fond. I will dilute with water," he said,
moving to the sink. But nothing came from the faucet save a
wheeze, a grind, and a trickle of rust.

"Ah, I had forgotten. Repairs; they had informed me. No
water for a while. So. Another liquid. Not alcoholic. What?
Ho!" He took up the small bottle of celery tonic. It was still
half full, and he pulled the odd stopper out of the odd bottle
and emptied the carbonated beverage into it. Swirled it several
times. Handed it to her.

Well! This certainly beat paying a drugstore, and it was
better than an injection! She closed her eyes and swallowed.
And swallowed. How did it taste? A little like celery and no
worse than she had expected. *Much* easier than *ex*ercises!
"How much do I owe you?" she asked.

Once again the liquid look. "Owe? Oh. Please pay me with
the pleasure of listening with me some of my maternally native
music. Here is one gramophone. I shall play some gamelan."

After quite some of this unusual music the doctor asked how
she felt. She said she felt sort of funny; he said he would
examine her again. She said she would go to the bathroom
first; and then, removing her shoes and holding them in her
hands, she silently left the premises of Songhabhongbhong
Van Leeuwenhoek, Dr Philosof., and went home.

After a night of odd and restless dreaming, in which she
seemed to be rather high up in a greenish place with lots of
grass and trees and some rather, well, *funny*-peculiar people,
Dorothy awoke with a faint sick-headache. Was it –? No, it
wasn't; wrong time of the month, for one thing, and it really
didn't feel like that anyway. She drifted back to sleep, this
time with no dreams, and awoke again. As she stirred in her

bed the thought came that she *did* feel heavier than usual. The medicine! Had it begun to work so soon? She hurried to the bathroom and hopped onto the scales. As she looked down she realized two things: For one, she *had* certainly gained weight! And, for another, her feet were covered with dark hair.

"Oh, my *God*!" she whimpered and, slipping off her nightie, she turned to face the full-length mirror.

It wasn't just her feet.

It was all of her.

As far as she could see, and even in the mirror she couldn't see all of her – she had turned into a gorilla.

It was certainly better than turning into a giant cockroach. But that was all she could think of in its favour.

The pounding on the door had been going on for a long time. Of course it was impossible to let anyone see her – and what good luck that her father had gotten one of the irregularly occurring jobs which kept the household going, and was away helping build sets on location somewhere. She'd better speak through the door. But someone was speaking through the door to *her*!

"I know you're in there, hairy!" the voice was shouting. *Hairy!* Then . . . then they already *knew*! How –? Who –?

She peered through a gap in her bedroom curtain, being careful not to move it, but in vain! Though she scuttled away in terror, whoever was outside began tapping, rapping on the bedroom window. Suddenly she remembered whom she'd seen. Not "hairy"! The man was shouting for "Harry", her father!

Dorothy's mother, smelling of whisky and perfume, had vanished from their lives some years ago – but she had left debts. Lots of debts. Dad had borrowed to pay the debts, then he borrowed to pay the money he had borrowed.

The whole thing had spiralled and doubled and tripled, and then fallen into the hands of the Greater Los Angeles Punitive Collection Agency. In fact, as she tiptoed into the living room she saw that another of the familiar cards had been slipped under the door. Bang! Bang! Bang! "*I know you're in there,*

Harry! Better open up and let me talk, Harry! We can't wait forever, Harry!"

On the card was printed the name of Hubbard E. Glutt, District Agent. Mr Glutt wasn't an entire stranger. He wore a once-white shirt and a once-grey suit, both with ingrown ketchup stains, and he had *extremely* hairy nostrils. It could not be said, even with the best of intentions, that he was a very nice man. His breath smelled, too.

"Go away, please go away," Dorothy said through the door. She was thankful to note that her voice was unchanged. She wasn't thankful for much else. "My dad's not in —"

"I don't care who's not in," yelped Mr Glutt. "Ya gunna pay sompthing?"

"But I have no money!"

Mr Glutt made a noise between a grunt and a snarl. "Same old story: 'My dad's not in and I have no money.' Huh? Still not in? Well, I gotta sudgestion." Here his voice sank and grew even nastier. "Lem*me* in, and I'll tell ya how we can, mmm, take mebbe twenny dollas affa the bill, liddle gurl, huh, huh, huh . . ."

Dorothy could stand it no longer. She jerked the door open and pulled Mr Glutt inside. The scream had not even reached his throat when Dorothy's new-formed fangs sank into it.

As though in a blur, she dragged the suddenly inert body into the breakfast nook. And feasted on it.

Moments passed.

The blur vanished. Oh God, what had she done? Killed and partially eaten someone, was what. But how? Gorillas don't eat people, gorillas eat bananas . . . *don't* they?

Therefore she wasn't even a gorilla. She was some sort of monster — like a werewolf? A were-gorilla? Trembling with shock and horror and fear, she stared at her image in the big front hall mirror . . . and gave a squeal of terrified loathing. The hair that covered her was now darker and coarser, and her facial features had coarsened, too. Her fingernails had become talons, although fragments of the Pearly Peach nail polish still remained. And examining her mouth as the squeal died away, she saw that it was full of yellow fangs. She began to sob.

How could something like this have *hap*pened to her? That's what girls always asked when they found themselves unwantedly pregnant – as if they didn't *know* how! But this was worse than pregnancy, a million times worse . . . and besides, pregnancy had a well-known cause, and she really couldn't imagine what had caused *this*.

Then a sudden thought came, echoing like a clap of thunder, illuminated as by a flash of lighting: that . . . that weird glandular-extract *med*icine which she had taken only yesterday! To make her figure fuller. Well, fuller it certainly was! But oh, at what a price! There was nothing to do but call the doctor and have him come over, and give her something to undo its effects. Only – only – would he make house calls? Well, she'd just have to see.

Only alas, she could not see. The most searching examination of the LA phone books, all several of them, failed to show any listing for a Doctor Van Leeuwenhoek . . . however spelled. Nor could she remember a phone in his small apartment. She was afraid to go out as she was now, at least by day. At night? Maybe. If anybody found out about what she'd done to Mr Glutt they'd have her jailed . . . or even killed . . . or put in a mental home. She'd have to conceal the body, run away and hide in the woods of Griffith Park, high in the Hollywood Hills, where she would roam and kill like a wild beast . . . until she was finally discovered and slain with a silver bullet.

At this thought she gave another tearful squeal.

Weeping, Dorothy cleaned the blood off the Spanish-style tiles in the entry hall and kitchen with her O-Cello sponge mop, and methodically put the remains of the collection agent in a large plastic bag, which she placed in the refrigerator to eat later. Oh, how lucky that her father wouldn't be home for another week! She had until then to decide what to do. Well, at least she had enough food.

Although, between weeping and listening to Jack Benny, the Whistler, and Stella Dallas on the radio, and watching Uncle Milton Berle and Kukla, Fran, and Ollie cavort on their prized new television set, she grew hungry again – she realized that she had no appetite at all for the rest of Mr Hubbard E. Glutt. Evidently she had partially devoured him out of mere rage and shock. Listlessly, Dorothy ate some lasagne instead.

And so passed the remainder of the week inside the pseudo-Spanish house in the Hollywood Foothills. A few times Angela or Luanne or other friends, and twice religious representatives of two different exclusive Truths, came to the door (besides phone calls) – Dorothy said (over the phone and through the door) that she had a highly contagious flu. She gave the same excuse to the newsboy, the Avon Lady, and the highly confused Welcome Wagon Woman.

As the week's end approached with no thoughts except flight into the hills, etc., her mood became almost frantic. Then one glorious morning she woke to find the hair vanished, her body lighter, and her teeth and nails returned to normal. She hastened to replace the Pearly Peach Polish.

But . . . wasn't there something *else* she had to do? The answer came at the week's absolute end, with her body again distressingly short and thin – but human. Clicking her tongue reproachfully at her forgetfulness, she dressed quickly and toted Mr Hubbard E. Glutt's very chilled remains in their plastic sack, and deposited them fairly late at night in a public trash bin.

Dad Harry returned on schedule, sunburned and exhausted, and demanding fried chicken and beer. Then he went to bed, and Dorothy, again in her padded bra, tight sweater, bouffant skirt, and (very) high heels, went back to school. She felt relieved, she felt worried. A visit to the place where Doctor Funny Name lived disclosed empty windows and a FOR RENT sign: Would the horrible condition recur? Oh, how she hoped not! Better to remain thin and skimpy all the days of her life – and never get into the movies at all!

Luanne and Angela were happy to see her again. They chattered away about the trifling things which had happened at Hollywood High during her absence, and now and again Dorothy squealed with interest which was only sometimes simulated. Would it happen again?

Early one night, about a month later, feeling vaguely ill at ease, she went for a stroll. The malaise increased; she thought a trip to a ladies' room would help, but the one in the park was now closed. There was nothing to do but go behind a bush; and it was there, as she adjusted her dress, that she felt her hands again come in contact with – a shaggy pelt. She let out a squeal of anguish. And fainted.

It was a lucky thing that her Dad was once again away, this time on his monthly week-long visit to his girlfriend in the unfashionable section of Malibu, the girlfriend's mother then making *her* monthly visit to her other daughter in Chula Vista.

Now it was impossible for Dorothy to fit into her clothes, so she made a bundle and dropped them into a debris receptacle as she passed it by. How to get home? Slinking was the only way, but as she sought out the most dimly lit streets, she only seemed to get further from home rather than nearer. And, oh! *Was* she suddenly hungry! She fought and fought against the desire for immediate food, but her stomach growled menacingly. Well, she knew how wasteful the average American family was. So of a sudden she lifted up the lid of a garbage can near a private home, with intent to delve into its contents.

No sooner had she lifted off the lid and bent over to examine what was inside, than there appeared suddenly, out of the *chiaroscuro*, the figure of a well-nourished early-middle-aged man with a small moustache. He had a large brown-paper bag in his hands which looked like garbage for disposal; astonishment was simultaneous. Dorothy squealed and dropped the lid with a clatter. The man said, "Gevalt!" and dropped the brown-paper bag, then recovered it almost immediately. Dorothy would have fled, but there was a high fence behind her. In theory she could have turned upon him with tooth and fang and claw, but unlike Mr Glutt, this man offered no gross importunity. And beneath the astonishment he seemed to have rather a kindly face.

"For a moment you had me fooled," said he. "A better-looking gorilla suit I never seen. What, you're embarrassed. Someone should see you rifling the garbage can, you should have what to eat?"

He shook his head from side to side, uttered a heavy sigh which seemed not devoid of sympathy.

"I'm not wearing a gorilla suit!" exclaimed Dorothy.

This time the shake of the head was sceptical. "Listen," said the man. "That LA has one weird what you might call ecology, this I know: possums, coyotes, escaped pythons, the weird pets some people keep because from human beings they don't find empathy: okay. But gori*ll*as? No. Also, gorillas don't talk. They make clicking noises is what, with an occasional guttural growl, or a squeal. Say. That was some squeal you gave just now. Give it again."

Dorothy, partly because of relief at finding the man neither hostile nor terrified, partly because of pride that *any*thing she could do should meet with approbation, obliged.

"Not bad. Not. Bad. At. All. I like it. I like it. Listen, why don't we do this? Come into the house, we'll have a little something to eat. I'm batching it right now; you like deli stuffed cabbage? Warming up now on the stove. Miffanwy ran away on me; luck with women I have yet to find, but hope I haven't given up yet, springs eternal in the human breast." Gently he urged Dorothy forward towards the house.

"Sandra hocked me a tchainik by day and by night, Shelley would gritchet me in kishkas until I could spit blood, I took up with Miffanwy. We'll eat a little something, we'll talk a little business – no commitments on either side. What we'll eat is anyway better than what's in the garbage can, although gourmet cooking isn't my line – listen, you wanna know something about shiksas? They never hock you a tchainik, they never gritchet you in kishkas, they don't kvetch in public places till you could drop dead from the shame; no. All they do is cheat. Watch out for the step."

Dorothy had seen better kitchens and she had seen worse. However, kitchen decor wasn't uppermost in her mind; what was uppermost was friendly human contact; also food. The man of the house ("Alfy is the name") filled her plate with stuffed-cabbage rolls and plied her with tangerines, asked if she preferred milk or cream soda and set out some Danish, pointed to a bowl of cut-up raw vegetables and pointed out that it kept away the dread scurvy, offered her a choice of seeded rye, pumpernickel, and egg-bread.

"Where there is no food, there is no religion. Where there is no religion, there is no food. So my first father-in-law used to say. What a gonnif. Eat, my shaggy friend. Eat, eat."

After quite some time, during which they both ate heartily and, truth to tell, noisily, Alfy gave grateful eructation. Gave a sudden exclamation. "Almost missed the news on the video! Finally I broke down and bought one. Many a movie big shot it will wipe out of business, they say, but me it wouldn't wipe out. Pardon my back," he said, as he turned to watch the small screen.

Dorothy gladly did so, for quite apart from her contentment in the immediate situation, she was also pleased to watch what many still called "video", which was not yet to be found in every room of every house, rather like an ashtray.

Neither black and white screen nor sound adjusted immediately, and Alfy adjusted the rabbit-ear antennas; at length a voice was heard to say: ". . . meanwhile, search continues for the so-called Monster of the Hollywood Hills."

"I'll give them yet a Monster of the Hollywood Hills," growled Alfy. "What are they trying to do with my property values? Communists! Holdupnikkes! Shut up, Alfy," he advised himself.

Two men, besides the television news personality, sat before a background of greatly enlarged photographs and plaster casts.

"Well, Dr William Wumple of the University of Southern Los Angeles Department of Primate Sciences, and Superintendent Oscar Opdegroof of the Country Police Bureau of Forensic Zoology, won't you tell us what your opinion is about all this?"

Professor Wumple said, "These photographs and plaster casts are of the foot-and-knuckle-prints of the increasingly rare Sumatran mountain gorilla of Sumatra, and –"

"I grant you, Professor Wumple," said Superintendent Opdegroof, "that there is certainly a resemblance. But the increasingly rare Sumatran mountain gorilla, a native of Sumatra in Indonesia, is vegetarian in its habitat. There is, as you know, no record of an increasingly rare Sumatran mountain gorilla, which inhabits the East Indies or Sumatra, ever having killed and eaten part of credit bureau representative and concealed his bones in a plastic bag. The diet of this otherwise harmless creature is mostly the stalk of the wild

celery plant which grows profusely on every wild mountain
slope of the archipelago of Sumatra."

"Depraved appetite," said Professor Wumple, "may be
found in any species. I refresh your memory with the fact
that pachyderms are also herbivorous, and yet there is the
classical case of the elephant named Bubi which fatally
trampled and ate a young woman named Anna O. in the
Zurich Zoo, who had heedlessly fed him leftover kümmelbrot
from the table of her employer, a dealer in low-priced watch
cases named Schultz."

The television news personality opened his mouth, but it
and the rest of him dwindled and vanished as Alfy switched off
the set. "Look, so now to business. Um, what did you say your
name was, unwilling though I am to force you out of your
chosen anonymity? *Dorothy?* A girl in a gorilla suit, this I
never encountered before," he said, surprised; but rallied
quickly. "My mother, she should rest in peace, told me that
in her own younger days, if a woman so much as smoked a
cigarette in the public street, she might as well have gone to
Atlantic City with a travelling salesman. But now we live in an
enlightened era. Lemme hear you squeal."

"Squeal?" asked Dorothy, somewhat lethargic from food
and rest.

Alfy nodded. "Yeah, squeal. Use your imagination. Say
you're strolling through your native jungle and you see, like,
reclining under a tree and fast asleep because she's lost from
her expedition – what then, a bewdyful young woman. You
never seen nothing like this in your *life* before! So naturally,
you give a squeal of astonishment. Lemme hear."

Dorothy, with only the slightest of thoughtful pauses, gave a
squeal. Of, she hoped, astonishment.

"Bewdyful," said Alfy.

Dorothy gave him a doubtful look. "No," he said. "I mean
it, I swear it. By my second mother-in-law's grave, she
should soon be inside of it. Hypocrisy is alien to my nature,
even though I never finished high school, but was cast out in
the midst of the teeming thoroughfares, what I mean *jungles*,
which are the streets of our large cities. But of this I needn't
bore you, Dotty. – Now use your imagination again. You and

this lovely young woman are going along a jungle trail in search of the mysterious Lost Temple of Gold. Her boyfriend, the head of the expedition, gets knocked on the head by a falling coconut, and as he sinks to the ground, simultaneously you – and you alone – become aware that an unfriendly tribe of rotten natives are slinking through the underbrush to attack: lemme hear you convey this information to your lovely human new-found lady friend with a series of intelligent squeals."

Dorothy did her best to oblige, and in the unpremeditated fervour of her performance, began to use gestures. Alfy was immensely pleased. "We'll dub it, we'll dub it!" he cried.

She was so excited that she found herself jumping up and down and scratching her pelt.

Alfy, watching her benignly, became concerned. "Even through your gorilla suit you're sweating," he said. "Let me get you some ice cubes for your cold drink." Running water over the old-fashioned all-metal tray, he turned and asked, "Why not take off your costume, you'll be more comfortable, Dotty?"

Even as she opened her mouth to repeat that she wore no costume, Dorothy observed a strange woman come running across the dimly lit dining room adjoining the kitchen; and as she ran, thus she screamed:

"I'll *give* you 'take off your costume,' I'll *give* you Dotty, I'll *give* you Shelley, I'll *give* you Miffanwy –"

"Sandra, if you hock me a tchainik, I'll –"

Dorothy reacted to Sandra with as little instinctive affection as she had to Hubbard E. Glutt; raising herself on her toes, extending her arms high and her hands out, her talons clawing and her fangs showing, she began to utter squeals of pure rage.

Sandra never for a moment showed the slightest sign of believing that she was confronted by someone in a gorilla suit; Sandra turned and fled, giving shriek after shriek of terror, horror and fright.

Dorothy pursued her down the street, sometimes erect, sometimes bounding along on all fours; till the lights of an oncoming car caused her to shinny up the nearest deciduous tree, whence she dropped upon a housetop, thence to another tree, and thence to another housetop. Until eventually she realized that she was absolutely lost.

Inadvertently scattering the inhabitants of a hobo jungle, she moodily drank their bitter black coffee and spent the night on a musty mattress in a culvert near their fire. The illustrated magazines of a certain type which those lonely and semihermitical men used to while away the hours of their solitude, she merely fed into the flames in disgust.

Much of the next day Dorothy spent in a eucalyptus grove destined soon to be "developed" into total destruction. She gave a lot of thought to her condition. It was no doubt the celery tonic in which the incompetent quack-doctor Songhabhongbhong Van Leeuwenhoek had administered the so-called glandular extract – containing as the soft drink must have done, certain elements very similar to the wild celery stalks eaten by the increasingly rare mountain gorilla of Sumatra – which had caused this change to come upon her. Of this she was certain.

Since it wasn't concurrent with her monthly cycle, and seemed not even to be identical with the full moon, she wondered if its occurrence might have something to do with her sign: Aries on the cusp. Vaguely she remembered hearing of a certain economically priced astrologer mentioned by her mother before she left to become an Avon Lady in Anaheim – or so her father said; perhaps (Dorothy now wondered for the first time) he had been shielding some less respectable occupation.

Her thoughts were interrupted with the utmost suddenness by the appearance in the grove of a simian-like creature who appeared equally startled. For a long moment both stood still, each staring at the other. Was this another increasingly rare Sumatran mountain gorilla? Another victim of the celery and hormone tonic? – No. It appeared to be a man in a flea-bitten gorilla suit! And it held a bottle of something wrapped in a brown paper bag.

"Listen," it said (or, though the voice was slightly slurred, it was a masculine voice – said *he*). "In times past, honey, when I was a well-known star of stage and screen, I drank nothing but the best Madeira, with a preference for *sercial*, but when you're down it's all over with the imported vintages. Any kind of sneaky pete will do. Go on, my dear. Go on and take a hit." His sunken snout came so near to her face that she sensed it wasn't his first drink of the day.

The well-known former star of stage and screen took the bottle and slid the top of it up high enough so that he could uncap it and drink of its contents, and yet quickly slide it back down inside the paper bag; for many people might object to someone blatantly imbibing alcohol in public – even in a eucalyptus grove which had formerly served as the site of a hobo jungle – for to do so is against the law.

Next, and though he had gallantly offered her a hit, he proceeded to do the following: turning slightly at an angle away from Dorothy, he fumbled his paw into his pelt and produced a second bottle, a smaller one with clear liquid in it; of this he swiftly drank and swiftly disposed of it once again in a pocket of some sort; and next he took a much longer tug of the cheap wine. *Then* he offered it to her again, and as she hesitated, thinking of a tactful refusal, he said, "It's only polite to offer, but to insist would be most *im*polite." – And jerked it away.

His voice had become increasingly slurred, and as he lurched off down the road, Dorothy considered the possibility that the clear liquid was vodka. It was only because he half-turned his head, and inclined it as though in invitation for her to accompany him, that she followed. Grotesquery prefers company, and she thought that she might as well go along – because she wasn't sure what else to do. So follow she did.

Now and then some of the passers-by looked at them, but nobody looked twice. Not only was this Hollywood, but this was the famous "Gower St Gulch", as outsiders in the know called it. To those on the inside it was merely "The Gully".

To outsiders *not* in the know it might have seemed as if preparations were being made for the annual cattle drive to Dodge City, so numerous were the men in cowboy outfits. There was a slight stir in their ranks, seemingly caused by a dark man wearing a soiled khaki shirt and faded dungarees, moccasins and a pair of reddened eyes, who was standing on the sidewalk and shouting:

"Slant-eyes folks and Mexicans and Very Light Coloured People, keep the hell outa the gully!" he yelled, in particular directing his cries to several people in war paint and feathers. "Leave the depiction of Native American Indian roles to jen-u-wine Native American Indians! – You, *you*, Marcus Garvey Doothit, professional name Marco Thunderhorse, I'm addressing myself ta *you*, don't gi' *me* no bull about yer Grandmother bein' a full-blood Cherokee Injin!"

M. G. Doothit, aka Marco Thunderhorse, gave a scornful pout and said, "All I have to say to *you*, Amos Littlebird, is that sticks and stones and arrows and musket balls may break my bones, but ethnic epithets merely reflect upon those who hurl them."

Scarcely had all this faded behind them when Dorothy and her lurching companion encountered a scowling young man bearing a sign which read:

SO-CALLED ``SCIENCE FICTION'' MOVIES/STOP LIBELLOUS
PORTRAYALS OF SO-CALLED ``MAD SCIENTISTS''. SCIENCE
IS THE HOPE OF THE PEOPLE!

It was not yet the 1960s, but the winds were full of straws.

By and by they came to a high wire fence surrounding a barracks-like compound; and here the senior simian figure paused to drain both of his bottles and hurl them away. Then he approached the gate in, for the first time, a fairly good simulation of an apelike lope. A grey-haired man stepped out of a booth, beaming.

"Gee, good *morn*ing, Mr Bartlett Bosworth," he exclaimed. "Only last night I was saying to my wife, 'Guess who I saw at AESSP this a.m., sugar?' And she says, 'Who?' And I told her, 'Remember Bart Bosworth who played Greeta Garbo's boy-friend and also he played Mree Dressler's grown-up hand-some son?' And she says, 'Sure! What's he doing *now*?' And I told her, 'He's imitating a gorilla for Alf Smatz, King of the D-Movies,' and she says, 'Oh gee, what a shame,' and –"

Thickly, from behind his gorilla mask, Bart Bosworth said, "Both of you just take your pity and divide it in two and then you can both shove it." And he lurched on through the gate.

The grey-haired man, no longer beaming, pointed to Dorothy and asked, "Who's this?"

"Who's it *look* like? Myrna *Loy*? My understudy."

The gateman turned his attention to other arrivals. Ahead of them was a sign reading: ALFRED EMMANUEL SMITH-SMATZ PRODUCTIONS. POPULAR ENTERTAINMENT AT POPULAR PRICES. The way seemed endless, but Bartlett Bosworth evidently knew his way.

By and by they came upon a clearing in a jungle. Scarcely had Dorothy time to express surprise in a single squeal, when Bart Bosworth, uttering a huge and hideous hiccup, fell full length upon the synthetic turf and began to snore.

This dull and repetitious sound was interrupted by a short, sharp slap: a man in the long-considered-obsolete uniform of a moving-picture director (including turned-around cap), had occasioned this by striking his forehead with the flat of his hand. "Again!" he cried. "Again! Drunk yesterday, drunk the day before – get him up! Hot coffee, bennies if anybody's got any, an ice pack. But get him *up*, get him *sober*!"

Although a shrivelled-looking chap with the air of a superannuated yes-man turned round and round like a dervish, shrilling: "Right, Chief! Yes, Chief! Hot coffee! Benzedrine! A nice pack!" others were not convinced.

" 'S no use, Mr Smatz," said the script girl.

"Wouldn't help, Alfy," called down the cameraman.

"We couldn't get him sober yesterday and we couldn't keep him sober the day before," declared a blond, youngish-looking fellow in short khaki pants and shirt, and a pith helmet.

And in a high, petulant voice, a bosomy blonde youngish-looking woman dressed similarly announced that she was "fed up with alla this stuff" – actually, she didn't say *stuff* – and in another minute would go sit in her dressing room.

"Get somebody else," advised somebody else, "for the ape part."

The man with the turned-around cap gave, through his megaphone, an anguished howl. "Even in a low-budget film no one could afford to maintain a shikker gorilla on the payroll! – Also," he said, giving the youngish-looking woman a baleful stare, "histrionics in high places I'm not appreciative of; also, furthermore, in low-budget films high places ain't so damn high. – *What*, 'Get somebody else?' *Who*, 'Get somebody else?' *Where*, 'Get somebody else for the ape part?' Ape-part-playing is a dying art, gorilla suits cost a fortune – and if I had a fortune would I be making D-films? No," he answered.

Then an odd expression came over his face. One hand he cupped around his ear; the other hand he used to shade his eyes. "Wait. Listen. Look. Just before shikker here, he plotzed, didn't I hear like a high-pitched squeal which clearly indicated astonishment and alarm? Sure I did. So. Okay. Who *squealed*?"

Voices were heard denying that he or she or they had squealed. Ears were cupped and eyes were shaded . . . It was very soon indeed that fingers were pointed. Dorothy, realizing that concealment was useless, shyly stepped forward.

Alfred Emmanuel Smith-Smatz – "Alfy" (for it was he) – clapped both hands together. "*Dotty!*" he exclaimed. "Not only did you chase away Sandra, that yenta; early this morning I get a phone call from my thirty-year-old stepson Sammy, the schmuck: 'Mommy is so terrified she swears she'll never leave Desert Hot Springs again' – but you are *still* giving out the intelligent squeals, with *expression*! Bartlett Bosworth never got no expression in his squeals; that's the way it is with them silent screen stars: squeak, yes; squeal, no. Are you a quick study, Dotty? Yeah? Good! So take a quick sixty seconds to study the next scene . . . You got it? Yeahh! Yeay! Lights! Camera! Dolly in on Dotty, this great little gorilla lady! ACTION! Let'm roll!"

The rest is Film History, even if much of it must be concealed from the fans and the gossip columns and the world at large. To be sure, Alfy Smatz ("King of the D-Movies") was a bit put out at first when he learned that Dorothy couldn't play gorilla roles week after week; but only during those weeks when the moon is full in central Sumatra.

But the month has, after all, more than one week. The first week Dorothy, in her own natural form (with artfully padded hips and bosom) plays the heroine in a science fiction film as the daughter of (despite feeble social protest) the mad scientist. The second week Dorothy is kidnapped from various wagon trains and restored to various wagon trains by, alternately, Marco Thunderhorse and Amos Littlebird. The third week Dorothy is, first, threatened by love-starved Arabs, and second, saved from same by the noble efforts of either Marco or Amos in jellabas. – But the *fourth* week in the AESSP shooting schedule: *Ahah!*

In the fourth week of every month Dorothy stars in one *STARRING JEANNIE OF THE JUNGLE, THE WORLD'S MOST LOVABLE LITTLE GORILLA* film after another after another after another. These movies have wowed the fans in every drive-in in North America, and break records in every box office from Tampa to Tahiti; and, boy! How the money rolls in!

Dorothy has paid off her father's debts and retired him on a personal pension, with modest privileges at the gaming tables in the poker palaces of Gardena.

Every now and then she and her blond, youngish-looking leading man of the moment get into her lemon-yellow Pighafetti-Zoom convertible to visit Luanne and Angela. They are green with envy. Again and again, separately and together, Luanne and Angela wonder. What is the secret of Dorothy's success? It isn't looks. It isn't figure. What? What? What?

It's showbiz, is what.

Dr Songhabhongbhong Van Leeuwenhoek has never been heard from again.

Serves him right.

THE AFFLICTION OF BARON HUMPFELHIMMEL

John Kendrick Bangs

John Kendrick Bangs (1862–1922) is another of those great humorists from the last century whose stories have pretty much been forgotten except for the frequently reprinted "The Water Ghost of Harrowby Hall" (1891), perhaps one of the best-known humorous ghost stories. In his day he enjoyed marked success in his ability to debunk well-known books and individuals. His greatest success came with A Houseboat on the Styx *(1895), in which the ghosts of various characters, real and literary, come together on their way to Hades. His most humorous stories will be found in* The Water Ghost and Others *(1894),* Ghosts I Have Met and Some Others *(1898),* Over the Plum-Pudding *(1901),* The Inventions of an Idiot *(1904) and the longer works* Alice in Blunderland *(1907) and* The Autobiography of Methuselah *(1909).*

Everybody said it was an extraordinary affair altogether, and for once everybody was right. Baron Humpfelhimmel himself would say nothing about it for two reasons. The first reason was that nobody dared ask him what he thought about it, and the second was that he was too proud to speak to anybody concerning any subject whatsoever, unless questioned. That he always laughed, no matter what happened, was the melancholy fact, and had been a melancholy fact from his childhood's earliest hour. He was born laughing. He laughed in church, he laughed at home. When his father spanked him he roared with laughter, and when he suffered from the measles he could not begin to restrain his mirth.

The situation seemed all the more singular when it was remembered that Rupert von Pepperpotz, the previous Baron Humpfelhimmel, and father of the Laughing Baron, as he was called, was never known to smile from his childhood's earliest hour to his dying day, and, strangest of all, was a far more amiable person, despite his solemnity, than the present Baron for all his laughter.

"What does it mean, do you suppose?" Frau Ehrenbreitstein once asked of Hans Pumpernickel, her husband's private secretary.

"I cannot tell," Hans had answered, "and I have my reason for saying that I cannot tell," he added, significantly.

"What is that reason, Hans?" asked the good lady, her curiosity aroused by the boy's manner.

"It is this," said Hans, his voice sinking to a whisper. "I cannot tell, because – because I do not know!"

And this, let me say in passing, was why Hans Pumpernickel was thought by all to be so wise. He had a reason always for what he did, and was ever willing to give it.

"They say," the good Lady Ehrenbreitstein went on – "they do say that when last winter the Baron while hunting boars was thrown from his horse, breaking his leg and two of his ribs, they could not be set because of his convulsions of laughter, though for my part I cannot see wherein having one's leg and ribs broken is provocative of merriment."

"Nor I," quoth Hans. "I have an eye for jokes. In most things I can see the fun, but in the breaking of one's bones I see more cause for tears than smiles."

And it was true. As Frau Ehrenbreitstein had heard, the

Baron Humpfelhimmel had broken one leg and two ribs – only it was while hunting wolves and not in a boar chase – and when the Emperor's physician, who was one of the party, came to where the suffering man lay he found him roaring with laughter.

"Good!" cried the physician, leaning over his prostrate form. "I am glad to see that you are not hurt. I feared you were injured."

"I am injured," the Baron replied, with a loud laugh. "My left leg – ha-ha-ha! – is nearly killing me – hee-hee! – with p-pain, and if I mistake not, either my heart – ha-ha-ha-ha! – or my ribs – hee-hee-hee! – are broken in nineteen places."

Then he went off into such an explosion of mirth as not only appeared unseemly, but also deprived him of the power of speech for five or six minutes.

"I fail to see the joke," said the physician, as the Baron's laughter echoed and re-echoed throughout the forest.

"Th-there – hee-hee! – there isn't a-any joke," the Baron answered, smiling. "Confound you – ha-ha-ha-ha! – oho-ho-ho! – can't you see I'm suffering?"

"I see you are laughing," the physician replied – "laughing as if you were reading a comic paper full of real jokes. What are you laughing at?"

"Ha-ha! I – I d-dud-don't know," stammered the Baron, vainly endeavouring to suppress his mirth. "I – I don't feel like laughing – hee-hee! – but I can't help it." And off he went into another gale. Nor did he stop there. The physician tried vainly to quiet him down so that he could set the fractured bones, but in spite of all he could do for him the Baron either would not or could not stop laughing. When he was able to move about again it was only with a limp, and even that appeared to have its humorous side, for whenever the Baron appeared on the public streets he was always smiling, and when the Mayor ventured to express his sympathy with him over his misfortune the Baron laughed again, and mirthfully requested him to mind his own business.

Then it was recalled how ten years before, when the famous Von Pepperpotz Castle was destroyed by fire, the Baron was found writing in his study by the messenger who brought the news.

"Baron," the messenger cried – "Baron, the chateau is burning. The flames have already destroyed the armoury, and are now eating their way through the corridors to the state banquet-hall."

The Baron looked the messenger in the eye for an instant, and then his face wreathed with smiles.

"My castle's burning, eh? Ha-ha-ha!" was what he said; and then, rising hurriedly from his desk, he hastened, shouting with laughter, to the scene, where no one worked harder than he to stay the devastating course of the flames.

"You seem to be pleased," said one who noticed his merriment.

The Baron's answer was a blow which knocked the fellow down, and then, striking him across the shoulders with his staff, he walked away, muttering to himself:

"Pleased! Ha-ha-ha! Does ruin please anybody – tee-hee-hee! If the churls only – tee-hee! – only knew – ha-ha-ha-ha!"

That was it! If they only knew! And no one did know until after the Baron had died without children – for he had never married – and all his possessions and papers became the property of the state. Through these papers the secret of the Baron's laughter became known to the good people of Schnitzelhammerstein-on-the-Zugvitz, and through them it became known to me. Hans Pumpernickel himself told me the tale, and as he has risen to the exalted position of Mayor of Schnitzelhammerstein-on-the-Zugvitz, an honour conferred only on the truly good and worthy, I have no reason to doubt that the story is in every way truthful.

"When Baron Humpfelhimmel died," said Hans, as he and I walked together along the beautiful sylvan path that runs by the side of the Zugvitz River, "I am sorry to say there were few mourners. A man who laughs, as a rule, is popular, but the man who laughs always, without regard to circumstances, makes enemies. One learns to love a person who laughs at one's jests, but one who laughs at funerals, at conflagrations, at beggars, at the needy and the distressed, does not become universally beloved. Such was the habit of Fritz von Pepperpotz, last of the Barons Humpfelhimmel. If you were to go to him with a funny story, none would laugh more heartily than he; but equally loud would he laugh were you to say to him that you had a racking headache, and should it chance that you were to inform him you had been desperately ill, his mirth would know no bounds. Even in his greatest frenzies of rage he would smirk and laugh, and so it happened that the popularity which you would expect would go with a mirthful disposition was the last thing in the world he could hope for. I do not exaggerate when I say that Baron Humpfelhimmel could not have been elected office-boy to the Mayor on a popular vote, even if there were no opposing candidate. Now that it is all over, however, and we know the truth, we have changed our minds about it, and already several hundred of our citizens have raised a fund of twenty marks to go towards putting up a monument to the memory of the Laughing Baron.

"Fritz von Pepperpotz, my friend," said Hans to me, in explanation of the situation, "laughed because he could not help it, as a statement found among his papers after he died showed. The statement contained the whole story, and in some of its details it is a sad one. It was all the fault of the grand-father of the late Baron that he could do nothing but laugh all his days, that he died unmarried, and that the name of Von Pepperpotz has died off the face of the earth forever, unless someone else chooses to assume that name, which, I imagine, no one is crazy enough to do. The only thing that could reconcile me to such a name would be the estates that formerly went with it, but now that they have become the property of the government the house has lost all of its attractions, retaining, however, every bit of its homeliness. Pumpernickel is bad enough, but it is beautiful beside Von Pepperpotz."

Here Hans sighed, and to comfort him, rather than to say anything I really meant, I observed that I thought Pumpernickel was a good strong name.

"Yes," Hans said, with a pleased smile. "It certainly is strong. I have had mine twenty-five years now, and it doesn't show the slightest sign of wear. It's as good as the day it was made, But to return to the Von Pepperpotz family and its mysterious affliction.

"According to the Baron's statement, while he himself could not restrain his mirth, no matter how badly he felt, his father, Rupert von Pepperpotz, could never smile, although he was a man of most genial disposition. Just as Fritz was ushered into the world, grinning like a Cheshire cheese –"

"Cat," I suggested, noting Hans's error.

"Cat, is it?" he said. "Well, now, do you know I am glad to hear that? I always supposed the term used was cheese, and positively I have lain awake night after night trying to comprehend how a cheese could grin, and finally I gave it up, setting it down as one of the peculiarities of the English language. If it's Cheshire cat, and not Cheshire cheese, why, it's all clear as a pikestaff. But, as I was saying, just as Fritz was born grinning like a Cheshire cat, his father Rupert was born frowning apparently with rage. He was the most ill-natured-looking baby you ever saw, according to the chronicles. Nothing seemed to please him. When you or I would have cooed, Rupert von Pepperpotz would wrinkle up his forehead until the furrows, if his nurse tells the truth, were deep enough to hide letters in.

"And yet he was rarely cross, and never disobedient. It was the strangest thing in the world. Here was a being who always frowned and never laughed, and yet who was as obliging in his actions as could be. As he grew older his active amiability increased, but his frown grew more terrible than ever. He became a great wit. As he walked through the streets of Schnitzelhammerstein-on-the-Zugvitz he was always merry, though none would have guessed it to look at him. He had a pleasant voice, and his neighbours all said it was a most startling thing to hear in the distance a jolly, roistering song, and then to walk along a little way and see that it was this forbidding-looking person who was doing the singing.

"How Rupert got Wilhelmina de Grootzenburg to become his wife, considering his seeming solemnity, which made him appear to be positively ugly, nobody ever knew. It is probable, however, that it was sympathy which moved her to like him, unless it was that his ugliness fascinated her. Rupert himself said that it was not sympathy for his inability to laugh or smile, because he did not want sympathy for that. He didn't feel badly about it himself. He never had smiled, and so did not know the pleasure of it. Consequently he didn't miss it. Smiling was an idiotic way of expressing pleasure anyhow, he said. Why just because a man thought of a funny idea he should stretch his mouth he couldn't see. No more could he understand why it was necessary to show one's appreciation of a funny story by shaking one's stomach and saying "Ha-ha!" On the whole, he said that he was satisfied. He could talk and could tell people he enjoyed their stories without having to shake himself or disturb the corners of his mouth. When little Fritz was born, and did nothing but laugh even when he had the colic, the solemn-looking Rupert observed that the baby simply proved the truth of what he said.

" 'What a donkey the child is,' he cried, 'to spoil his pretty face by stretching his mouth so that you almost fear his ears will drop into it! And those wild whoops, which you call laughter, what earthly use are they? I can't see why, if he is glad about something, he can't just say, "I'm glad about so and so," mildly, instead of making me deaf with his roars. Truly, laughter is not what it is cracked up to be.'

" 'Ah, my dear Rupert,' Wilhelmina, his wife, had said, 'you do not really know what you are talking about! If you could enjoy the sensation of laughing once you would never wish to be without it.'

" 'Nonsense!' replied the Baron. 'My father never laughed, so why should I wish to?'

"Now, then," continued Hans, "according to Fritz von Pepperpotz's statement, there was where Rupert was wrong. Siegfried von Pepperpotz had known what it was to laugh, but he had not known when to laugh, which was why the family of Von Pepperpotz was afflicted with a curse, which only the final dying-out of the family could remove, and there lay the solution of the mystery. It seems that Siegfried von Pepperpotz, grandfather of Fritz and father of Rupert, had been a wild sort of a youth, who smiled when he wished and frowned when he wished, no matter what the occasion may have been, and he smiled once too often. A miserable-looking figure of a man once passed through the village of Schnitzelhammerstein-on-the-Zugvitz, selling sugar dolls and other sweets. To

Siegfried and his comrades it seemed good to play a prank on the old fellow. They sent him two miles off into the country, where, they said, was a rich countess, who would buy his whole stock, when in reality there was no rich countess there at all, so that the old man had his trouble for his pains.

"That he was a magician they did not know, but so he was, and in those days magicians could do everything. Of course he was angry at the deception, and on his return to Schnitzelhammerstein-on-the-Zugvitz he sent for the young men, and got all of them to apologize and buy his wares except Siegfried. Siegfried not only refused to apologize and buy the old man's candies, but had the audacity to laugh in his face, and tell him about a wealthy old duke who lived two miles out on the other side of the village, which the magician immediately recognized as another attempt to play a practical joke upon him.

" 'Enough, Siegfried von Pepperpotz!' he cried, in his rage. 'Laugh away while you can. After today may you never smile, and may your son never smile, and may your son's son, willing or unwilling, smile smiles that you two would have smiled, and so may it ever go! May every third generation get the laughter that the preceding two shall lose, according to my curse!'

"This made Siegfried laugh all the harder, for, not knowing, as I have said, that the old man was a magician, he had no fear of him. Next day, however, he changed his mind. He found that he could not laugh. He could not even smile. Try as he would, his lips refused to do his bidding.

"It ruined his disposition. Siegfried von Pepperpotz grew ill over it. The greatest doctors in the world were summoned to his aid, but to no avail. If the curse had ended with him he might not have minded it so much, but after the discovery that from the day of his birth his son Rupert was no more able to laugh than himself he began to brood over the affliction, and shortly died of it; and when Fritz found out from a paper he discovered in a secret drawer in the old chest in the chateau what the curse was – for Siegfried never told his son, and alone knew from what it was he suffered, and that it was perpetual – he resolved that there should be no further posterity to whom it should be handed down.

"That," said Hans, "is the story of Baron Humpfelhimmel's affliction."

"And a strange story it is," said I.

"Though I don't know that it has any particular moral."

"Oh yes, it has!" said Hans. "It has a good moral."

"And what is that?" I asked.

"Don't laugh at your own jokes," he replied. "If Siegfried von Pepperpotz had not laughed when the magician came back, he never would have been cursed, and this story never would have been told."

THE CASE OF THE FOUR AND TWENTY BLACKBIRDS

Neil Gaiman

Neil Gaiman (b. 1960) is best known as the author of the Sandman series of graphic novels, but he is equally adept at the full works. His recent books include Neverwhere *(1996) (based on his TV serial),* Stardust *(1998), an enchanting fairy tale, and the collections* Angels and Visitations *(1993) and* Smoke and Mirrors *(1998). The following story is one of Gaiman's earliest, and the first he feels worthy of resurrection. It suitably leads off our little duo of gangster stories.*

I sat in my office, nursing a glass of hooch and idly cleaning my automatic. Outside the rain fell steadily, like it seems to do most of the time in our fair city, whatever the tourist board say. Hell, I didn't care. I'm not on the tourist board. I'm a private dick, and one of the best, although you wouldn't have known it; the office was crumbling, the rent was unpaid and the hooch was my last.

Things are tough all over.

To cap it all the only client I'd had all week never showed up on the street corner where I'd waited for him. He said it was going to be a big job, but now I'd never know: he kept a prior appointment in the morgue.

So when the dame walked into my office I was sure my luck had changed for the better.

"What are you selling, lady?"

She gave me a look that would have induced heavy breathing in a pumpkin, and which shot my heartbeat up to three figures. She had long blonde hair and a figure that would have made Thomas Aquinas forget his vows. I forgot all mine about never taking cases from dames.

"What would you say to some of the green stuff?" she asked in a husky voice, getting straight to the point.

"Continue, sister." I didn't want her to know how bad I needed the dough, so I held my hand in front of my mouth; it doesn't help if a client sees you salivate.

She opened her purse and flipped out a photograph – a glossy eight by ten. "Do you recognize that man?"

In my business you know who people are. "Yeah."

"He's dead."

"I know that too, sweetheart. It's old news. It was an accident."

Her gaze went so icy you could have chipped it into cubes and cooled a cocktail with it. "My brother's death was no accident."

I raised an eyebrow – you need a lot of arcane skills in my business – and said: "Your brother, eh?" Funny, she hadn't struck me as the type that had brothers.

"I'm Jill Dumpty."

"So your brother was Humpty Dumpty?"

"And he didn't fall off that wall, Mr Horner. He was pushed."

Interesting, if true. Dumpty had his finger in most of the crooked pies in town; I could think of five guys who would have preferred to see him dead than alive without trying.

Without trying too hard, anyway.

"You seen the cops about this?"

"Nah. The King's Men aren't interested in anything to do with his death. They say they did all they could do in trying to put him together again after the fall."

I leaned back in my chair.

"So what's it to you? Why do you need me?"

"I want you to find the killer, Mr Horner. I want him brought to justice. I want him to fry like an egg. Oh – and one other *little* thing," she added, lightly. "Before he died Humpty had a small manila envelope full of photographs he was meant to be sending me. Medical photos. I'm a trainee nurse, and I need them to pass my finals."

I inspected my nails, then looked up at her face, taking in a handful of waist and Easter-egg bazonkas on the way up. She was a looker, although her cute nose was a little on the shiny side. "I'll take the case. Seventy-five a day and two hundred bonus for results."

She smiled; my stomach twisted around once and went into orbit. "You get another two hundred if you get me those photographs. I want to be a nurse *real* bad." Then she dropped three fifties on my desktop.

I let a devil-may-care grin play across my rugged face. "Say, sister, how about letting me take you out for dinner? I just came into some money."

She gave an involuntary shiver of anticipation and muttered something about having a thing about midgets, so I knew I was onto a good thing. Then she gave me a lopsided smile that would have made Albert Einstein drop a decimal point. "First find my brother's killer, Mr Horner. And my photographs. *Then* we can play."

She closed the door behind her. Maybe it was still raining but I didn't notice. I didn't care.

There are parts of town the tourist board don't mention. Parts of town where the police travel in threes if they travel at all. In my line of work you get to visit them more than is healthy. Healthy is never.

He was waiting for me outside Luigi's. I slid up behind him, my rubber-soled shoes soundless on the shiny wet sidewalk.

"Hiya, Cock."

He jumped and spun round; I found myself gazing up into the muzzle of a .45. "Oh, Horner." He put the gun away. "Don't call me Cock. I'm Bernie Robin to you, Short-stuff, and don't you forget it."

"Cock Robin is good enough for me, Cock. Who killed Humpty Dumpty?"

He was a strange-looking bird, but you can't be choosy in my profession. He was the best underworld lead I had.

"Let's see the colour of your money."

I showed him a fifty.

"Hell," he muttered. "It's green. Why can't they make puce or mauve money for a change?" He took it, though. "All I know is that the Fat Man had his finger in a lot of pies."

"So?"

"One of those pies had four and twenty blackbirds in it."

"Huh?"

"Do I hafta spell it out for you? I . . . *Ughh* . . ." He crumpled to the sidewalk, an arrow protruding from his back. Cock Robin wasn't going to be doing any more chirping.

Sergeant O'Grady looked down at the body, then he looked down at me. "Faith and begorrah, to be sure," he said. "If it isn't Little Jack Horner himself."

"I didn't kill Cock Robin, Sarge."

"And I suppose that the call we got down at the station telling us you were going to be rubbing the late Mr Robin out – here; tonight – was just a hoax?"

"If I'm the killer, where are my arrows?" I thumbed open a pack of gum and started to chew. "It's a frame."

He puffed on his meerschaum and then put it away, and idly played a couple of phrases of the *William Tell Overture* on his oboe. "Maybe. Maybe not. But you're still a suspect. Don't leave town. And Horner . . ."

"Yeah?"

"Dumpty's death was an accident. That's what the coroner said. That's what I say. Drop the case."

I thought about it. Then I thought of the money, and the girl. "No dice, Sarge."

He shrugged. "It's your funeral." He said it like it probably would be.

I had a funny feeling like he could be right.

"You're out of your depth, Horner. You're playing with the big boys. And it ain't healthy."

From what I could remember of my schooldays he was correct. Whenever I played with the big boys I always wound up having the stuffing beaten out of me. But how did O'Grady – how *could* O'Grady have known that? Then I remembered something else.

O'Grady was the one that used to beat me up the most.

It was time for what we in the profession call "legwork". I made a few discreet enquiries around town, but found out nothing about Dumpty that I didn't know already.

Humpty Dumpty was a bad egg. I remembered him when he was new in town, a smart young animal trainer with a nice line in training mice to run up clocks. He went to the bad pretty fast though; gambling, drink, women, it's the same story all over. A bright young kid thinks that the streets of Nurseryland are paved with gold, and by the time he finds out otherwise it's much too late.

Dumpty started off with extortions and robbery on a small scale – he trained up a team of spiders to scare little girls away from their curds and whey, which he'd pick up and sell on the black market. Then he moved on to blackmail – the nastiest game. We crossed paths once, when I was hired by this young society kid – let's call him Georgie Porgie – to recover some compromising snaps of him kissing the girls and making them cry. I got the snaps, but I learned it wasn't healthy to mess with the Fat Man. And I don't make the same mistakes twice. Hell, in my line of work I can't afford to make the same mistakes once.

It's a tough world out there. I remember when Little Bo Peep first came to town . . . but you don't want to hear my troubles. If you're not dead yet, you've got troubles of your own.

I checked out the newspaper files on Dumpty's death. One minute he was sitting on a wall, the next he was in pieces at the bottom. All the King's Horses and all the King's Men were on the scene in minutes, but he needed more than first aid. A medic named Foster was called – a friend of Dumpty's from his Gloucester days – although I don't know of anything a doc can do when you're dead.

Hang on a second – *Dr Foster!*

I got that old feeling you get in my line of work. Two little brain cells rub together the right way and in seconds you've got a twenty-four-carat cerebral fire on your hands.

You remember the client who didn't show – the one I'd waited for all day on the street corner? An accidental death. I hadn't bothered to check it out – I can't afford to waste time on clients who aren't going to pay for it.

Three deaths, it seemed. Not one.

I reached for the telephone and rang the police station. "This is Horner," I told the desk man. "Lemme speak to Sergeant O'Grady."

There was a crackling and he came on the line. "O'Grady speaking."

"It's Horner."

"Hi, Little Jack." That was just like O'Grady. He'd been kidding me about my size since we were kids together. "You finally figured out that Dumpty's death was an accident?"

"Nope. I'm now investigating three deaths. The Fat Man's, Bernie Robin's and Dr Foster's."

"Foster the plastic surgeon? His death was an accident."

"Sure. And your mother was married to your father."

There was a pause. "Horner, if you phoned me up just to talk dirty, I'm not amused."

"Okay, wise guy. If Humpty Dumpty's death was an accident and so was Dr Foster's, tell me just one thing.

"Who killed Cock Robin?"

I don't ever get accused of having too much imagination, but there's one thing I'd swear to. I could *hear* him grinning over the phone as he said: "You did, Horner. And I'm staking my badge on it."

The line went dead.

★   ★   ★

My office was cold and lonely, so I wandered down to Joe's Bar for some companionship and a drink or three.

Four and twenty blackbirds. A dead doctor. The Fat Man. Cock Robin . . . Heck, this case had more holes in it than a Swiss cheese and more loose ends than a torn string vest. And where did the juicy Miss Dumpty come into it? Jack and Jill – we'd make a great team. When this was all over perhaps we could go off together to Louie's little place on the hill, where no one's interested in whether you got a marriage licence or not. "The Pail of Water", that was the name of the joint.

I called over the bartender. "Hey. Joe."

"Yeah, Mr Horner?" He was polishing a glass with a rag that had seen better days as a shirt.

"Did you ever meet the Fat Man's sister?"

He scratched at his cheek. "Can't say as I did. His sister . . . huh? Hey – the Fat Man didn't have a sister."

"You sure of that?"

"Sure I'm sure. It was the day my sister had her first kid – I told the Fat Man I was an uncle. He gave me this look and says, 'Ain't no way I'll ever be an uncle, Joe. Got no sisters or brothers, nor no other kinfolk neither.' "

If the mysterious Miss Dumpty wasn't his sister, who *was* she?

"Tell me, Joe. Didja ever see him in here with a dame – about so high, shaped like this?" My hands described a couple of parabolas. "Looks like a blonde love goddess."

He shook his head. "Never saw him with any dames. Recently he was hanging around with some medical guy, but the only thing he ever cared about was those crazy birds and animals of his."

I took a swig of my drink. It nearly took the roof of my mouth off. "Animals? I thought he'd given all that up."

"Naw – couple weeks back he was in here with a whole bunch of blackbirds he was training to sing 'Wasn't that a dainty dish to set before *Mmm Mmm*'."

"*Mmm Mmm*?"

"Yeah. I got no idea who."

I put my drink down. A little of it spilt on the counter, and I watched it strip the varnish. "Thanks, Joe. You've been a big help." I handed him a ten-dollar bill. "For information received," I said, adding, "Don't spend it all at once."

In my profession it's making little jokes like that that keeps you sane.

I had one contact left. I found a pay phone and called her number.

"Old Mother Hubbard's Cupboard – Cake Shop and Licensed Soup Kitchen."

"It's Horner, Ma."

"Jack? It ain't safe for me to talk to you."

"For old time's sake, sweetheart. You owe me a favour." Some two-bit crooks had once knocked off the Cupboard, leaving it bare. I'd tracked them down and returned the cakes and soup.

". . . Okay. But I don't like it."

"*You* know everything that goes on around here on the food front, Ma. What's the significance of a pie with four and twenty trained blackbirds in it?"

She whistled, long and low. "You really don't know?"

"I wouldn't be asking you if I did."

"You should read the Court pages of the papers next time, sugar. Jeez. You are out of your depth."

"C'mon, Ma. Spill it."

"It so happens that that particular dish was set before the King a few weeks back . . . Jack? Are you still there?"

"I'm still here, ma'am," I said, quietly. "All of a sudden a lot of things are starting to make sense." I put down the phone.

It was beginning to look like Little Jack Horner had pulled out a plum from this pie.

It was raining, steady and cold.

I phoned a cab.

Quarter of an hour later one lurched out of the darkness. "You're late."

"So complain to the tourist board."

I climbed in the back, wound down the window, and lit a cigarette.

And I went to see the Queen.

★   ★   ★

The door to the private part of the palace was locked. It's the part that the public don't get to see. But I've never been public, and the little lock hardly slowed me up. The door to the private apartments with the big red heart on it was unlocked, so I knocked and walked straight in.

The Queen of Hearts was alone, standing in front of the mirror, holding a plate of jam tarts with one hand, powdering her nose with the other. She turned, saw me, and gasped, dropping the tarts.

"Hey, Queenie," I said. "Or would you feel more comfortable if I called you Jill?"

She was still a good-looking slice of dame, even without the blonde wig.

"Get out of here!" she hissed.

"I don't think so, toots." I sat down on the bed. "Let me spell a few things out for you."

"Go ahead." She reached behind her for a concealed alarm button. I let her press it. I'd cut the wires on my way in – in my profession there's no such thing as being too careful.

"Let me spell a few things out for you."

"You just said that."

"I'll tell this my way, lady."

I lit a cigarette and a thin plume of blue smoke drifted heavenwards, which was where I was going if my hunch was wrong. Still, I've learned to trust hunches.

"Try this on for size. Dumpty – the Fat Man – wasn't your brother. He wasn't even your friend. In fact he was blackmailing you. He knew about your nose."

She turned whiter than a number of corpses I've met in my time in the business. Her hand reached up and cradled her freshly powdered nose.

"You see, I've known the Fat Man for many years, and many years ago he had a lucrative concern in training animals and birds to do certain unsavoury things. And that got me to thinking . . . I had a client recently who didn't show, due to his having been stiffed first. Doctor Foster, of Gloucester, the plastic surgeon. The official version of his death was that he'd just sat too close to a fire and melted.

"But just suppose he was killed to stop him telling something that he knew? I put two and two together and hit the jackpot. Let me reconstruct a scene for you: You were out in the garden – probably hanging out some clothes – when along came one of Dumpty's trained pie-blackbirds and *pecked off your nose*.

"So there you were, standing in the garden, your hand in front of your face, when along comes the Fat Man with an offer you couldn't refuse. He could introduce you to a plastic surgeon who could fix you up with a nose as good as new, for a price. And no one need ever know. Am I right so far?"

She nodded dumbly, then finding her voice, muttered: "Pretty much. But I ran back into the parlour after the attack, to eat some bread and honey. That was where he found me."

"Fair enough." The colour was starting to come back into her cheeks now. "So you had the operation from Foster, and no one was going to be any the wiser. Until Dumpty told you that he had photos of the op. You had to get rid of him. A couple of days later you were out walking in the palace grounds. There was Humpty, sitting on a wall, his back to you, gazing out into the distance. In a fit of madness, you pushed. And Humpty Dumpty had a great fall.

"But now you were in big trouble. Nobody suspected you of his murder, but where were the photographs? Foster didn't have them, although he smelled a rat and had to be disposed of – before he could see me. But you didn't know how much he'd told me, and you still didn't have the snapshots, so you took me on to find out. And that was your mistake, sister."

Her lower lip trembled, and my heart quivered. "You won't turn me in, will you?"

"Sister, you tried to frame me this afternoon. I don't take kindly to that."

With a shaking hand she started to unbutton her blouse. "Perhaps we could come to some sort of arrangement?"

I shook my head. "Sorry, Your Majesty. Mrs Horner's little boy Jack was always taught to keep his hands off royalty. It's a pity, but that's how it is." To be on the safe side I looked away, which was a mistake. A cute little ladies' pistol was in her hands and pointing at me before you could sing a song of sixpence. The shooter may have been small, but I knew it packed enough of a wallop to take me out of the game permanently.

This dame was *lethal*.

"Put that gun down, Your Majesty." Sergeant O'Grady strolled through the bedroom door, his police special clutched in his ham-like fist.

"I'm sorry I suspected you, Horner," he said dryly. "You're lucky I did, though, sure and begorrah. I had you trailed here and I overheard the whole thing."

"Hi, Sarge, thanks for stopping by. But I hadn't finished my explanation. If you'll take a seat I'll wrap it up."

He nodded brusquely, and sat down near the door. His gun hardly moved.

I got up from the bed and walked over to the Queen. "You see, toots, what I didn't tell you was who *did* have the snaps of your nose job. Humpty did, when you killed him."

A charming frown crinkled her perfect brow. "I don't understand . . . I had the body searched."

"Sure, afterwards. But the first people to get to the Fat Man were the King's Men. The cops. And one of them pocketed the envelope. When any fuss had died down the blackmail would have started again. Only this time you wouldn't have known who to kill. And I owe you an apology." I bent down to tie my shoelaces.

"Why?"

"I accused you of trying to frame me this afternoon. You didn't. That arrow was the property of a boy who was the best archer in my school – I should have recognized that distinctive fletching anywhere. Isn't that right," I said, turning back to the door, " . . . 'Sparrow' O'Grady?"

Under the guise of tying up my shoelaces I had already palmed a couple of the Queen's jam tarts, and, flinging one of them upwards, I neatly smashed the room's only light bulb.

It only delayed the shooting a few seconds, but a few seconds was all I needed, and as the Queen of Hearts and Sergeant "Sparrow" O'Grady cheerfully shot each other to bits, I split.

In my business, you have to look after number one.

Munching on a jam tart I walked out of the palace grounds

and into the street. I paused by a trash-can, to try to burn the manila envelope of photographs I had pulled from O'Grady's pocket as I walked past him, but it was raining so hard they wouldn't catch.

When I got back to my office I phoned the tourist board to complain. They said the rain was good for the farmers, and I told them what they could do with it.

They said that things are tough all over.

And I said. Yeah.

THE MAN WHO HATED CADILLACS

E. K. Grant

E. K. Grant claims he doesn't exist, and that he is really someone else. Just who is a little hard to define. I can only repeat what he's told me. E. K. Grant says he is the prose pseudonym of a minor US scriptwriter, whose lack of importance in the Great Scheme of Things is clearly demonstrated by the fact that he earns the vast majority of his wages as an electrical engineer and computer scientist. Mind you, he also told me that he was "abandoned as a child in the Serengeti and raised by vegetarian baboons", that he "has been married for at least 2,000 years to a mysterious woman he met inside a pillar of fire", and that "DNA analysis has verified that he is the only known son of Anastasia Nikolaevna and the heir presumptive to the throne of Imperial Russia." I'm rather dubious about all of this although, having dealt with him, I'm inclined to accept the bit about the vegetarian baboons!

Clients and bill collectors knock.

Gunsels and hit men come in shooting.

When somebody charges in unannounced and empty-handed, he's either a cop or someone who's mistaken my office for the men's room. (One door farther down the hall, on the left, if you're interested. The principal difference is that the door of the men's room has been recently refinished, and the sign is more neatly painted. Smells better in there, too.)

My present visitor hadn't knocked, and his hands were empty.

The suit, the clean-cut all-American-boy face and hairstyle, and the bulge under the armpit were sufficient to announce his profession. One of the federal boys, slumming in my part of town.

He came in so fast that I didn't have time to tell him about the loose rug. He damn near broke his neck when he tripped.

I'll give him this: he recovered before he landed on the carpet, displaying a bit of fancy footwork that indicated either football or ballet training. I decided football was the safer bet. He walked over to the desk gingerly, with an occasional leery glance at the floor. He towered over me and glared imposingly.

Fortunately, I don't impose easily. When he growled, "You could be sued over that rug," I just smiled up at him.

"Sure I could," I said. "And if you'd knocked, like the sign on the door says, I'd have called out a warning." I motioned over my shoulder. "See those pockmarks on the wall? Machine pistol. The laddy with the elderly Schmeisser would have gotten me, if tripping on the rug hadn't distracted him. I'll risk being sued."

His expression went neutral. He pulled out an ID folder and flashed it with a condescending gesture. I took it out of his hand before he realized I'd moved, and motioned him to the one rickety chair that lives in front of my desk, swaying back and forth in the fitful breezes from the intermittent air conditioner. His micro-momentary expressions while he decided he didn't need to jump me and take it back were interesting.

He gingerly eased his way into the chair while I picked up the phone and punched buttons. The other end was answered on the first ring; but then, the people in that office always move fast. Unlike me, they're on a good salary.

"Hello, Harvey," I said. "This's Jake Larsen. I've got one of your people down here, or at least the ID that belongs to him. Describe Rodney Z. Bevans for me, will you?"

Harvey Lemnitz is the head of the local federal office for which I do occasional odd jobs. He described my visitor to a nicety, including the retired boy-scout look, and said, "I sent him down with a job for you. We're short-handed again, tracking down all the leads you broke loose for us on the Scarponi thing last month. Knew you'd be calling in to check him, so I didn't bother to tell you he was coming; you're so paranoid you'd still call."

I said, "I'm not paranoid. It's just, people keep shooting at me. Thanks for the kind thoughts." I hung up and tossed Bevans his ID folder, backhand. It landed neatly in his lap. "What does the 'Z.' stand for?"

He put the folder carefully back in his pocket and said "Zebulon". He took another folder, eight by eleven, out of his inside coat pocket and tossed it backhand onto my desk, probably to show that he could toss things too. The gesture was ruined when his movement nearly collapsed the chair.

He said, "I won't say anything about the chair. I suppose someone tried to draw on you while he was sitting in it."

I gestured at the perforations in the ceiling. "Nine millimetre tracks. He moved way too fast, and it sort of disintegrated out from under him."

My attention was only half on my reply. The folder on my desk had landed open, showing a picture I recognized.

"So you want me to check up on Doctor Frayley," I said. "Seems simple enough." I fixed him with the iciest glare I could muster, though it didn't seem to faze him, and demanded, "Is this likely to end up like the last one? All I was supposed to do was find one of Scarponi's hot-money couriers, a guy named Scammer. No one warned me about his girlfriend."

Bevans looked politely bored, so I elaborated. "Scammer's girlfriend. Seventeen years old, and the best, fastest shot with a .44 Magnum I've ever seen or heard of."

He gave up and looked interested again. "Mr Lemnitz told me about her. You know, he really thought it was Scammer who was killing all those people. He's been saying he's very much indebted to you for solving the case for him." His expression indicated that I was supposed to be favourably impressed by the apology. I wasn't.

He realized it and said, "This one shouldn't be any difficulty. All we want is a tail and a report. We'd do it ourselves if we weren't so short of personnel right now, but we had to re-assign a lot of people in the last few weeks. You're authorized full-scale expenses, and probably up for a completion bonus if you can find out where the good Doctor Frayley gets his money."

I rubbed the bridge of my nose. Bevans picked up on my fatigue instantly. "You feeling okay?"

"Fine," I said. "Just lack of sleep. My neighbourhood's got a problem, an idiot child named Nigel. Nigel has an old Cadillac with no muffler. He likes to drive it up and down the street in the wee small hours. ALL the wee small hours." Getting back to the subject, I asked, "Why does someone care where Frayley gets his dough?"

Bevans shrugged. "We have to clear him for a new job, and Internal Revenue reports that he always declares a good twenty grand above what he makes at the university. Calls it 'gambling winnings'." He made a wry face, incongruous on one of his stolid demeanour.

"So it's illegal for a man to gamble, as long as he declares the winnings and pays his taxes?"

"It is if he's never been near Nevada, doesn't frequent any gambling joints in this town, and doesn't make book by telephone. IRS doesn't care where the money comes from, as long as he pays taxes on it. But we have to know where he gets it before we can report he's clean."

"Can you tell me what this job is, that he has to be cleared for?"

He smiled at me. One up. "Nope," he said. "You may assume that it pertains to his profession, physics. Period. Your sole concern is the source of his extra income."

"Okay," I said. "I don't have to tell you things have been

sparse lately." Hell, a look around the rat-hole I euphemistically called an office would tell anybody that. The Subsidiary Service Act, which allowed government agencies to employ private investigators with adequate clearances, was the only thing that had kept me going this long. With the liberalization of the state's divorce laws, there was little clientele for the average investigator; and television to the contrary, divorce snooping is bread and butter to your average private eye.

God knows I'd preferred divorce work, dirty and underhanded as most of it is; nobody had been shooting at me in those days.

I closed the folder he'd thrown me and slipped it into my inside right coat pocket, opposite the worn Colt .45 that nestles under my left arm. He nodded, as if to say, "That's it, then," and left the room without saying another word. His exit was slightly marred by another trip on the edge of the rug. I heard muttering as he passed down the hall.

It took all of thirty seconds to lock the desk, set the booby traps, and avoid the rug on the way out. When I'm broke and money beckons, a rabbit couldn't catch me.

Doctor Thaddeus Frayley, possessor of two earned PhDs and a couple of honorary ones, lived in a nice, respectable brownstone about three stone-throws from the edge of the state university campus. In my own somewhat chequered college career – before I'd been expelled for a few trivial escapades involving a couple of young ladies who'd rather inconveniently turned out to be related to humourless members of the administration – I had taken a few of Frayley's physics courses. He was one of the small group of teachers for whom I'd retained any real respect and liking.

As I walked up the flagstone path, I began to realize why Uncle Sam was nervous about him. The place was good for at least three hundred grand on the open market. There was a great deal more house than was obvious from the street, and the fancy topiary landscaping looked good for another thirty thou. To the side was a huge fenced yard with high oleander hedges. In this neighbourhood, real estate wasn't cheap, and I seemed to remember a house on that lot. Frayley must have bought it and razed it to get more room. Curiouser and curiouser.

The door was answered by platinum blonde hair, limpid blue eyes, and the face of an angel. I couldn't see the rest; she was wearing a thick flannel housecoat. When I finished looking at her, I looked at the interior of the house. It was nice, richly furnished, but not up to the competition. I looked back at her.

"Yes?" she said. The voice was that of a cello, warm and rich. I was in love for the third time that week, so completely smitten that I couldn't recall whom I'd fallen for on Tuesday. That should have rung a warning bell deep inside; normally I have a memory like an elephant where ladies are concerned.

"Talk some more, please," I said. "I love the sound of your voice, and what are you doing tonight?"

She turned her head aside and called. "Father! One of your students is here."

I was still digesting that when Doctor Frayley entered the room, finger stuffed in the edge of a book, reading glasses low on his nose. He was balder than I remembered, but he looked fit and his eyes were the same clear blue. He looked me up and down. "Not one of mine," he said. "Looks familiar, but none of mine wears a shoulder holster. Tell him to go away." He turned to leave the room, then spun back before I could protest, his eyes sparkling with sudden interest.

He said, "Would you by any chance be one of those people who've been following me for the last few weeks? If you are, by all means come in and explain why. I've been very curious."

He strode over without waiting for my answer, gently reached past his daughter, politely grabbed my arm, and firmly escorted me into the library–study. While I knew the floor plan of the far end of the house (a kitchen, a bathroom, a couple of bedrooms, but let's not get into personal historical digressions) I'd never seen the study before. The framed military decorations included European Theatre medals from World War Two, a Bronze Star, and a Silver Star with cluster. I was positive that one of the photos was a much younger Frayley flanked by General Wild Bill Donovan and Doctor Stanley Lovell. Dead centre, in the place of honour over the fireplace, was an original animation cel, Marvin the Martian, signed by Chuck Jones. Live and learn, I guess.

He was pouring me brandy and pushing cigars at me before I could get a word in edgeways – good brandy and expensive cigars. I accepted the brandy, just to be polite, and held the glass out for a refill.

"Well?" he said. "Have I broken some law? Are you some kind of busybody looking for a handout? I assure you that I have little money."

"That's exactly the problem," I said. "I'm a private investigator" – I showed him my identification – "certified for auxiliary duty with certain government agencies. Maybe you don't think you have much money, but a lot of people are very concerned about where you get an average of twenty thousand a year in addition to the salary you earn."

"You mean my gambling winnings?"

"Bull," I said. "Scarponi's people own all the gambling in the state, and they wouldn't tolerate someone who won that consistently. They'd have taken you for a ride and planted you in a cornfield a long time ago. Besides which, I distinctly remember your lectures on gambling. Unless you've had a stroke in the last fifteen years, you're not a gambler."

He looked straight at me, and said, "Until you said that, I hadn't connected. I saw the name Jake Larsen on your licence, and it slipped right past me. I must be getting old." He looked me up and down, appraisingly. "Of course, you have changed considerably."

"Still healthy, though," I said. "Thanks in large part to having been taught not to gamble." He nodded, pleased.

"So," I said, "would you like to tell me about the money, or do I have to do it the hard way, and snoop around for weeks?"

My approach may seem ridiculous, but I have seen far too many investigators poke around a situation for weeks, even months, when somebody would have been glad to explain if he'd only been asked. Shaking a tree to see if something falls out is often effective, if occasionally dangerous, investigative technique.

Frayley frowned. I remembered that expression from physics lectures; he wasn't annoyed, he just couldn't think of a simple answer. He brightened, and said, "What the heck. For all the good it'll do, come on down to the rec room, and I'll show you." He crossed the room with a bouncing stride, and led the way down a flight of stairs that had been hiding behind a row of potted plants luxurious enough to masquerade as an outdoor hedge.

The "rec room" was lit up like the Mojave at high noon, and if it was a recreation room, then I wear lavender undies. Just because I got tossed out of school before I could finish my junior year doesn't mean I'm too dumb to know a lab when I see one. The electron microscope and the NMR spectrograph were impressive enough, but when I saw the computer he'd set up to do the data acquisition from the lab gear, I knew he was far wealthier than we'd suspected. I'd seen a G-7 Micro-Cray before, and I knew what they sold for.

What bothered me was the pentagram set into the floor in contrasting tiles. Having had a few rather strangely orientated lady friends, I'd seen those before, too.

He followed my gaze, and beamed. "That's right. Black magic. Or, at least, magic."

He walked over to a workbench and picked up a glittering device I couldn't identify. While he fiddled, I stood there trying to decide whether he was putting me on, or just cruising for semi-permanent installation in the nearest loony bin.

He bent to root around in a pile of stuff heaped up next to the workbench, and came up with a two-faced chess clock, the kind used in tournaments. He walked to the centre of the pentagram, set it down, stepped back, and pointed the strange instrument at it.

The clock wavered.

I don't have any better way to describe it – the clock wavered. There was a glowing polychrome ripple in the air around the chess clock, and then it wasn't there any more. There was a small pile of bills, normal greenbacks, topped by a few cents in change.

He grinned, and gestured for me to pick up the money.

It was new. Crisp and clean.

Frayley said, "It's not parlour magic. It's the real thing. A simple application of potential equivalency. That clock," he pointed at the money I was holding, "Was worth a little under twenty bucks. All I did was make it directly equivalent instead of potentially equivalent. Simple, when you know how. I could probably teach you how to do it in a couple of hours."

He frowned briefly. "Of course, sometimes I get pre-1963 Silver Certificates and silver money; there's a lot I don't understand."

I bent down and rapped on the centre tile. Solid. I hadn't thought it was an illusion, anyway. The lights were pretty bright.

"Simple, I doubt," I said. "Otherwise someone else would have found out how to do it a long time ago."

Frayley's silvery eyebrows arched, giving him a quizzical, cherubic expression. "But someone did. "If I have seen farther than others, it is because I have stood on the shoulders of giants . . .""

He was still quoting Newton. He'd always idolized the man.

I said, "You mean Isaac Newton invented . . ."

"Of course not!" he snapped. "If Newton had found this, he'd have gone on to quantify the rules of magic as rigorously as he did for physics and mathematics. No, I found the clues in a manuscript – written by a minor alchemist who worked under the patronage of Frederick of Wuertzburg."

"The famous Frederick? The one who hung every alchemist that showed up?" I asked.

He nodded approval. "The same. Apparently he developed his allergy to alchemists from his association with that first one. I think he stumbled on this effect without noticing the principle of potential equivalence. Every time he converted ten bucks' worth of lead into gold for his patron, all he got was ten bucks' worth of gold. Hard to make a profit on that."

He brought over the shiny gismo for me to examine, and said, "My first working model. Won't operate without the pentagram, and isn't reliable during certain phases of the moon. Tried it during an eclipse, once, and got mirror-image silver roubles from the late 1800s."

I handled it gingerly, afraid of setting it off. There weren't any moving parts, just a random agglutination of silvery metallic whatsits stuck together at odd angles.

"You don't have to be so gentle with it," he said. "Part of the spell is mental, and it won't work on anything outside a pentagram."

I said, "I see why you claimed you got the dough from gambling. Are you going to tell me what you've been converting, to get that much money?"

He was suddenly diffident. Then he grinned like a bashful schoolboy. "Cadillacs."

I exploded with laughter. "Do you know how many cops around here are looking for a hot Cadillac ring? This isn't a very big town, and somebody's gotten at least fifty Caddies in the last year. You?"

"Yes," he said. "I don't like them. Big, ostentatious, and wasteful. You could build three or four Volkswagens for what it costs to put together a Cadillac, and we can't afford that kind of waste these days. Do you realize" – anger was replacing the defensive tone – "that the average Cadillac converts into less than three hundred dollars? Shows what they're really worth!"

"What about the money you cost the insurance companies? That wasn't very ethical."

He wasn't defensive at all, any more. "Ridiculous. Insurance companies buy all the politicians they need to legislate mandatory car insurance at whatever rates they feel like setting. Presuming I cost them any money they'll miss, they'll just jack up everyone's premiums a fraction of a cent per year. I'm only augmenting my salary at public expense, and most of those insurance customers are the same idiots who've been voting against raising teachers' salaries for the last thirty years. I haven't been paying myself any more than I could get, working a lot less, as an industrial consultant."

I probably looked a bit dubious at that point, because he went on.

"I wanted to put my daughters through school, and pay off my house, something any competent auto mechanic or plumber can do, but no honest professor! If Karla hadn't managed to graduate 'summa' and nail a teaching scholarship, I'd probably have had to start going after Chryslers, too."

Shrugging his rationalizations aside, I said, "So you've got a portable version of that gismo."

He pulled out a flat leather pouch, something like an over-sized watch-fob with knotted tassels attached.

"Certainly," he said. "Completely portable. Independent of pentagrams, planetary conjunctions, and state of mind."

"Take it easy, Professor. You're not selling it to me. I don't even know why you're showing it to me."

He shrugged. "Who would you tell? If you'd like to try and broadcast it, be my guest. I promise to use my influence to help you get into the most comfortable asylum in the state."

Frayley stopped to look me directly in the eye, and grinned that bashful, disarming grin again. "But the main reason I told you, is that I need help to cook up a story to explain the money, and I remembered your sense of humour. It was bizarre even for an undergraduate."

How could I say no, after a compliment like that? We talked about possible explanations while he walked me out to my car, and I silently considered ways to check and verify his story, just to make sure he wasn't taking me for a ride.

It was balmy, late-summer twilight, and I let my guard down for just a second as we walked down the sidewalk. Trouble arrived in the form of squealing tyres, rapid-fire shots, and Frayley grabbing a handful of my jacket just below the nape of the neck to toss me to safety behind a convenient car. I hit on my left shoulder, rolled tight, and came up with my Colt in my right hand, wincing at the pain in my left shoulder as I racked the slide. I leaned around the hood just in time to get a clear shot at the vaguely familiar guy with the machine-gun, and he slumped, part-way out the car window. As it veered away, I got off a few more shots, taking out both tyres on the near side. It was a big glossy black Cadillac, and I recognized the plates. Scarponi's boys. It skidded, spun, and slammed sideways into another car parked farther down the street. I was taking careful aim at the opening driver's-side door when the car suddenly shimmered, rippled with a multi-coloured glow, and became a heap of money lying in the street.

I lowered my gun and looked over my shoulder to see Frayley straightening up next to the parked car behind mine, pocketing his magic watch-fob. We walked over to examine the remains of the vanished car. There was a lot more money there than a miserable three hundred bucks; it must have had an expensive engine or accessories. To one side of the heap of greenbacks was a human forearm, its hand still gripping the pistol grip of a Thompson sub-machine-gun. Its stock was missing from about as far back as the end of the amputated arm. I recognized the ruby pinkie ring; "Pinkie" Fuller had liked to brag about how he'd taken it from his very first victim. I said, "Pinkie Fuller. One of Scarponi's more psychotic gunsels. Dunno who was driving, probably Fat Buford, since they always work together."

Frayley made a surprised noise, and pulled out his gismo again. He looked around to make sure he was unobserved, pointed it, and the Thompson and the arm wavered, glowed, and blurred into nice clean money. Even the small puddle of blood vanished neatly. He shook his head, sadly.

"Hated to do that. That Thompson looked like a collector's item." He caught my expression and went on. "Didn't you notice? Charging handle on the top. Pre-1928. Interesting; till now I'd had no idea this would work on people, since it never occurred to me to use a living test subject." He looked at me directly. "Scarponi?"

I explained, "Minor local Mafioso. Wants me dead, keeps sending out people to see to it."

I cut off the conversation at that point, since a number of heavily armed neighbours were emerging to investigate the gunfire. At least a couple appeared to have personal, proprietary interests in the damaged cars we'd used as shields.

Fortunately, Frayley was on good terms with his neighbours, and was able to convince them we'd turn in the appropriate reports, sans any mention of the rapidly divvied-up funds on the street. He gave copies of his card to the two families whose cars had been shot up and broadsided, and wrote the name and number of an auto-body mechanic on the backs. He said, "If the insurance doesn't cover it completely, don't worry about it, I will. My friend and I would be dead if we hadn't been able to use your cars for protection, and I'm taking personal responsibility for getting them into factory-new shape. This is the best auto-body man in town. He's a good friend of mine; after all, I raised three lead-footed daughters. Their driving habits put *his* kid through college."

Following the impromptu block party, obligatory socialization, handshaking, and mutual head-shaking over "What The World Was Coming To", we managed a late-evening retreat to Frayley's house.

"Father, where have you . . . Oh!" She hastily belted the flannel housecoat shut when she saw me. I was pleased with her choice of lounging garments, short and transparent. The legs were every bit as good as the rest of the package.

Frayley said, "Nothing to worry about, my dear. The undesirable elements have left the neighbourhood, and the police will be duly notified. Why not just hit the sack? We're grabbing a snack in the kitchen, we'll try to keep it quiet." She didn't look convinced, but disappeared back into the hallway.

I followed him out to the kitchen. He was fast; he already had a coffee pot on, there were two brandies sitting on the sideboard, and he was cracking eggs into a frying pan.

"How do you like your eggs?" He was completely matter-of-fact, as though he dealt with drive-by shootings every day. Then I noticed a trace of dampness in an empty glass by the stove and saw that the seal on the brandy bottle on the sideboard was freshly broken. There were at least three glasses' worth missing from it. Professor Frayley was even faster than I had thought.

I helped myself to one of the filled glasses and said, "Any way you're cooking them is fine with me." It was the same excellent brandy as before, and the glow helped to mask the pain from my sidewalk-bruised shoulder. I was feeling fairly human by the time we sat down to eat, and gave voice to the thought uppermost in my mind.

"That is your daughter Karla, isn't it? I can't believe how much she's grown."

He grinned at me as he lathered a piece of toast with low-fat butter. "You always did like my daughters. I recall a time when you were dating two of them alternately. They were quite fond of you, too."

I started to protest and he waved me into silence with the half-piece of toast left after his first bite. He chewed it into

submission and said, "I had no objection. Truth be known, I'd
sooner either of them had ended up with you than the twerps
they did marry. Karla's my youngest, but she's old enough,
and intelligent enough, to look out for herself. I admit I don't
like the idea of her being near someone who's apparently a
target for organized crime."

He changed the subject. "Why did you quit school? It's
been a number of years, but I seem to remember that you were
one of my better students."

I laughed. It almost didn't hurt any more. "After they threw
you out of school, back then, you got drafted. That took me
out of circulation for a few years, and then I earned a commis-
sion and worked for one of Uncle Sam's spook outfits for a few
more years, because there were some things I'd learned to
hate. When my face got too well known, it was either fly a desk
in Langley, or come home and find honest work. Since all I
really knew was snooping, I got my PI licence." I shrugged.
"Did all right until they liberalized the divorce laws. Now I
can't even afford an office with a working air conditioner.
Every time I get a big case, I seem to step on Scarponi's toes,
which means he keeps sending out people to shoot at me."

He raised his eyebrows by way of inquiry. I responded,
"Edward Scarponi. Scion of a fine old Italian Mob family.
Went to all the best schools, managed to marry a rich society
dame. Bound and determined to own and operate the entire
state some day. But he's not doing too well with his career, and
he keeps blaming me."

Professor Frayley looked properly sympathetic. He refilled
my glass and said, "I don't want to see you in a position where
you could be charged with conflict of interest. However, like
all professional academics, I owe a debt to the community that
pays my salary, and it occurs to me that removing Mr Scarponi
from circulation would probably be a Good Thing. Particularly since he seems to be willing to shoot up residential
neighbourhoods, including mine. What would be the best
way to go about it?"

"Well," I said, "I gutted his operating funds last month, so
he can't buy the politicians he needs to get the dam construction contract he was depending on. Right now, he's nearly

broke, and since he doesn't have legal ownership of his wife's mansion and property yet . . ."

"Hold on," he said. "Explain that."

"Scarponi's rich society wife disappeared a couple of years ago. He's still waiting for her to be declared legally dead so he can take over the estate, but her family is holding out for the full seven years. He's been able to float a couple of loans with the mansion as security, but he's having trouble with the payments because the federal boys are after his gambling and drug operations."

"Excellent," he said. "We'll gut his mansion, for starters. Clean it out, maybe even convert the whole thing. If it's security for his operating capital, let's see if we can get the loan called in. Then maybe we can find out where his illegal property is, and zap that as well. I'd love to convert a truckload of drugs. We'd need another truck to carry the money."

Scarponi's mansion was surrounded by guards, a fence, and carnivorous German Shepherds and Dobermans. It didn't look like he bothered with burglar alarms; all the burglars in the state worked for him.

It was about three a.m. when we scrambled to the base of the ten-foot fence. Frayley was impressing me more and more. He had to be at least thirty years older than my thirty-five, but he was moving like a commando, not even breathing hard after our run. I was panting like a dog, and trying not to make any noise. I made a mental note to ask him how he stayed in shape, and then cancelled it; I probably didn't want to know.

He had some kind of small test equipment out, and was examining the fence electronically. "Just high voltage, and maybe a continuity alarm. No sign of any kind of active scanning, no sonar, no infra-red. Trivial stuff. Could he be such a fool that he depends on just his public image to keep people out?"

"Either that, or we're walking into a really stupid trap," I said softly. "Remember, he could be sitting in there with all kinds of passive motion detectors, light amplifiers, body-heat spotters, you name it. When his carload of gunsel didn't come back, he could have blown the state, or dug in here. Remember, just because my source *said* he wasn't staying here doesn't mean he's not, and there might be inside guards, no matter what we've been told.''

Frayley pulled a roll of thin rubbery sheeting from his rucksack, unrolled it next to the fence, and knelt on it while he cut several strands, having first jumpered around the spots where he made the cuts. He produced a few lengths of plastic tubing, slit lengthwise, and slipped them over the wire strands to prevent an accidental grounding.

We slipped through and arranged things so the fence would look undamaged to superficial examination.

Another ten minutes of stealthy approach got us to the house. No signs of alarms on the doors or windows, no guards. Scarponi liked it quiet, and the guards were all down by the gates in the fence, out of the immediate picture; but not so far out that they couldn't get back into it in a hurry if we made any noise. With any luck they wouldn't notice that someone had tossed soporific-drenched chunks of raw meat over the fence for the dogs. We probably hadn't gotten them all, but we could hope.

The lights were on, dimly.

The converter Frayley had given me fitted reassuringly in my hand. It was a small leather pouch containing the major elements of the equivalency spell: several symbol-ridden diagrams on parchment, a few random semiconductors strung together in a circuit that made no sense to me, and a couple of glued-in coloured pebbles.

I cleared my mind, focused my attention on a large, over-stuffed chair, pointed the amulet, and ran through the symbolic manipulations Frayley had taught me. I waited, not really expecting much, but what I got was over six hundred bucks. That chair must have been upholstered in real leather.

Frayley grinned proudly. We split up and began converting things – furniture, rugs, paintings, doorknobs, doors – glee-fully stuffing the paper money into Frayley's rucksack. We left the coinage where it fell; confusion to the enemy. We left the drapes intact and closed to avoid attracting attention from outside.

Except for Mrs Scarponi's collection of rare books, it took

less than twenty minutes to clean out the first floor. We had a brief, whispered argument over a first edition of Newton's *Principia Mathematica*. Frayley wouldn't condone converting it, and it ended up in the rucksack, along with the money.

On the second floor, I disturbed a guard who was very fast on the draw. So much for no guards in the house.

As the muzzle of his revolver lined up on a spot between my eyes, I made a mental note to come back and haunt my contact. Or worse, if I could manage to poltergeist it. I saw his thumb pulling back the hammer in that time-stretching unreality that takes hold when you know you're going to die.

And then both the guard and his revolver rippled, coruscated mildly, and became a surprisingly respectable heap of greenbacks.

I turned to Frayley, who was just lowering his converter, and whispered, "He couldn't have been worth that much. Even with inflation prices, the chemicals that make up a human body are only worth a few bucks."

"I quite agree," he whispered, scooping up the money. "I hadn't expected this effect, since I haven't converted living things before. We could be looking at the black-market value of his kidneys and corneas, his potential earning power over the rest of his lifespan, or even an outstanding inheritance from his Aunt Phoebe. Certainly explains the anomalously high take from that Cadillac this afternoon. I'd love to look into this; perhaps we could find a correlation to the amounts we get, using standard actuarial tables. Hmm. Need to convert a large number of people, to get a statistically valid sample."

He moved away, very quietly humming Gilbert and Sullivan, "I've got a little list . . ."

We finished the floor and moved up to the third. We didn't know the layout here – none of my acquaintances had ever visited above the second floor. Well, maybe Sylvia had, but she never talked about the cash customers. It was quiet, as dimly lit as the lower floors had been.

We stripped a few rooms, and I found what looked like the master bedroom. I tiptoed in, hoping for a safe. The lights flared to full brightness, and I wheeled to find Scarponi glaring across the sights of a rock-steady Smith and Wesson

Model 39. He completely missed the Professor slipping into the room behind him. Frayley pointed his converter, and Scarponi was suddenly threatening me with a fistful of money.

At that point, Scarponi got a bit comical; I'd never seen so many expressions on one face in so few seconds. He started across the room toward me, still waving the bills.

I don't know what he intended; possibly he was going to try to beat me to death with a sheaf of paper money. From where Frayley stood, it may have looked as though Scarponi were attacking. Or maybe Frayley just didn't need the excuse.

The Professor raised his converter and Scarponi wavered in mid step. There was a glowing shimmer in the air, and then only a huge heap, four or five feet tall, of paper money.

Strange money.

It was printed in white ink on green paper, and it writhed as though a breeze were stirring it. There was no breeze.

I looked to Frayley for an explanation. He looked just as puzzled as I felt. Suddenly his face paled. He backed away from the heap, jumped back into the hall.

"Get away from it!" His voice was thin, tight. I hugged the wall, moving fast, trying to join him. It didn't work, because the strange money spilled out across the floor in a curling wave, sweeping around toward me. I jumped onto a convenient desk, still five or six feet from the door.

From the hall, Frayley said, "I had a hint of this from some of my calculations. That stuff is negative money. Short half-life, and it has to combine with normal money to decay. It *might* be able to cancel against the positive value of anything else."

I wasn't quite sure what he was talking about until I saw one of the strange bills hump itself across the carpet and touch the leg of a couch. There was a blur, a mild purple flash, and a huge, rough-edged bite was missing from the corner of the couch. It teetered on the remaining legs and leaned onto several more of the questing bills. As it touched each bit of negative money, it fell lower and lower, and then it was gone, without appreciably reducing the amount of the stuff swirling around on the floor. The rest of the furniture had begun to sink away, and I was pretty sure I was seeing occasional flashes of bare floorboard through the questing whitebacks. My desk lurched and settled a bit. Frantically, I kicked everything off the top of the desk, watching it vanish in small purple flares as it fell into the writhing sea of negative money.

The desk lurched again and I shoved my converter into my pocket and jumped for the chandelier. It had to be a modern reproduction, since no real chandelier would have been mounted with such chintzy small screws. They started coming loose with little tinkling noises, and small pieces of plaster rained on my head.

I looked down, and wished I hadn't. I caught one last glimpse of the top of Mrs Scarponi's heirloom oak desk as it disappeared forever from mortal ken. The negative money swirled hungrily, seeking something else to combine with.

Wads of normal money flew across the room to fall at the far end; Frayley was tossing in bunches of money from the hallway. The negative money mounded up, sliding over in a cresting wave to engulf the real stuff, but directly under me some of the whitebacks bulged up toward my toes, managing to look as hungry as underfed piranhas. I remembered "Pinkie" Fuller's detached arm and had a momentary vision of my own two arms swinging ridiculously from the chandelier sans the rest of me. The stuff made an evil rustling noise as it surged up and down, trying to touch me. I raised my knees a bit, and was rewarded by more creaking noises as a few more mounting screws fell past me.

"Swing!" I heard Frayley shout. "Jump across while it's mostly over there!"

I really didn't like the idea of trying to swing on that chandelier, but the anticipatory rustling beneath me was a huge incentive. Hell, Errol Flynn got away with it. I swung my legs back and forth and let go at the same instant that the chandelier came loose and fell behind me. I swear I heard slurping noises as the anti-money engulfed it.

I didn't quite make it to the door but Frayley got a hand under the small of my back and boosted me across the threshold, while slamming the door shut. The door lasted a fraction of a second, vanishing in a purple flare. Out through the space poured a flood of the questing whitebacks, like an all-devouring lava flow that had forgotten what colour it was supposed to be.

Frayley led the way toward the stairs, running on his toes like a professional sprinter. A couple of fast-moving negative ten-dollar bills zoomed past me, like hunting dogs trying to pull down a fleeing deer. They seemed to be focused on his rucksack, and I realized the concentration of money must be a prime attractant, just like opposite-polarity electrostatic charge.

I said, "Drop the pack!" He responded by pulling it higher and running faster, and the leaping bills got just high enough to take out the seat of his pants, disclosing the fact that he had atrocious taste in polka-dot shorts. His burst of speed was enough to get him to the head of the stairs while the slower-moving ones and fives sank into the hallway carpet, eating away circular patches in little purple flares.

I made it to the stairs and tried to keep up with him on the way out of the house. Running for the fence, I realized Frayley wasn't with me, and turned to see why he'd stopped. He pointed at the mansion, which was crumbling in on itself with ponderous dignity, accompanied by a few sound effects of the creaking and rending variety. I yanked on his jacket, urging him toward the fence, but he held his ground, watching the place collapse inward with occasional flickers of eerie purple glow.

As the last of the mansion teetered into nothingness, Frayley whispered, "Impressive. He must have been hugely in debt, to have that great a negative value. Or maybe it was just a reflection of his value to society." He shrugged. "I really need to accumulate a lot more experimental evidence."

We heard guards yelling obscenity-laden queries to each other, and took off to weasel out through Frayley's private gate, which he patched neatly behind us. Half an hour later we quietly entered his house.

The lights snapped on before he could hit the switch, and there was Karla again. Her robe was belted shut; but it was much thinner than the earlier housecoat, and fitted tightly enough to do her justice. The frown on her face was magnificent.

"Daddy, I don't know who this man is, but I can tell you're up to no good. Again!"

He handed me the rucksack, walked over to her, took her by the shoulders, kissed her on the forehead, and spun her round to urge her from the room with a gentle spank. He said, "I never ask what you're up to when you stay out all night. Kindly extend me the same courtesy."

She looked back as she left. I was gratified to see that she was looking for my reaction to her father's statement, and blushing. That tickled me. I've known very few ladies who even knew how. I did wonder how she'd react to seeing the situation from my point of view, since she wasn't in a position to see those bilious polka-dot shorts.

A few minutes later, we were safely ensconced in the kitchen, with Frayley turning out a quick batch of waffles and sausage.

As he dished it up, he said, "I think Karla likes you. If my opinion matters, I approve. I'd also like to make a donation to the Jake Larsen Scholarship Fund. I figure about half of tonight's take ought to be appropriate?"

I looked at him for a moment. "Scholarship?" He wasn't a man given to euphemisms, and I remembered his comments about conflict of interest.

He blinked, surprised that I hadn't got it. "I should think it would be obvious. You were kicked out of school on trumped-up charges. And I doubt it was impartially tried, considering the make-up of the board of trustees in those days. Why didn't you just come back to school on the GI Bill?"

I poured myself another brandy, and looked at the pile of cash on the table. The PI business would never earn enough to retire on, assuming I lived that long. I nodded.

He said, "Good. For your own information, strictly off the record, I'm being considered for a government post – running a new section of the State Department, ostensibly to provide data retrieval liaison between the Russian space programme and our own. Actually we'll be pooling spy-satellite data on areas of mutual interest. I'll have to spend a good deal of time in Russia being diplomatic, and I'd like someone stateside to keep an eye on the place, and on Karla."

He paused, and added, "Later we'll be expanding the department, and it would be easier to justify hiring you if you have a technical degree or two. I'm going to need people with your kind of experience and special aptitudes. For one thing, you learned how to operate the value converter in half an hour last night. It took me months to get it under control, even though I invented it." My kind of experience? Uh-oh. I made a mental note to be very leery of any future full-time job offers from Professor Frayley.

Hell, just thinking up an explanation for his extra income that wouldn't land us both in jail was going to be dangerous enough.

He cautioned me about my night's "gambling winnings" as he escorted me to the door. "Be sure you declare every penny of that on your income tax. I don't want those Internal Revenue people after you. Those people are terrifying!" He shivered.

"Look on the bright side," I said. "Russian cars are as gross and ridiculous as Detroit battleships. When you convert a Zil or a Moskva, will you get dollars or roubles?" He walked away with a happily puzzled expression.

I chuckled and started down the walk. It was that perfect time of early morning when it's still dim, but the birds are starting to get raucous in preparation for the coming dawn; the air smelled good. There was someone there, barely visible in the early morning half-light. Karla.

"Excuse me, but I was listening to you and father talk. I thought I heard him call you Jake Larsen?" She ended with a disbelieving, questioning tone.

"Guilty as charged. I'm me. Does it make a difference?"

Her hands played nervously with the belt of her robe. ". . . We all thought you were dead."

"So did I, a couple of times. Especially after the Cong captured what was left of my outfit. But the NVA didn't watch us quite closely enough, and one night several friends of mine and I managed to get loose and go home. Took us a while, but we made it."

"Oh," she said. "My father's chess club is tomorrow night, and I have all the papers graded for my Friday classes.

Nothing to do and I hate to watch TV. Would you like to come over for dinner?"

I wasted about a twelve-thousandth of a second considering the answer to that one, and found out what time to show up.

She scampered back inside, and I walked away in the brightening morning. Things were looking up, on several counts.

First, I was going to have a nice little discussion with the contact who'd told me Scarponi wouldn't be home, and that there were no guards inside the mansion. I rubbed my knuckles in happy anticipation.

Then, I was going to do a little private experimentation in paraphysics; after all, Noisy Nigel, the Problem Child With No Muffler, drove a Cadillac, and I knew where he parked his car.

And Professor Frayley hadn't thought to ask for his gadget back.

THE ULTIMATE

Seamus Cullen

Seamus Cullen (b. 1927) is an American author resident in Ireland. He has written a number of bawdy fantasies, of which Astra and Flondrix *(1976) is probably the best known. He has also produced two Arabian fantasies,* A Noose of Light *(1986) and* The Sultan's Turret *(1986). The following story has been extensively revised by the author from an episode in* The Sultan's Turret.

In the thirteenth century, Spain was still divided between Christians and Muslims. Solomon ha-Levi was adviser and physician to the Sultan of Granada. It was he who fostered the cooperation between the sultan and San Fernando of Castille to overthrow the brutal Muslim rulers of Seville.

Solomon's granddaughter, the precocious Dinah, has been dabbling in magic in her grandfather's laboratory; a careless mistake almost unleashed a powerful fiend originally imprisoned by King Solomon of Israel. The story opens with Dinah plotting the rescue of her father, Moses, and her two cousins who have been captured with their caravan while returning to Spain from far Cathay. This episode follows the adventures of the rescue team. Dinah summons her adoring gnome, Bubbi, by pouring a few drops of special wine into the mouth of a carved frog.

"Momo, why are you being so stubborn? I wouldn't say I had a lot of gardening to attend to if I didn't, why would I do that?" Bubbi's hat was lying on the small table in the centre of the room; without it, he looked hopelessly young, his wife Momo always thought. Particularly with that short, straight hair standing up like needles on a porcupine. She adored his merry brown eyes and the stubby little nose which became glaringly red whenever he was excited.

Momo looked up from the homespun woollen jerkin she was embroidering for him with threads of gold and silver. Although it was by no means overly warm, she had removed her sleeveless blouse and sat on the chair wearing only her ample pyjama-bottom trousers. Uncomfortable, Bubbi noticed the enticing tilt of her small, flirtatious nipples. They would swell, he whimpered silently to himself, entasis was not far off. Hooo-hooo, why else would she have removed her blouse? This is sheer provocation, he concluded.

"Why would you do that?" she repeated at last. "To run away from your proper duties, that's why. You want to get back to that spoilt brat, Dinah, that's why. You probably think she's prettier than I am."

"Dinah?" he gasped, visibly shocked by the accusation. Immediately, as though hearing an echo, he was shocked by his shock. Would she see through him, through his indignant protests? "Momo," he reasoned, "she's a little girl, may the Lord forgive you for such terrible thoughts."

"Ah-ha!" the female gnome exploded, slamming the sewing down on a small table next to her chair. "She's a little *girl*, huh? May the Lord forgive *you*," she mimicked. "May I remind my fine upstanding scholar of a husband that Abishag the Shunammite was also a little girl. A young virgin. Do you remember who was Abishag, Don Scholar?"

Bubbi brushed a bit of dried mud from his leather britches, which came to just below the knees. Unthinkingly, he picked up his hat – a gesture of habit.

"Put down that hat while I'm talking to you, Don Gardener!" she fairly shouted at him. The hat hit the table and his hand shot back as though the crown contained a serpent's fangs. Momo harrumphed her satisfaction, then her eyes narrowed. "All right, so who was she?"

"Who was who . . . what?" he asked miserably, scratching furiously through what his wife described as porcupine quills.

"Abishag the Shunammite, that's who! We were talking about someone else, maybe, Don Memory?" She vaulted out of the chair and stood face to face with him. "Abishag the Shunammite!" Her voice was a roar.

Bubbi cupped a protective hand over his offended ear. What was all this about Shunammites, he wondered? What was she trying to prove? He shrugged, holding his palms up before him.

"They brought her to King David in his old age, that's what," Momo chortled, wagging an accusing finger under her husband's nose. "You know what for?" she demanded. He shook his head vigorously, denying all knowledge of such biblical carryings-on. "To put the fire back in his old chest, that's what for. But remember, the scriptures are often misleading when it comes to anatomy. To bring back the fire of youth to an old man . . . you understand, Don Puzzled Face?"

"What's the matter with you, Momo, since when am I an old man?" Bubbi was showing the first signs of temper, of patience wearing thin. But Momo was a sound strategist.

"You're supposed to know your Torah, no? You study the Talmud, don't you? Well, no good student would forget who is Abishag. But you *are* getting old," she declared, wagging the scolding finger again. "And why? Because you are always neglecting your duty, that's why. I am a sad person, can't you see that? I'm the only gnome lady my age who has no children . . . yet. What do you think that makes me? A freak, that's what! How long do you expect me to live with this shame?"

"Why do you always make out it's *my* fault?" he sobbed. His nose was turning red, slowly but surely, she noticed between swipes at her copious tears. "Look around you," he commanded. "Only a good husband would provide you with such a fine house." His hand swept the room in a grand gesture. "There's even an extra bedroom waiting for our 'Little Stranger' . . ."

"Somebody said you were a *bad* husband?" Her eyebrows rose, daring him to say such words had ever passed her lips. "Your Jewish Andalusian Princess gave us a splendid garden plot that is mirrored here, in our dimension . . . please don't think I'm ungrateful. You built us a dream house here, our neighbours come for miles to eat their hearts out." She paused to take a deep breath, warning him with a shake of her finger not to interrupt. "Bubbi . . . charity begins at home, remember? Your gardening chores for the princess can wait a little."

Momo grabbed Bubbi's hand before he could protest or escape. She dragged him toward the open bedroom door. He nearly lost his balance reaching back for his old conical hat.

Still holding his hand, Momo applied surprising strength; he did a complete somersault, landing on his back in the middle of the bed. With a sigh of defeat, he slipped off his leather jerkin and stretched out, inching over to his side of the bed, his left arm raised over his head. Momo cuddled up beside him, with her feet toward the head of the bed. Bit by bit, they adjusted their torsos and arms until Bubbi nodded that the position was perfect. The raised left arms began to intertwine until the armpits were locked in an airtight embrace.

"Oh, Bubbi," she whispered with tremulous delight, "it's so wonderful, you do it so nicely, so tenderly, so passionately, I'm in heaven already . . . is it good for you?"

"Perfect," he gurgled, his voice purring. He tried hard to keep his thoughts concentrated on the here and now. Dinah, the gorgeous swords he had liberated, young Joseph, the secret

room in Solomon's house, the difficulty in contacting Musa,
the demon . . . even more so that crazy Djinn, Musa's father
. . . it all went spinning madly on and on in his head, distracting him . . .

"Bubbi, Bubbi, do you feel how intense it's getting? This is
going to be the most fantastic one ever, we're going to reach
Blissies together, I know it, we won't be childless any longer, I
tell you, this is the Biggy!"

A brilliant flash of light above nearly blinded him . . .
Momo's eyes were closed. Immediately, it was replaced by
the figure of a huge, open-mouthed frog. Brilliant red wine
was splashing into that wide maw and a thunderous drumbeat
sounded his name with every splashing drop.

"Dinah is summoning me," he shouted. He levitated
straight up to the ceiling, jamming the hat onto his head
and the jerkin over it. He didn't hear the sickening sound,
the echo of the broken suction from their torn-apart armpits.
His hat cleaved through the beamed ceiling like a red-hot knife
through butter. But he heard Momo's plaintive voice following him even after the ceiling resealed itself at the end of his
preternatural passage.

"Bubbi, Bubbi, don't leave me now, this is IT . . . I'm
almost there . . . Bubbi, do not leave me . . ." The words cut
into him even as he reached the surface of Dinah's garden in
the palace.

"Are you all right?" Dinah asked sweetly, closing the lid of
the tiny casket containing the carved frog and the small vial of
wine. "Were you peacefully sleeping when I called?" she
asked.

"Er – not exactly," he answered evasively. "I – er . . .
hmmmmn." He stopped talking and hopped from one bare
foot to the other. "Maybe next time you summon me, maybe
just one tiny drop of wine, yes? Very tiny, then wait a bit,
please? I nearly forgot my hat in the scramble."

"I'm sorry, I still haven't the knack." Quizzically, she
brushed some tiny clods of earth from his shoulder. Then
she giggled. "Hat? It's so warm and you worry about . . ."

"It has to do with getting here," he interrupted. "Can't get
here without my hat." He pointed to a spot between two rows

of carrots, the spot where he had just appeared. "It cuts through everything, the hat. You didn't see me arrive?"

"You weren't here, then the next moment you were. You suddenly appeared, but not from anywhere in particular." She shrugged her shoulders. "I'm afraid I'm still pretty dim about the small details of magic."

Dinah rose from the carpet and stepped closer to the gnome. He ignored her and studied the fine silk carpet. Just right.

"Where do you think I came from?" he asked, walking back to the carrots. He pressed one big toe into the soft earth and two fabulous swords appeared. Dinah gasped. He pointed to the ground.

"You came through the ground . . . from under the garden? You live down there . . . in a hole?"

"In a house!" he snorted, hopping up and down again. "A very nice house, too. Even my wife Momo says so."

"B-b-but," she stammered, "how did you get a house all the way down there, what do you breathe, where does the smoke go . . ."

"Dinah, you are being too literal. Only humans are so picky about up, down, this side, that side. It's another dimension, it only looks 'down'. And no, if you dug a hole, you couldn't find my house. If you dug a hole and kept at it for a couple of centuries, you might get to Cathay . . . but not to my house."

"How is that possible?" she moaned; her head began to ache.

"Don't fret, don't fret," he pleaded, patting her little hand. "It's possible because the earth is round . . . Hooo-hooo, don't ask more questions. The earth is . . ." he paused, bounded to an orange tree and picked an orange, "round, believe me. Here is Granada . . ." he pointed to one side of the orange, ". . . and here is Cathay." He turned the fruit over. "Simple . . . yet I go straight down and I'm home. Now let's wrap up these swords, we're wasting time."

In a few moments he had the lovely swords securely and inconspicuously wrapped in the carpet and cleverly tied with the lengths of rawhide she had brought with her. He took off his hat and placed the bundle on his head. He instructed her to hold the centre rawhide binding. They walked through the glorious gardens, skirting the piles of rubble. Workmen busied themselves furiously. The sultan wanted his new city within a city completed; Alhambra it was called, because of the reddish stone.

When they reached the gates, her escort was waiting. Her grandfather and the sultan were taking no chances on a second abduction attempt. Of course, the guards never saw Bubbi hoist the carpet up to Dinah's saddle, nor his amazing, gravity-defying leap up onto the horse's rump. Dinah alone could see her devoted helper.

"Where is young Joseph?" Bubbi whispered.

"Are you referring to that Blackamoor of my grand-father's?" she asked haughtily.

"An ignorant thing to say," he reprimanded. He started waxing so elegantly about word definitions that she lost him in a labyrinth of floridly academic Hebrew.

"Could you put all that simply, say in the local language we usually use? You sound like you're writing a commentary for the Babylonian Talmud."

"Oh? Do I now? You might be interested to know, my dear princess, that they spoke Aramaic. I merely said, Blackamoor is a misnomer. The Moors are from the north-west of Africa and they are not black. Joseph is from far south of the desert . . . far south." He was twirling his hat on one finger when she looked over her shoulder. And wearing a superior, self-satis-fied look.

"By the beard of the Prophet," she breathed with heavy resignation . . . in Arabic. "Africa is Africa, is it not? As for your precious Bla – Joseph, he was dispatched to our house some while ago with a chest of my things."

The street door was ajar when they arrived. How unusual, Dinah thought. Lax security save when one was entering or leaving. The troop dismounted and the captain helped Dinah. He was about to reach up again for the carpet resting on her pommel. It was now settled on a muscular shoulder, a decid-edly black muscular shoulder. Where had *he* come from? the captain wondered, looking toward the door; it was now fully opened.

Dinah told the captain she would feel safer if they ranged

themselves along the ridge above the house. She would send a household servant when they were ready to leave.

Inside Solomon's secret alchemical and magical laboratory, Dinah pointed imperiously to the centre of the last chalk circle she had inscribed in the middle of the stone floor. Joseph dropped the burden disdainfully, irritated by her attitude. There was a very loud clank.

"Be careful!" the girl ordered.

"Just how old are you to be giving *me* orders, child?" Joseph gritted through clenched teeth.

"Old enough to give slaves orders . . . I'm thirteen." Before Joseph could riposte, she glared at a spot on the floor. "Bubbi, will you teach this slave some manners, please?"

"Hooo-hooo, you better be careful, princess, Joseph is now assistant court physician, a master of the Sacred Qabbala and maybe the best swordsman in all of Andalusia . . ."

"I wouldn't care if he were the king of the Blackamoors . . ."

Neither Bubbi nor Joseph was listening. Joseph was sitting on his heels, shaking Bubbi's hand gleefully.

"*He* can see you, Bubbi?" she spluttered with indignation.

"Of course," Bubbi answered, as though to a backward child. "How can we work together, fight together, if he can't see me?"

Dinah opened her mouth to protest . . . after all, Bubbi was her own personal gnome, how could this – this – upstart . . . But Bubbi's upraised arm aborted the tirade.

"We have more things to do than time to do them in. Stop all the bickering, you can sort yourselves out when this is over."

Dinah went to work on the magic circle and Joseph helped her; she was so amazed at his knowledge and swift capability that shivers of admiration suffocated her rage.

When the circle was complete, dedicated to Yesod, the Foundation, a lighted charcoal brazier in place along with a vial of incense, and a chalk triangle drawn outside the circle, Bubbi undid the thongs, opened the carpet and displayed the two enchanted swords. With a gasp of astonishment, Joseph dropped to his knees. He touched one briefly, then picked up the other with overwhelming joy.

"Is *that* the one you choose?" Bubbi asked evenly. "You reject the other?"

"Oh, no, but I thought it was for Dinah . . . its nature is positively female. Is this one truly for me?" He couldn't believe it.

"Dinah?" the girl muttered. "Dinah . . . who does he think . . ."

"Yours!" roared the gnome in simulated pain. "Stolen from the Khalif's treasury in Baghdad, guards searching far and wide and what do you think they will do to the thief when they catch him? Torn limb from limb, even if he is but a small gnome. For the time being, Joseph, but don't become too attached to it."

Even as Bubbi finished his admonishment, Joseph had already created two sets of harnesses from the thongs. Proudly, he suspended the scabbard of his sword from one, offering the other to Dinah. She took it and smiled her gratitude. His heart nearly stopped. It was the first time she had smiled at him and he was helplessly, hopelessly in love.

Briefly, Dinah explained to them how grave the problem was. Her dear father and the two boob cousins, as she called them, had been returning from the borders of India and Cathay with the richest caravan ever. The last message they had sent speeding homewards located them between Bactria and Baghdad. Her strongest intuition told her they had been waylaid, robbed and imprisoned . . . no doubt for ransom. The three of them had to rescue Moses, her father. Now!

"Hooo-hooo!" The wailing sound made the brazier flare up. Bubbi leapt up and seemed more to float toward the ceiling. He pressed his fingers against it and remained suspended for a second or two, then wafted slowly back to the floor.

"Bubbi, how did you do that? It was wonderful, can you teach me . . . ?"

Bubbi ignored the Nubian and glared at Dinah.

"What was all that about?" she asked, feeling rather naked under his stare.

"You're a girl!" he accused, as though that explained everything.

"You never noticed before?" Joseph half-whispered to himself. "Lord, that ravishing red hair, those unearthly green eyes, that – those – you know . . . a girl!"

"What are you getting at?" she demanded, paying no attention to Joseph's paean.

"Don't you see?" Bubbi hit the ceiling again, but came right down. "Only three of us, we have to free the prisoners . . . wherever *they* are . . . we don't even know that and one of us three is a gorgeous young girl, and what have you got? Every fiend, pervert, rapist and God alone knows what else . . . we'll be spending all our time defending *you*, never mind your father and the boobs, as you call them."

"You're not leaving me behind and that is that!" She crossed her arms over her bosom and glared back at the gnome.

"We're not taking you as a girl . . . and that is that!" the gnome retorted.

"You want me to wear men's clothing?"

"Exactly!" Joseph and Bubbi sang out in unison.

"All right, I'll go change now."

"Just a moment," Joseph smiled and held up his hand. "Your face is so beautiful, so totally feminine, a beggar's tatters could not disguise your sex."

She smiled shyly and blushed, shrugging her shoulders.

"Tell one of the servants to shear off just enough of your lovely hair to make a small beard on the chin and a moustache." Bubbi described the lines artistically on his own lip and chin. "Tell her to glue it in place firmly, we can't have it dropping off – Hooo-hooo, would that be trouble."

When Dinah left, Joseph started hopping from one foot to the other, mimicking Bubbi without realizing it.

"What was that you did before?" he asked beseechingly . . . you know, as though you had no weight at all . . . what is it called . . . how do you . . ."

"Sha-sha-sha," Bubbi admonished, "you're hurting my ears. It's called Szappo, all gnomes have to learn it if they wish to reach this plane, the humans' plane. You can't do it everywhere, you need a good strong magnetic force . . .". He pointed down at the floor, as if afraid an eavesdropper might steal the information. "You attune to the magnetic force, attune your vibrations and it's like the force grabs your weight and leaves you free. No more questions. I'll try to teach you when we get back – *if* we get back. Now, no more questions, let's check every detail of this magical working."

They had just finished a careful inspection when Dinah returned. They both jumped back, Joseph's sword nearly clear of the scabbard before he recognized Dinah. The long cloak with a hood covering most of her face made a frame for a fierce red beard.

"Let's get going," she hissed, "time is running out. Not only that, if Grandfather returns before we're back . . . Well, let's say it will be most unpleasant."

"Ready whenever you are, Princess ha-Levi," Joseph intoned mischievously.

She drew her sword and handed it to him. He stood directly behind her and crossed his sword with hers in front of her. She told them to visualize the four pentagrams she was creating in the cardinal compass points, linking them together with blue flame. As soon as the banishing ceremony was complete and she began the invocation to bring them out on the astral plane, Joseph felt his perceptions expand in all directions with the speed of light.

All three began to feel the pull of some great force drawing them upwards and outwards. Suddenly, a new and distinctly terrifying shift occurred. A terrible moan broke from Bubbi's throat. Lad and girl saw a horrid brown foot-like appendage grow more distinct in the triangle to the north of the circles. Three great toes began to extend dragon-like talons out; in the blink of an eye they were pressing down on one of Bubbi's vulnerable, naked feet. The talons started to sink in.

The sword in Joseph's right hand flashed with blinding speed. Before it could reach the offending appendage, Musa, the demon, appeared and kicked the member out of existence. Joseph looked around. The laboratory was gone and they were all standing on a great field of strange, purple grass. The tops of a dozen blades of it had been hewn down by the young man's sword.

This strange land extended to infinity in all directions. The sky above was a pale lavender, yet it created as much light as their own sky. Dinah narrowed her eyes. In the distance, huge fountains sprayed upwards, blazing like jewels. Further on there were uncountable numbers of trees, with that same jewel-like aspect. She knew that the strangeness, the tightness in her stomach, was her own inability to comprehend a realm without limits of time or space.

"No time for daydreaming, little girl," Musa ordered. She looked up, again surprised. Vision was enhanced, hearing as well. The green demon had little Bubbi locked in his arms. The gnome was grimacing vilely, growling like a maddened dog. As he struggled, Dinah saw the ugly red marks on his foot begin to turn a sickly green.

"Yes," Musa apparently read her mind with ease, "that was Azazel trying to get back into your laboratory . . . *again*. Remember the first time? Our proud, *careless* little magician nearly freed him and what a bad encounter for her poor grandfather. Azazel knows there is a weakness in the fabric between the worlds, right there in Solomon's magic workshop. The mighty Solomon of ancient Israel bound him over and banished him. Now he wants this Solomon to set him free . . . or his careless granddaughter."

Speechless and deeply shamed by Musa's words, Dinah hung her head and furiously fought back the tears. She felt Joseph's strong hand on her shoulder, reassuring her.

"Joseph, run quickly to that fountain and let the jewel-like shower fall on the tip of your sword. But, on pain of death, do not let it splash you." Musa pointed to a fountain on their left.

Moments later, Musa had Bubbi pinned to the ground and Joseph applied the tip of the sword to the festering foot like a cauterizing iron. There was a bright flash, the momentary stench of burning flesh, and the wound disappeared. Musa was on his feet with no apparent motion, the Nubian's sword was sheathed. The dazed Bubbi was swung up on Musa's shoulders and told to grip his hair firmly; he was not to let go for any reason. When Bubbi began shouting to know what they had done to him, Musa slapped his leg and told him to hush. A gnome and a demon might slip through undetected, but the Djinni, whose realm this was, could detect humans over great distances.

Musa told the two young ones to stand on his feet, one on either side, and wrap their arms about his waist. "Hold on tightly," he ordered.

Their eyes burnt so fiercely that they had to close them. The sensation of upward, then forward motion moved from speed to something beyond that; to Dinah it was like entering a soundless vacuum. Even so, she was aware that the speed increased every second. An urge to scream nearly overpowered her; then she realized no sound was possible. Next, the vertigo made it seem all her insides were being pressed up toward her throat. They were plummeting downwards like a fiery meteor.

One moment Dinah was whirling down with the others, now she was crouching on the ground, her sword in her hand. They had landed . . . but where? And the noise of running feet gave her no time for further reflection.

"Remember what I told you," Joseph whispered, close to her side, his sword making practice flicks before him, "watch their eyes, not their swords. When I engage them, you crack shins or ankles – that will disable them adequately. No unnecessary bloodshed."

"*You told me?*" she cried, bewildered, but it was too late, the first two guards were rushing them. Bubbi turned his face to the wall and braced his hands against it. One foot shot out behind him and one guard tripped, did a forward flip just as the flat of Joseph's blade sent him to sleep. The next guard chose Joseph and Dinah chose his ankle. The loud ringing sound of her blade blended with his howl of pain. Then Joseph put him to sleep and he joined his stricken companion.

Four more guards rounded the corner. Bubbi was busy tying up the unconscious guards' hands and feet with their own turbans. The leader of the next four hesitated, wondering why their fallen companions were twitching so; of course, they could not see the gnome.

"There they are!" shouted the leader. "Attack them, don't

let them escape. The Kadi will reward us well." With a howl of glee, he raced forward, menacing the young couple with the sword whirling above his head.

With a frightful roar, the heavy wooden door of a dungeon at the end of the dark passageway blew off its hinges and flattened all four of the advancing guards. The door splintered when it struck the far wall. As the four guards lay groaning, a whip-like vine snaked out of the dungeon and, with four loud cracks, encircled an ankle of each man. They were lifted off the ground and whizzed through the doorless entrance so swiftly that they seemed mere blurs. A whole chorus of moans and cries suddenly stopped.

"What was all that?" Joseph breathed unevenly.

"All that was Musa, I believe," Dinah answered, shuddering.

"I'm glad he's on our team," Bubbi added.

A sudden blaze of light filled the doorway; a magnificent, brightly sparkling apparition stepped lightly into the passageway, bending his head under the eight-foot ceiling. A wail rose from Bubbi, who darted behind Dinah and wrapped his arms about her knees in terror.

"Wrong again, young princess," the apparition stated flatly. "But then, you do make a habit of careless mistakes. It was not Musa, but his father. Allow me to introduce myself . . . Hutti at your service. As for that miserable earthworm hiding behind a woman's – excuse me, a *man's* trousers, you can tell him I'm *not* on *his* team."

"I am Dinah ha-Levi," she replied, trying to pull herself up to her full height and regain her dignity, which was not easy with the gnome clamped onto her knees.

"Of the Jewish persuasion, I presume?" the Djinn enquired, his face suffused with delight as his eyes almost literally devoured Dinah limb by limb. Dinah nodded assent.

"Not only that, but a delicious young virgin to savour . . . a *very* young virgin, I'd say." Hutti smiled and bowed with appreciation. "Twelve, going on thirteen, would be my guess, and my guesses are never wrong. I shall really enjoy *knowing* you, my dear."

"See here, whoever you are," Joseph shouted, his sword halfway out of its sheath, "touch but one hair and you will answer to . . ."

The Djinn turned and glared at Joseph. All the mischievous glints faded in his eyes and they became yellow as topaz, cold, and filled with anger.

"In the first place, I was not talking to you. Further, you must be exceedingly deaf: 'Whoever you are?' You didn't hear me? What a pity. Things like that irritate me. MY – NAME – IS – HUTTI. H-U-T-T-I."

To Dinah and Bubbi, the words penetrated painfully, though the Djinn was not speaking that loudly. Joseph was crouched over his bent knees, his hands clapped over his ears. The sounds stopped and Joseph removed his hands, though his body continued to vibrate visibly.

"There, now," the Djinn announced in a pleasant voice, "Let's see if that doesn't improve matters. Hear that shuffling sound? Over behind that tiny hole at the base of the wall." He pointed, but the passageway was too dark to detect a hole, much as they tried.

"It seems you're subnormal on a few counts," the Djinn said, more to himself. He gestured at Joseph and the lad threw one hand over his eyes, the other over his nose.

"Now, can you see the hole?" Hutti asked him. The Nubian nodded, a bit stunned. "Can you hear what's going on back there?" Again, the lad agreed. "And how about the smell?" Joseph put a hand to his nose. He looked about to throw up.

"You not only heard two mice mating, you smelled it as well. With such enhanced facilities, you will be more useful on such dangerous adventures. Better able to – er – protect our lovely young princess . . . Yes?"

Dumbfounded, Joseph nodded.

"Isn't it funny about most humans?" he asked Dinah, smiling broadly again. "You give them a precious gift and they simply nod. Do they say 'thank you'? My dear, when you have the time, see if you can put some manners in him, yes?"

Before the bewildered Joseph could find his tongue, Hutti

pointed at the two guards Bubbi had tied up and then flicked his finger toward the doorless dungeon. Joseph got the first on one shoulder and, with help from Dinah and Bubbi, hoisted the second. Joseph in the lead, they followed the Djinn.

It was too dark to see until the Djinn gestured with an extended forefinger, tracing a line where ceiling and wall joined. Soft fairy lights appeared and brightened. The six unconscious guards lay in a pile in the centre of the floor. Three shadowy figures sat still and listlessly against the wall opposite the doorway; they were chained to the wall. Dinah ran there, sobbing. Her father and cousins sat with heads hanging, tongues bluish and distended from lack of water.

Hutti thrust an earthenware ewer and wooden spoon into her hands. "Very slowly," he said softly, "only a bit at a time or they will get violently ill."

Food and wine appeared, guards were stripped and the clothing closest in size to their own was exchanged with the prisoners. Moses and the cousins were recovering rapidly. Dinah thought it might have to do with the sparkling clear beverage, perhaps not wine as she had at first thought.

Hutti sent Joseph and Bubbi on a mission and then stood in the middle of the dungeon, his chin resting on one hand. Dinah had the sudden intuition that only the body was here, the mind communicating with another sphere entirely. She looked at him, studying him intently while holding her father's cold, inert hand.

Hutti's deeply burnished coppery hair hung in waves and curls to his shoulders. From his brow sprang two splendid golden horns. His body was absolutely perfect, covered with an almost translucent skin of pale, pale emerald with a tracery of golden lines, a network coursing over his entire form. These boasted bright silver dots along the network and it all seemed to do with the incredible energy he radiated.

Suddenly, across the passageway and clearly visible through the doorway, appeared a tall, very lean figure covered in a copious, cowled robe that even hid the face. A long bony finger poked from one sleeve, gesturing to her. Hutti was oblivious. As she passed him she wondered if he had, in fact, stopped breathing. There wasn't a flicker as she left the dungeon.

Dinah didn't realize she had run the last few steps; she would have stumbled had not strong hands caught her. Without the sensation of footfalls, she was swept away from the vicinity of the doorway to another part of the passageway. She looked up. The cowl fell back and she was staring up into the most inspiring face she had ever seen. A beautiful face with a long beard, auburn-blanched and burnt pale with the light of a thousand suns. Such a sublime, such a serene face, it made her want to bask and bask. The magical, almost divine man held her two hands cupped in his.

"I am Isa ben Maryam," he whispered. "I have come here to help you . . . and you will need that help very soon indeed."

"Isa – ben – Maryam?" she breathed, hardly able to get her vocal cords working. "He who is the messiah of the Gentiles, the one they say is the son of . . . ?"

"No, no," he smiled, his mouth hardly seeming to move; his mind was speaking to hers. "The one you mean is Yehoshua ha-Mashiah . . . in Arabic he is known as Isa ben Maryam. I am a different Isa, my spiritual mother a different Maryam."

"You are a Muslim, then?" she fairly squeaked.

"I am a true believer in God . . . as you are, Dinah. Nothing separates us, believe me. A great saint, my godfather, is very interested in your well-being. You remind him so much of his granddaughter when she was your age. You see, she was ravished by a Djinn and, as a result, she produced the demon, Musa. Her life was destroyed and my godfather Anwar does not want this to happen to you."

"Was it – that – Djinn?" She pointed down the passage, unable to control her voice. Her eyebrows lifted as far as they could and he nodded affirmation. "Ohhhh . . ." The breath left her body and she would have sagged to the floor had Isa not supported her.

"Here," he said, placing a minute object in her hand. She looked down and saw six tiny hexagrams joined point to point to fashion a perfect little box. Something ephemeral shimmered inside, a force of some sort held captive, she imagined. A sphere that throbbed with a life of its own.

"That sphere has a life of its own, like Hutti's skin," she murmured.

"Similar in substance," Isa agreed, "but quite different in nature. And that difference is precisely what will protect you when the crucial moments come."

"Moments?" she queried nervously. "There will be . . . more than one?"

"Musa, who has been very good, very reasonable so far, considering he is a demon, found out that what would be needed to free your family was a bit over his head and beyond his powers. So, he called in Hutti, his father. That means they will both want the price of a young virgin's favours . . . namely yours," Isa sighed mournfully.

"Oooohhh." She shook for a moment like a distempered dog. "What does *this* do . . . what do I do with *it*?"

"When the time comes," he intoned, "you place it under your tongue until it seems fiery hot. Then clench it between your teeth and compress your lips until air can escape only through the hexagrams."

"And what does *that* do?" Her hair tossed from side to side with her bewilderment.

"Do you know where you are now?" Isa asked gently. She shook her head. "We are in the dungeons of the Khalif's palace in Baghdad. A very long way from Granada, is it not? You will have to cross that same astral plane in order to return home as quickly as you got here. On that journey, you will be met and spirited away briefly. Neither Hutti nor Musa will realize you are, in a sense, absent."

"Whom will I meet . . . I mean, who will spirit me away?" Dinah was tripping over her words.

"Anwar, my saintly godfather, or Aysha. She is the fiercest female Djinn of them all and Hutti is terrified by her. However, she is also the mother of his full Djinn son. And . . . Anwar's guardian angel. She will take good care of you."

"But – but . . ."

"Shhh," he soothed her. "Find a pocket and hide your talisman carefully. Also, make sure you and Joseph find safe hiding places for your swords. They were stolen for you from this very treasury by the very, very brave little gnome, Bubbi. And they do have magical properties."

Before she could even form another question, Isa faded away, and she was sitting on the hard bench in the doorless dungeon. Her father and cousins were still in trances and Hutti hadn't moved.

Noises outside made her head turn. In walked Joseph and Bubbi, their arms piled high with princely clothing.

"All right," Hutti barked, suddenly animated, "let's get the three ex-prisoners stripped and re-clothed. In the most royal of the garments."

Dinah, and her companions worked feverishly, responding to a flow of orders from the huge Djinn. When Moses and his nephews were dressed, the unconscious guards were re-dressed.

"What is the matter with my father and cousins?" Dinah cried, glaring at Hutti. "They're like sleep-walkers."

"Exactly," Hutti agreed affably. "Getting them out of here unrecognized requires that not one careless word be spoken. Once safely on their way, they will snap back to normal." Hutti placed his fists on his hips and laughed down at her mockingly. "You do want them to finish the journey safely, don't you? With all that wealth they were bringing back to Granada?"

"Of course I do . . . I came all this way for just that reason . . ."

"Then imagine what would happen to our splendid illusion if those two dummies, your cousins, began blurting out their true identities. Everybody back in chains, that's what."

"What are you going to do?" she whispered, her irritation changing to awe.

"Temptation. We shall tempt the little judge, the Khalif's Kadi. We shall blind him with a treasure beyond belief. And make him the new Khalif of Baghdad. Never mind, just keep still and watch. I believe you will be dazzled." Hutti smiled, pleased with himself and his master plan.

The Djinn tore one of the chains free of the stone wall and opened the neck-iron with ease. He slipped it around his neck and fastened it tight, then threw the end of the chain at Moses' feet. He stared at Moses, then at the cousins. "Understood?" he said aloud. All three nodded.

Moses picked up the end of the chain and gave it a fierce, imperious yank. Hutti bounded forward, crouching and fawning. The three men led the suddenly buffoon-like creature away.

Bubbi hopped from one foot to the other, nearly hitting the ceiling each time. "Why did Musa do it, why did he call on his father?" The gnome was wringing his hands as he spoke. "Musa owes me favours, he would not dare demand Dinah pay the – er – ah – price. Hooo-hooo, what will we do, Hutti will insist."

Joseph's hand slapped the hilt of his sword. Dinah's hand slipped inside her robe and into the little pocket where the talisman nestled.

Before they could speak, a tremendous uproar approached, doubling in volume as the clatter of many feet rounded the bend in the passageway. They heard boots, weapons clashing against the walls and voices all trying to outdo one another.

As though lifted up physically, Dinah found herself on the bench with Joseph, side by side with the entranced guards. They assumed the same mute stillness and Bubbi cowered under the bench, clutching the hem of Dinah's robe.

". . . All of which you will behold presently," Moses intoned as he made his grand entrance. Dinah looked at him with admiration. He gave her the very slightest of winks before continuing. My, she thought, he was like a king, tall as his father, Solomon, his black beard showing only a small amount of silver.

A short, portly man entered the dungeon and courtiers scurried about, arranging carpets on the floor, cushions and low tables with sweetmeats.

"Kadi," Moses addressed him from his noble height, "if you will accept our offer and assume the recently vacated Khalif's throne, one of the world's greatest treasures shall be yours."

Moses fascinated his listeners with his tale of the sacking of King Solomon's temple, which had contained a horde of riches never before equalled. If the Kadi accepted the throne they would be his. All he had to do was free the poor captive merchants and their goods and chattels. He made a grand gesture toward the occupants on the bench.

At this moment, the two cousins, Abraham and Ichabod, entered triumphantly, Hutti following on the end of his chain.

The Kadi shuddered and stepped back from the sight of such a monster. "You are absolutely positive the Khalif – er – the former Khalif was tried and condemned for . . . heresy?" he asked in a rather high-pitched voice.

"I saw him with these very eyes . . . he was seized on the boat from Mecca and taken in chains to Basra." Moses took the chain from the boys and pulled Hutti close to him.

"Now, good sir, we must begin our return journey immediately, there is no time to spare. May we have your answer?"

The Kadi licked his lips nervously and looked at the Djinn. Hutti made a sound deep in his throat and spat out a ruby the size of a large melon. It rolled about the dirt floor, painting the walls with streaks of vivid red. The Kadi leaned forward, his face glowing with greed. And nodded.

"Now, you bold creature, whom I have bound over with the power of Solomon which has been vested in me, yield up that which you have pledged in return for your freedom. Do it now, I command you!"

Hutti shambled forward, his head rolling and bobbing, his tongue protruding grotesquely. Then he began to expand his lungs. More and more his bulk filled the room, forcing attendants out into the passage. Then there was a roar like a thousand thunderbolts striking a blackened sky. The far wall was shattered and reduced to fine rubble.

A gasp went up from every throat as a huge tidal wave of gold, jewels, crowns and silver plate rolled out into the dungeon. The more it came the more the ceiling-high horde behind never seemed to diminish. The new Khalif was seated on a cushion, fondling an enormous, emerald- and diamond-encrusted crown. The guards dressed as merchants filed out, followed by Dinah, Joseph and Bubbi. The youths had already hidden their precious swords under their garments.

Moses stood in the doorway and intoned a warning in a voice of great authority. He warned that if anyone tried to renege on their agreement, that great supernatural monster

would return, the treasure would disappear and they would all
be turned to stone.

When Moses joined them outside the nearest palace gate, an
army of camels and horses began to arrive, the camels laden
down with the treasures the wily Kadi had stripped from them
without the knowledge of the Khalif. Dinah found herself
mounted on a camel without the vaguest notion of how she got
there. She decided she better stop wondering and questioning
and simply accept that where Djinns and demons strode,
nothing was ever what it seemed.

"Ready?" She looked up and Hutti still towered over her as
though she were standing on the ground. "Father and cousins
free, the vast treasure back in the family's hands, a trusty
Nubian with a magic sword to protect them on the long voyage
home . . . what more could you ask, my delicious princess?"

Hutti was grinning like a cat admiring a canary.

"Why can't we all go home together . . . the way we came?"
She was addressing Hutti but her eyes were fixed on Joseph.

"Only those who came on that unearthly route can return
that way. You could take Joseph but who would protect your
family?" Hutti laughed good-naturedly. "Poor Dinah. Surely
they will find a fast ship and be home in less than two
months."

She knew arguments would gain nothing. Hutti was man-
oeuvring her, she could sense that. "What about that vast
treasure you claim was from the temple in Jerusalem . . . has it
disappeared by now?"

"Are you as naive as your Nubian hero? That will be here
until tomorrow at midnight. Musa has instructions to return it
to its – hmmm – normal place of residence. By that time, your
family will be beyond pursuit."

"And that little man? I don't believe that story of the Khalif
my father told . . . that was *your* idea. What will happen to
him?" Hutti saw her concern was real.

"Your head is full of date stones, my dear," he commented
dryly. "That 'little man', as you affectionately call him,
captured your father and his caravan behind the Khalif's back.
He does not deserve your maudlin sympathy. But don't worry,
he will be warned soon enough to give up his new costume and

airs by the time al-Abbasi, the real Khalif, returns. It may teach our greedy little judge a lesson he won't forget."

"Oh." Dinah felt thoroughly deflated. She looked up at Hutti once more, a puzzled expression on her face. "Well, what happens now?"

"Wait and see," he answered enigmatically. "Whatever, I do look forward to our next meeting." Her next question had no chance to form; there was a brilliant flash of blue and Hutti was gone. But his voice could still be heard, the words directed at Joseph.

"Listen carefully, Joseph," Hutti called out. "Straight on, no unnecessary stops, the beasts will not need forage or water for a good long while. Cross the river at a point just below Hit, no further south than that. Press on to the oasis of Ghadir as-Sufi. A short refreshment rest there and on to Bir Sejri oasis. Skirt Damascus to the south and on to Tyre, where you will find a very swift ship waiting. These guards will awaken some hours after your departure. Dinah's camel will lead them back to Baghdad."

There was another blue flash and both Dinah and Bubbi were lifted and dizzily hurtled skyward.

The totally alien scene exploded before her eyes with such brilliant splendour that Dinah was momentarily blinded. Yes, that same purplish grass, the flashing trees with jewels for fruit, the vault of bright yet soft lavender overhead. It was all too stunning to take in at one glance. They had been moving with such speed on the race to Baghdad that she had hardly been able to take in a single detail. Bubbi's rebellious screech roused her.

Musa had suddenly appeared and was clasping the struggling gnome tightly to his chest. With an incredible bound the demon rose and his head carved an opening in the fabric – of – something. It was gone, the body following, and by the time Dinah shouted and leapt up herself to catch the feet, they were gone too. She heard a soft chuckle as she landed, somewhat painfully.

"In a hurry to leave?" Hutti taunted her. He had appeared from behind the nearest tree holding a handful of the sparkling fruit. "Don't try to follow Musa, you're much safer here. He is still so young and impetuous. *I'll* look after you."

Dinah leapt back and drew her sword, aiming at his groin.

Hutti threw the last jewel over his shoulder and began slapping his knees with glee.

"Are you going to split me down the middle? Perhaps sever my head from my body? My dear, why are you human females always so tedious? What is virginity . . . a lack of something, nothing more. And we are about to rectify that. Take your clothes off!"

"I most certainly will not!" she defied him, raising the tip of the sword to menace his heart.

The many windings of her head-covering flew about as though caught in a cyclone. The end of the cloth ripped the sword from her hand, the scabbard from its thongs; her robe and undergarments flew straight up in the air. Weapon, clothing and the traitorous head-covering landed in a neat pile atop the tree over Hutti's head.

Suddenly naked, she gasped, then screamed, collapsing to sit on her heels and bend forward, one hand over her bright coppery maiden-hair, the other shielding the small but exquisitely shaped breasts. The girl sobbed piteously; the Djinn rocked on his heels and laughed.

Looking up, Dinah saw a vague outline begin to take shape in the tree, on a limb below her clothing. Hutti's desire-mad eyes were riveted on her alone. A disembodied arm reached out with a small ewer. Fine, jewel-like drops descended to land atop Hutti's head. He seemed not to notice. But his knees did. They began to quaver, then collapse. In a few seconds, the entire gigantic body was sprawled on the ground. A gentle, happy snoring filled the air.

Now, two disembodied arms extended and extended. Dinah felt the gentle hands lift her and seat her on the limb above. Next to her, a shimmering angel began to materialize. Complete with perfect wings.

"Anwar sent me," the glorious vision announced, "to help you through your ordeal. We have a great deal to do and little time, those few drops from the Fountain of Forgetfulness will not keep my mate down there in dreamland too long."

She became aware of a great feeling of bliss filling every bit of her, as though God himself had blessed her. Only then did she feel a small pearl-like object in the palm of her hand.

"We must insert this inside your most secret of secrets, my dear. Anwar, who is Isa ben Maryam's godfather – and Musa's great-grandfather – says you must be protected from the fate of his beloved granddaughter. You must wear this at all times save during the days of the moon. Hutti is my mate, yes. But in earth terms he can be most dangerous. A woman who gives birth to a demon is shunned in all society."

Dinah tried to protest but Aysha, as she was called, had such sensitive, delicate hands that the girl never felt a thing. Aysha held out the tiny hexagon box that had been hidden inside Dinah's robe. Even before Dinah wondered about that, she realized there was nothing Aysha could not achieve . . . absolutely nothing.

A moment later and they were standing in a clearing far from the sleeping Hutti.

"When we return and Hutti awakens, he will undertake to ravish you. You will prevent that in the only way known: you will perform The Ultimate." Aysha smiled encouragement at the girl, easing her panic.

"The Ultimate? Me? Wha-what is The Ultimate?" Dinah pleaded.

"Yes, you . . . I shall teach you. There is no string of words in any language that can describe The Ultimate. But when you perform it, you will see the results and, really, that is all you need know."

Aysha made a thrilling sound deep in her throat. Dinah thought of birds, of paeans, of beautiful music performed on the strings of many instruments. Nothing described it. Try as she might, she simply could not imitate the sound. Then Aysha stroked her throat lightly with the tips of her fingers and Dinah felt something expand inside her larynx and, before she knew it, she was making the sound.

"To give it its full power," Aysha explained, "you must place the talisman Isa ben Maryam gave you in your mouth and pass that sound through the hexagrams and around the ephemeral sphere in the tiny cage. Now, for the dancing."

It seemed to take endless hours but Aysha assured her pupil that in earth time, it was mere minutes. Aysha's body was too exquisite for mere words, Dinah felt. How would she, thin and not yet a fully formed woman, ever recreate those haunting, erotic movements?

"Beautiful, my dear," the female Djinn assured the exhausted girl. "Hutti will never know what hit him. He will never forget it. He will spend endless hours dreaming of having it again. You will see."

"Oh, Aysha, if that is true then I will never be safe," the girl moaned.

"Yes, you will." Aysha explained that all Dinah had to do if under a future attack was warn Hutti that The Ultimate could be performed only under a new moon during the summer solstice. And only by a virgin who had never even been touched in her secret places. That would stop him in his tracks. Still, prudence demanded she never forget the protective device she now wore in that secret place.

Instantaneously, they were back beside Hutti's prone body. Aysha began to fade away. Dinah took a deep breath and looked up longingly toward her clothes. She felt a sharp slap on her buttock and jumped.

"All right, Hutti, are you ready? I don't like to be kept waiting, you gorgeous hunk." As she said it, her clothing dropped to the ground, still neatly piled and folded.

Hutti sat up, startled, blinking and rubbing his eyes.

"Here," she patted the pile of clothing. "Put your head down on my sweetly scented clothes, stretch out so I can reach every delicious part of you, so I can show you how much I desire you, my wonderful lover."

His body shot straight up in the air and he made a perfect landing, his head on her clothes. Dinah stretched luxuriously, swaying and undulating as she did. Softly at first, the sounds came through the talisman, quavering, insinuating, luring him to watch her dance.

The frenzied movements, the glorious sounds soon had him helplessly roaring for more and more and more. The volume of her voice rose and flashes of lightning appeared, increasing in strength and volume until it seemed the astral plane would be split asunder.

The Djinn's body rose erratically, as though jerked skywards on invisible ropes. He dwindled to nearly nothing, then came crashing down to land on the exact same spot. His limbs were twisted and tortured but before Dinah could despair, she saw the vibrant look of total ecstasy on his face.

"Tuck your clothing under your arm, we must be off to pay your debt to Musa now," Aysha's disembodied voice instructed. Next to her stood Bubbi, straight as a ramrod, his eyes closed. Aysha's soft giggle told Dinah he was in a trance and would stay so until he was safely home.

"Oh, Aysha, I couldn't go through that again . . . I'm exhausted," Dinah exclaimed. She felt Aysha's lips on her brow and a rush of renewed energy coursed through her. "Let's go," she said, "I think I'm going to enjoy this one."

Clothing under one arm, the other wrapped around Aysha, she blinked once and was standing in a vast hall. A palace, she assumed, taking in the carpets, furniture and decorations. Then she saw the demon, lying upside down on his back, as though they were up and he was down. She noted, her breath catching in her throat, that he was in a high state of arousal.

"What took you so long?" he roared in ever greater oestrus. "Was my father as insatiable as ever, my pretty ex-virgin?"

"Stop wasting time," Dinah shouted back. "Get down here where I can get my hungry, greedy hands on you, you delicious green brute of a lover." Her sinuous movements and the sounds from her talisman matched the passion she expressed.

Dinah sat straight up . . . in her own bed. Then, it all came flowing back. Bubbi was dropped in the garden and disappeared below the earth, muttering something about Momo having his guts for garters. Then Aysha – then Aysha – but all she could conjure up was the sensation of ecstasy, the feeling of mind and soul expansion, a feeling that, for many brief moments, she had actually entered paradise. She heard the creak of a door, the door of her grandfather's chamber . . .

Lord! Here she was at home and she hadn't even thought to . . .

Pulling a silken robe about her nakedness, Dinah flew down the stairs and raced to Solomon's bedroom. She paused at the door, listening to rather strange sounds. Then a spirit-like hand touched her elbow.

"Your beloved grandfather arrived home this evening, after a long and gruelling journey. Hepzie bathed him in the warm kitchen and now your servant Farida is anointing him with warm oils to ease the pains in his aged joints. He deserves whatever small pleasure this gives him. Be kind and wait until the morning, after he has had a good night's rest."

Aysha was gone again. Dinah hesitated, longing to see Solomon, then she turned and retraced her steps.

"What is this insane obsession with Abishag the Shunammite?" Solomon croaked, his body feeling ease from the warm, aromatic oils.

"She was a fair and comely virgin, she was brought to the king to lie upon his breast and bring the fire back to him," Farida explained. Before he had a chance to protest, she was in the bed, trying to cover his body with her own.

"Adonai, save me," he gasped.

"I've lost so much weight, just to make myself pleasing . . . to you," she protested.

"And to whom else?" he asked, with a touch of sarcasm.

"Do you not think me fair and comely?" she hummed into his ear, moving her body temptingly.

"Fair, yes. But we have to stop short on the virgin part."

"Well, I'm practically a virgin . . . almost." Her soft crying threatened to build into a wail of despair.

"All right, all right, don't cry, you can stay for a few minutes more, until your tears cease," he conceded. Reaching out to pat her back reassuringly, he misjudged and found himself stroking a buttock. His response shocked him; he thought all that was over long ago. She raised her bottom invitingly and his hand slipped between her thighs.

"What is this!" he demanded. "You are a Christian in a Jewish household and you shave your pubic hair like a Muslim?"

"Don't beat me, Master. In this crazy place you have to be prepared to be all things to all people," she confided ingenuously for an almost virgin.

"Well," he admonished sternly . . . without releasing his grip . . . "I hope you haven't been too many things to too many people, my dear, because there are some ailments even I can't cure."

THE STAR OF
THE FARMYARD

Terry Jones

*Terry Jones (b. 1942) will always be known as one of the
Monty Python team, even though he has produced a significant
body of work on his own. This ranges from the thoroughly
academic* Chaucer's Knight *(1980) to the delightful story
collections* Fairy Tales *(1981) and* Fantastic Stories
*(1992). The following is one of his favourite stories from the
latter collection.*

There was once a dog who could perform the most amazing
tricks. It could stand on its head and bark the Dog's
Chorus whilst juggling eight balls on its hind paws and
playing the violin with its front paws. That was just one of
its tricks.

Another trick it could do was this: it would bite its own tail,
then it would roll around the farmyard like a wheel, balancing
two long poles on its paws – on top of one of which it was

balancing Daisy the Cow and on the other Old Lob the Carthorse – all the while, at the same time, telling excruciatingly funny jokes that it made up on the spot.

One day Charlemagne, the cock, said to Stanislav, the dog: "Stan, you're wasted doing your amazing tricks here in this old farmyard – you ought to go to the Great City or join the circus."

Stan replied: "Maybe you're right, Charlemagne."

So one bright spring morning, Stanislav the Dog and Charlemagne the Cock set off down the road to seek their fortunes in the Great City.

They hadn't gone very far before they came to a fair. There were people selling everything you could imagine. There was also a stage on which a troop of strolling players were performing.

So Charlemagne the Cock strode up to the leader of the troop and said: "Now, my good man, this is indeed your lucky day, for you see before you the most talented, most amazing juggler, acrobat, ventriloquist, comedian and all-round entertainer in the whole history of our – or any other – farmyard . . . Stanislav the Dog!" And Stanislav, who all this time had been looking modestly down at his paws, now gave a low bow.

"Can't you read?" said the leader of the troop. "No dogs!"

And without more ado, Charlemagne the Cock and Stanislav the Dog were thrown out.

"Huh!" said Charlemagne, picking himself up and shaking the road-dust out of his feathers. "You're too good for a troop of strolling players anyway."

Stanislav climbed wearily out of the ditch. He was covered in mud, and he looked at his friend very miserably.

"I'm tired," he said. "And I want to go home to my master."

"Cheer up, my friend!" replied Charlemagne the Cock. "We're going to the Great City, where fine ladies and gentlemen drip with diamonds, where dukes and earls sport rubies and emeralds, and where the streets are paved with gold. With your talents, you'll take 'em by storm. We'll make our fortunes!"

So the cock and the dog set off once more down the long, dirty road that led to the Great City.

On the way they happened to pass a circus. Charlemagne the Cock strode up to the ringmaster, who was in the middle of teaching the lions to stand on their hind legs and jump through a ring.

"Tut! Tut! Tut! My good man," said Charlemagne the Cock. "You needn't bother yourself with this sort of rubbish any more! Allow me to introduce you to the most superlative acrobat and tumbler – who can not only stand on his hind paws, but can jump through fifty such rings . . . backwards and whilst balancing one of your lions on his nose . . . and do it all on the high wire . . . *without a safety net!*"

"I only do tricks with lions," said the ringmaster.

"But Stanislav the Dog has more talent in his right hind leg than your entire troop of lions!"

"These are the best lions in the business!" exclaimed the ringmaster. "And they'd eat you and your dog for supper without even blinking. In fact they need a feed right now!" And he reached out his hand to grab Charlemagne the Cock. Stan the Dog saw what was happening, however, and nipped the ringmaster on the ankle.

"Run, Charlemagne!" he yelled.

And Charlemagne ran as fast as he could, while Stan the Dog leapt about – nipping people's ankles – as the entire circus chased them down the road.

"Help!" squawked Charlemagne, as the circus folk got closer and closer and hands reached out to grab him by the neck.

But Stan the Dog ran under everyone's legs and tripped them up. Then he said to Charlemagne: "Jump on my back! I can run four times as fast as these clowns!"

And so they escaped, with Charlemagne the Cock riding on Stan the Dog's back.

*   *   *

That night they slept under a hedge. Charlemagne the Cock was extremely nervous, but Stan the Dog curled himself around his friend to protect him. Stan himself, however, was not very happy either.

"I'm hungry," he murmured, "and I want to go home to my master."

"Cheer up!" said Charlemagne. "Tomorrow we'll reach the Great City, where your talents will be appreciated. Forget these country yokels. I'm telling you – fame and fortune await you and . . ."

But his friend was fast asleep.

Well, the next day, they arrived in the Great City. At first they were overawed by the noise and bustle. Many a time they had to leap into the gutter to avoid a cart or a carriage, and on one occasion they both got drenched when somebody emptied a chamber pot from a window above the street, and it went right over them.

"Oh dear, I miss the farmyard," said Stan the Dog. "And nobody here wants to know us."

"Brace up!" cried Charlemagne. "We're about to make our breakthrough! We're going straight to the top!" And he knocked on the door of the Archbishop's palace.

Now it so happened that the Archbishop himself was, at that very moment, in the hallway preparing to leave the palace, and so, when the servant opened the door, the Archbishop saw the cock and the dog standing there on the step.

"Your Highness!" said Charlemagne, bowing low to the servant. "Allow me to introduce to you the Most Amazing Prodigy Of All Time – Stanislav the Dog! He does tricks you or I would have thought impossible! They are, indeed, miracles of . . ."

"Clear off!" said the servant, who had been too astonished to speak for a moment. And he began to close the door.

But Charlemagne the Cock suddenly lost his temper.

"LISTEN TO ME!" he cried, and he flew at the servant with his spurs flying.

Well, the servant was so surprised he fell over backwards,

and Charlemagne the Cock landed on his chest and screamed: "THIS DOG IS A GENIUS! HIS LIKE HAS NEVER BEEN SEEN OUTSIDE OUR FARMYARD! JUST GIVE HIM A CHANCE TO SHOW YOU!"

And Stan the Dog, who had nervously slunk into the hallway, started to do his trick where he bounced around on his tail, juggling precious china ornaments (which he grabbed off the sideboard as he bounced past) whilst barking a popular Farmyard Chorus that always used to go down particularly well with the pigs.

"My china!" screamed the Archbishop. "Stop him at once!" And several of the Archbishop's servants threw themselves at Stan the Dog. But Stan bounced out of their way brilliantly, and grabbed the Archbishop's mitre and started to balance a rare old Ming vase on the top of it.

"Isn't he great?" shouted Charlemagne the Cock.

"Grab him!" screamed the Archbishop, and the servants grabbed Charlemagne.

"But look at the dog!" squawked the cock. "Don't you see how great he is? Do you know anyone else who can juggle like that?"

But just then – as luck would have it – all the butlers and chambermaids and kitchen skivvies and gardeners, who had heard all the noise, came bursting into the Archbishop's hall. They stood there for a moment horrified, as they watched a barking dog, bouncing around on his tail, juggling the most precious pieces of the Archbishop's prize collection of china.

"Stop him!" roared the Archbishop again. And without more ado everybody descended on poor Stan, and he disappeared under a mound of flailing arms and legs. As a result, of course, all the Archbishop's best china crashed to the floor and was smashed into smithereens.

"Now look what you've done!" yelled Charlemagne.

"Now look what we've done!" exclaimed the Archbishop. "Listen to me! You're both filthy, you look as if you slept in a hedge, you stink of the chamber pot and you dare to burst into my palace and wreck my best china! Well! You're going to pay for it! Throw them into my darkest dungeons!"

And the Archbishop's servants were just about to do so, when suddenly a voice spoke from above them.

"Silence, everybody!" said the Voice.

Everybody froze. Then the Voice continued: "Don't you know who this is? Archbishop! Shame on you! This is the Voice of God!"

The Archbishop fell to his knees, and muttered a prayer, and everyone else followed suit.

"That's better!" said the Voice of God. "Now let Stan the Dog go free. He didn't mean no harm."

So they let go of Stan the Dog.

"And now," continued the Voice of God. "Let Charlemagne the Cock go!"

So they let go of Charlemagne the Cock.

"Now shut your eyes and wait for me to tell you to open them again!" said the Voice of God.

So they all shut their eyes, and Stan the Dog and Charlemagne the Cock fled out of the Archbishop's palace as fast as their legs could carry them.

I don't know how long the Archbishop and his servants remained kneeling there with their eyes shut, but I am certain that the Voice of God never told them to open their eyes again. For, of course, the Voice wasn't the Voice of God at all – it was the Voice of Stan the Dog.

"You are, as I say, a very talented dog," said Charlemagne as they ran down the road. "But I'd almost forgotten you were a ventriloquist as well!"

"Luckily for us!" replied Stan. "But look here, Charlemagne, I'll always be talented – it's just the way I am. Only I'd rather use those talents where they're appreciated, instead of where they get us into trouble."

"Stanislav," said Charlemagne, "maybe you're right."

*   *   *

And so the two friends returned to the farmyard. And Stanislav the Dog continued to perform his astounding tricks for the entertainment of the other farm animals, and they always loved him.

And even though Charlemagne occasionally squawked a bit at night, and said that it was a waste of talent, Stan the Dog stayed where he was – happy to be the Star of the Farmyard.

DIAMONDS – BLACK AND WHITE

Anthony Armstrong

Anthony Armstrong – the pseudonym of British author George Willis (1897–1976) – is the last of the old-timers I've selected for this anthology, and another of the unjustly neglected humorists. Armstrong was at his best and most prolific in the 1920s and 1930s, and at that time bore comparison with P. G. Wodehouse. Whereas Wodehouse is (deservedly) remembered, Armstrong is (undeservedly) forgotten. His collections The Prince Who Hiccupped *(1932) and* The Pack of Pieces *(1942) – with stories selected from* The Strand, Pearson's, Punch *and other popular magazines of the day – contain some of the best fairy-tale spoofs you'll ever read. Here's one of them.*

Once upon a time there was a woman who lived in a cottage near a forest. She had a husband of a sort, whom she found quite useful to chop logs and fetch water from the well and to keep the wolf from the door by carving little wooden likenesses for sale to travellers. Many of these, incidentally, were bad enough to have kept a whole pack of wolves at quite a distance. She had also an elder daughter, named Grummilla, by another husband and a younger daughter who was called Nada. She had no sons; but she had a tom-cat called Rumpelstiltskin after a distant cousin twice removed and now put away for good, and there was a girl called Squab who came in on Monday mornings to oblige with the washing. Oh, and there was a puppy called Joseph, but he doesn't really matter. I think that's all.

The two daughters were very different indeed, both in looks and manners, as half-sisters generally are. Grummilla was tall and raven-haired, and though she had good looks in a hard sort of way, she was both lazy and surly. Her father had been, before his death, Keeper of the Royal Wild Boar (there *was* only one) in the neighbouring forest, and it had gone to his head.

Nada, on the other hand, was very sweet-tempered and kind to animals – even to Rumpelstiltskin, who was about as foul an animal as one could find in a day's march. She was a platinum blonde with shining hair. Her mother disliked her and always favoured her elder sister. Ladies prefer brunettes. Anyway what with that and Grummilla's laziness, Nada always had to do all the dirty work about the home.

At the time when my story begins this household was in a great state of excitement, for news had just reached them that no less a person than the son of the Vizier of the country would be passing close by them on his return from a visit to a foreign country. He had been sent there, as everyone knew, to bring back a wife for his young master the Prince, for he was a very sharp fellow and was reputed to have a good eye for a deal whether in food or furniture or wives.

"And," said Mushla (for that was the woman's name) to her husband, "he may hear of your wood-carving and stop here to have his head done in teak."

"Mps!" remarked her husband, meaning "And what the dickens is the good of that?" He was not much of a fellow for the light chit-chat. I have forgotten what his name was;

everyone simply called him "Mushla's husband"; she was that sort.

"He might – er – notice Grummilla," continued Mushla, who was ambitious, and knew well that the Vizier's son was unmarried. Her eye took on the faraway look of the woman who perceives a prospective son-in-law of high birth before he perceives it himself.

"Well, he might notice Nada," countered her husband, who generally took Nada's side, partly because she was his own daughter, but chiefly because his wife didn't.

"Oh, he might notice Squab," retorted Mushla, nettled, and banged the kitchen door. And that was that.

In the kitchen, however, Mushla began to think some very ambitious thoughts. She knew well that people married queerly in those days. It was nothing out of the common for a Vizier's son to fall in love with the daughter of a wood-carver on sight and even go so far as to marry her; indeed, it was quite usual. Mushla smiled to herself and thought again of Grummilla.

One day, soon after this, a messenger brought the information to Mushla's house that the Vizier's son, as she had hoped, was actually intending to pay them a visit that very evening with the object of having Mushla's husband carve his likeness – or at any rate his as-near-like-as-possible.

Mushla's ambition flamed up immediately. All at once in her mind's eye she saw Grummilla affianced that very night to the young man and going back with him to Court. And much as she liked her elder daughter she would not be sorry. At Court Grummilla's rather troublesome disinclination for work would have full scope. So instantly she was all bustle.

First she made her husband find his collar, sponge it, and even put it on. Then she broke the news to her daughter. Grummilla didn't seem very interested, till her mother pointed out that Viziers' sons, being rich and aristocratic, were popularly supposed to make good husbands for the lower classes, when she brightened up and asked what she had better wear.

They had a long discussion as to ways and means and whether they should shorten the skirt of her blue and silver or wear the pink sack-cloth just as it was. Mushla took a very serious view of the forthcoming meeting, going so far as to suggest that Grummilla should have a special wash for it, including the ears – even though it was only Thursday.

Grummilla demurred at this, her line of argument being first, that there was no water and the well was such a long way off, and second, that it didn't seem much good being dark and raven-haired if one had to wash on odd days of the week, even for a Vizier's bachelor son.

Mushla, however, at last induced her daughter to make the effort by promising to send Nada to the well for the water, and by pointing out that once she was a Vizier's daughter-in-law and a lady, she needn't wash any more, but could use cold cream at night and powder in the daytime and call it Care of the Skin instead.

So poor Nada, who had already been set to work by Mushla to clean up the cottage, was sent off to the well with a bucket, and injunctions to put a snap in it or she knew what.

She was just hauling the bucket to the top again when the slip-knot she had tied proved to be more of a slip than a knot and the bucket fell back into the depths. This frightened Nada very much, for it was her mother's favourite bucket; so after some thought she climbed down the rope into the well to fetch it up.

Now all sorts of extraordinary things used to happen in the good old days – in fact, any era in which fairies and magicians and witches and so on wandered round at large was bound to provide incidents out of the common. So that Nada was not particularly surprised when, reaching the water's surface, she saw facing her in the side of the well a magic door. It was a swing door, bearing the legend "Pull!" Nada, being feminine, pushed. The door, being magic, opened. She went in.

A path lay before her and she walked curiously along it for some distance till she met an old crone with two tired boxes of matches clutched in a grimy paw, seated on a bank.

"Spare-a-copper-lidy-for-a-poor-old-woman-what-only-wants-tuppence-more-to-get-a-bed-for-the-night," began the old crone who, as no doubt you have guessed, was a fairy in disguise, but who occasionally did this sort of thing when she found fairyland a bit boring. Also, she quite frequently made a trifle out of it, to salt away in the fairy sock.

Now Nada hadn't got many coppers and certainly didn't want to lose them, but since she regularly read her fairy books and had her suspicions, she took care to give the old thing her blessing instead. A very wise course of procedure, besides being a cheap way of getting out of it. At the words the old woman suddenly changed back into fairy shape, and Nada of course pretended politely to be terribly surprised, displaying much confusion and even making a curtsy.

"Dear child!" purred the fairy. She loved unsophisticated people. The world, she considered, was getting rather too full of a sharp younger generation who recognized her through all her disguises, and this, as you can well believe, must be dashed annoying. "Can I help you, my pretty girl?" she continued beneficently.

"I dropped my mother's favourite bucket down the well," said Nada, "and I'm looking for it."

"Oh, is that all," replied the fairy, and waved her wand. "You'll find it at the top when you go back. Now because you've been so good-hearted and spoken so kindly to one whom you thought was but an old woman, I shall give you a present."

She thought a minute, waved her wand experimentally, said to herself: "No, that won't do!" washed it out and waved again. Then she announced with some pride: "For every word you speak when you return to earth a diamond, a sparkling white diamond to match your shining hair, shall fall from your lips. There, what about that?" She paused to study the effect of this statement on the girl. "Rather a novel idea don't you think, my dear?" she asked a trifle anxiously.

"Very," agreed Nada, who certainly did feel it was a handsome thing to happen to anyone when looking for a bucket; then she said goodbye very prettily.

When she got back (having found the bucket at the top), her mother at once began to blame her for the delay, till Nada tried to explain and large white diamonds dropped from her lips. After that it took a very long time to tell the story because Nada's parents and Grummilla were on their hands and knees scrabbling for her lightest remark, and her father kept saying "What?" in the hopes of getting a bigger one. And then it was discovered that Joseph the puppy – for you know what puppies are – had swallowed quite a long word and that took up more time still.

When at last Mushla grasped more or less what had happened, she hurried Grummilla into an apron, thrust a bucket, an old one, into her hand and told her to be off to the well as quick as she could and do the same. With a true mother's instinct she had realized that under present circumstances even an ordinary Vizier's son, let alone one so sharp as this one was reputed to be, would not be able to help preferring Nada to Grummilla. And while she didn't mind Grummilla leaving her, if the girl made a good match, Nada was far too useful about the house to be allowed to go, for she could cook and sew and clean, and even get a fair amount of work out of Squab, who was pretty hopeless at anything except washing stockings.

So Grummilla raced off, reaching the well in something under fifty seconds, and the bucket had barely touched the bottom before she had slid down the rope herself and was crawling through the magic door (which, by the way, now bore the legend "Pull and Let Go!" because it *was* a magic door).

She hurried along the path till she came to the old woman who promptly asked her for coppers. Now Grummilla was rather high and mighty and did not read fairy stories, nor in the excitement had Nada had time to say much else than that she had met a fairy. Grummilla, therefore, was looking out for something snappy in white chiffon with a wand and wings. So she retorted angrily: "I've got nothing for you: get out of my way!"

Naturally she was a bit startled when the old woman changed into her proper shape, and tried to retrieve her error by remarks about the weather while hurriedly fumbling for her purse. The fairy, however, was no fool.

"What do *you* want?" she said crossly.

"Well, to tell you the truth," replied Grummilla, taking this as an offer, "there's nothing I'd like so much as to have – er – something come out of my mouth with each word I speak. Say

– er – little shining stones?" she added skilfully, feeling she had better not display too great a knowledge of what had happened to her sister.

The fairy waved her wand with what was, for a fairy, of course, quite a malevolent grin. "Granted as soon as asked," she said, for she had nice manners. But she looked searchingly at Grummilla's raven-dark tresses as she did so and chuckled once more to herself.

Grummilla was off again like a shot, and found her mother waiting at the door.

"Well?" she cried.

"All right, mother, I've got it," returned Grummilla. But though half a dozen shining lumps fell from her lips as she spoke, to the surprise of both of them they were black – as black as Grummilla's raven hair.

Mushla looked suspiciously at her. Then she picked up a couple of her daughter's words and examined them. Whatever they were, and Mushla didn't know or care, they were by no means diamonds.

"Here, what's this?" she asked angrily.

"Don't ask me!" snapped Grummilla, equally annoyed, and she loosed off three more, as black as the others.

The subsequent argument brought out Mushla's husband, who had been indoors listening to his younger daughter more eagerly than ever before in his life and now had his pockets full. He, too, was surprised and secretly not a little pleased that Grummilla hadn't got anything as good as Nada. He didn't like his surly step-daughter.

"They're quite pretty," he said at last by way of soothing everybody. He picked one of the black lumps up and fingered it carefully. "Now I would . . ."

"Pretty be hanged!" snarled Mushla. "They're not diamonds."

"No," agreed her husband judicially, "but on the other hand . . ."

"Just dirty common stones!"

"Of course they may . . ."

"Oh, shut up!"

"Mps!" went her husband and shut up. He retired into the

house, leaving the two women wrangling together and already ankle-deep in a litter of the black lumps.

Poor Nada came in for more hard words than before when it was at last discovered that nothing could be done. Her sister taxed her with greed, double-dealing and selfishness, and Mushla nearly broke a blood vessel trying to accuse her of taking the better gift for herself and at the same time endeavouring to point out how much better Grummilla's gift really was after all. Every time Nada opened her mouth to reply she evoked a fresh tirade by producing more diamonds, and every time her father opened his mouth to defend her he was told to shut up.

At last things settled down a bit. It was agreed that the only thing to do when the Vizier's son came was for Grummilla not to talk if she could possibly help it. What sounded like a sarcastic laugh at this point was traced to Mushla's husband, who had great difficulty in persuading his wife that he had only been clearing his throat. Then Grummilla got into her prettiest dress, the blue and silver, and shortened the skirt so much that she might almost have been mistaken for a society lady already. Nada was kept in her rags and set to the hardest work her mother could find, which, of course, was shovelling out into the courtyard any comments her sister saw fit to pass, before the expected visit.

Towards evening the Vizier's son arrived. He was met with many bowings by Mushla's husband and welcomed into the cottage by Mushla herself, resplendent in a fur pelisse she had won ten years before in a raffle. Behind her was Grummilla, looking rather handsome and determined not to speak. Nada had been sent into the back kitchen, where she was dealing with Joseph the puppy, who had shown a decided partiality for her sister's conversation and now had indigestion.

The Vizier's son was tall and dark with large lips, a larger nose, and keen, very keen black eyes. As I said, he had the reputation of being a sharp young man and he looked it. He had one servant accompanying him.

"I have heard of your fame at carving wooden likenesses," began the Vizier's son patronizingly.

Mushla's husband revolved his hat rapidly in his hands and mumbled something that was drowned by his wife's effusive answer, as she shooed Rumpelstiltskin, who, being a cat, had of course taken the best chair, out into the courtyard.

The Vizier's son, whose name was Baran, sat down and began to talk pleasantly about the weather and a dragon they had seen while coming through the wood and the prevalence of magicians in that part of the country and other items of local interest. Mushla very carefully placed Grummilla where the light fell on her to best advantage. Grummilla kept her lips tightly closed, but nodded and smiled whenever the Vizier's son made a remark, thus giving him, in the way women do, the impression that she was a brilliant conversationalist. Her mother noticed with satisfaction that Baran appeared at least impressed if not attracted. She could not help feeling pleased that Nada was safely tucked away in the kitchen and was unable to flaunt her diamonds in front of the Vizier's son. There was a businesslike look in the young man's keen eyes, and the nose reminded her of a pedlar who had once sold her husband a so-called magic wand which had turned out to be valueless. He certainly was a sharp young man, the kind of person, Mushla decided, who wouldn't care what sort of wife he had if she could produce diamonds as fast as she could talk.

She was still congratulating herself on her strategy, and her husband had just recovered from his nervous embarrassment sufficiently to be able to handle his knives without cutting himself, when the kitchen door sprang open and Joseph appeared, hotly pursued by Nada.

Mushla was furious and sprang at her.

"Didn't I tell you to stay in the kitchen and clear it up?" she rapped; then, as she saw Baran looking with interest at Nada, she added, with swift recollection: "Don't dare say a word!"

But it was too late. A few large diamonds rolled from Nada's lips as she began to reply. The Vizier's son jumped and looked a trifle startled – even in those days of magic. But he came up again to it bravely and tried politely not to notice anything. He was quite good at not noticing things. In fact, he had recently had a good deal of practice. A friend of his at Court, one of the Equerries, had for some time been suffering from a pair of donkey's ears instead of his own and no one had been better than Baran at not noticing the disability – even though all his friend's hats had to have two holes cut in the top.

Mushla, however, seeing that it had happened, tried to pass it off.

"Poor girl!" she whispered loudly to Baran. "Such a misfortune! Lumps of glass you know, sir," she added mendaciously, being determined not to spoil Grummilla's chance. "It's not as if it were anything valuable."

She turned swiftly round, caught her amazed husband just about to speak, and drove his explanatory protest deep down into him again with a super-powerful frown worked by both eyebrows at once.

"What a pity!" remarked Baran courteously, but eyeing with curiosity a word which had fallen close to his chair.

Mushla again rounded on Nada and sent her back into the kitchen, triumphing in her skilful retrieving of an awkward situation. But when she turned round once more Baran had picked up the diamond near his foot and was looking at it through a little microscope which he had taken from his pocket and fixed in a practised eye.

"Merely glass, sir," said Mushla again, a trifle anxiously.

"Oh – er – quite," returned the Vizier's son carelessly, and made as if to throw it away with scorn, but checked himself. He then said even more carelessly: "But quite a curio!" And put it disdainfully in his pocket instead.

"Here, I say . . ." began Mushla's husband but stopped and plunged into his carving, as once again he caught his wife's eye. Mushla's eye would have stopped a dragon in mid charge.

There was a pregnant silence. Then Baran said, looking towards the kitchen.

"Charming girl, your daughter. She ought to be at the Court. Great opportunities there for a girl of her – er – gifts."

This, felt Mushla, was dangerous.

"Beautiful black hair like hers, sir, is wasted here," she replied in a loud whisper. She did not intend that there should be any mistake about which daughter she considered the charming one.

"Oh – er – yes," said the Vizier's son in puzzled fashion,

looking vaguely round till his eye fell on Grummilla. Then he
said, "Oh – er – yes" again – in quite a different tone of voice
and not very enthusiastically. Then once more he stared at the
kitchen door.

"Let me see," he added after a while to Mushla's annoyance. "Lumps of glass, I think you said?"

"Yes," she replied shortly, feeling she had better stick to it.

The Vizier's son smiled at her amiably but incredulously.
He certainly was sharp. Mushla's husband said nothing. He
always became very preoccupied with his work as time went
on, and at the moment he was concentrating on the problem of
whether to incline to truth or flattery in the delineation of his
client's remarkably large nose. He decided at last in favour of
flattery, principally because the other would take so long and
use such a lot of wood.

"Lumps of glass," the Vizier's son began again, as though
he couldn't leave the subject, "have always interested me."

At this moment, Mushla, realizing that he was distinctly
neglecting Grummilla in favour of her sister, felt called upon
to invent further.

"Oh, that in itself is nothing, sir. What makes it all so bad is
that my daughter Nada is – er – well, she's really not quite all
there if you know what I mean."

Baran did appear to know what she meant. The statement,
in fact, Mushla was pleased to observe, shook him considerably. "Her sister, now," she continued rather pleased, "is as
charming as they make 'em."

"Oh, quite, quite," agreed Baran thoughtfully.

"Now if only," continued Mushla who was nothing if not
bold, "anyone was looking for a wife."

"Well," replied Baran with rather a sly look and glancing for
the first time at his servant standing behind him with a box,
"to tell you the truth, *I am –*"

Mushla was so amazed at this answer that she sat down
heavily on a chair. At which she had to get up very quickly,
and soothe Rumpelstiltskin, who, sneaking in unnoticed, had
again got there first.

"I beg your pardon?" stammered Mushla at last when she
had got her voice. She despatched a look towards Grummilla

which meant if anything did, "Keep your mouth shut and you've got him."

"I must have a wife and by tomorrow," continued Baran. "Reasons of State and so on," he explained. "You see it's . . ."

But at that minute there came four heavy bangs from a sword hilt on the door. There were really five bangs, but Baran's servant, who was trying to be very efficient, opened it so quickly that he got the last one himself, and before he could recover Baran had kicked him angrily for being a fool. It wasn't much fun being a servant in those days.

Outside the door was a young man in fine clothes, who strode imperiously into the cottage. To Mushla's surprise Baran, looking very startled, made a low bow.

"Your *Highness!*" he said, and a quick pallor spread all over his lips and as far down his nose as it could get in the time.

"Ah, Baran! Didn't expect me, did you?" said the other masterfully. "I rode out to your camp to meet you and heard you were here." He appeared to notice Mushla and her husband for the first time, and said patronizingly: "Stand at ease, good people! You may carry on." There was no doubt that he was a Prince.

Mushla was too surprised at his sudden arrival to do anything except sink into a chair for the second time in five minutes. On this occasion, however, Rumpelstiltskin, who believed in learning by experience, just made his getaway in time.

"Now Baran," said the Prince, sitting down in the best chair, "about this wife you went to get for me. Where is she?"

Baran stammered and stuttered.

"Don't dare tell me you haven't brought one!" snapped the Prince.

Baran hesitated then began glibly:

"Well, Your Highness, it's a long story . . ."

At that moment the servant, who had been revengefully rubbing his last point of contact with his master, suddenly handed the Prince the box he held with a vindictive grin. Baran recoiled, and whispering fiercely "You're sacked!" went even paler than before.

The Prince opened the box, and a large purple toad with yellow spots crawled out and gazed up at him.

"Hey! What's this?" he gasped, hastily averting his eyes and reciting rather a good exorcism.

Baran collected himself desperately. "Frankly, it *was* Her Royal Highness the Princess of Slovo-Carmania . . ."

The Prince's mouth fell open and he gazed in amazement at the animal. The purple toad looked slightly coy.

"The lady you were bringing back to be my wife?" he demanded.

"Yes. She – er – met with an accident yesterday," continued the Vizier's son, nervously moistening a good deal of his large lips. He had been hoping to avoid this unpleasant scene, but had not expected to see his master so soon, nor had he anticipated his servant's treachery. "A witch," he went on, "with cross-eyes, passed by and appeared to cause Her Highness a good deal of amusement . . ."

"What the dickens," thundered the Prince, "do you think you're at?" He shook the toad, who looked very huffy and then tried to make up for it with a winning smile. It was not a great success. "Are you trying to insinuate that I'm to marry this?" he continued, getting very red about the edges of the face.

As the Prince stood six-foot-two in his hunting boots and was supposed to be the best battleaxe expert in the kingdom, the Vizier's son hurriedly said he wasn't trying to do anything of the sort, in fact nothing had been further from his mind, in fact he . . .

"That's all right then," returned His Highness, mollified, and handed the simpering toad back to the underling who was now keeping well out of range of his late master. "Now, what's it all about?"

"I can explain easily," said Baran, looking wildly round for an explanation. "You see, I . . ."

It was at this point that his eye fell on Grummilla. "It's like this," he said more easily. "Since the accident, I made other arrangements. *This* is Your Highness' future wife." And he indicated Grummilla, who instantly smiled and nodded hopefully.

Mushla drew a deep breath and so far forgot herself as to pat Rumpelstiltskin, who had during the conversation attained the chair once more. Her husband was too astonished to do more than cut a large slice off the forehead of his carving, which suddenly gave it a singularly unprepossessing, not to say sinister, appearance.

"Well, well, well," said the Prince, standing back and surveying Grummilla with great interest. "*That's* more like it." He appeared attracted. "What is your name, my dear?"

Grummilla incautiously replied, and a lump of black stone leapt out onto the floor.

"Great Battleaxes!" cried the Prince, while Baran this time was quite unable to conceal his amazement. He had covered his surprise at Nada's conversational adjuncts fairly well, but now it began to look rather like an epidemic. He passed his hand apprehensively over his own lips to see if he had caught it too.

"Slight indisposition," murmured Mushla, much over-come, trying to smile at the Prince and frown at Grummilla and stare down her husband (who was still absently carving bits off his work with his mouth open) all at the same time.

But the Prince had recovered and was obviously becoming interested in the girl, though politely ignoring her conversational concomitants. He engaged Grummilla in talk, and she, feeling the worst was now known and also having a lot of time to make up, talked till the floor was like a beach. Baran, however, who had picked up one or two words (including one which had fallen on his foot and, as it was "incomprehensibilities", had rather hurt), was studying them closely, looking narrowly at Mushla as he did so.

"Of course," the Prince said at last, trying to stem the output of which he was now rather tired, "I quite understand, Baran, it's certainly a novelty; but you must admit – I mean it'd be awfully inconvenient at Court. Think of the carpets. It's neither ornamental nor useful. I'm sorry," he added to Mushla, "but there it is."

Baran, who, as you have realized by now, was a sharp young man, agreed and added swiftly: "Of course that's only to show Your Highness the idea."

"What idea?"

"Well," cried Baran, as one working up to his big scene, "what about this?"

He flung open the kitchen door to Mushla's dismay and brought in Nada. "*Here* is the wife I really intend for you. She possesses the same – er – trait but in both a useful and ornamental fashion. Just say a few words, my dear," he added anxiously to Nada.

Nada complied, and at her first remark the Prince, as he afterwards put it, fell in love.

Within a few minutes everything was arranged – I said they were quick in those days – and the Royal visitor prepared to depart, having graciously inspected what was left of Mushla's husband's carving and remarked, somewhat tactlessly, that he had often longed to carve gargoyles himself.

Mushla, however, seemed far from pleased at losing Nada and her help in the house, and being left with Grummilla.

"What about Grummilla?" she said anxiously to Baran. "Didn't you say *you* were looking for a wife?"

"So I was," agreed the young man carelessly, "but as you may have guessed, it was for him, not for myself."

"But – but . . ."

"Look here, my good woman," whispered Baran, still in the careless take-it-or-leave-it manner of the true businessman. "I'll tell you what I'll do. If you like to give me a good dowry with this girl, I'll marry her myself. There!"

Mushla thought it over. If Nada was going she was quite anxious to get rid of Grummilla, who would make work in the household and not do it.

"All right," she said.

"What about the dowry?"

"Get a bag," replied Mushla, quite smartly for her, "and I'll ask Nada to recite 'The Wreck of the Hesperus' before she goes . . ."

"No. Something with longer words in it," countered the Vizier's son swiftly.

And that was the end of it. But, as I said, Baran was a very sharp young man. He had realized that diamonds soon ceased to be valuable if they could be made in large sentences. While *coal* was always *coal* – a fact Mushla and her husband had not realized, for coal was both scarce and valuable in that kingdom and practically unknown among the lower classes.

So he married Grummilla as soon as possible and founded the Baran Fuel Supply Company Limited, and did very well. Indeed, in hard winters he used to stay out late at nights so as to get told off at length by his wife when he returned, and thus always had large supplies on hand at favourable prices to cope with the increased seasonal demand.

MALOCCHIO

Eliot Fintushel

Eliot Fintushel (b. 1948) is a teacher and performer of mask and mime and has twice won the US National Endowment for the Arts Solo Performer Award. His short stories and essays have been appearing in American science fiction and literary magazines since 1993. The following story is brand new.

I am a perfect pacifist, but I once gave Joe Galucci the Evil Eye. It was the summer before I entered college, and I was working for Mandrake & Kinsey Seed Company (now defunct). As I sat beside Joe figuring out how many nasturtiums and portulacas to send to the Spend-'n'-Saves of Jasper, Illinois, I whistled discordant sections of *Le Sacre du Printemps*. I tightened my lips for strange oboe solos that only he and I could hear.

"You know, Joe," I'd coo, "every day young people are dying suddenly of unknown causes." Then more whistling.

One time Joe called his mother at coffee break. Meyer, my only friend there, overheard. "*Malocchio*, Mama!" Joe whis-

pered, and Meyer duly reported. He asked her to prepare the
herbal unguent she would rub into his scalp to ward off my
killing gaze. "I'll come right home from work. Don't tell Pop.
Have it ready, okay?"

The bastard did his Spend-'n'-Saves faster than I did – it's a
wonder the efficiency that a lack of grey matter can engender –
and he bragged to me about it constantly. Worse, he had leered
at Helen Wojtczak the day she had met me for lunch; he'd even
had the nerve to come up and introduce himself to her, sidling
between us as if I didn't exist.

Downstairs at the vending machines – Sara Lee crumb-
cakes, hot chocolate, java, Beechies, Life Savers – Joe would
jawjack with the regulars, happily among remedial readers
who knew batting averages and car models (male) or what
lovers hung off what cliffs on which soaps (female). They
laughed, flirted, backslapped, and sneaked out at lunch for a
beer at Slim's. I couldn't go there; I was seventeen, a year shy
of legal. Joe was *eighteen*.

"Hey Al," he japed as he scooped a roll of tropical-flavoured
Life Savers from the maw of the candy machine, "you'll never
be in with the in-crowd, you know that? Never." Suddenly,
my quarters felt like brass knucks in the palm of my hand. I
clenched. I unclenched.

"Don't be mean, Joe," someone scolded. The in-crowd
laughed as I pocketed my knucks and slinked back to my
baloney sandwich and chess with Meyer. Forget the Beechies.
Pax in terra.

When Joe was in the mood, he liked to slap me. Working
beside me at the same long table, looking up numbers on the
same charts, he would cuff me on the back of the head, and
when I turned to look, he'd be smirking in his tote sheets. Our
supervisor never saw a thing.

Myself, I wasn't brought up to be violent. I'd just give Joe a
look. Or whistle.

I think that's why the Imp came to me, empowered me –
instead of a Joe Galucci. When you abstain from things, like
me from fisticuffs, it creates a kind of potential somewhere in
your brain, an unresolved energy that actuates as Imps and
Poltergeists and suchlike. That's how I figure it.

The Imp sneaked up on me while I snoozed in a toilet stall – my quarter-to-noon ritual. I heard him before I saw him: "That Galucci's an imbecile, ain't he?"

"Meyer, is that you?" I woke so suddenly it took me a moment to remember what I was doing sitting on a toilet with my pants up.

"No, I ain't Meyer." It had a voice like a gutted muffler. "Come on out. I got a offer to make you."

I unlatched the stall door. I pushed it open, slipped out, then fell back against it – and whistled.

The Imp winced. "Cut that out!" He was three feet tall and shaped like a clove of garlic. His features were splits in the garlic paper. His eyes were cracks with tiny star anise flowers stuck in them. His crack of a mouth had a pimento peeking out for a tongue. "I hate that. I can't stand that high-pitched ruckus."

His clothes: pissed-on, smoke-stained drapery, from the pompon at the point of his cap to the one at the tip of each slipper. Two ruffled fins snug to the lunule of his piddling bod served for arms, I gathered. What hands he had, if any, were in his pockets.

"Don't upchuck, prithee," he said. "Faint if you like – some do. Help you jetsam old Galooch, is what I'm good for – if you ain't too chickenshit to let me." He slug-slimed nearer on those slick crescent dogs – a neat performance, Disney on ice except for the condom dispenser upstage left.

"What . . . what are you?"

"Deep!" he said. "Take me to Slim's for a gin and tonic, why don'tcha, and I'll draw you a picture." Exactly like magic, the buzzer sounded for lunch. My mind at that point was as lucid as a shovelful of slush. I closed my mouth and led the thing to Slim's.

We took a booth. Nobody ID'ed me – the Imp winked. He ordered us gin and tonics.

"Hey! Who's the chicky?" Galucci sidled by with his Neanderthal pals. "Hubba hubba!" A couple of them winked or blew kisses. The Imp smiled sweetly. They laughed and bellied up to the bar for their lunch.

"They see you as a girl!" I said.

"Deep," he said. "I'm gonna enjoy doing business with you." The drinks came, and he swallowed them both, swizzle-sticks and all. "Call me Buck. I'm an Imp. I seen what you been laying on Joe there, the Evil Eye and that. 'Amateurish stuff,' I tell myself, 'but the kid's got potential.' You got potential, Al. I'm interested in taking you on."

"Taking me on?"

"Thing is – and this is my loss leader, I'm gonna tell you this much strictly gratis – thing is, to give a good Evil Eye, you gotta know the guy you're eyeballing. Every human soul is bound by exactly *three knots*. You gotta see two of a guy's particular knots before you can give 'im an effective Evil Eye."

"Knots?"

"Want another drinky?" He called out an order for another two gin and tonics. "Okay. I'll give you a f'rexample. You. Knot Number One: you always gotta think you're smarter than everybody else, but you actually got the IQ of a turnip, no offence. Knot Number Two: even though you are among the horniest bipeds on Planet Earth – this is Planet Earth, right? – you're gonna die a virgin."

He looked up and smacked his lips. The waitress, than whom I was smarter, and whom I was dying, *per impossibile*, to deflower, spun Buck's tumblers onto the table. He threw them down his throat, insinkerated the swizzle-sticks in his tiny maw, and washed it all down with three or four cardboard coasters that said "Bass Ale" in red and blue. "Them are two of your three knots. Tough luck, kid, but every human's got 'em. Wretched race! Imps rule. Cheers!" He chomped down the glasses.

"Imps rule," I muttered, my heart dark within me. I thought, (1) I do not just imagine that I'm smarter than other people; I *am* smarter. I can't help that. (2) Horny, yes! But I am not going to die a virgin. Matter of fact, I am practically up to second base with Helen Wojtczak, and there are still seven weeks before I leave for college.

So I voiced my thought (3): "Those aren't *my* knots, Buck."

He smiled a petite cedilla of a smile, fading even as it appeared. "Sure, sure! I musta been thinking of somebody else. That's it! I was thinking of somebody else, Al. You got me

dead to rights, buddy! I can't get one past you! But anyways, you
see what I mean. If you wanna do a proper Evil Eye on that
Galucci sap, you gotta find out his knots, see?"

"What's my third one?" I said.

"Damn me if you ain't a Einstein and Solomon rolled into
one, kid! 'What's my third'! You knock me out. Flat cold!
What a horse-trader! Tell you what. You go case Galucci.
Figger his knots, see? Throw him a genuine pro *malocchio*.
Prove yourself. Then I'll give you free access to my entire
brain. Introductory offer. One time only . . . Hey, beautiful,
two more gin 'n' tonics!"

"Wait a minute. I don't want to actually hurt anyone, you
know."

He guffawed pulverized glass onto the tablecloth. "You
crack me up, Al. Drink my gins. I gotta take a powder. When
you done your homework, you know where to find me."

"I mean it. I'm not interested. I don't hate him, Buck. I
don't hate anybody."

A circumflex of a smile. An umlaut of a twinkle. Buck
vanished.

The waitress brought me the two drinks and the tab. I
smiled my irresistibly sexy smile. She grimaced and departed.
I looked at the bill. It was my lunch and bus money.

That evening I played chess with Meyer up by the reservoir.
We squatted between the fluted columns of the Water Authority, right in the middle of the compass engraved on the portico,
me at E, Meyer at W. It was rosy twilight, and from up there
on Weber's Hill we could have watched the city skyline darkle,
if we had cared to look past our pawns and pieces.

"You're nuts, Al," – casually sliding his rook along my first
rank – "but as for the two knots, I gotta say, it rings true.
Check."

"Stupid move." I took his rook.

"Check," he said, moving in from the queen's side.

"Dumb," I said. I took his other rook. "He was a million
miles off. You're nearly as smart as me, Meyer – I know that.
And as for the virgin thing . . . here comes Helen."

"Checkmate," he said. I hadn't seen the knight move. I was

beat after walking home from Mandrake & Kinsey's. I never lost to Meyer unless I was half-asleep. Besides, I'd been thinking about Helen. "Anyway, Al, don't do anything stupid. The summer's half over, you're going to NYU, and Joe's gonna be an office clerk for the rest of his life. Just ignore him. Lay off the Stravinsky. You don't really hate him, do you?"

"Of course not! I don't hate anybody, Meyer. But what if you could really give somebody the Evil Eye? Wouldn't the experiment be worth it?"

"No. Here she comes. Two's company, buddy. See ya!" He scooped the chess pieces into his satchel, folded the board under his arm, and ran off.

I galloped down the sunset side of Weber's Hill to Helen. She was beautiful. She made a blue work shirt and cutoffs look like Cinderella's gown. Her frizzy blonde hair floated like a halo above a Botticelli angel's face. Her nose was a little bigger than Venus' maybe, but I like them that way. Helen Wojtczak had been the queen of my dreams since I almost kissed her at New Year's, and she almost let me.

We walked together up the stone steps of the Water Authority, crossed north, north-west, west-north-west, and I kissed her. "Don't," she said.

I knitted my brows. Helen squeezed my hand with a sisterliness I found alarming, and led me to the circular walk around the reservoir.

"I have something to tell you." She stared down into our long shadows.

"I have something to tell *you*." It was motel night, I'd decided. I wanted to make a liar out of Buck the Imp as soon as possible.

"Al, there's somebody else."

I dropped her hand. I stopped walking. I looked out across the reservoir, through the chain link fence to the fountain spraying antibacterially in the waning light. "Who?"

"It doesn't matter who, Al."

"Yes it does. Tell me who."

"A guy you work with. Remember the day I met you for lunch . . . ?"

★   ★   ★

"I knew you'd come round, Al my boy. Now, to find two of
Galucci's knots – and mind you, I could tell 'em to you, one,
two, but it wouldn't do you no damn good, because you gotta
see 'em for yourself – to find two of them knots of his – and
they're double squares, believe you me, solid as a frigging
Gordian – you just watch him, savvy? Down in the bushes and
tight to the windows, watch his life, Al. Shadow the jerk.
Where he tightens up – that's your baby! You'll see them
knots, four days max . . . How about we get some more of
them gin 'n' tonics at Slim's?"

"No thanks, Buck – what's in this for you?"

"For me? I'm like a big league scout, champ. You'll be a
feather in my cap, see?"

"What league is that?"

"Do you hate this Galucci's guts or not?" He crinkled his
little face. The pale epithelium puckered, split, and curled like
wood shavings. Where they parted, a crimson inner skin
showed through.

"I hate him, all right."

"Then waddaya care about leagues, huh? I'll tell you
everything-plus when Galooch goes down." The lunch
buzzer sounded. Buck chose a new way to disappear. He
collapsed into his own body like a custard pie falling in.
His hat funnelled down his cranium. His head went down
his throat, the throat down his torso, and so on to the pair
of pompons at the tips of his feet. The feet imploded,
sucking in the pompons with a pop! All that remained was
a faint sulphurous odour. Also, the condom machine was
gone.

On the way home from work, on the No. 66 bus, Meyer tried
to console me about Helen. Plenty of fish in the sea, he said.
No skin off my teeth, I said, honest, but I couldn't play chess
that night – some homework to do.

"You think I'm stupid, don't you, Al? I know what you're
up to. You're doing what the damned Imp told you to do.
You're shadowing Joe." He shook his head and moved to
another seat.

I stayed on the bus past Meyer's stop, past mine, and all the
way to midtown. From there I transferred to the one that

would take me across the tracks to Joe Galucci's neighbour-hood.

The first knot was easy. I could hear the ruckus halfway down the block. People on the street looked embarrassed. Mothers hurried their children past the Galuccis' house. Neighbours shut their windows.

Not me. I made straight for Joe's. Down in the bushes, tight to the windows, I watched Joe Galucci's life.

Next day Buck debriefed me by the bathroom sink. "His father's a drunk, right?" I said.

"And . . . ?"

"He beats Joe's mother. I heard her cry. I heard him yell."

"And . . . ?" Buck plumbed a hole I took to be a nostril and produced a small diamond. He examined it briefly, then flicked it onto the floor, where it turned into a dustball and skittered away.

"And – what?" I said.

"What about Joe?"

"Joe shouted at his father. He tried to break it up. There were a few slaps and broken dishes; then Mr Galucci stomped out. I listened by the back window – Joe tried to get his mother to leave the bum. Joe and his mom were both crying."

"His father beats her up all the time, Buck. Joe's desperate to stop it."

"He can't," Buck crowed. "That's the knot. He wants to save her, but he never will, because she don't wanna be saved. It's a beaut, ain't it? That's Number One."

"I think it's kind of sad."

"Don't give me that crap!" Buck started undulating, bottom to top, and each time the wave reached the tip of his conical hat, a puff of smoke came out. "You want me to tell you what he did after you left? Her initials are *Helen Wojtczak* . . ."

"That bastard!"

"Exactly. He took the pot with all your ante sittin' there, Al. He shot the moon."

"Yeah, well, I'll euchre him!"

"That's the spirit! One more knot to go!" Just like a Cocteau movie, Buck dissolved into the mirror over the sink, gooey

black and white rippling surface and all. I saw him dwindle
into that strange world where there was a league in which I was
about to be a rookie.

The lunch buzzer sounded. I had a big appetite.

"I'll beat you at chess." Meyer sidled in next to me on the No.
66 bus and fished out his wallet chess set – tiny, flat leather
pieces in a square of slots.

"Dream on," I said, and I pushed the king's pawn.

"Galucci looks bad. He was quiet today. Did you do it, Al?
Did you give him the Eye?"

"No. I'm gonna, though, as soon as I figure out one of his
other knots."

"He's got a date with Helen at the main library at six. I
heard him on the phone – watch your queen, Al."

"I am watching my queen. You watch your queen . . . The
library? What would Galucci do at a library?"

"Back issues of *The Auto Trader* – who knows? . . . There it
goes: you lost it, Al." He slid a rook pawn next to my queen.
My queen had nowhere left to go.

"I don't wanna play any more." I slapped the chess set
closed. "I have to think about something."

Meyer frowned. "You wanna know what your third knot is,
Al?"

"No, I don't. How would you know, anyway?"

"I know." He got up and stood by the rear door until his
stop. I stayed on till the library.

I spotted them in Business and Finance. I slipped among
the shelves and cleared a view between the SATRAPY–TORT and
XYZ volumes of a legal encyclopedia. They sat at a table by a
window overlooking the river. She was more beautiful than
ever, the way girls get when they're next to another guy, as if
the guy were a kleig light shining right on her.

I could see her dimpled knees under the table, pressed
against Galucci's. The way I was feeling, I could have im-
pregnated Helen all the way from Philosophy, Religion and
Education, fifty yards distant. And I could have decked Joe
from Geography and History on the next floor.

He was wearing glasses. I'd never seen him wear glasses. He

stared into a thick book and jotted down notes in a spiral pad next to it. Helen talked, turned pages for him, and stroked his hair. At one point he slammed the book shut, pulled off his glasses, and marched to the window in a huff. Helen followed him. She slid her arm around his waist. He laid his head on her shoulder. They disappeared into an aisle that connected to Sports and Recreation.

I sneaked up to their table to see what Joe had been squinting at – *Principles of Accountancy* by Warren and Beasley.

"That's Number Two!" Buck straddled the transom, trimming his fingers – his fingers, not his nails – trimming them to the middle joint of their seven. For the Imp, this was nonchalance. I watched the fingertips fall to the floor where they dried and curled in seconds, like a time-lapse film of desiccating carrots. "He ain't up to accountancy. Not enough smarts. He'll die feeling like a failure on account of he'll never get the hang of double entries. Wretched race! Imps rule." Snip! Snip!

"Poor bastard!"

"Tell me again what they was doing in Sports and Recreation . . . ?"

It was burned into my memory: Helen and Joe like DNA strands – God forbid! – double-helixing between bound volumes of *Sports Illustrated*. "Right!" I said. "*Malocchio!*"

"That's my boy! Just dig into him with them lovely weepers of yours. The knots are like landmarks on a bombardier's map." Snip!

For the first time in weeks, I was at my desk when lunchtime came. Joe moped beside me. He hadn't struck me for days. You could almost take him for a human being, sitting there dragging a pencil across the order forms.

I figured it was time to elicit some of Galucci's ill-will, just to remind me what I was in it for: "Hey, Galooch! How's the CPA today?"

He half smiled. For a moment I thought he was going to cry. Then the buzzer sounded for lunch. He just sat there as everyone else filed out. "Joe," I said, "aren't you going to Slim's with your friends?"

"They ain't my friends. Nobody gives a flying petootie about me, Al. I'm sick of playing the game."

And there it was – Knot Number Three. He wasn't in with the in-crowd.

When I went out onto the loading dock for a smoke after lunch, Buck was there, sucking the air from the tyres of parked cars. He'd balloon up like a blood-pressure band and his little feet would start to levitate while he French-kissed a valve. Then he'd let go and jet around the parking lot, insanely laughing.

After four or five cars, he slid over to the loading dock and sat down next to me. He clicked valve caps palm to palm as if they were a rosary. "So, are we ready for action or what?"

I watched my cigarette smoulder. "I found the third knot . . ."

Buck backfired. Black smoke billowed from his pores. "You dumb human! Damn your race! Two, I told you! Two!"

"But I couldn't help it, Buck. It was right there . . ."

"Don't tell me! I don't wanna hear it!" He stuffed his fingers into his ears all the way up to the fourth joint. The valve caps tumbled. "I know all about it, damn it! I know everybody's knots, you dumb human! Imps rule! Just clam up! Go do the *malocchio*, is all! Don't think about it, Al! Do it now!"

"I can't go through with it, Buck."

"You what?" He stopped hiccuping. "I knew it! Damn your race!" His eyes widened like little missile silos. The sulphur smell intensified. The air between us seemed to yellow.

"Listen, Buck. I appreciate all your help, but now that I really know Joe, now that I see his three knots, I can't hate him any more. I don't want to give him the Evil Eye, Buck."

A thin stream of black smoke issued from the pompon at the peak of Buck's hat. "You know what happens to people who get the Evil Eye? Things go wrong, Al, things that are no-body's fault, see? Little things can make a big difference, Al. Half a second crossing the street. The wrong knob on a stove top. You catch my drift, Al? Look . . ."

Buck levelled his gaze at a pigeon gliding down toward the

loading dock. It fluttered erratically, then slammed into a concrete pier and dropped straight down, its neck broken.

"Y'see," Buck said, "that can happen to humans too. It could happen to you, Al, if you ain't careful – say, if you rubbed me the wrong way or something. Not that you'd be that stupid."

"Jesus, Buck, don't you ever feel sorry for anybody? Don't Imps have knots?"

"Yeah, but just one, not three, and nobody ever finds out. Ever. Imps rule. Galucci gets *malocchioed*, or you do. Think about it, Al. I'll see you after."

I butted my smoke and shoved through the bumpered double doors into the shipping room. Meyer was there. His chessboard dangled by a corner from one hand. The pieces littered the floor at his feet. "I saw him. I heard everything. I can't believe it. He's an Imp! He's really an Imp!" The chessboard fell.

"Yeah, so now what?" I walked past him toward the corridor and the vending machines.

"Wait up!" He ran after me, leaving the chess pieces where they lay. He grabbed my shoulder. "Imps don't rule, Al. You got him! Don't you see that? He's completely helpless!"

"You're nuts, Meyer. If I don't do what he wants, he'll do a *malocchio* on me. I'll end up like the pigeon. What am I supposed to do – get Joe Galucci's mother to rub oil in my hair? I've got to give Joe the Evil Eye, and that's that." I pulled my shoulder from under Meyer's hand.

He stepped in front of me and blocked my way. I could hear people chattering by the vending machines now. I looked past Meyer to see if I could spot Joe.

"Don't you get it, Al? Don't you know why he wouldn't let you tell him about Joe's third knot?"

"Get out of my way, Meyer." Through a doorway, I saw Joe's brogues sticking out under a chair by the coke machine. I pushed Meyer out of my way and walked to the doorway. Joe looked up. I looked down.

He slapped me, I thought. *He makes fun of me. He thinks he's smarter than I am, faster than I am. He stole my girl.*

I hurtled through his eyes. Everything grew as hazy and dim

as the sun to a deep-sea diver. In the tunnel behind Joe Galucci's eyes, I saw neon figures – his drunken father raging, the bruised mother weeping. I sped in past a phantom Joe Galucci beating his fists against the tunnel wall and tearing incomprehensible pages out of a thick book. At the tunnel's end was a soft red spot like a target painted on a rifle-range dummy.

I hesitated. At my back I heard Meyer's voice – "Don't, Al!" – and for the briefest moment I saw the third knot: Joe Galucci alone in himself, Joe Galucci blinkering himself to his loneliness and despair, aching to blend in with the in-crowd. He had fallen behind while they laughed over Seven-and-Sevens at Slim's . . .

"What do you want, Al?" A pained expression crossed Joe's face.

"You got change of a dollar?" I couldn't do it.

The coke bottle in Joe Galucci's hand boiled over into his lap. A thick, bubbling, yellow fluid seethed down his legs and onto the floor. He stood.

"Run, Joe!" I yanked him up by the elbow. Searing fumes rose from the puddle. The three or four people who had been grazing at the candy machines stampeded out. I pushed Joe out along with them – he didn't resist. Meyer stood beside me as the fumes congealed into a child-sized clove of garlic.

"You've had it!" Buck levelled his smoky red eyes at me, and I felt that my world was haemorrhaging. Everything turned bad and drained away.

"No," Meyer shouted. "*You've* had it, Imp! My friend Al has a temper like nobody's business. He keeps it on a leash. He's fooled everybody. He's even fooled himself. He thinks he's a pacifist! He thinks he can't hate. But you better look out, Mr Imp!"

Buck staggered backwards. His face twitched. He looked at me, then covered his eyes with a freshly defingered paw. He seemed to cave in as my world swelled back into existence. "Wretched race!" he spat, but now there was pity in it, as if he perceived the precious eye of a needle through which I could never squeeze, because I was a barren, hateful egotist: my three knots!

Knots or no, I could still whistle. I remembered how it had made him wince. I whistled a glissando from as low and loose as I could pucker, sliding up in pitch until the plaster walls and concrete floor of that basement room resonated. The vending machines and the fluorescents kicked in, and the room became one large tuning fork. Buck's little face scrunched like a burnt raisin.

"Humans rule!" Meyer crowed.

"Stop it! Stop it!" Buck swirled down into the puddle like a tornado in reverse. The puddle of Buck froze, shattered, and vanished.

Meyer and I sat together on the No. 66 bus.

"That's the last we'll see of Buck," Meyer sighed. "We found the Imp's knot, don't you see? Same as you, Al: to do a *malocchio*, he has to know his victim, but the more he knows him, the less he wants to hurt him. It's a razor's edge. Two knots is just enough to be able to do his dirt. That's why he got so worked up when you were about to tell him Joe's third."

"Same as with *my* knots. He only pretended to know the third one."

"Now you're getting it!"

"I figured that all along, Meyer, you sap."

"When I told Buck your third knot, he was finished. He didn't have the heart to hurt you any more. Even Imps have feelings, Al."

"I hope the little shit comes back. I'll give him something to feel, all right."

Meyer flipped open his pocket chess set and pushed the white king's pawn two spaces forward. "Better do it quick, before you get to know him."

Here's the falling action: I was best man at Joe Galucci's wedding. God knows what Helen sees in him! I've been trying to lure her into adultery ever since, but she hasn't bitten yet. I live alone in the next town, a pillar of the local chapter of the Fellowship of Reconciliation. I work for Meyer, whom I'd still beat regularly at chess, him and all his sons, if the bastards didn't cheat.

I've had no further commerce with Imps. Sometimes I wonder if the whole thing ever really happened. After all, those "knots" of mine were complete baloney. In fact, I'd be one happy fellow if whoever lets the air out of my tyres every morning would just lay the hell off.

THE METROGNOME

Alan Dean Foster

*In the previous volume I reprinted one of the Mad Amos
Malone stories by Alan Dean Foster (b. 1946). Foster is so
prolific and so diverse it was difficult to know what to select
from the richness of his work, and in the end I have chosen the
title story from his collection* The Metrognome and Other
Stories *(1990). For a while Foster was probably best known
as the novelizer of major sf and fantasy movies including* Dark
Star *(1974) and* Alien *(1979), but he proved he had his own
voice in the popular Spellsinger series – Spellsinger at the
Gate *(1983), The Day of the Dissonance *(1984), The
Moment of the Magician *(1984), The Path of the Peram-
bulator *(1985), The Time of the Transference *(1986), Son
of Spellsinger *(1993) and Chorus Skating *(1994). He has
also edited the anthologies of humorous fantasy* Smart Dragons, Foolish Elves *(1991) and* Betcha Can't Read Just One
(1991). You may also want to check out Mad Amos *(1996)
and* Jed the Dead *(1996).*

Charlie Dimsdale stared at the man in front of him. Even under ordinary circumstances Charlie Dimsdale would have stared at the man in front of him. However, this confrontation was taking place in the lowest level of the Fifty-Second Street Bronx subway line, a good many metres beneath the hysterical surface of Manhattan. It was just short of preordained that Charlie Dimsdale would stare at the man in front of him.

The man in front of Charlie Dimsdale stood slightly over a metre high. He was broad out of all proportion in selected places. His head especially was even larger than that of a normal-sized man. Its most notable feature was a proboscis that would be flattered by the appellation bulbous. This remarkable protuberance was bordered by a pair of huge jet-black eyes that hid beneath black eyebrows a Kodiak bear would have been proud of. Two enormous floppy ears, the shape and colour of dried apricots, fluttered sideways from the head, their span a truly impressive sight.

The pate itself was as bald and round as the bottom of a china teacup. A good portion of it was covered by a jaunty red beret set at a rakish angle to the left. Huge black muttonchop whiskers rambled like a giant caterpillar across his face.

Arms that were too long for the short torso ended in thick, stubby fingers. Black hair, well cultivated, grew there in profusion. In addition to the beret, he wore a double-breasted pinstripe jacket with matching trousers. His black Oxfords were immaculately polished.

Had such a confrontation occurred anywhere else in the world with an appropriate Dimsdale substitute, it is likely that said Dimsdale substitute would have fainted quickly away. Charlie Dimsdale, however, merely gulped and took a step backward.

After all, this was New York.

The little man put his hirsute hands on his hips and stared back at Charlie with undisguised disgust.

"Well, you've seen me. Now what are you going to do about it?"

"Seen you? Do? Look, mister, I'm only . . . my name's Charles Dimsdale. I'm second assistant inspector to the undercommissioner for subway maintenance and repair. There's a misaligned track down here. We've had to make three consecutive computer reroutings up top" (this was official slang, of course) "for three different trains. I'm to see what the trouble is and to try and correct it, is all."

Charlie was a rather pleasant if unspectacular-appearing young man. He might even have been considered attractive if it weren't for his mousy attitude and those glasses. They weren't quite thick enough to double as reactor shielding.

"Uh . . . did I just see you walk out of that wall?"

"Which wall?" the man asked.

"That wall, behind you."

"Oh, that wall."

"Yes, that wall. I didn't think there was an inspection door there, but . . ."

"There isn't. I did."

"That's impossible," said Charlie reasonably. "People don't go around walking through walls. It isn't done. Even Mr Broadhare can't walk through walls."

"I don't doubt it."

"Then how can you stand there and maintain you walked through that wall?"

"I'm not human. I'm a gnome. A metrognome, to be specific."

"Oh. I guess that's okay, then."

At that point, New Yorker or no, Charlie fainted.

When he came to, he found himself staring into a pair of slightly glowing coal-black eyes. He almost fainted again, but surprisingly powerful arms assisted him to his feet.

"Now, don't do that to me again," said the gnome.

"It's very rude and disconcerting. You might have hit your head on the rail and hurt yourself."

"What rail?" asked Charlie groggily.

"That one, there, in the middle."

"Ulp!" Charlie took several steps back until he was standing on the walkway. "You're right. I really could have hurt myself. I won't do it again." He looked disapprovingly at the gnome. "You aren't helping things any, you know. Why don't you vanish? There're no such things as gnomes. Even in New York. Especially in New York."

"Ha!" grunted the gnome. He said it in such a way as to imply that among those assembled, there was one possessed of about as many brains as a stale pretzel. The big, soft kind, with plenty of salt. Someone was full of dough. Charlie had no trouble isolating him.

"Look," he said imploringly, "you simply can't *be!*"

"Then how the deuce am I?" The gnome stuck out a hairy paw. "Look, my name's Van Groot."

"Charmed," said Charlie, dazedly shaking the proffered palm.

Here I am, he thought, thirty metres below the ground in the middle of Manhattan, shaking hands with a character who claims to be out of the Brothers Grimm named Van Groot who wears Brooks Brothers suits.

But he *had* seen him walk out of a wall.

This suggested two possibilities.

One, it was really happening and there were indeed such creatures as gnomes. Two, he'd been breathing subway exhaust fumes too long and was operating on only one cylinder. At the moment he inclined to the latter explanation.

"I know how you must feel," said Van Groot sympathetically. "Come along with me for a bit. The exercise should clear your head. Even if, De Puyster knows, there's probably not much in it, anyway."

"Sure. Why not? Oh, wait a minute. I've got to find and clear that blocked switch."

"Which switchover is it?" the gnome inquired.

"Four-six-three. It's been jumped to indicate a blocked track, and thus the computer automatically —"

"I know."

"— several alternate programs . . . you know?"

"Sure. I'm the one who set it."

"*You* reset it? You can't do that!"

Van Groot said "Ha!" again, and Charlie decided that if nothing else he was not overwhelming this creature with his precision of thought.

"Okay. *Why* did you move it?"

"It was interfering with the smooth running of our mine carts."

"*Mine carts!* There aren't any mi–" he hesitated. "I see. It was interfering with your mine carts." Van Groot nodded approvingly. Charlie had to hop and skip occasionally to keep up with the gnome's short but brisk stride.

"Uh, why couldn't your mine carts just go over the switch when it was correctly set?"

"Because," the gnome explained, as one would to a child, "that way, the metal kept whispering 'blocked! blocked!' This upset the miners. They work very closely with metal, and they're sensitive to it. With the switch thrown this way, the rails murmur 'open, open', and the boys feel better."

"But that seems like such a small thing."

"It is," said Van Groot.

"That's not very polite."

"Now, why should we be polite? Do you ever hear anyone say, 'Let's take up a collection for needy gnomes'? Is there a Save the Gnomes League? Or a Society for the Prevention of Cruelty to Gnomes? When was the last time you heard of someone doing something for a gnome, any gnome!" Van Groot was getting excited. His ears flapped, and his whiskers bristled. "Canaries and fruit-fly researchers can get government money, but us? All we ask are our unalienable rights to life, liberty, plenty of fights, and booze!"

This isn't getting me anywhere, thought Charlie cogently.

"I admit it seems inequitable," he said. Van Groot seemed to calm down a little. "But I'd still appreciate it if you'd let me shift the track back the way it belongs."

"I told you, it would be inconvenient. You humans never learn. Still, you seem like such a nice, pleasant sort . . . for a human. Properly deferential, too. I may consider it. Just consider it, mind."

"That's very decent of you. Uh," (how does one make small talk with a gnome?) "nice weather we're having, isn't it?" Someone had thrown a beer can out of a subway car window. Charlie stepped down off the walkway to remove the can from the tracks.

"Not particularly."

"I thought all you people lived in Ireland and places like that."

"Ireland, my myopic friend, is cold, wet, rainy, uncivilized, and full of crazy American émigrés. About the only thing you can mine there in quantity is peat. Speaking as a miner, let me tell you that it's pretty hard to take pride in your profession when all you mine is peat. Did you ever see a necklace made of peat? A queen's tiara? And it takes a lousy facet. Ireland! That's our trade, you know. We're mostly miners and smiths."

"Why?"

"That's about the stupidest question I've ever heard."

"Sorry."

"Do you think we'd ignore a whole new world and leave it to you humans? When your noisy, sloppy, righteous ancestors paddled across, we came, too. Unobtrusively, of course. Why, there were gnomes with Washington at Valley Forge! With Jones on the –"

"Well, I can certainly understand that," said Charlie hastily, "but I thought you preferred the country life."

"By and large most of us do. But you know how it is. The world's becoming an urban society. We have to change, too. I've got relatives upstate you wouldn't *believe*. They still think they can live like it's Washington Irving's day. Reactionaries."

Charlie tried to conceive of a reactionary gnome and failed.

"And good gem mines are getting harder and harder to find out in the country. All the surface ones are being turned into tourist traps. It's hard enough to find a decent place to sleep any more, what with one petroleum engineer after another doing seismic dowsing. Any idiot could tell you there's no oil at ninety percent of the places they try. But will they learn? No! So it's boom, boom, boom, night after night. The subways are mild and consistent by contrast."

"Whoa. You mean you do mining . . . right here in Manhattan?"

"*Under* Manhattan. Oh, we've found some excellent spots! Go down a little way and the gem-bearing rock is plentiful. Check your New York history. Excavators often turn up fair-quality stones. But no one bothers to dig farther because their glass tomb or pyramid or whatever is on a deadline. Tourmaline, beryl, the quartz gems . . . they've turned up in the foundations of some pretty famous buildings. The rarer, more valuable stuff is buried farther down. Even so, the Empire State Building almost did become a mine. But we got to the driller who found the diamonds."

Charlie swallowed.

"And there's plenty of scrap metal. We turn it into sceptres and things. Mostly to keep in practice. There isn't much of a market for cast-iron sceptres."

"I can imagine," said Charlie sympathetically.

"Still, you never know when you'll need a good sceptre. Or a proper Flagan-flange."

"Pardon my ignorance –"

"I've been doing that for half an hour."

"– but what is a Flagan-flange?"

"Oh, they're used to attract . . . but never mind. About that scrap metal and such. We're very concerned about our environment. Gnomes are good for the ecology."

"Uh." Charlie was running a possible scenario through his mind. He saw himself reporting to Undercommissioner Broadhare. "I've fixed that jammed switch, sir. The gnomes moved it because it was interfering with their mine carts. But I don't want you to prosecute them because they're good for the ecology."

"Right, Dimsdale. Just stand there. Everything's going to be all right."

Oh, yeah.

"But I would have imagined . . ." He waved an uncertain hand at Van Groot. "Well, just look at yourself!"

The gnome did. "What did you expect? Green leaves, lederhosen, and a feather cap? You know, Manhattan is one of the few places in the world where we can occasionally slip out and mix with humans without starting a riot. Always at night, of course. Are you sure you haven't seen any of us? We're very common around Times Square and the theatre district."

Charlie thought. Below the Flatiron Building at one a.m.?

On a bench in Washington Square? A glimpse here, a reflection in a window there? Who *would* notice?

After all, this was New York.

"I see. Do all you city gnomes –"

"Metrognomes," corrected Van Groot placidly.

"Do all you metrognomes dress like that?"

"Sharp, isn't it? Cost me a pretty penny, too. Double-knit, special cut, of course. I can't exactly wear something right off the rack. No, it depends on your job. I'm sort of an administrator. An executive, if you will. Dress also depends on where you live. The gnomes that work under Dallas affect Stetsons and cowboy boots. Those that live under Miami are partial to sun shorts and big dark glasses. And you should *see* the gnomes that live under a place called the Sunset Strip in Los Angeles!" He shook his Boschian baldness. "We're here."

They'd halted in front of a switching section of track. Charlie could see the red warning light staring steadily up-tunnel, a baleful bloody eye.

The silence was punctuated abruptly by a low-pitched rumbling like thunder. It grew steadily to a ground-shaking roar.

A clumsy, huge old-fashioned mine cart, built to half scale, came exploding out of the far wall. Two gnomes were pushing it from behind while another pulled and guided the front. The lead gnome had pure white hair and a three-foot beard that trailed behind him like a pennant.

The cart careened crazily down and over the tracks, threatening to overturn every time it hit the ground. Somehow it seemed to flow over the rails. The three gnomes wore dirty coveralls and miners' hard hats with carbide lamps. The cart was piled high with gleaming, uncut gemstones and what looked like an archaic washer-dryer. The lead gnome had just enough time for a fast wave to them before the apparition disappeared into the near wall. The rumble died away slowly. It reminded Charlie of the sound his garbage disposal made when it wanted to be petulant.

"Well, what are you waiting for? Switch it back."

"What?" said Charlie dazedly. "You mean I can?"

"Yes. Now hurry up, before I change my mind."

Charlie stumbled over and threw the manual switch. The heavy section of track slid ponderously into place, and the warning light changed to a beneficent leafy green. It would show green now on the master layout in the controller's office.

"Now," said Van Groot with enough force to startle Charlie, "you owe *me* a favour!"

"Yeah. Sure. Uh . . . what did you have in mind?" said Charlie apprehensively, calling up images of blood-sucking and devil sacrifice.

"I don't mind telling you that things have been getting rather edgy down here. What with one skyscraper after another going up. And now you're expanding the subways again. I can't promise what might happen. One of these days someone's going to drive a shaft right down into one of our diggings and we'll have another strike on our hands."

"Happen? Strike?"

"Boy, you sure are eloquent when you get humming. Sure. Gnomes aren't known for their even tempers, you know. When gnomes go on strike, they've got nothing to do but cause mischief. The last one we had was back in . . ." He murmured a date that momentarily had no meaning to Charlie.

Then, "Hey, wasn't that the week of the big blackout, across the north-east?"

"Well, you know how strikes spread. The boys under Pittsburgh and Boston got together with some power plant gnomes and . . . It was a terrible mess! Most awkward!"

"Awkward! Good grief, another few days of that and . . ."

Van Groot nodded soberly. "Exactly. Some of us finally appealed to the boys' reason, moral fibre, and good nature. When that didn't work, we got most of 'em dead drunk, and the executive committee repaired a lot of the damage."

"No wonder the engineers could never figure out what caused it."

"Oh, they made up excuses. Didn't stop them from taking credit for fixing the trouble," said Van Groot. "But then, who expects gratitude from humans?"

"You expect something like that might happen again? That would be awful!"

The gnome shrugged. "That depends on your point of view." He flicked away cigar ash daintily. "As a matter of fact, it so happens that this new addition to your system –"

"It's not *my* system!"

"Yes. Anyhow, we've got a pretty nice chrysoberyl and emerald mine –"

"Emerald mine!"

"– right under the intersection of Sixth Avenue and Sixteenth Street. That mean anything to you?"

"Why no, I . . . no, wait a minute. That's where . . .?" He goggled at Van Groot.

"Yep. The new Bronx-Manhattan tunnel is going through just south of there. That's not the problem. It's the new express station that's set to go in –"

"Right over your mine," whispered Charlie.

"The boys are pretty upset about it. They read the *Times*. It's a pretty explosive situation, Dimsdale. Explosive." He looked hard at Charlie.

"But what do you expect *me* to do? I'm only second assistant inspector to the undercommissioner for subway maintenance and repair. I haven't got the power to order changes in things like station locations and routings and stuff!"

"That's not *my* problem," said Van Groot.

"But they're scheduled to start blasting for that station . . . my God, the day after tomorrow!"

"That's what I hear." Van Groot sighed. "Too bad. I don't know what'll happen this time. There's been talk of getting together with the Vermont and New Hampshire gnomes. They want to pour maple syrup into all the telephone cables and switches between Great Neck and Ottawa. A sticky situation, I can tell you!"

"But you can't –" Van Groot looked at Charlie as though he were examining a special species of earthworm.

"Yes, you can."

"That's better," said Van Groot. "I'll do what I can. But while I disagree with the boys' methods, I sympathize with their sentiments. They took an emerald out of there once that was . . ." He paused. "Best I can give you is about twenty-four hours. No later than twelve o'clock tomorrow night."

"Why twelve?" asked Charlie inanely.

"It's traditional. If you've managed to help any, I'll meet you back here. If not, go soak your head."

"Look, I told you, I'm only a second assistant to —"

"I remember. I'm not responsible for your failings. Your problem."

"Tomorrow's Saturday. On Sundays I always call my mother in Greenville. If you gum up the telephone lines, I won't be able to."

"And the chairman of the board of General Computers, who usually calls his mistress in Geneva on Sunday mornings, won't be able to, either," said Van Groot. "It'll be a very democratic crisis. Remember, midnight tomorrow."

Puffing mightily on the cigar and ignoring Charlie's entreaties, the gnome executive disappeared into the near wall of the tunnel.

The morning was cool and clear. On Saturday mornings Charlie usually went first to the Museum of Natural History. Then off to the Guggenheim to see if anything new had come in during the week. From there it was down to the Village for a quick tour through Heimacker's Acres of Books bookstore. Then home, where he would treat himself to an expensive TV dinner instead of the usual fried chicken or Swiss steak. Out to a film or concert and then home.

Today, however, his schedule was markedly altered. He went to the museum on time. The usual thrill wasn't there. Even the exhibits of north-western Indian dugouts failed to excite him as they usually did. Instead of envisioning himself perched in the bow, harpoon poised for the whale kill, he saw himself crouched in the rear, paddling furiously to escape the hordes of angry gnomes that were chasing him in birch-bark canoes. And when he looked at the always imposing skeleton of the Tyrannosaurus Rex and saw Undercommissioner Broadhare's sour puss in the grinning skull, he decided it was definitely time to depart.

He made up a speech. He'd walk straight into Commissioner Feely's office, powerful and insistent, and say, "Look here, Feely. You've got to shift the new Sixth Avenue station from the north to the south side of the tracks, because if you don't, the gnomes will destroy our great telephone network with maple syrup and —"

Charlie moaned.

He was still moaning when he stumbled out of the museum. The stone lions that guarded the portals watched him go. He headed for the Guggenheim out of habit but found himself instead wandering aimlessly through Central Park.

Let's see. He could sneak into the planning office and burn the station blueprints. No, that wouldn't do. They were bound to have plenty of copies. Charlie had to fill out three copies of a form himself just to requisition a box of paper clips.

He could sneak into the station site and try to sabotage the construction machinery. That would delay things for a while. Except he didn't think he knew enough about the machinery to successfully bust any of it. He'd never been very mechanically inclined. In fact, he'd failed handicrafts miserably in high school. Everything he had tried to make had turned out to be a napkin holder.

How about using the site to stage a rally for the admission of Nationalist China to the UN? That was always sure to draw a noisy, rambunctious crowd. They might even sabotage the construction gear themselves! He knew a friend who was faintly associated with the John Birch Society who might . . . no, that wouldn't work. Rightist radicals would hardly be the group to get to try to halt construction of *anything*.

Besides, they were all only temporary. Delaying tactics. Also, he could go to jail for any one of them. A prospect that enthralled him even less than missing his regular Sunday call to his mother in Greenville.

Dinnertime rolled around, and he still hadn't thought of anything. He was reminded of the real world by the smell of incinerating frozen veal cordon bleu. The delicately carbonized odour permeated his tiny living room. The unappetizing result in his stove was not calculated to improve his humour, already bumping along at a seasonally low ebb.

What he did was most unusual. For Charlie it was unique. He dug down, deep, deep into the bowels of his cupboards, past countless cans of Mr Planter's peanuts, down past an immaculate cocktail shaker, never used since its purchase three years ago, down past things better left unmentioned, until he found a hair of the dog.

Never more than a social drinker – mostly at official company functions – Charlie thought a few sips might sharpen his thoughts. It seemed to work for old Agent X-14 regularly every Friday evening on channel 3. So he sipped delicately and carefully. For variety, he alternated bottles. They were friendly dogs, indeed. Warm and cuddly, like a Maltese. Shortly thereafter they were rather more like a couple of playful Saint Bernards. And very shortly thereafter he was in no condition to aspire to any analogies at all.

Actually, he hadn't intended to get drunk. It was, however, an inescapable by-product of his drinking. He ran out of sippables in what seemed indecently short order.

He threw on his raincoat – it wasn't raining, but you never knew, he thought belligerently – and headed in search of more follicles of the pooch. It was sheer good fortune he didn't start for the pound.

On the way he had the fortune and misfortune to encounter Miss Overshade in the hallway. Miss Overshade occupied the apartment across the hall from Charlie, on the good side of the building. She was a local personality of some note, being the weather lady on the early news on channel 8. She had at one time been voted Miss Continental Shelf by the Port of New York Authority and currently held the title Miss High-Pressure Area from the New York Council of Meteorologists.

In point of fact she actually *was* constructed rather along the lines of an especially aesthetic gathering of cumulus clouds. She noticed Charlie, sort of.

"Good evening, Mister . . . uh, Mister . . ."

"Dimsdale," mumbled Charlie. "Dimsdale."

"Oh, yes! How are you, Mister Dimsdale?" Without pausing to learn if he was on the brink of a horrible death, she vanished into her apartment. That voice was calculated to bring on the monsoon. For all she cares, he thought, I might as well be a . . . a gnome.

He hurried down the stairs, insulting the elevator.

*   *   *

At seven sharp Charlie was perusing the soluble delights of an aged and not-so-venerable establishment known as Big Swack's Bar. Currently, he existed in a state of blissful inebriation that followed a thin path betwixt nirvana and hell. For the nonce, nirvana prevailed.

Charlie had a thought, grappled with it. It was brought on by something Van Groot had said. He looked at it hard, piercingly, turning it over in his mind and searching for cracks. It squirmed, trying to get away. He was careful, because he'd seen other things tonight that hadn't been at all real. This thought, however, was.

He left so fast, he forgot to collect the change from his last drink. An occasion that so astonished the proprietor, "Big Swack" – whose real name was Hochmeister – that he talked of nothing else for days afterward.

"Jonson, Jonson! Bill Jonson!" Charlie hammered unmelodically on the door.

Bill Jonson was a sandy-haired, rather sandy-faced young geologist who occasionally shared with Charlie a pallid sandwich in the equally pallid Subway Authority cafeteria. He did not need minutes to observe that his friend was not his usual bland self.

"Charlie? What the hell's the matter with you?"

Now, Charlie was somewhat coherent because on the way up to his friend's abode he'd had enough sense to ingest three Sober-ups. These were chased downstream consecutively by water, half a Pepsi, and an orange drink of sufficient sweetness to destroy any self-respecting molar inside a month. As a result, his mind cleared at the expense of his stomach, which was starting to cloud over.

"Listen, Bill! Can you take a . . . a sounding, a reading, a . . . you know. To determine if there's something special in the ground? Like a big hollow place?"

"I suspect a big hollow place, and it's not in the ground. Come back tomorrow maybe, Charlie, huh? I've got company, you know?" He sort of tried a half grin, half blink. It made him look like a man suffering an attack of the galloping gripes.

"Bill, you've got to take this sounding! You *can* take one?

I've heard you mention it before. Pay attenti – hic! – man! This is important! Think of the telephone company!"

"I'd rather not. I got my bill two days ago. Now, be a good chap, Charlie, and run along. It can wait till Monday. And I *have* got company."

Charlie was desperate. "Just answer me. Can you take a sounding?"

"You mean test the substrata, like I do for the Subway Authority?"

"Yeah! That!" Charlie danced around excitedly. This did not inspire Bill to look on his friend with favour.

"You've got to take one for me!"

"A reading? You're drunk!"

"Certainly not!"

"Then why are you leaning to the left like that?"

"I've always been a liberal. Listen, you know the new station they're planning to build for the extended Bronx–Manhattan line? The one at Sixth and Sixteenth?"

"I've heard about it. That's more your department than mine, you know."

"Indirectly. You've got to come down and take a reading there. Now, tonight. I . . . I've reason to suspect that the ground there is unstable."

"You are crazy. There's no real unstable ground in Manhattan unless you count some of the bars in the Village. It's practically solid granite. Do you have any idea what time it is, anyway?" He looked pointedly at his watch. "My God, it's nearly eight-thirty!"

This unsubtle hint did not have the intended effect on Charlie.

"My God," he echoed, looking in the general vicinity of his own timepiece, "it *is* nearly eight-thirty! We've got to hurry! We've only got till twelve!"

"I'm beginning to think you've got even less than that," said Bill.

"Who does?" came a mellifluous voice from behind the door.

"Who's that?" Charlie asked, trying to peer over his friend's shoulder.

"The television. Now look, go on home and I'll do whatever you ask. Monday, huh? Please?"

"Nonsense, Bill," said the voice. The door opened wider. A young lady in rather tight slacks and sweater came into view behind Bill. "Why don't you invite your friend in? Charlie, wasn't it?"

"Still is," said Charlie.

"I can't think of a single reason," said Bill in a tone that would have sufficed to tan leather. He opened the door with great reluctance, and Charlie slipped inside.

"Hi. My name's Abigail," the girl chirped.

"Abigail?" said Charlie in disbelief.

"Abigail," replied Bill, nodding slowly.

"My name's Charlie," said Charlie.

"I know."

"You do? Have we met before?"

"Get to the point," said Bill.

"Abigail, you've got to help me. I must enlist Bill's inexhaustible fount of scientific knowledge. In an enterprise that is vital to the safety of the city of New York!" Abigail's eyes went wide. Bill's got hard, like dumdum bullets.

"I have reason to believe," he continued conspiratorially, "that the ground at Sixth Avenue and Sixteenth Street is unstable. If this is not proved tonight, lives will be endangered! But I must buttress my theory with fact."

"Don't swear. Gee, that's fantastic! Isn't that fantastic, Bill?"

"It sure is," Bill replied. In a minute he would fantasize her further by strangling his own friend right before her fantasized eyes.

Charlie began to prowl around the living room, his own oculars darting right to left. "Well, don't just stand there, Bill! We've got to assemble your equipment. Now. Don't you agree, Abigail?"

"Oh, yes. Hurry, Bill, let's do!"

"Yes," murmured Bill tightly. "Just let me get my *hat* and my *coat*." He took another look at his friend. "Is it raining out?"

Charlie was on his hands and knees, peering under the

couch. "Raining out? Don't be absurd! Of course it isn't raining out. What makes you think it's raining out?"

"Nothing," said Bill. "I can't imagine where I got the idea."

Sixth Avenue and Sixteenth Street was not a very busy intersection, even late on a Saturday night. Especially since it had been blocked off in spots by the construction machinery. On the other hand, it wasn't exactly a dark alley, either. The winos, comfortably tucked into their favourite corners, were no problem. But there were enough pedestrians about to make Bill feel uncomfortable and conspicuous with his heavy field case.

"Why can't we go in there?" he asked, pointing to an assemblage of heavy earth movers.

"Because the construction area is protected by a three-metre-high wire fence topped with three rows of barbed wire with triple alarms on the gates and is patrolled by vicious large-fanged guard dogs, is why."

"Oh," said Bill.

"Can't you do whatever you have to do right here?" asked Abigail.

"Yeah, you're not going to set off a very *big* explosion, are you?" Charlie blurted.

It is true that Charlie was still fairly intelligible. But the effects of the Sober-ups were wearing off, and he tended to talk rather louder than normal.

So the word "explosion" did have the useful effect of sending several couples scurrying to the other side of the street and clearing a broad space around them.

"For cryin' out loud," whispered Bill, "will you shut up about explosions! You want to get us arrested?" He turned to survey the wooden fence that closed off the vacant lot behind them. "There's bound to be a loose board or a gate in this fence. All I'm going to do inside is set off the smallest cap I've got. You'll get the briefest reading I can take, and that's it!"

While Bill and Charlie screened her from the street, Abigail slipped under the hinged plank they'd found. Charlie followed, and Bill came last, after slipping through his field kit. They stood alone in the empty lot.

"Oooo, isn't this *exciting*!" Abigail whispered.

"One of the most thrilling nights of my life," growled Bill. He'd long since resigned himself to the fact that the only way he was going to get rid of his friend, short of homicide, was to go through with this idiocy.

"Only let's be ready to get out of here quick, huh? I don't feel like trying to explain to any of New York's finest what I'm doing taking seismic readings in a vacant lot at nine o'clock Saturday night."

"Is it that late already?" yelled Charlie, oblivious to his friend's attempts to shush him. "Hurry, hurry!"

"Anything, if you'll only *shut up*!" Bill moaned nervously. The others watched while he proceeded to dig a small hole with a collapsible spade. He put something from his case into it, then filled in the dirt, tamping it down tightly with the flat of the spade. He walked back to them, trailing two thin wires.

"This is exciting!" said Abigail. Bill gave her a pained look while Charlie fairly hopped with impatience.

Bill hit the small push-button device the wires led from. There was a muffled *thump!* Clods of earth were thrown several metres into the tepid air of the New York night. They were accompanied by a non-organic shoe and several long-empty tuna fish cans.

"Well?" asked Charlie. He said it several times before he realized Bill couldn't hear him through the earphones. Finally he tapped him on the shoulder. "How long will it take?"

"Too long," said Bill, mooning at Abigail, who was inspecting the midget crater. "It was a very small bang. I've got to amplify and reamplify the results and wait for a proper printout from the computer. Maybe an hour, maybe two."

"That *is* too long!" Charlie whimpered piteously.

"That – is – too – *bad*!" Bill was just about at the end of his good humour.

"Well, okay, but hurry it up, will you?"

Bill chewed air and didn't reply.

"I don't believe it!" There was a peculiar expression on the young geologist's face.

"What is it, what's happened?" said Abigail.

Bill turned slowly from his instruments, looked up at Charlie.

"You were right. Son of a bitch, you were right! I don't believe it, but . . . unstable! Jeez, there's a regular *cave* down there!"

"Will it affect the tunnel?"

"No, not the line, but as for putting a station down here . . . The whole thing could collapse under other sections of the block. And I couldn't begin to predict what blasting here might do. I don't think anyone would get hurt, but the added *expense* . . . to ensure the safety of the crane operators and such . . ."

"Now, that *would* be serious," said Charlie. "Hey, what time is it?"

" 'Bout twenty to twelve," Bill replied, glancing down at his watch.

Charlie looked askance at his watch. "Heavens, it's twenty to twelve! I've got to run! See you soon, Bill!"

"Not likely," the geologist murmured.

"And thanks, thanks a million! You'll report your results to the commissioner's office, won't you?"

"Yeah, sure!" shouted Bill as his friend slipped through the loose board. No reason not to. He'd get a lot of credit for his foresight in detecting the faulted area. Maybe a paper or journal article out of it, too. And he'd take it after what he'd gone through tonight.

"Now, don't be bitter," whispered Abigail, kissing him selectively. "You were marvellous! It wasn't that difficult. Besides, I think it was fun. And different. I've never been invited out for a seismic reading before."

Bill squinted glumly into the bright light that had settled on them. "And you'll be the first girl to be arrested for it, too." He sighed, kissing her right back.

"Van Groot! Hey, Van Groot!" Charlie had been stumbling through the tunnel for what seemed like hours. He'd wandered off and on the inspectors' walkway, unmindful of the fact that at any moment a train could have come roaring down the subterranean track to squash him like a bug.

"Here, gnome, here, gnome!" That sounded even worse. If he ran into a night inspector, he might be able to alibi away "Van Groot!" He didn't think he was clever enough to explain away "Here, gnome!"

Could he? Well, could he?

"De Puyster!" came a familiar voice. "Stop that shouting! I can hear you."

"Van Groot! I've found you!"

"Eureka," the gnome said dryly. "I'd sure be distressed if you'd found me and I turned out to be someone else."

Tonight the gnome administrator was wearing blue shark-skin. The beret was gone, replaced by a gunmetal-blue turban. A gold silk handkerchief protruded from the jacket pocket, matched to the gold shoes of water buffalo hide.

"Well?"

Charlie tried to catch his breath. It occurred to him that the steady diet of booze and exercise he'd been existing on all night did not go together like, say, chocolate chip and cookie.

"It's . . . it's all right! Everything's going to be okay. You can tell the relatives up north they can leave their maple syrup in the trees and not black out cities or any of that kind of stuff! Your mine won't be harmed."

"Why, that's merry marvellous!" said Van Groot. "How-ever did you manage it? I admit I didn't have much confidence in you."

"Friend . . . friend of mine will present enough evidence to the Subway Planning Board showing that the ground, the area for the proposed station, is unstable. Unsuitable for practical excavation. If they think it'll cost them another five bucks, they'll move it to the south side of the tunnel. It was all a matter of just using the fact of your mine, not trying to pretend it wasn't there. They don't know it's a mine, of course."

"Seismic test?"

"Yeah. How did you know?"

"Reasonable. Three of my best pick-gnomes reported in earlier this evening with migraines."

"Sorry."

"Don't give it no mind. Serves 'em right." Van Groot chuckled with satisfaction.

"Anyway," Charlie continued, "lives, time, and difficulty cannot stop the New York Subway Authority. But money . . . yeah, your mine is safe, all right."

"And so are your phone lines. So is that of the chairman of the board of General Computers."

"It'll be an express station, anyway. It shouldn't bother you too much," Charlie added. He was getting groggy again. His stomach and brain were ganging up on him.

"You've done very well, indeed, my boy. I'm surprised at you. It's been a long time since any human traded favours with us."

"Aw, I'll bet you set the whole thing up. Anyway, I've got to be honest about it. I didn't do it for you. I didn't do it for me, either. I – I did it –" and here he stood very tall, straight, and patriotic, "– for the telephone company!" It was all he could do not to salute.

"Bravo! I wish there was something we could give you. A little token, a remembrance. I don't suppose you could use a nice sceptre."

"I'm afraid not. No coronations for a month at least. I'm going on the wagon."

"Too bad. Well, here. Take this, anyway."

"Sure," said Charlie agreeably. The gnome thrust something into his raincoat pocket. "So long, Veen Grat! It was nice knowing you. Stop up at my place sometime. Play a couple games o' gi . . . o' gin!"

"I may do that," replied Van Groot. "Some night. I'll bring my own djinn."

Charlie was halfway up the tunnel when he whirled at a sudden thought and shouted back. "Hey, Van Greet!"

"Yes?" The voice floated down faintly from the distant blackness.

"What did you give me?"

"Why, a Flagan-flange, of course."

Charlie giggled as he thought about it. He couldn't stop giggling. However, it wasn't so funny. This made him nervous, and he stopped. He was just about to enter into a symbiotic relationship with his mattress when there was a knock at his door. It repeated insistently. It refused to go away.

Grumbling, he stumbled blindly to the door and peered through the peephole – no one just opens his door at two in the morning in New York. Suddenly he was sure he'd actually gone to sleep four hours ago and was now dreaming. But he opened the door.

It was Miss High-Pressure Area.

She had a robe draped loosely over a nightgown no self-respecting spider would have owned up to. Cumulus formations were disturbingly apparent.

"Can I come in, Mister . . . uh . . ."

"Dimsdale," mumbled Charlie. "Charlie Dimsdale." He took two steps backward. Since he was still holding on to the knob, the door came with him.

She stepped inside, closed it behind her. The robe opened even more. So did Charlie's pupils. Proportionately.

"You're going to think I'm just *terrible*," (this was a blatant falsehood) "but . . ." She was staring at him in the strangest way. "I really can't . . . explain it. But, well, if you could just . . ."

She took a quick step forward and threw her arms around him. For someone out of practice, Charlie reacted well. She whispered something in his ear. It wasn't a weather report. What she said, softly, was, "It'll be okay. He thinks I'm in Geneva."

Charlie hung on and directed her into the apartment, kicking the door shut behind them. He listened gravely.

Now he knew what a Flagan-flange attracted.

THE EYE OF TANDYLA

L. Sprague de Camp

Although Lord of the Rings *had a lot to do with it, it is not far from the truth to say that the modern revival of interest in fantasy fiction owes much to L. Sprague de Camp (b. 1907). He began writing fantasy for John W. Campbell's legendary magazine* Unknown *in the 1940s, which first published his Harold Shea stories (written with Fletcher Pratt), later collected as* The Incomplete Enchanter *(1941), and other titles. De Camp also edited and revised a number of Robert E. Howard's stories about Conan the Barbarian, bringing together the first comprehensive series of Conan books. Much of de Camp's solo work is in the vein of comic fantasy, and I would highly recommend* The Goblin Tower *(1968),* The Clocks of Iraz *(1971),* The Unbeheaded King *(1980), the* Fallible Fiend *(1973),* The Incorporated Knight *(1987),* The Pixillated Princess *(1991) and* The Purple Pterodactyls *(1979) – the last being a collection of "the adventures of W. Wilson Newbury, ensorcelled financier". The following is one of de Camp's early fantasy adventures, long overdue for revival.*

One day – so long ago that mountains have arisen since, with cities on their flanks – Derezong Taash, sorcerer to King Vuar the capricious, sat in his library reading the Collected Fragments of Lontang and drinking the green wine of Zhysk. He was at peace with himself and the world, for nobody had tried to murder him for ten whole days, by natural means or otherwise. When tired of puzzling out the cryptic glyphs, Derezong would gaze over the rim of his goblet at his demon-screen, on which the great Shuazid (before King Vuar took a capricious dislike to him) had depicted Derezong's entire stable of demons, from the fearful Feranzot down to the slightest sprite that submitted to his summons.

One wondered, on seeing Derezong, why even a sprite should bother. For Derezong Taash was a chubby little man (little for a Lorska, that is) with white hair framing a round youthful face. When he had undergone the zompur-treatment, he had carelessly forgotten to name his hair among the things for which he wanted eternal youth – an omission which had furnished his fellow magicians with fair scope for ribald ridicule.

On this occasion, Derezong Taash planned, when drunk enough, to heave his pudgy form out of the reading chair and totter in to dinner with his assistant, Zhamel Seh. Four of Derezong's sons should serve the food as a precaution against Derezong's ill-wishers, and Zhamel Seh should taste it first as a further precaution. After they had consumed a few jars more of wine, Derezong would choose three of his prettiest concubines and stagger off to bed. A harmless programme, one would have said. In fact Derezong Taash had already, in his mind, chosen the three, though he had not yet decided upon their order.

And then the knock upon the door and the high voice of King Vuar's most insolent page: "My lord sorcerer, the king will see you forthwith!"

"What about?" grumbled Derezong Taash.

"Do I know where the storks go in winter? Am I privy to the secrets of the living dead of Sedo? Has the North Wind confided to me what lies beyond the ramparts of the Riphai?"

"I suppose not." Derezong yawned, rose, and toddled

throneward. He glanced back over his shoulders as he went, disliking to walk through the halls of the palace without Zhamel to guard his back against a sudden stab.

The lamplight gleamed upon King Vuar's glabrous pate, and the king looked up at Derezong Taash from under his hedge of heavy brows. He sat upon his throne in the audience chamber, and over his head upon the wall was fastened the hunting-horn of the great King Zynah, Vuar's father.

On the secondary throne sat the king's favourite concubine Ilepro, from Lotor: a dumpy middle-aged Lotri, hairy and toothy. What the king saw in her . . . Perhaps in middle age he had become bored with beauty and sought spice from its antithesis. Or perhaps after the High Chief of Lotor, Konesp, had practically forced his widowed sister upon the king after Ilepro's husband had died of a hunting accident, the monarch had fallen truly in love with her.

Or perhaps the hand of the wizard-priest of Lotor was to be discerned behind these bizarre events. Sorcery or its equivalent would be needed to account for King Vuar's designating Ilepro's young son by her Lotri husband as his heir, if indeed he had done so as rumour whispered. Derezong was thankful that the youth was not present, though that quartet of Lotri women, swathed in their superfluous furs, squatted around the feet of Ilepro.

Derezong was sure there was something here that he did not understand, and that he would not like any better when he did understand it. Despite the present peace-treaty between Lotor and Lorsk, he doubted that the Lotris had forgotten the harrying that King Zynah had inflicted upon them in retaliation for their raids.

After his preliminary prostration, Derezong Taash observed something else that had escaped his original notice: that on a small table in front of the throne, which usually bore a vase of flowers, there now reposed a silver plate, and on the plate the head of the Minister of Commerce, wearing that witlessly blank expression that heads are wont to do when separated from their proper bodies.

Evidently King Vuar was not in his jolliest mood.

"Yes, O King?" said Derezong Taash, his eyes swivelling nervously from the head of the late minister to that of his sovereign.

King Vuar said: "Good my lord, my concubine Ilepro, whom I think you know, has a desire that you alone can satisfy."

"Yes, sire?" Jumping to a wrong conclusion, Derezong Taash goggled like a bullfrog in spring. For one thing, King Vuar was not at all noted for generosity in sharing his women, and for another thing, of all the royal harem, Derezong had the least desire to share Ilepro.

The king said: "She wishes that jewel that forms the third eye of the goddess Tandyla. You know that temple in Lotor?"

"Yes, sire." Although he retained his blandest smile, Derezong's heart sank to the vicinity of his knees. This was going to prove even less entertaining than intimacy with Ilepro.

"This small-souled buckster," said Vuar, indicating the head, "said, when I put the proposal to him, that the gem could not be bought, wherefore I caused his length to be lessened. This hasty act I now regret, for it transpires that he was right. Therefore, our only remaining course is to steal the thing."

"Y-yes, sire."

The king rested his long chin upon his fist and his agate eyes saw distant things. The lamplight gleamed upon the ring of grey metal on his finger, a ring made from the heart of a falling star, and of such might as a magic-repellent that not even the sendings of the wizards of Lotor had power to harm its wearer.

He continued: "We can either essay to seize it openly, which would mean war, or by stealth. Now, although I will go to some trouble to gratify the whims of Ilepro, my plans do not include a Lotrian war. At least, not until all other expedients have been attempted. You, therefore, are hereby commissioned to go to Lotor and obtain this jewel."

"Yes indeed, sire," said Derezong with a heartiness that was, to say the least, a bit forced. Any thoughts of protest that he might have entertained had some minutes since been banished by the sight of the unlucky minister's head.

"Of course," said Vuar in tones of friendly consideration,

"should you feel your own powers inadequate, I'm sure the King of Zhysk will lend me his wizard to assist you . . ."

"Never, sire!" cried Derezong, drawing himself up to his full five-five. "That bungler, far from helping, would be but an anchor stone about my neck!"

King Vuar smiled a lupine smile, though Derezong could not perceive the reason. "So be it."

Back in his own quarters Derezong Taash rang for his assistant. After the third ring Zhamel Seh sauntered in, balancing his big bronze sword by the pommel on his palm.

"Some day," said Derezong, "you'll amputate some poor wight's toe showing off that trick, and I only hope it will be yours. We leave tomorrow on a mission."

Zhamel Seh grasped his sword securely by the hilt and grinned down upon his employer. "Good! Whither?"

Derezong Taash told him.

"Better yet! Action! Excitement!" Zhamel swished the air with his sword. "Since you put the geas upon the queen's mother we have sat in these apartments like barnacles on a pile, doing nought to earn King Vuar's bounty."

"What's wrong with that? I plague none and nobody plagues me. And now with winter coming on, we must journey forth to the ends of rocky Lotor to try to lift this worthless bauble the king's sack of a favourite has set her silly heart upon."

"I wonder why," said Zhamel. "Since she's Lotri by birth, you'd think she'd wish to ward her land's religious symbols instead of raping them away for her own adornment."

"One never knows. Our own women are unpredictable enough, and as for Lotris . . . But let's to the task of planning our course and equipage."

That night, Derezong Taash took only one concubine to bed with him.

They rode east to fertile Zhysk on the shores of the Tritonian Sea, and in the city of Bienkar sought out Derezong's friend, Goshap Tuzh the lapidary, from whom they solicited information to forearm them against adversity.

"This jewel," said Goshap Tuzh, "is about the size of a small fist, egg-shaped without facets, and of a dark purple hue. When seen from one end, it displays rays like a sapphire, but seven instead of six. It forms the pupil of the central eye of the statue of Tandyla, being held in place by leaden prongs. As to what other means, natural or otherwise, the priests of Tandyla employ to guard their treasure, I know not, save that they are both effective and unpleasing. Twenty-three attempts have been made to pilfer the stone in the last five centuries, all terminating fatally for the thieves. The last time I, Goshap Tuzh, saw the body of the thief . . ."

As Goshap told the manner in which the unsuccessful thief had been used, Zhamel gagged and Derezong looked into his wine with an expression of distaste, as if some many-legged creeping thing swam therein – although he and his assistant were by no means the softest characters in a hard age.

"Its properties?" said Derezong Taash.

"Considerable, though perhaps overrated by distant rumour. It is the world's most sovereign antidemonic, repelling even the dread Tr'lang himself, who is of all demons the deadliest."

"Is it even stronger than King Vuar's ring of star-metal?"

"Much. However, for our old friendship, let me advise you to change your name and take service with some less exacting liege lord. There's no profit in seeking to snatch this Eye."

Derezong Taash ran his fingers through his silky-white hair and beard. "True, he ever wounds me by his brutally voiced suspicions of my competence, but to relinquish such luxe as I enjoy were not so simple. Where else can I obtain such priceless books and enrapturing women for the asking? Nay, save when he becomes seized of these whimsies, King Vuar's a very good master indeed."

"But that's my point. When do you know his caprice notorious may not be turned against you?"

"I know not; betimes I think it must be easier to serve a barbarian king. Barbarians, being wrapped in a mummy-cloth of custom and ritual, are more predictable."

"Then why not flee? Across the Tritonian Sea lies lordly Torrutseish, where one of your worth would soon rise –"

"You forget," said Derezong, "King Vuar holds hostages: my not inconsiderable family of fourteen concubines, twelve sons, nine daughters, and several squalling grandchildren. And for them I must stick it out, though the Western Sea swallow the entire land of Pusaad as is predicted in the prophecies."

Goshap shrugged. " 'Tis your affair. I do but indigitate that you are one of these awkward intermediates: too tub-like ever to make a prow swordsman, and unable to attain the highest grade of magical adeptry because you'll not forswear the delights of your zenana."

"Thank you, good Goshap," said Derezong, sipping the green wine. "Howsoever, I live not to attain pre-eminence in some austere regimen disciplinary, but to enjoy life. And now, who's a reliable apothecary in Bienkar from whom I can obtain a packet of syr-powder of highest grade and purity?"

"Dualor can furnish you. What semblance do you propose upon yourselves to cast?"

"I thought we'd go as a pair of traders from Parsk. So, if you hear of such a couple traversing Lotor accompanied by vast uproar and vociferation, fail not to show the due surprise."

Derezong Taash bought his syr-powder with squares of gold bearing the stamp of King Vuar, then returned to their inn where he drew his pentacles and cast his powder and recited the Incantation of the Nines. At the end, both he and Zhamel Seh were both lying helpless on the floor, with their appearance changed to that of a pair of dark hawk-nosed fellows in the fluttery garb of Parsk, with rings in their ears.

When they recovered their strength, they rode forth. They crossed the desert of Reshape without suffering excessively either from thirst, or from the bites of venomous serpents, or from attacks of spirits of the waste. They passed through the Forest of Antro without being assailed by brigands, sword-toothed cats, or the Witch of Antro. And at last they wound among the iron hills of Lotor.

As they stopped for one night, Derezong said: "By my reckoning and according to what passers-by have told us, the temple should lie not more than one day's journey ahead. Hence, it were time to try whether we can effect our direption by surrogate instead of in our own vulnerable persons." And he began drawing pentacles in the dirt.

"You mean to call up Feranzot?" asked Zhamel Seh.

"The same."

Zhamel shuddered. "Some day you'll leave an angle of a pentacle unclosed, and that will be the end of us."

"No doubt. But to assail this stronghold of powers chthonian by any but the mightiest means were an even surer passport to extinction. So light the rushes and begin."

"I can fancy nothing riskier than dealing with Feranzot," grumbled Zhamel, "save perhaps invoking the terrible Tr'lang himself." But he did as he was bid.

They went through the Incantation of Br'tong, as reconstructed by Derezong Taash from the Fragments of Lontang, and the dark shape of Feranzot appeared outside the main pentacle, wavering and rippling. Derezong felt the heat of his body sucked forth by the cold of the daev, and felt the overwhelming depression the thing's presence engendered. Zhamel Seh, for all his thews, cowered.

"What would you?" whispered Feranzot.

Derezong Taash gathered his weakened forces and replied: "You shall steal the jewel in the middle eye of the statue of the goddess Tandyla in the nearby temple thereof and render it to me."

"That I cannot."

"And why not?"

"First, because the priests of Tandyla have traced around their temple a circle of such puissance that no sending or semblance or spirit, save the great Tr'lang, can cross it. Second, because the Eye itself is surrounded by an aura of such baleful influence that not I, nor any other of my kind, nor even Tr'lang himself, can exert a purchase upon it on this plane. May I return to my own dimension now?"

"Depart, depart, depart . . . Well, Zhamel, it looks as though we should be compelled to essay this undelightsome task ourselves."

Next day they continued their ride. The hills became mountains of uncommon ruggedness, and the road a mere trail cut into cliffs of excessive steepness. The horses, more accustomed to the bison-swarming plains of windy Lorsk, misliked the new topography, and rubbed their riders' legs painfully against the cliffside in their endeavour to keep away from the edge.

Little sun penetrated these gorges of black rock, which began to darken almost immediately after noon. Then the sky clouded over and the rocks became shiny with cold mist. The trail crossed the gorge by a spidery bridge suspended from ropes. The horses balked.

"Not that I blame them," said Derezong Taash, dismounting. "By the red-hot talons of Vrazh, it takes the thought of my fairest concubine to nerve me to cross!"

When led in line with Zhamel belabouring their rumps from the rear, the animals crossed, though unwillingly. Derezong, towing them, took one brief look over the side of the bridge at the white thread of water foaming far below and decided not to do that again. Feet and hooves resounded hollowly on the planking and echoed from the cliffsides, and the wind played with the ropes as with the strings of a great harp.

On the other side of the gorge, the road continued its winding upward way. They passed another pair, a man and a woman, riding down the trail, and had to back around a bend to find a place with room enough to pass. The man and the woman went by looking sombrely at the ground, barely acknowledging with a grunt the cheerful greeting Derezong tossed at them.

Then the road turned sharply into a great cleft in the cliff, wherein their hooffalls echoed thrice as loud as life and they could scarcely see to pick their way. The bottom of the cleft sloped upward, so that in time they came out upon an area of tumbled stones with a few dwarfed trees. The road ran dimly on through the stones until it ended in a flight of steps, which in turn led up to the Temple of Tandyla itself. Of this temple of ill repute, the travellers could see only the lower parts, for the upper ones disappeared into the cloud floor. What they could see of it was all black and shiny and rising to sharp peaks.

Derezong remembered the unpleasant attributes ascribed to the goddess, and the even more disagreeable habits credited to her priests. It was said, for instance, that the worship of Tandyla, surely a sinister enough figure in the Pusaadian pantheon, was a mere blind to cover dark rites concerning the demon Tr'lang, who in elder days had been a god in his own right. That was before the towering Lorskas, driven from the mainland by the conquering Hauskirik, had swarmed across the Tritonian Sea to Pusaad, before that land had begun its ominous subsidence.

Derezong Taash assured himself that gods and demons alike were not usually so formidable as their priests, from base motives of gain, tried to make them out. Also, that wild tales of the habits of priests usually turned out to be at least somewhat exaggerated. Although he did not fully believe his own assurances, they would have to suffice for want of better.

In front of the half-hidden temple, Derezong Taash pulled up, dismounted, and with Zhamel's help weighted down the reins of their beasts with heavy stones to hinder them from straying.

As they started for the steps Zhamel cried: "Master!"

"What is't?"

"Look upon us!"

Derezong looked. The semblance of traders from Parsk had vanished, and they were again King Vuar's court magician and his assistant, plain for all to see. They must have stepped across that line that Feranzot had warned them of. Derezong took a sharp look at the entrance. Half-hidden in the inadequate light, two men flanked the doorway. His eye caught the gleam of polished bronze. But if these doorkeepers had observed the change in the looks of the visitors, they gave no sign.

Derezong Taash drove his short legs up the shiny black steps. The guards came into full view, thick-bodied Lotris with beetling brows. Men said they were akin to the savages of Ierarne in the far North-East, who knew not horse-taming and fought with sharpened stone. These stood staring straight ahead, each facing the other like statues. Derezong and Zhamel passed between them.

They found themselves in a vestibule where a pair of young Lotri girls said: "Your boots and swords, sirs."

Derezong lifted off his baldric and handed it to the nearest, scabbard and all; then pulled off his boots and stood barefoot with the grass he had stuffed into them to keep them from chafing sticking out from between his toes. He was glad to feel the second sword hanging down his back inside his shirt.

A low remark passed between Zhamel and one of the girls – a girl who, Derezong observed, was not bad-looking for a Lotri, in a plump moon-faced way.

"Come on," said Derezong Taash, and led the way into the naos of the temple.

It was much like other temples: a big rectangular room smelling of incense, with a third of the area partitioned off by a railing, behind which rose the huge black squat statue of Tandyla. The smooth basalt of which it was carved reflected feebly the highlights from the few lamps, and up at the top, where its head disappeared into the shadows, a point of purple light showed where the jewel in its forehead caught the rays.

A couple of Lotris knelt before the railing, mumbling prayers. A priest appeared from the shadows on one side, waddled across the naos behind the railing. Derezong half expected the priest to turn on him with a demand that he and Zhamel follow him into the sanctum of the high priest, but the priest kept on walking and disappeared into the darkness on the other side.

Derezong Taash and his companion advanced, a slow step at a time, towards the railing. As they neared it, the two Lotris completed their devotions and rose. One of them dropped something that jingled into a large tub-like receptacle behind the railing, and the two squat figures walked quickly out.

For the moment, Derezong and Zhamel were entirely alone in the big room, though in the silence they could hear faint motions and voices from other parts of the temple. Derezong brought out his container of syr-powder and sprinkled it while racing through the Incantation of Ansuan. When he finished, there stood between himself and Zhamel a replica of himself.

Derezong Taash climbed over the railing and trotted on the

tips of his plump toes around behind the statue. Here in the shadows, he could see doors in the walls. The statue sat with its back almost but not quite touching the wall behind it, so that an active man, by bracing his back against the statue and his feet against the wall, could lever himself up. Though Derezong was "active" only in a qualified sense, he slipped into the gap and squirmed into a snugly fitting fold in the goddess' stone draperies. Here he lay, hardly breathing, until he heard Zhamel's footfalls die away.

The plan was that Zhamel should walk out of the temple, accompanied by the double of Derezong. The guards, believing that the temple was now deserted of visitors, would relax. Derezong would steal the stone; Zhamel should raise a haro outside, urging the guards to "Come quickly!" and while their attention was thus distracted, Derezong would rush out.

Derezong waited a while longer. The soft footsteps of another priest padded past and a door closed. Somewhere, a Lotri girl laughed.

Derezong began to worm his way up between the statue and the wall. It was hard going for one of his girth, and sweat ran out from under his cap of fisherfur and down his face. Still no interruption. He arrived on a level with the shoulder and squirmed out onto that projection, holding the right ear for safety. The slick stone was cold under his bare feet. By craning his neck, he could see the ill-favoured face of the goddess in profile, and by stretching he could reach the jewel in her forehead.

Derezong Taash took out of his tunic a small bronze pry-bar he had brought along for this purpose. With it he began to pry up the leaden prongs that held the gem in place, carefully lest he mar the stone or cause it to fall to the floor below. Every few pries, he tested it with his finger. Soon it felt loose.

The temple was quiet.

Around the clock he went with his little bar, prying. Then the stone came out, rubbing gently against the smooth inner surfaces of the bent-out leaden prongs. Derezong Taash reached for the inside of his tunic, to hide the stone and the bar. But the two objects proved too much for his pudgy fingers to handle at once. The bar came loose and fell with a loud ping – ping down the front of the statue, bouncing from breast to belly to lap, to end with a sonorous clank on the stone floor in front of the image.

Derezong Taash froze rigid. Seconds passed and nothing happened. Surely the guards had heard . . .

But still there was silence.

Derezong Taash secured the jewel in his tunic and squirmed back over the shoulder to the darkness behind the statue. Little by little, he slid down the space between statue and wall. He reached the floor. Still no noise save an occasional faint sound such as might have been made by the temple servants preparing dinner for their masters. He waited for the diversion promised by Zhamel Seh.

He waited and waited. From somewhere came the screech of a man in the last agonies.

At last, giving up, Derezong Taash hurried around the hip of the statue. He scooped up the pry-bar with one quick motion, climbed back over the railing, and tiptoed toward the exit.

There stood the guards with swords out, ready for him.

Derezong Taash reached back over his shoulder and pulled out his second sword. In a real fight, he knew he would have little hope against one hardened and experienced sword-fighter, let alone two. His one slim chance lay in bursting through them by a sudden berserk attack, then to keep on running.

He expected such adroit and skilful warriors to separate and come at him from opposite sides. Instead, one of them stepped forward and took an awkward swipe at him. Derezong parried with a clash of bronze and struck back. Clang! Clang! went the blades, and then his foe staggered back, dropped his sword with a clatter, clutched both hands to his chest, and folded up in a heap on the floor. Derezong was astonished; he could have sworn he had not gotten home.

Then the other man was upon him. At the second clash of blades, that of the guard spun out of his hand, to fall ringingly to the stone pave. The guard leapt back, turned and ran, disappearing through one of the many ambient doors.

* * *

Derezong Taash glanced at his sword, wondering if he had not known his own strength all this time. The whole exchange had taken perhaps ten seconds, and so far as he could tell in the dim light, no blood besmeared his blade. He was tempted to test the deadness of the fallen guard by poking him, but lacked both time and ruthlessness to do so. Instead, he ran out of the vestibule and looked for Zhamel and the double of himself.

No sign of either. The four horses were still tethered a score of paces from the steps of the temple. The stones were sharp under Derezong's bare and unhardened soles. Derezong hesitated, but only for a flash. He was in a way fond of Zhamel Seh, and his assistant's brawn had gotten him out of trouble about as often as Zhamel's lack of insight had gotten them into it. But to plunge back into the temple in search of his erratic aide would be rash to the point of madness. And he did have definite orders from the king.

He sheathed his sword, scrambled onto the back of his horse, and cantered off, leading the other three beasts by their bridles.

During the ride down the narrow cleft, Derezong had time to think, and the more he thought the less he liked what he thought. The behaviour of the guards was inexplicable on any grounds but their being drunk or crazy, and he did not believe either. Their failure to attack him simultaneously; their failure to note the fall of the pry-bar; the ease with which he, an indifferent swordsman, had bested them; the fact that one fell down without being touched; their failure to yell for help . . .

Unless they planned it that way. The whole thing had been too easy to account for by any other hypothesis. Maybe they wanted him to steal the accursed bauble.

At the lower end of the cleft, where the road turned out onto the side of the cliff forming the main gorge, he pulled up, dismounted, and tied the animals, keeping an ear cocked for the sound of pursuers echoing down the cleft. He took out the Eye of Tandyla and looked at it. Yes, when seen end-on it showed the rayed effect promised by Goshap Tuzh. Otherwise, it exhibited no special odd or unnatural properties. So far.

Derezong Taash set it carefully on the ground and backed

away from it to see it from a greater distance. As he backed, the stone moved slightly and started to roll towards him.

At first he thought he had not laid it down on a level enough place, and leapt to seize it before it should roll over the edge into the gulf. He put it back and heaped a little barrier of pebbles and dust around it. Now it should not roll!

But when he backed again, it did, right over his little rampart. Derezong Taash began to sweat anew, and not, this time, from physical exertion. The stone rolled toward him, faster and faster. He tried to dodge by shrinking into a recess in the cliff-wall. The stone swerved and came to rest at the toe of one of his bare feet, like a pet animal asking for a pat on the head.

He scooped out a small hole, laid the gem in it, placed a large stone over the hole, and walked away. The large stone shook and the purple egg appeared, pushing aside the pebbles in its path as if it were being pulled out from under the rock by an invisible cord. It rolled to his feet again and stopped.

Derezong Taash picked up the stone and looked at it again. It didn't seem to be scratched. He remembered the urgency with which Chief Konesp was said to have pressed his sister upon King Vuar, and the fact that the demand for the stone originated with this same Ilepro.

With a sudden burst of emotion, Derezong Taash threw the stone from him, towards the far side of the gorge.

By all calculation, the gem should have followed a curved path, arcing downward to shatter against the opposite cliff. Instead, it slowed in mid flight over the gorge, looped back, and flew into the hand that had just thrown it.

Derezong Taash did not doubt that the priests of Tandyla had laid a subtle trap for King Vuar in the form of this jewel. What it would do to the king and to the kingdom of Lorsk if Derezong carried out his mission, he had no idea. So far as he knew, it was merely an antidemonic, and therefore should protect Vuar instead of harming him. Nevertheless, he was sure something unpleasant was planned, of which he was less than eager to be the agency. He placed the gem on a flat rock, found a stone the size of his head, raised it in both hands, and brought it down upon the jewel.

Or so he intended. On the way down, the stone struck a projecting shelf of rock, and a second later Derezong was capering about like a devil-dancer of Dzen, sucking his mashed fingers and cursing the priests of Tandyla in the names of the most fearful demons in his repertory. The stone lay unharmed.

For, Derezong reasoned, these priests must have put upon the gem not only a following-spell, but also the Incantation of Duzhateng, so that every effort on the part of Derezong to destroy the object would rebound to his own damage. If he essayed some more elaborate scheme of destruction, he would probably end up with a broken leg. The Incantation of Duzhateng could be lifted only by a complicated spell for which Derezong did not have the materials, which included some very odd and repellent substances indeed.

Now, Derezong Taash knew that there was only one way in which he could both neutralize these spells and secure the jewel so that it should plague him no more, and that was to put it back in the hole in the forehead of the statue of Tandyla and hammer down the leaden prongs that held it in its setting. Which task, however, promised to present more difficulties than the original theft. For if the priests of Tandyla had meant Derezong to steal the object, they might show greater acumen in thwarting his attempt to return it, than they had in guarding it in the first place.

One could but try. Derezong Taash put the jewel into his tunic, mounted his horse (leaving the other three still tethered) and rode back up the echoing cleft. When he came out upon the little plateau upon which squatted the temple of Tandyla, he saw that he had indeed been forestalled. Around the entrance to the temple stood a double row of guards, the bronze scales of their cuirasses glimmering faintly in the fading light. The front rank carried shields of mammoth hide and big bronze swords, while those in the rear bore long pikes which they held in both hands and thrust between the men of the front rank. They thus presented a formidable hedge to any attacker, who had first to get past the spear-points and then deal with the swords.

One possibility was to gallop at them in the hope that one or two directly in one's way would flinch aside, opening a path by which one could burst through the serried line. Then, one could ride on into the temple and perhaps get the gem back into place before being caught up with. If not, there would be a great smash, some battered guards, a wounded horse, and a thoroughly skewered and sliced sorcerer all tangled in a kicking heap.

Derezong Taash hesitated, then thought of his precious manuscripts and adorable concubines awaiting him in King Vuar's palace, which he could never safely enter again unless he brought either the gem or an acceptable excuse for not having it. He kicked his mount into motion.

As the animal cantered toward the line, the spear-points got closer and larger and sharper-looking. Derezong saw that the guards were not going to flinch aside and obligingly let him through. Then, a figure came out of the temple and ran down the steps to the rear of the guards. It wore a priest's robe, but just before the shock of impact Derezong recognized the rugged features of Zhamel Seh.

Derezong Taash hauled on his reins, and the horse skidded to a halt with its nose a scant span from the nearest point. Derezong – living in a stirrupless age – slid forward until he bestrode the animal's neck. Clutching its mane with his left hand, he felt for the gem with his right.

"Zhamel!" he called. "Catch!"

He threw, Zhamel leapt high and caught the stone before it had time to loop back.

"Now put it back!" cried Derezong.

"What? Art mad?"

"Put it back, speedily, and secure it!"

Zhamel, trained to obey commands no matter how bizarre, dashed back into the temple, albeit wagging his head as if in sorrow for his master's loss of sanity. Derezong Taash untangled himself from his horse's mane and pulled the beast back out of reach of the spears. Under their lacquered helmets, the heads of the guards turned this way and that in evident perplexity. Derezong surmised that they had been given one simple order – to keep him out – and that they had not been told how to cope with fraternization between the stranger and one of their own priests.

As the guards did not seem to be coming after him, Derezong sat on his horse, eyes on the portal. He'd give Zhamel a fair chance to accomplish his mission and escape, though he thought little of the youth's chances. If Zhamel tried to push or cut his way through the guards, they would make mincemeat of him, unarmoured as he was. And he, Derezong, would have to find and train another assistant, who would probably prove as unsatisfactory as his predecessor. Still, Derezong could not leave the boy utterly to his fate.

Then, Zhamel Seh ran down the steps carrying a long pike of the kind held by the rear-rank guards. Holding this pike level, he ran at the guards as though he were about to spear one in the back. Derezong, knowing that such a scheme would not work, shut his eyes.

But just before he reached the guards, Zhamel Seh dug the point of the pike into the ground and pole-vaulted. Up he went, legs jerking and dangling like those of a man being hanged, over the lacquered helmets and the bronze swords and the mammoth hide shields. He came down in front of the guards, breaking one of their pikes with a loud snap, rolled to his feet, and ran towards Derezong Taash. The latter had already turned his horse around.

As Zhamel caught hold of the edge of the saddle pad, an uproar arose behind them as priests ran out of the temple shouting. Derezong drummed with his bare heels on the stallion's ribs and set off at a canter, Zhamel swinging along in great leaps beside him. They wended their way down the cleft while the sound of hooves wafted after them.

Derezong Taash wasted no breath in questions while picking his way down the trail. At the bottom, where the cleft ended on one side of the great gorge, they halted for Zhamel to mount his own horse, then continued on as fast as they dared. The echoes of the pursuers' hooves came down the cleft with a deafening clatter.

"My poor feet!" groaned Zhamel Seh.

At the suspension bridge, the horses balked again, but Derezong mercilessly pricked and slapped his mount with his sword until the beast trotted out upon the swaying walkway. The cold wind hummed through the ropes, and the daylight was almost gone.

At the far end, with a great sigh of relief, Derezong Taash looked back. Down the cliffside road came a line of pursuers, riding at reckless speed.

He said: "Had I but time and materials, I'd cast a spell on yonder bridge that should make it look as 'twere broken and dangling useless."

"What's wrong with making it broken and useless in very truth?" cried Zhamel, pulling his horse up against the cliffside and hoisting himself so that he stood upon his saddle.

He swung his sword at the cables. As the first of the pursuers reached the far side of the bridge, the structure sagged and fell away with a great swish of ropes and clatter of planks. The men from the temple set up an outcry, and an arrow whizzed across the gap to shatter against the rock.

Derezong and Zhamel resumed their journey.

A fortnight later, they sat in the garden back of the shop of Goshap Tuzh the lapidary in sunny Bienkar. Zhamel Seh told his part of the tale:

". . . so on my way out, this little Lotri cast her orbs upon me once again. Now, thought I, there'll be time in plenty to perform the Master's work and make myself agreeable in this quarter as well —"

"Young cullion!" growled Derezong into his wine.

"— so I followed her. And in truth all was going in most propitious and agreeable wise, when who should come in but one of these chinless wonders in cowl and robe, and went for me with a knife. I tried to fend the fellow off, and fear that in the fracas his neck by ill hap got broke. So, knowing there might be trouble, I borrowed his habit and sallied forth therein, to find that Master, horses, and Master's double had all gone."

"And how time had flown!" said Derezong Taash in sarcastic tones. "I trust at least that the young Lotri has cause to remember this episode with pleasure. The double no doubt, being a mere thing of shadow and not a being rational, walked straight out and vanished when it crossed the magical barrier erected by the priests."

"And," continued Zhamel, "there were priests and guards rushing about chittering like a pack of monkeys. I rushed about as if I were one of them, saw them range the guards around the portal, and then the Master returned and threw me the stone. I grasped the situation, swarmed up the statue, popped Tandyla's third eye back into its socket, and hammered the prongs in upon it with the pommel of my dagger. Then I fetched a pike from the armoury, pausing but to knock senseless a couple of Lotris who sought to detain me for interrogation, and you know the rest."

Derezong Taash rounded out the story and said: "Good Goshap, perchance you can advise our next course, for I fear that should we present ourselves before King Vuar in proper persons, without the gem, he'd have our heads set tastefully on silver platters ere we our explanation finished. No doubt, remorse would afterwards o'erwhelm him, but that would help us not."

"Since he holds you in despite, why not leave him, as I've urged before?" said Goshap.

Derezong Taash shrugged. "Others, alas, show a like lack of appreciation, and would prove no easier masters. For had these priests of Tandyla confided in my ability to perform a simple task like carrying their gemstone from Lotor to Lorsk, their plot would doubtless have borne its intended fruit. But fearing lest I should lose or sell it on the way, they put a supernumerary spell upon it –"

"How could they, when the stone has anti-magical properties?"

"Its anti-magical properties comprise simple antidemonism, whereas the following-spell and the Incantation of Duzhateng are sympathetic magic, not sorcerous. At any rate, they caused it to follow me hither and thither, thus arousing my already awakened suspicions to the fever pitch." He sighed and took a pull on the green wine. "What this sorry world needs is more confidence. But say on, Goshap."

"Well, then, why not write him a letter setting forth the circumstances? I'll lend you a slave to convey it to Lorsk in advance of your persons, so that when you arrive, King Vuar's wrath shall have subsided."

Derezong pondered. "Sage though I deem your suggestion, it faces one obstacle insurmountable. Namely: that of all the men at the court of Lorsk, but six can read; and among these King Vuar is not numbered. Whereas of the six, at least five are among my enemies, who'd like nought better than to see me tumbled from my place. And should the task of reading my missive to the king devolve on one of these, you can fancy how he'd distort my harmless pictographs to my discredit. Could we trick old Vuar into thinking we'd performed our task, as by passing off on him a stone similar to that he expects of us? Know you of such?"

"Now there," said Goshap, "is a proposal indeed. Let me cogitate . . . Last year, when the bony spectre of want came upon the land, King Daior placed his best crown in pawn to the Temple of Kelk, for treasure wherewith to still the clamourings of his people. Now, this crown bears at its apex a purple star sapphire of wondrous size and fineness, said to have been shaped by the gods before the Creation for their own enjoyment, and being in magnitude and hue not unlike that which forms the Eye of Tandyla. And the gem has never been redeemed, wherefore the priests of Kelk have set the crown on exhibition, thereby mulcting the curious of further offerings. But as to how this well-guarded gem shall be transferred from this crown to your possession, ask me not, and in truth I had liefer know nought of the matter."

Next day, Derezong Taash cast upon himself and Zhamel Seh the likeness of Atlantes, from the misty mountain range in the desert of Gautha, far to the East across the Tritonian Sea, where it was said in Pusaad that there were men with snakes for legs and others with no heads but faces in their chests.

Zhamel Seh grumbled: "What are we, magicians or thieves? Perhaps if we succeed in this, the King of Torrutseish across the Tritonian Sea has some bauble he specially fancies, that we could rob him of."

Derezong Taash did not argue the point, but led the way to the square fronted by the Temple of Kelk. They strode up to the temple with the Atlantean swagger, and into where the crown lay upon a cushion on a table with a lamp to illuminate it and two seven-foot Lorskas to guard it, one with a drawn sword and the other with a nocked arrow. The guards looked down over their great black beards at the red-haired Atlanteans in their blue cloaks and armlets of orichalc who pointed and jabbered as they saw the crown. And then the shorter Atlantean, that was Derezong Taash beneath the illusion, wandered out, leaving the other to gape.

Scarcely had the shorter Atlas passed the portal than he gave a loud squawk. The guards, looking that way, saw his head in profile projecting past the edge of the doorway and looking upward as though his body were being bent backward, while a pair of hands gripped his throat.

The guards, not knowing that Derezong was strangling himself, rushed to the portal. As they neared it, the head of the assailed Atlantean disappeared from view, and they arrived to find Derezong Taash in his proper form strolling up to the entrance. All the while behind them the powerful fingers of Zhamel Seh pried loose the stone from King Daior's crown.

"Is aught amiss, sirs?" said Derezong to the guards, who stared about wildly as Zhamel Seh came out of the temple behind them. As he did so, he also dropped his Atlantean disguise and became another Lorska like the guards, though not quite so tall and bushy-bearded.

"If you seek an Atlas," said Derezong in answer to their questions, "I saw two such issue from your fane and slink off into yonder alley with furtive gait. Perhaps it behoves you to see whether they have committed some depredation in your hallowed precincts?"

As the guards rushed back into the temple to see, Derezong Taash and his assistant made off briskly in the opposite direction. Zhamel Seh muttered: "At least, let's hope we shall not have to return this jewel to the place whence we obtained it!"

★   ★   ★

Derezong and Zhamel reached Lezohtr late at night, but had not even finished greeting their loving concubines when a messenger informed Derezong Taash that the king wanted him at once.

Derezong Taash found King Vuar in the audience room, evidently fresh-risen from his bed, for he wore nought but his crown and a bearskin wrapped about his bony body. Ilepro was there, too, clad with like informality, and with her were her ever-present Lotrian quarter.

"You have it?" said King Vuar, lifting a bushy brow that boded no good for a negative answer.

"Here, sire," said Derezong, heaving himself up off the floor and advancing with the jewel from the crown of King Daior.

King Vuar took it in his fingertips and looked at it in the light of the single lamp. Derezong Taash wondered if the king would think to count the rays to see if there were six or seven; but he reassured himself with the thought that King Vuar was notoriously weak in higher mathematics.

The king extended the jewel towards Ilepro. "Here, Madam," he said. "And let us hope that with this transaction ends your incessant plaint."

"My lord is as generous as the sun," said Ilepro in her thick Lotrian accent. " 'Tis true I have a little more to say, but not for servile ears." She spoke in Lotrian to her four attendants, who scuttled out.

"Well?" said the king.

Ilepro stared into the sapphire and made a motion with her free hand, meanwhile reciting something in her native tongue. Although she went too fast for Derezong Taash to understand, he caught a word, several times repeated, that shook him to the core. The word was "Tr'lang".

"Sire!" he cried. "I fear this northern witch is up to no good –"

"What?" roared King Vuar. "You vilipend my favourite, and before my very optics? I'll have your head –"

"But sire! King! Look!"

The king broke into his tirade long enough to look, and never resumed it. For the flame of the lamp had shrunk to a bare spark. Cold eddies stirred the air of the room, in the midst of which the gloom thickened into shadow and the shadow into substance. At first, it seemed a shapeless darkness, a sable fog, but then a pair of glowing points appeared, palpable eyes, at twice the height of a man.

Derezong's mind sought for exorcisms while his tongue cleaved to the roof of his mouth with terror. For his own Feranzot was but a kitten compared to this, and no pentacle protected him.

The eyes grew plainer, and lower down horny talons threw back faint highlights from the feeble flame of the lamp. The cold in the room was as if an iceberg had walked in, and Derezong smelt an odour as of burning feathers.

Ilepro pointed at the king and cried something in her own language. Derezong thought he saw fangs as a great mouth opened and Tr'lang swept forward towards Ilepro. She held the jewel in front of her, as if to ward off the daev. But it paid no attention. As the blackness settled around her, she gave a piercing scream.

The door now flew open again and the four Lotri women rushed back in. Ilepro's screams continued, diminuendo, with a curious effect of distance, as if Tr'lang were dragging her far away. All that could be seen was a dwindling shapeless shape of shadow in the middle of the floor.

The foremost of the Lotris cried "Ilepro!" and sprang towards the shape, shedding wraps with one hand while tugging out a great bronze sword with the other. As the other three did likewise, Derezong Taash realized that they were not women at all, but burly male Lotris given a superficially feminine look by shaving their beards and padding their clothes in appropriate places. The first of the four swung his sword through the place where the shape of Tr'lang had been, but without meeting resistance other than that of air. Then he turned toward the king and Derezong.

"Take these alive!" he said in Lotrian. "They shall stand surety for our safe departure."

The four moved forward, their swords ready and their free hands spread to clutch like the talons of the just-departed demon. Then the opposite door opened and in came Zhamel Seh with an armful of swords. Two he tossed to Derezong Taash and King Vuar, who caught them by the hilts: the third he gripped in his own large fist as he took his place beside the other two.

"Too late," said another Lotri. "Slay them and run's our only chance."

Suiting the deed to the declaration, he rushed upon the three Lorskas. Clang! Clang! went the swords as the seven men slashed and parried in the gloom. King Vuar had whirled his bearskin around his left arm for a shield and fought naked save for his crown. While the Lorskas had an advantage of reach, they were handicapped by the king's age and Derezong's embonpoint and mediocrity of swordsmanship.

Though Derezong cut and thrust nobly, he found himself pushed back towards a corner, and felt the sting of a flesh-wound in the shoulder. And whatever the ignorant might think of a wizard's powers, it was quite impossible to fight physically for one's life and cast a spell at the same time.

The king bellowed for help, but no answer came, for in these inner chambers the thick stone walls and hangings deadened sound before it reached the outer rooms of the palace where King Vuar's guards had their stations. Like the others, he, too, was driven back until the three were fighting shoulder to shoulder in the corner. A blade hit Derezong's head flatsides and made him dizzy, while a metallic sound told that another blow had gotten home on the king's crown, and a yelp from Zhamel Seh revealed that he also had been hurt.

Derezong Taash found himself fast tiring. Each breath was a labour, and the hilt was slippery in his aching fingers. Soon they'd beat down his guard and finish him, unless he found some more indirect shift by which to make head against them.

He threw his sword, not at the Lotri in front of him, but at the little lamp that flickered on the table. The lamp flew off with a clatter and went out as Derezong Taash dropped on all fours and crept after his sword. Behind him in the darkness he could hear the footsteps and the hard breathing of men, afraid to strike for fear of smithing a friend and afraid to speak lest they reveal themselves to a foe.

Derezong Taash felt along the wall until he came to the hunting-horn of King Zynah. Wrenching the relic from the wall, he filled his lungs and blew a tremendous blast.

The blast of the horn resounded deafeningly in the confined space. Derezong took several steps, lest one of the Lotris locate him by sound and cut him down in the dark, and blew again. With loud tramplings and clankings, the guards of King Vuar approached. The door burst open and in they came with weapons ready and torches high.

"Take them!" said King Vuar, pointing at the Lotris.

One of the Lotris tried to resist, but a guardsman's sword sheared the hand from his arm as he swung, and the Lotri yelled and sank to the floor to bleed to death. The others were subdued with little trouble.

"Now," said the king, "I can give you the boon of a quick death, or I can turn you over to the tormentors for a slower and much more interesting one. Do you confess your plans and purposes in full, the former alternative shall be permitted you. Speak."

The Lotri who had led the others when they entered the room said: "Know, King, that I am Paanuvel, the husband of Ilepro. The others are gentlemen of the court of Ilepro's brother Konesp, High Chief of Lotor."

"Gentlemen!" snorted King Vuar.

"As my brother-in-law has no sons of his own, he and I concocted this sublime scheme for bringing his kingdom and yours under the eventual united rule of my son Pendetr. This magician of yours was to steal the Eye of Tandyla, so that, when Ilepro conjured up the daev Tr'lang, the monster would not assail her as she'd be protected by the gem's powers; it should, instead, dispose of you. For we knew that no lesser creature of the outer dimensions could assail you whilst you wear the ring of star-metal. Then she'd proclaim the child Pendetr king, as you've already named him heir, with herself as regent till he comes of age. But the antisorcellarious virtues of this jewel are evidently not what they once were, for Tr'lang engulfed my wife though she thrust the gem in's maw."

"You have spoken well and frankly," said King Vuar, "though I question the morality of turning your wife over to me as my concubine, yourself being not only alive but present here in disguise. However, the customs of the Lotris are not ours. Lead them out, guards, and take off their heads."

"One more word, King," said Paanuvel. "For myself I care little, now that my beloved Ilepro's gone. But I ask that you make not the child Pendetr suffer for his father's faulty schemes."

"I will think on't. Now, off with you and with your heads." The king turned to Derezong Taash, who was mopping at his flesh-wound. "What is the cause of the failure of the Eye of Tandyla?"

Derezong, in fear and trembling, told the true tale of their foray into Lotor and their subsequent theft of the sapphire in Bienkar.

"Aha!" said King Vuar. "So that's what we get for not counting the rays seen in the stone!"

He paused to pick up the jewel from where it lay upon the floor, and the quaking Derezong foresaw his own severance, like that which the Lotris were even now experiencing.

Then Vuar smiled thinly. "A fortunate failure, it seems," said the king. "I am indebted to you both, first for your shrewdness in penetrating the plans of the Lotris to usurp the throne of Lorsk, second for fighting beside me to such good purpose this night.

"Howsoever, we have here a situation fraught with some slight embarrassment. For King Daior is a good friend of mine, which friendship I would not willingly forego. And even though I should return the gem to him with explanation and apology, the fact that my servants purloined it in the first place would not sit well with him. My command to you, therefore, is to return at once to Bienkar –"

"Oh, no!" cried Derezong Taash, the words escaping involuntarily from him under the impetus of strong emotion.

"– return to Bienkar," continued the king as if he had not heard, "and smuggle the jewel back to its original position in the crown of the King of Zhysk, without letting anyone know that you are involved either in the disappearance of the stone or in its eventual restoration. For such accomplished rogues as you and your apprentice have shown yourselves to be, this slight feat will pose no serious obstacle. And so goodnight, my lord sorcerer."

King Vuar threw his bearskin about him and tramped off to his apartments, leaving Derezong and Zhamel staring at one another with expressions of mingled horror and a vast dismay.

THE OUTPOST UNDISCOVERED BY TOURISTS

A Tale of Three Kings and a Star for this Sacred Season

Harlan Ellison

When future generations look back at the twentieth century and can view things in perspective, I suspect they will highlight only a handful of writers whose dynamism and creativity made them amongst the most original and influential in the genres of fantasy and science fiction. I would be very surprised (and disappointed) if Harlan Ellison is not amongst them. Ellison (b. 1934), who is far better known in America than he is in Britain, has produced some of the most startling and incisive stories of the last forty years, the best of which will be found in The Essential Ellison *(1987). His stories are often so bleak and harrowing that it is easy to forget he also has a puckish sense of humour, and I can think of*

*no better way to close this book than with Ellison's story of the
Three Kings.*

They camped just beyond the perimeter of the dream and
waited for first light before beginning the siege.

Melchior went to the boot of the Rolls and unlocked it. He
rummaged about till he found the air mattress and the inflatable television set, and brought them to the cleared circle.
He pulled the cord on the mattress and it hissed and puffed up
to its full size, king size. He pulled the plug on the television
set and it hissed and firmed up and he snapped his fingers and
it turned itself on.

"No," said Kaspar, "I will not stand for it! Not another
night of roller derby. A King of Orient I are, and I'll be
damned if I'll lose another night's sleep listening to those
barely primate creatures drop kicking each other!"

Melchior glowed with his own night light. "So sue me," he
said, settling down on the air mattress, tidying his moleskin
cape around him. "You know I've got insomnia. You know
I've got a strictly awful hiatus hernia. You know those *latkes*
are sitting right here on my chest like millstones. Be a person
for a change, a *mensch*, it couldn't hurt just once."

Kaspar lifted the chalice of myrrh, the symbol of death, and
shook it at Melchior. "Hypochondriac! That's what you are, a
fake, a fraud. You just like watching those honkytonk bimbos
punching each other out. Hiatus hernia, my fundament! You'd
watch mud wrestling and extol the aesthetic virtues of the
balletic nuances. Turn it off . . . or at least, in the name of
Jehovah, get the Sermonette."

"The ribs are almost ready," Balthazar interrupted. "You
want the mild or the spicy sauce?"

Kaspar raised his eyes to the star far above them, out of
reach but maddeningly close. He spoke to Jehovah: "And this
one goes ethnic on us. Wandering Jew over there drives me
crazy with the light that never dims, watches institutionalized

mayhem all night and clanks all day with gold chains . . . and Black-is-Beautiful over there is determined I'll die of tertiary heartburn before I can even find the Saviour. Thanks, Yahweh; thanks a lot. Wait till *you* need a favor."

"Mild or spicy?" Balthazar said with resignation.

"I'd like mine with the mild," Melchior said sweetly. "And just a *bissel* apple sauce on the side, please."

"I want dim sum," Kaspar said. His malachite chopsticks materialized in his left hand, held far up their length indicating he was of the highest caste.

"He's only being petulant," Melchior said. "He shouldn't annoy, Balthazar sweetie. Serve them cute and tasty ribs."

"Deliver me," Kaspar murmured.

So they ate dinner, there under the star. The Nubian king, the Scrutable Oriental king, and the Hebrew king. And they watched the roller derby. They also played the spelling game called *ghost*, but ended the festivity abruptly and on a rancorous note when Balthazar and Melchior ganged up on Kaspar using the word "pringles", which Kaspar contended was *not* a generic but a specific trade name. Finally they fell asleep, the television set still talking to itself, the light from Melchior reflecting off the picture tube.

In the night the star glowed brightly, calling them on even in their sleep. And in the night early warning reconnaissance troops of the Forces of Chaos flew overhead, flapping their leathery bat-wings and leaving in their wake the hideous carbarn monoxide stench of British Leyland double-decker buses.

When Melchior awoke in the morning his first words were, "In the night, who made a ka-ka?"

Balthazar pointed. "Look."

The ground was covered with the permanent shadows of the bat-troops that had flown overhead. Dark, sooty shapes of fearsome creatures in full flight.

"I've always thought they looked like the flying monkeys in the 1939 MGM production of *The Wizard of Oz*, special effects by Arnold Gillespie, character make-up created by Jack Dawn," Kaspar said ruminatively.

"Listen, Yellow Peril," Balthazar said, "you can exercise

that junk heap memory for trivia later. Unless the point is lost on you, what this means is that they know we're coming and they're going to be ready for us. We've lost the element of surprise."

Melchior sighed and added, "Not to mention that we've been following the star for exactly one thousand nine hundred and ninety-nine years, give or take a fast minute, which unless they aren't too clever, should have tipped them off that we were on the way some time ago."

"Nonetheless," said Kaspar, and fascinated by the word, he said it again, "nonetheless."

They waited, but he didn't finish the sentence.

"And on that uplifting note," Balthazar said, "let us get in the wind before they catch us out here in the open."

So they gathered their belongings – Melchior's caskets of Krugerrands, his air mattress and inflatable television set, Kaspar's chalice of myrrh, his Judy Garland albums and fortune-cookie fortune calligraphy set, Balthazar's wok, his brass-bound collected works of James Baldwin and hair-conking outfit – and they stowed them neatly in the boot of the Rolls.

Then, with Balthazar driving (but refusing once again to wear the chauffeur's cap on moral grounds), they set out under the auspices of power steering, directly through the perimeter of the dream.

The star continued to shine overhead. "Damnedest thing I ever saw," Kaspar remarked, for the ten thousandth time. "Defies all the accepted laws of celestial mechanics."

Balthazar mumbled something.

For the ten thousandth time.

"What's that, I didn't hear?" Melchior said.

"I said: at least if there was a pot of gold at the end of all this . . ."

It was unworthy of him, as it had been ten thousand times previously, and the others chose to ignore it.

At the outskirts of the dream, a run-down section lined with fast food stands, motels with waterbeds and closed circuit vibrating magic fingers cablevision, bowling alleys, Polish athletic organizations and used rickshaw lots, they encountered the first line of resistance from the Forces of Chaos.

As they stopped for a traffic light, thousands of bat-winged monkey-faced troops leaped out of alleys and doorways with buckets of water and sponges, and began washing their windshield.

"Quick, Kaspar!" Balthazar shouted.

The Oriental king threw open the rear door on the right side and bounded out into the street, brandishing the chalice of myrrh. "Back, back, scum of the underworld!" he howled.

The troops of Chaos shrieked in horror and pain and began dropping what appeared to be dead all over the place, setting up a wailing and a crying and a screaming that rose over the dream like dark smoke.

"Please, already," Melchior shouted. "Do we need all this noise? All this *geshrying*! You'll wake the baby!"

Then Balthazar was gunning the motor, Kaspar leaped back into the rear seat, the door slammed and they were off, through the red light – which had, naturally, been rigged to stay red, as are all such red lights, by the Forces of Chaos.

All that day they lay siege to the dream.

The Automobile Club told them they couldn't get there from here. The speed traps were set at nine miles per hour. Sects of religious fanatics threw themselves under the steel-belteds. But finally they came to the Manger, a Hyatt establishment, and they fought their way inside with the gifts, all tasteful.

And there, in a moderately priced room, they found the Saviour, tended by an out-of-work cabinet-maker, a lady who was obviously several bricks shy of a load who kept insisting she had been raped by God, various shepherds, butchers, pet store operators, boutique salesgirls, certified public accountants, hawkers of T-shirts, investigative journalists, theatrical hangers-on, Sammy Davis, Jr, and a man who owned a whippet that was reputed to be able to catch two frisbees at the same time.

And the three kings came in, finding it hard to find a place there in the crowd, and they set down their gifts and stared at the sleeping child.

"We'll call him Jomo," said Balthazar, asserting himself.

"Don't be a jerk," Kaspar said. "Merry Jomomas? We'll call him Lao-Tzu. It flows, it sings, it soars."

So they argued about that for quite a while, and finally settled on Christ, because in conjunction with Jesus it was six and five, and that would fit all the marquees.

But still, after two thousand years, they were unsettled. They stared down at the sleeping child, who looked like all babies: like a small, soft W. C. Fields who had grown blotchy drinking wine sold before its time, and Balthazar mumbled, "I'd have been just as happy with a pot of gold," and Kaspar said, "You'd think after two thousand years someone would at least offer me a chair," and Melchior summed up all their hopes and dreams for a better world when he said, "You know, it's funny, but he don't look Jewish."